Silver Splendor

"How curious," he mused, crouching beside her. "This isn't the season for camellias to bloom."

Her rapt gaze studied the many-petaled blossom. "In America we'd call it a maverick. Something wild and rare and free."

Like you, Nicholas wanted to say. He felt the sudden fierce desire to shower her with flowers, to see her lying naked in a bed of blooms . . .

He reached for the stem. "Why don't you take it?"

Her quick fingers caught his wrist. Beseeching and beautiful in the gaslight, her eyes met his. A deluge of desire swamped his senses. Her lush scent mingled with the odors of damp earth and untamed undergrowth. He could think of little else save the nearness of her body, the firmness of the fingers enclosing his wrist . . . and the need throbbing heavily in him.

Silver Splendor

BARBARA DAWSON SMITH

AVON BOOKS ◆ NEW YORK

SILVER SPLENDOR is an original publication of Avon Books. This work has never before appeared in book form. This work is a novel. Any similarity to actual persons or events is purely coincidental.

AVON BOOKS
A division of
The Hearst Corporation
105 Madison Avenue
New York, New York 10016

First Avon Books Printing: August 1989

AVON TRADEMARK REG. U.S. PAT. OFF. AND IN OTHER COUNTRIES, MARCA REGISTRADA, HECHO EN U.S.A.

Printed in the U.S.A.

K–R   10   9   8   7   6   5   4   3   2   1

To my parents

Acknowledgments

I am deeply indebted to the following:

Merri Ferrell, Associate Curator, The Museums at Stony Brook, Long Island, for sharing her extensive knowledge of carriages; Arthur Goddard, instructor of Latin, The Kinkaid School; Pat Foley, sculptor-in-residence, The Kinkaid School; the people at the Art Students League of New York; Joyce Bell, Alice Borchardt, Arnette Lamb, and Susan Wiggs, whose criticism and support have meant so much to me; my husband for his unflagging patience; and my daughter, Jessica, for making it so easy for daddy to be patient.

Chapter 1

London, 1880

He was still following her.

Frowning, Elizabeth Hastings returned her gaze to the mist-hung street ahead, where a gas lamp cast a hazy sulfur circle over the cobblestones. In the distance Big Ben chimed eight times. In fair weather the sky would be a palette of pinks and purples, the byways crammed with laborers and tradesmen. But tonight a veil of vapor brought an early dusk, the chilly June drizzle driving all but a few hardy Londoners indoors.

Elizabeth shivered, uneasy and cold. Rounding the corner onto Maiden Lane, she darted another glance behind her. Half a block away, through the scattering of pedestrians, she glimpsed the man again. His thickset shoulders were hunched inside a tattered frock coat, his crudely drawn face shadowed by a porkpie hat. She'd first noticed him while boarding the Strand omnibus, then again when he'd disembarked at her stop. Intent on reaching home before nightfall, she had afforded him scant notice, filing away an absentminded catalogue of his bulldog features.

But now her senses were sharpened.

Clutching her artist's satchel with cold-numbed fingers, Elizabeth forced herself to remain calm. She was being overimaginative, that was all. The stranger had made no threatening gesture; their paths merely lay in a similar direction.

Still, she quickened her pace. A hansom cab rattled past, its high-perched driver huddled against the bleak drizzle. The misty twilight softened the edges of buildings and made poetry of the dingy brick tenements on the fringes of Covent Garden. The scents of cooking cabbage and rotting garbage mingled in the damp, smoke-laden air. From somewhere came a burst of male laughter.

A ragged urchin darted past and vanished into a shadowed alleyway. Elizabeth felt a sudden longing for Kipp's company, but as usual, when wanted, the unkempt boy was nowhere to be seen. Like so many other street Arabs roaming this section of the city, he was probably haunting the marketplace in hope of scrounging some supper.

The tap of her footsteps sounded louder on the wet pavement now that she'd left the clatter of traffic on the Strand. The main roads were well lit by gas lamps, but here in the narrow side streets, the slate gray of dusk rapidly yielded to the charcoal of night. An occasional passerby carried a torch or lantern, but for the most part her way lay in shadow.

Elizabeth considered seeking refuge in a coffee house or tavern. But if she tarried, her father might worry needlessly. She felt a familiar rush of affection laced with concern. Provided, of course, her father was at home and not drowning his sorrows in drink at The Lion and the Lamb.

She glanced back again. The man had gained ground. A shudder prickled her skin. Yet even as she watched he paused to peer into the window of a boot maker's shop.

It was fanciful to think he was stalking her, Elizabeth told herself firmly. If the stranger were bent on robbery, he'd be lurking about the nearby marketplace and awaiting a chance to waylay one of the rich gentlemen who came there to taunt the porters or buy nosegays.

Her worn leather satchel contained only a few farthings and her sketch pad.

Not for the first time she chided herself for lingering so late in the magnificence of Westminster Abbey. Daring another look around, Elizabeth found to her relief that the stranger was gone. Still, she wouldn't rest easy until she was safely within her own lodgings.

The chilly mist penetrated her shawl and curled tendrils of hair around her face. Gripping her satchel tightly, she hurried over the rain-slick cobbles toward the quiet, shabby street where she lived. From a window high above, someone's laundry hung pale and limp against the darkened brick like white chalk drawings on a blackboard. Her anxiety began to abate as the familiar shape of Mrs. Chesney's lodging house loomed through the night. The glow of a gaslight inside promised warmth and safety—

Something scraped within the inky interior of an alleyway ahead. Her heart vaulted in alarm. Elizabeth swung toward the sound. But the shadows were deep, the narrow passageway eerily silent.

Pausing no more than an instant, she walked on swiftly, avoiding the alley. She was being foolish, jumping at a noise probably made by a prowling tomcat—

In a sudden rush of movement something barreled out of the darkness at her. A stocky man, a porkpie hat . . . *him!*

A scream tore from her throat. She turned, already running. Rough hands clamped onto her shoulders and jerked her back around. The stench of fetid breath struck her face. Through the gloom, she glimpsed his coarse features.

Wildly she swung the satchel. Its sharp edge caught him hard under the chin. He grunted in pain, his grip loosening just enough for her to wrench free.

Sobbing with panic, she darted toward the rooming house. Her shawl dropped somewhere along with the satchel. Over her gasping breath she heard the thud of footsteps.

Her feet slipped on cobbles slick with moisture. Terrified, she fought for balance. The hands of her pursuer bit into her shoulders again.

With a ragged cry, she tried to twist away. But he was too strong. Another scream swelled within her. Suddenly his fingers were tightening around her neck and cutting off her air.

She struggled, kicking and pummeling. His hands were a closing noose, squeezing and strangling. Blood roared in her ears; pain seared her lungs. A tide of darkness poured over her, drowning her strength.

The brougham negotiated the traffic at the Piccadilly intersection and carved a path through the congestion of fine carriages and hansom cabs. The coachman shook his whip at a slow-moving cart, his curse lost in the clatter of hooves and the shouts of tradesmen. At the rear of the vehicle two liveried footmen stood stiff as statues, seemingly oblivious of the cold drizzle.

Inside, Lord Nicholas Ware, Earl of Hawkesford, leaned against the luxurious leather seat and glared out the window. He saw not the bleak night but the obstinate face of his sister. By God, Cicely had gone too far this time. She had never been one to heed propriety. Yet skipping a French lesson or letting loose a frog at Lady Foster's soiree was nothing compared to what Cicely had done now.

The news of her scandalous behavior had taken a day to reach him. The maid told the footman, the footman told the butler, the butler told the valet, and the valet—quite gingerly—told the earl.

Appalled and angry, Nicholas had canceled his plan to escort Cicely and Aunt Beatrice to the theatre. He'd wrested the details of the transgression from Cicely and then laid down the law. She had been penitent...far too penitent. And entirely too eager to promise more circumspect behavior in the future.

Nicholas was well acquainted with that soulful smile and those appealing blue eyes. Rather than trust his sister's word, he meant to put a stop to this latest indis-

cretion once and for all. Tonight, before she ruined her
reputation and soiled the Ware family honor.

Consorting with artists, for God's sake! His mouth
tightened. It was sheer luck only the maid caught Cicely stealing back into the house, her gown speckled
with dried sculpting clay. Sheer luck that no one of
consequence had spied his sister in the company of this
immoral bohemian artist.

The fact that his sister's mentor was female did nothing to mollify Nicholas's sense of outrage. If Cicely's
gushing testimony could be credited, Elizabeth Hastings was a sculptress of incredible talent and impeccable repute. More likely, Nicholas reflected with distaste,
Miss Hastings was a bluestocking of vulgar manners
and doubtful virtue.

The distant chime of Big Ben tolled the hour of eight.
The brougham jolted more slowly over the cobblestones, the coachman apparently searching for the artist's address. Nicholas peered outside. The coach
lanterns afforded him a glimpse of shadowy tenements
and sinister alleyways; the mist lent an unearthly quality to the scene. The damp air had crept up from the
Thames, hastening nightfall and clearing the streets of
all but those on the most urgent of errands.

Errands as urgent as his own.

Nicholas felt his sense of purpose intensify as he
gazed at the seedy district so unlike the discreetly elegant homes to which he was accustomed. Laundry
hung pale and ghostly against the shabby buildings
outside. Despite the brougham's closed windows, he
could detect the stench of rubbish.

The thought of Cicely frequenting such a hellhole—
unchaperoned, no less—angered Nicholas anew. Yet
he could not place the entire blame for this affair on his
sister's pretty shoulders. For all her air of sophistica-
tion, Cicely was only seventeen and naive in the ways
of the world. Doubtless she had been duped . . . duped
by an artist who sought to take advantage of Cicely's
rank.

Staring moodily across the darkened interior of the

carriage, Nicholas clenched his jaw against a twist of affection and frustration. Perhaps this present predicament was a direct result of his soft-hearted desire to see his sister happy. Perhaps if the responsibility of the earldom had not been thrust upon him at so young an age—

From somewhere nearby came the piercing cry of a woman.

Nicholas started. Whipping his eyes back out into the night, he told himself she was none of his concern, that he needn't entangle himself in what was likely a commonplace family squabble.

Yet he found the thought of a woman being abused intolerable.

He rapped sharply on the front glass. The coachman brought the pair of matched grays to a quick halt.

Before the footman could open the door, Nicholas slid down the window and thrust his head into the drizzle. "Greaves!"

The stout coachman twisted on his perch and aimed a startled look down at Nicholas. "Yes, m'lord?"

"Did you hear that scream?"

Greaves nodded. "Came from 'round about there as best I could tell." He pointed his whip toward the far end of the darkened street.

"Drive on down there."

"M'lord?" In the lamp glow the coachman's beetle-browed eyes went wide with surprise and doubt. "Beggin' your pardon, but it's likely just some doxy—"

"Do as I say," Nicholas snapped. "And be quick about it."

"Yes, m'lord."

Greaves cracked his whip and the carriage started with a jolt. Heedless of the cold mist, Nicholas peered ahead into the gloom and sought some sign of the woman. But he could see little beyond the circle of light cast by the twin coach lamps, and he could hear nothing but the swift clop of hooves on the cobblestones.

Then, as the brougham neared the end of the block, he spied a black shape half-swallowed by the shadows of a tenement. The shape moved, transforming itself into the hulking figure of a man. A man whose hands encircled a woman's throat.

Rage rose in Nicholas. Before the carriage came to a complete halt, he flung open the door and sprang out.

The man whirled; the light of the lanterns caught the surprise on his brutish features. He hurled the woman aside and she crumpled to the wet ground.

He made a move to dart off into the night. Nicholas's fists closed around the rough tweed of the man's coat and jerked him around. The cutthroat fell sprawling to the rain-slick cobbles. For a second he lay there, his porkpie hat askew. Then he leapt to his feet again. In his hand flashed the deadly gleam of a knife.

Nicholas swung aside. The plunging blade met the sleeve of his frock coat and rent the velvet cuff. In one swift motion he sliced the edge of his palm onto the ruffian's wrist. The man howled in pain; the knife clattered to the wet pavement and skittered into the shadows.

In the blink of an eye, the burly man scuttled pell-mell into the darkness, like a rat seeking shelter.

"I'll nab him!" shouted one of the footmen. Nicholas turned to see Dobson scooping up the knife from a gutter and bolting after the villain.

The earl shot a look at the other lanky footman, who stood beside the brougham, staring as if dumbstruck. "Assist him, Pickering!" Nicholas commanded. "Take one of the lamps."

Pickering gulped, his Adam's apple bobbing. "M-me, m'lord?"

Nicholas glared a reply and Pickering hurried to fetch a lantern. Then he dashed off, the yellow light wavering over the impeccable blue and gold of his livery.

Nicholas hastened to the woman. Heedless of the damp, dirty pavement, he dropped to his knees beside her. Her face lay in shadows, her body deathly still. "Miss?" he called softly.

She gave no response. Alarmed, he touched her

throat, seeking a pulse beat. She moaned and stirred restlessly.

At least, he thought grimly, she was alive.

"Greaves, bring that light here."

The carriage springs creaked as the coachman clambered from the elevated front seat; then the glow of the remaining lamp shone over the woman's slight form. Quickly Nicholas examined her for injury. She wore a neat but shabby violet gown embroidered with fanciful silver flowers; its soft and flowing folds were peculiar yet pleasing. The bodice was cut far too demurely to brand her a whore. Was she perhaps an actress at one of the nearby Drury Lane theatres? Or a shop girl attacked on her way home from work?

He turned his eyes to her face... and felt a weakening rush inside him, as if the ground had dropped away.

Like a blow to his midsection, the uncommon sensation left him momentarily without breath. She was strikingly lovely, yet certainly he knew women of more classic beauty. Disciplining his reaction with cold logic, he analyzed her features. There was nothing unusual about the jet-black spill of her hair, nothing singular in the milky hue of her complexion, nothing exceptional in the fine line of her cheekbones or the pale curve of her lips. She brought to mind the wildness of a gypsy; he preferred a woman to be more polished.

So why did he feel this absurd elation, as if he had unearthed a rare jewel buried in a rubbish heap?

The feeling of wonder evaporated as he spied the red marks bruising the swanlike curve of her throat. The sight fired his fury and quickened his concern. He swiftly removed his frock coat and wrapped it around her.

"D'you suppose she's dead, m'lord?"

Greaves's voice startled Nicholas; he had forgotten the coachman's presence. "Of course she isn't dead," the earl said curtly. "But as soon as the footmen return we must get her to a doctor."

"Yes, m'lord."

His mission concerning Cicely could wait, Nicholas decided. Taking great care, he tunneled a hand into the woman's tumbled hair and the other beneath her knees, lifting her against him. She felt warm and pliant, childishly light and alarmingly limp. Her scent was redolent of herbs and damp earth, an oddly pleasing combination.

As he turned toward the brougham, she made a small sound and shifted in his arms. He halted expectantly. Her eyelids fluttered; her lashes lifted.

His insides took another heart-stopping plunge.

Her eyes were a luxurious lavender, entrancing and intelligent. She looked up at him without a trace of surprise or shyness, as if awakening to find herself cradled in a strange man's arms were nothing unusual. Her gaze drifted over his face, scrutinizing every detail, and her dark brows quirked into a fascinating frown.

Unexpectedly she put a hand to his jaw. The subtle brush of her fingers along his skin ignited a fire in him that flared fiercer than any sparked by a more intimate caress.

"Perfect," she murmured, her voice as soft and unique as the rest of her. "You have the most perfect bone structure I've ever seen."

Nonplussed, he stared down at her. She stared back, those remarkable lavender eyes unblinking. He had braced himself for hysterics, for tears, for a fit of the vapors . . . for anything but this unnervingly frank assessment.

Brusquely he asked, "How are you feeling?"

The question seemed to surprise her. Her brow furrowed and her lashes flickered. "My throat hurts," she said slowly, touching tentative fingers to the reddened area. A shudder coursed through her slender frame; comprehension washed over her face like a cloud over the sun. "That man"—her voice broke, sounding husky and exotic—"he tried to strangle me!"

"You needn't worry," Nicholas said to allay the alarm in her eyes. "He won't harm you anymore. I've seen to that."

"But why did he attack me? I haven't anything of value."

"Perhaps he didn't realize that."

With inbred chivalry Nicholas didn't voice his guess about her assailant's probable intent. He started toward the brougham, Greaves trotting behind at a respectful distance, the light from the lantern swaying. She wriggled; Nicholas shifted his grip.

"Where are you taking me?" she asked.

"Out of the rain."

She squirmed again. "I want to go home."

"I'm taking you to a doctor."

"Put me down!"

The fine edge of panic in her tone broke through to him. Beside the carriage Nicholas lowered the woman to her feet. She retreated a few steps, half slipping on the wet cobbles, looking lost in the dark folds of his frock coat. Her eyes were wide and wary and winsome, her hair a stunning spill of inky silk around her shoulders.

"I don't mean you any harm," he said gently. "I'm only trying to help you."

She seemed to relax. "Thank you. I do appreciate your coming to my rescue, but there's no need to make a fuss."

"I'm not making a fuss, I'm only being logical," he said with a trace of annoyance. "You've had a bad shock. I insist that you get into my carriage and sit down."

She made no move to accept his proferred hand. "I don't want to appear ungrateful, but I'm really all right. Truly I am."

Her refusal of support was disconcerting. The other women of his acquaintance would have been milking the situation for all it was worth, wilting and clinging and weeping.

"Then I insist on escorting you home."

She waved at the nearest tenement. "I live right over there." She glanced at the brougham, where Greaves stood holding the door open, his bushy-browed eyes focused into the darkness, his fleshy face barren of expression. Her hand went to her mouth; her gaze went to Nicholas. "My apologies, sir. I hope I haven't caused you to be late for an appointment."

"Nothing that couldn't wait."

"I'm sorry to have been such a bother."

A bother... *her*? "Think nothing of it."

She drew in a breath. "Well, then, I suppose I should go."

But she didn't go; she just stood there in the cold damp air, gazing at him with those lovely lavender eyes.

Again Nicholas had the unnerving impression that she was committing every detail of his face to memory. For the first time in many, many years he found himself blessing the whim of heredity that had graced him with physical handsomeness. Only belatedly did he remind himself the opinion of a common street woman was of no consequence.

No, *common* was the wrong word for her. She was rare, remarkable, standing there with his coat enveloping her slight form, her hair tumbled around her shoulders. She looked as poised and proud as a queen, as fragile and fanciful as a nymph.

And like a nymph she might melt into the mist, never to be seen again. The thought filled him with the most peculiar sense of desolation.

From the alley came the crunch of footsteps and the sway of a light. The footmen emerged onto the street, Dobson stepping smartly in the lead, Pickering trailing with the lantern.

"We lost him, m'lord," Dobson said, looking disappointed.

"Too many dark alleyways," Pickering added, looking relieved.

"I was ready to beat the bugger to a bloody pulp," Dobson said, loudly smashing his fist into his palm.

"Er... me, too," Pickering concurred, furtively running a finger inside his collar.

"Never mind," Nicholas said. "There must be a

thousand holes around here where a rat could hide."

He turned to address the woman. "This incident must be reported at once. Since I got a good look at the scoundrel, I'll take you to Scotland Yard."

"Thank you, but there's really no need to bother. I'll sketch a likeness for the police in the morning."

"Sketch?"

"Yes, I'm an artist, you see. In fact, I was just returning from Westminster Abbey...oh, dear!" Without warning, she darted into the gloom near the alleyway and appeared to be searching for something.

An artist? And with that husky-soft American accent? A suspicion tugged at the back of his mind, a suspicion so preposterous Nicholas summarily rejected it.

He followed her into the shadows, motioning to Pickering to bring the lantern. "Have you lost something, miss?"

She flashed a dismayed look over her shoulder. "My satchel! I dropped it when that man attacked me. Oh, dear, all the drawings I did of those lovely tombs... Henry the Seventh, Mary Queen of Scots—"

"Is this it?" Nicholas inquired, plucking a sadly worn leather case from the foul gutter.

"Yes! Oh, thank you so much!"

Her eyes shining, she seized the satchel and hugged it close, mindless of the mud spatters. Nicholas found himself wishing she'd displayed as much enthusiasm when he'd rescued her.

"You're welcome," he said stiffly. Spying something else lying in the shadows, he picked up a heap of damp, dark wool. "Perhaps this is also yours?"

Smiling, she took the shawl. "Thank you again. You've been so kind." She bit her lip and added, "I only wish I could repay you."

Nicholas had a thought at that, a thought he repressed mercilessly. "There's no need," he said politely.

"Wait!" she said as if he hadn't spoken. "I know how I can thank you. I shall do your bust!"

He frowned. "My bust?"

"Yes!" She took an excited step toward him. "You must sit for me. I'd meant to sculpt you from memory alone, just for myself, but instead I shall give you the bust. It will be so much easier if you'll agree to pose for me. Might we set a time, sir?"

Suspicion resurrected inside Nicholas, as cold as the mist. Disregarding good manners, he asked bluntly, "Who are you?"

"Oh, I doubt you've heard of me," she said apologetically, clutching the satchel close. "It's difficult for a woman to make a name for herself in the arts. Besides, I've only been in London a short while. But you have such perfect bone structure, such marvelous character to your face, I promise you, you'll love what I—"

"Your name, miss."

He'd employed that chilling tone to great advantage on certain recalcitrant members of parliament. Her color rose and her smile wilted.

"Elizabeth Hastings," she murmured.

Despite his anticipation of her answer, Nicholas felt thunderstruck. So this was the dissolute artist Cicely was constantly stealing away to visit. The woman looked so solemn, so anxious. Ruthlessly he conquered the inane impulse to kiss away the grave pucker marring her brow.

"Well," she said with a sigh, "I knew you wouldn't have heard of me. Very few people have."

"Oh, but I have, Miss Hastings," he said with stern softness. "Indeed, I have."

Her smile reappeared in full glory, like a rose unfurling to the sun. "Truly? I just completed a bust of a Mr. Darby Lovett in Chelsea. He's a barrister—perhaps you know him?"

"Not personally," Nicholas said with deliberate evasion. "However, your reputation may be more far-reaching than you imagine."

Wistful pleasure shone on her face. "Do you really suppose so? I've sold a few things here and there, you know. Most people aren't interested in the sort of sculpture I do—the bust for Mr. Lovett only paid the rent—but I would so much like to bring beauty into other people's lives."

Her enthusiasm stirred something tender inside Nicholas. Tightening his jaw, he said coldly, "Quite so. I find myself intrigued by your offer to sculpt me, Miss Hastings. Might we discuss the matter further in the privacy of your lodgings?"

Her eyes rounded. "Now?"

"If it isn't inconvenient . . ."

"Oh, no, it would be a pleasure."

Indeed, Nicholas thought contemptuously as she led him toward the nearby rooming house. All of his suspicions about her were wellfounded. No woman of virtue would so blithely receive a strange man without a chaperon present. Doubtless Miss Hastings was in the habit of entertaining men. The notion vaguely disturbed him. Good God, why should he care one way or the other?

Because of Cicely, he reminded himself firmly. His impressionable sister must not be allowed to associate with someone of such loose moral character.

Pickering walked ahead, holding the lantern high to light the way up a narrow flight of steps, the wooden risers creaking. Doors opened off each landing; the sounds of laughter and the smells of cooking emanated from inside. The stairwell was dingy but swept clean, Nicholas noted. Still, he felt appalled at the incongruous notion of such a lovely woman living in poverty.

Five flights up, at the top floor, Miss Hastings inserted a key in the lock and tilted her head at Nicholas. "My father may be home." The door swung open to darkness. "Oh, I guess he's not."

She sounded nervous, as if the impropriety of the situation had just occurred to her. Pickering brought the lantern inside until she lit an old-fashioned oil lamp, then Nicholas motioned the footman out.

The door closed with a quiet click. Miss Hastings removed his frock coat and tossed it over the back of a rush-bottomed nursery chair, on which she had already set her shawl and satchel.

The room was small but cozy, the few furnishings a clever blend of the mundane and the unique. Half visible behind a bamboo screen was an ancient iron bedstead. Near it stood a rickety washstand bearing a Chinese ginger jar in lieu of a pitcher. A gothic hall table harbored a collection of antique musical instruments: dulcimer, lute, and mandolin. Whimsically adorning one bare wall was a lifesized charcoal sketch of an armchair and tea table. The overall effect was as quaint and gypsylike as Elizabeth Hastings herself.

Beneath a row of tall, darkened windows, a worktable held an array of odds and ends, chisels and mallets and clay. Statues littered the floor, along with piles of books, while mud-spattered cloths draped the tops of several pedestals. Walking to the hall table, he idly rubbed a finger over the gold embossed letters on a royal blue book: *Elizabeth Templeton Hastings*. Obeying an odd impulse, he opened the volume and found himself gazing at the sketch of a laughing woman. For an instant he thought she was Elizabeth Hastings, for the features were remarkably similar. Then he noted the fine lines bracketing the mouth and eyes.

"My mother," she murmured, coming beside him. "She died last autumn."

The sadness in her voice curled around his heart. "I'm sorry."

Over the smoke of the lamp he caught a whiff of her country garden scent. In the flickering light the red marks on her throat were already darkening to bruises; the sight aroused the sudden sharp urge to protect her. Unexpectedly his groin tightened. Her mist-curled hair cascaded in unruly waves to her waist and brought to mind a sudden, vivid picture of what she would look like with only that lavish jet black mantle veiling her body, her breasts full and milky smooth, her hips lush and feminine.

Forcing his eyes from her, he snapped the book shut. For Cicely's sake he must not stray from his purpose.

Miss Hastings struck a match to light another oil

lamp, this one on the washstand. Bending, she adjusted the wick.

"There," she said in satisfaction, straightening. "Now I can see you better."

She seemed to have recovered from the brief bout of uneasiness at the door. For some obscure reason, the very serenity of her manner set Nicholas's teeth on edge.

"You don't even know my name," he said, his voice quietly harsh, "yet you invite me here alone with you. How do you know I won't do worse to you than that ruffian?"

She gazed at him with those vast violet eyes and for the life of him he couldn't tell what she was thinking. Then, in a small voice, she asked, "What *is* your name?"

"Lord Nicholas Ware."

With stern pleasure he watched comprehension flit across the wild beauty of her face. Her eyes lit up and her lips curved into the most intriguing smile. "Ware! Why, then, you must be Cicely's brother, the Earl of . . ."

"Hawkesford."

Her hand went to her bodice. "What an extraordinary coincidence that you of all people would happen along at such a moment . . . or *was* it coincidence? Were you coming to see me?"

"Quite astute, Miss Hastings."

Her smile bloomed brighter. "Then you must have been intending to commission me to sculpt you. Cicely said she would convince you to do so."

"Indeed," Nicholas said dryly. "That is precisely the sort of grandiose promise I would expect of my sister."

"What a peculiar turn of fate—me offering to sculpt you, I mean." Elizabeth Hastings gave a merry laugh. "You see, I knew you weren't the sort of man to treat a woman unkindly. I can tell a great deal about a person by looking at his face. You have both strength of character and faultlessly handsome features. I can't wait to capture your likeness in clay." Tilting her head to the side, she studied him, tapping a finger against the curve of her lip.

Nicholas squelched a sudden, almost violent urge to kiss that adorable mouth. "You mistake my purpose, Miss Hastings," he said in his most chilling tone. "I have not come here to participate in any artistic endeavor."

"Oh." Her eyes clouded, then cleared. "Well, I understand if you haven't the time to sit for me. But perhaps if you could give me just a few minutes to do some sketches..."

Before he could speak, she dashed to the worktable and returned with a copybook and pencil. "If it's not too much trouble, I'll do some studies of you from different angles, then use a caliper to make sure of the measurements..."

"Miss Hastings."

The steely softness of his voice failed to halt her swift strokes interspersed with studious glances at his face. "Mmm-hmm?" she murmured.

"*Miss Hastings.*"

This time his grimly gentle tone penetrated; the pencil stilled and her eyes met his. "Is something wrong?" she asked, looking quite charmingly flustered. "I'm sorry, how remiss of me! Of course, you'd rather sit." Tossing aside her copybook and pencil, she started to drag over a chair.

"No, I should not like to sit. What I have to say will take only a moment."

"Say?"

"Contrary to the conclusion to which you have leapt, Miss Hastings, I did not come here to ask you to sculpt me."

"You didn't?"

Her crestfallen face almost made Nicholas regret what must be done. Almost. "I came here to discuss your association with my sister. Or shall I say, your exploitation of her."

A tiny furrow appeared on her brow. "Exploitation?"

"Quite." With effort, he curbed the most curious

urge to avoid her eyes. "Under your influence, Cicely
has come to the ludicrous conclusion that she wishes to
study art."

"What's so ludicrous about studying art?"

"She is a lady, Miss Hastings. She should be spend-
ing her time in gentler, more womanly pursuits. I shall
not stand by and see her reputation destroyed for the
sake of a passing whim."

He could tell by the paling of her cheeks that his
opinion of the morality of artists was not lost on Elizabeth Hastings. Turning in a swirl of violet skirts, she
walked to her worktable and reached into an oil cloth-
covered bucket, drawing forth a small ball of clay.

She swung toward him. "What makes you so certain
Cicely's interest in art is solely a whim? She has talent,
you know."

Nicholas caught himself watching her nimble fingers
working the clay; he forced his mind back to duty. "You
don't know my sister as I do. She's young and foolish,
easily influenced by silly, romantic notions."

"As you, sir, are not."

The trace of mockery made him tighten his jaw. He
realized Elizabeth Hastings wasn't as flighty as she
seemed on the surface.

"Undoubtedly," he went on icily, "the well-stocked
shelves of Mudie's lending library have filled Cicely's
head with eccentric ideas. Ideas you've fostered to suit
your own purpose."

"Just what purpose do you mean?"

The proud tilt of her chin made Nicholas feel
vaguely abashed. "Cicely is not without influence. I
suspect you'd planned to use that influence to obtain
art commissions."

Her fingers stilled on the clay. "You are mistaken,
sir," she murmured. "I intended nothing of the sort. All
I want is to foster her talent rather than see it wither in
a stuffy drawing room."

Her aura of quiet dignity again gave him the disconcerting sense of having misjudged her. Yet even if she
had no nefarious designs on Cicely, Nicholas firmly re-

minded himself, the principal issue remained. Elizabeth Hastings belonged to an unacceptable world. If anyone of consequence learned of his sister's association with the artist, Cicely's reputation would be in shambles. She would be shunned by polite society and relinquish hope of a decent marriage. He could not—would not—allow one imprudent act to destroy her future.

"Regardless of what you intended, Miss Hastings, I must insist that you cease encouraging my sister."

She regarded him coolly; her supple fingers manipulated the clay absently. "Then we seem to be at an impasse, sir, for I will go on tutoring Cicely. *Your* endorsement is not necessary to me."

Her unruffled manner incensed Nicholas beyond reason. Discarding all pretense of politeness, he snapped, "Might I point out, Miss Hastings, you are indebted to me for your rescue. The least you might do to repay me is to offer your cooperation."

He had the brief satisfaction of seeing smudges of color leap to her cheeks. She thrust the ball of clay into her pocket and marched to the chair. "I must ask you to leave, sir," she said, snatching up his crumpled coat. "Dear me!" Her lips parted in surprise as she stared at the slash rending the dark velvet cuff. "How did this happen?"

"The man who attacked you had a knife."

She paled, lifting her gaze to Nicholas. The concern he saw there was absurdly gratifying. "You might have been killed," she said in a small voice.

"So might you."

Nibbling her lip, Miss Hastings looked away. Suddenly she lay down the frock coat and drew a thin silver chain from beneath her bodice. Carefully removing something from the necklace, she held out her hand.

"I'm sorry to have caused the ruin of your expensive coat. I haven't the money to repay you, but perhaps this will compensate for the damage; it belonged to my grandfather."

Cradled in her palm was a man's silver signet ring. Nicholas felt curiously ashamed. Did Elizabeth Hastings so heartily resent being indebted to him that she would part with something of such obvious sentimental value?

"I can't accept that," he stated.

"Take it, please." Stepping closer, she boldly thrust the ring into the pocket of his waistcoat. "It's all I have of value to offer you."

The tilt of her chin bespoke pride and character; the fire in her eyes conveyed passion and conviction. Nicholas stared down at her gypsy beauty and felt a powerful tide of longing, a longing that both baffled and bedeviled him. Why did he feel drawn to a woman so far removed from his own world? Her fragrance evoked a stirring reminder of wild herbs and lush earth. He wanted to learn the scent and taste and touch of every part of her. She was fresh and free, unfettered by the conventions that bound him.

Logic warned him against the imprudent thoughts crowding his mind. He could have any one of a hundred lovely women more acceptable to a man of his rank. He should walk away from temptation; he should retain control of the urges burning inside him.

He could ... he should ... and yet ...

"But you can offer me something of far greater value than a ring," Nicholas said slowly. "You can offer me yourself."

Chapter 2

Shock numbed Elizabeth. She should have anticipated this proposal; Lord Nicholas Ware had made
his opinion of her morals plain enough. An angry flush
stung her cheeks. Papa had been right to warn her
against the hypocrisy of the nobility. And she had been
wrong to place so much trust in the strength of character she saw in the earl's face.

Yet she could not deny he fascinated her. Despite
that polished arrogance of manner, that austere set to
his jaw, Lord Nicholas looked the epitome of chiseled
perfection. His hair was as brown as fired clay, his eyes
as gray as granite beneath fierce brows. His white shirt
and charcoal waistcoat failed to disguise the power of
his body. For a man who led the pampered life of an
aristocrat, his muscles looked superbly fit. His body
had the vitality of a Michelangelo, the sensuousness of
a da Vinci.

Elizabeth longed to duplicate in clay the shape and
texture and vigor of Nicholas Ware. She wanted to ap-
praise the breadth of his muscles and the smoothness
of his flesh, to measure the contours of his cheekbones
and the sweep of his jaw. But by doing so she would
confirm his base opinion of her. He wouldn't understand that her interest was purely artistic curiosity.

"Miss Hastings?" he prompted, studying her with
guarded gray eyes. "Perhaps I should make myself
clearer. I'm asking you to become my mistress."

Feeling the urge to slap his flawless face, Elizabeth

21

reached into her pocket for her clay, digging her fingers into the soft ball. She would not behave like the street woman he believed her to be. "I see," she said coolly.

His dark brows lifted. "No, I don't believe you do see. I'll provide you with a house in St. John's Wood, servants to fulfill your every need, a wardrobe to befit your station." His voice lowered. "It promises to be a mutually satisfying arrangement... Elizabeth."

Resentment choked her. Did he expect her to fall at his feet in humble gratitude? "Why me, your lordship? I thought you despised artists."

He shifted his weight impatiently. "I disapprove of my sister's interest in art. That has nothing to do with my attraction to you."

"Yet you expect me to give up my work, to become your paramour."

"On the contrary, you may certainly pursue your sculpting..." The earl paused, then added in a caressing murmur, "Whenever I'm not with you."

The intensity of his gaze kindled an unexpected fever within her; the ball of clay softened under the sudden heat of her hands. Flustered, Elizabeth lowered her eyes to his starched collar and neatly knotted cravat. Despite her antipathy, it was gratifying to know the earl's passion for her burned fiercer than his scruples... that such a stunningly attractive man desired her.

He came closer and the gentle pressure of his fingers tipped her chin up. "I'm offering you a better life, Elizabeth, a safer place to live." His eyes as soft as smoke, he tenderly brushed his fingertips over her cheek. "I find myself most impatient to become your protector. I await only your permission to do so."

Lord Nicholas appeared supremely confident of her acceptance. Her throat ached as much from bitterness as from bruises. She assured herself his mistaken opinion of her morals didn't matter, so why did she feel so hurt?

Elizabeth stepped back, out of his reach. "You intend

to rob me of my good name. That's hardly the role of a *protector*."

Startled displeasure flitted over his features; his face hardened and his hands clenched. "I made you a sincere offer. You're not likely to get a better one."

"*I* would term your proposal selfish, not sincere, Mr. Ware."

"Lord Hawkesford."

His terse insistence on the title incensed her. "Oh, but you're not *my* lord. In America, terms of respect are for those who earn them."

His jaw tautened. "You're being rather judgmental, Miss Hastings. You hardly know me."

"I know hypocrisy. You'd keep a mistress tucked away while you waltz into society with your oh-so-proper wife and pretend to be a respectable, God-fearing man."

"I have no wife."

For some unfathomable reason her heart sang at his curt disclosure. "Regardless," Elizabeth stated, her fingers molding the clay, "the fact that I was not born into your British aristocracy makes me no less a lady. And the fact that you were doesn't make you a gentleman." She paused, disillusionment underlying her anger. "The best I can say of you, Lord Hawkesford, is that you have a pleasing face. Beyond that, nothing about you interests me."

He stood as stiff and cold as a marble statue. "That's quite enough, Miss Hastings. There's no need to belabor your rejection of my offer."

Abruptly he strode toward her. Fear leapt inside Elizabeth; he looked furious enough to kill. Her hand covered her bruised throat as she retreated a step.

He stopped in front of her. His eyes were as gray and unfathomable as a London fog. Her heart tripped wildly, though somehow she could not believe he meant her harm.

"My coat, miss," he said, sending a pointed glance at the garment lying on the chair directly behind her.

The alarm drained away, leaving Elizabeth feeling slightly foolish. "Of course."

Reasoning that the garment was already ruined, she reached for it without regard for her clay-smudged fingers. The fabric felt smooth and expensive to the touch, as polished and elegant as Lord Nicholas himself. Awkwardly she presented the coat to him.

He draped it over his arm, but made no move to depart. His eyes studied her intently and fascination kept her rooted. He stood so close she could see the individual strands of dark hair at his temples, the chiseled line of his cheekbones, the sleek strength of his jaw. To her delight she could not detect a single physical flaw. Even his faint, tangy scent held an uncommon appeal. The finely drawn grooves bracketing his mouth warmed the stern beauty of his face. The sudden disconcerting desire to press her lips there swept over her. How could she let this Adonis walk out of her life?

"Forgive me for having offended you, Miss Hastings. You may rest assured that I shall not trouble you again."

Stunned by the quiet apology, Elizabeth could only gape. Surely the regret on his face was impossible to trust. Lord Nicholas Ware might be handsome on the surface, but he lacked substance beneath.

Yet somehow she wanted to believe him.

Footsteps sounded outside; the doorknob rattled. The tap of a walking stick and the low whistling of a hymn preceded her father's entrance.

Her heart jolted. His shoulders were slumped beneath his Inverness cape, his billycock hat tilted back on his gray hair. She knew the instant Owen Hastings saw them; the mournful melody ceased in mid note. His hazel eyes widened, focusing first on Elizabeth, then on Lord Nicholas.

Her father's back went rigid. "What's going on here? What are you doing alone with this stranger, Libby?"

Pocketing the ball of clay, Elizabeth hastened to his side. "Everything's fine, Papa. I'd like you to meet Lord

Nicholas Ware, Cicely's brother. Lord Hawkesford, may I present my father, Owen Hastings."

Lord Nicholas inclined his head in a regal nod. "It's a pleasure, Mr. Hastings."

Her father glared. "I don't care if you're the Prince of Wales." Grasping Elizabeth's shoulder, he scrutinized her face. "Are you all right? Has he insulted you in any way?"

Shocked and shamed by her father's rudeness, she tilted her head at him. The sour smell of rye whiskey told her he'd been drinking, but alcohol usually made him melancholy, not malicious. "Of course I'm all right. Lord Nicholas came to discuss his sister—"

"What's this?" Owen's whiskered face went taut with horror as he spied her reddened throat. Abruptly he brandished the walking stick and sprang at Lord Nicholas. "You bloody scoundrel! What in holy hell have you done to my Libby?"

The earl neatly sidestepped the assault. Heedless of the coat over his arm, he wrenched the cane from Owen's hand. The stick went flying onto the worktable. Bits of clay scattered and a mallet thunked to the floor.

Her father doubled his fists, despite Lord Nicholas's superior height. "I'll kill you for harming my daughter. By God, I will!"

"Papa, no!" Shaken by his violence, Elizabeth took hold of his rough tweed sleeve. "You don't understand. Lord Hawkesford didn't hurt me—he saved my life!"

Her father started visibly and swung to her. "What?"

"A man followed me home tonight." Lifting a hand to her throat, she swallowed hard, conscious of the bruising soreness. "I was coming down the street outside when he leapt from a dark alleyway and tried to throttle me."

"Bless my soul!" Owen muttered, touching her cheek, his face gray with horror. "I knew it wasn't a good idea to come to London. Are you all right?"

Elizabeth nodded shakily. "Only because Lord Hawkesford happened upon me in time. So you see, we owe him a debt of gratitude."

"On the contrary, Miss Hastings," the earl broke in, "you may consider any debt between us cancelled."

His steady eyes caught hers. Suddenly Elizabeth felt flushed and discomfited . . . and inexplicably regretful. So he had settled for her grandfather's ring as payment, after all.

Taking off his hat, Owen raked his fingers through his graying hair. "I thank you for helping my daughter," he said brusquely. "But if you're of a mind to demand a lewd reward from her, you'll have me to answer to."

"Papa!" Though he'd struck uncomfortably right on the mark, Elizabeth was appalled. "You're embarrassing me—and Lord Hawkesford."

His expression stern, her father patted the back of her hand. "I'm sorry to address such matters in front of you, Libby, but you're far too trusting—you always have been." He aimed another glower at the earl. "There's no telling what sort of liberties a man of his position will take. Why else do you think the good Lord says 'It is easier for a camel to go through the eye of a needle, than for a rich man to enter the kingdom of God'?"

Lord Nicholas arched a dark brow. " 'Judge not, and ye shall not be judged.' "

Owen scowled. "A high-and-mighty English lord quoting the Bible? I'm surprised you'd leave your mistress's bed long enough to attend church."

"And where were you when your daughter needed help?"

A dull flush tinged Owen's whiskered cheeks. "That's none of your concern."

"Circumstance has made it my concern. I'd caution you to watch over her better in the future. This is not the sort of neighborhood a woman should be roaming alone."

"I can take care of my Libby! I don't need your advice."

"Indeed," Lord Nicholas drawled, his voice heavy with irony. With unperturbed civility, he swept Elizabeth a formal bow, then gave her father a curt nod. "It's been a pleasure."

Bemused by his self-possession, Elizabeth said, "Thank you."

The coat draped over his arm, he walked past her scowling father. At the door the earl paused to look back, his eyes as cool as the mist. "Pray keep in mind what I said about Cicely. My decision regarding her association with you is irrevocable."

The words struck Elizabeth like sleet, driving all warmth from her heart. Despite admitting his mistake about her morals, he still regarded her as an unsuitable mentor. Before she could form a reply, Lord Nicholas left, the door closing.

"Good riddance, I say!" Owen Hastings slammed his felt hat onto a wall hook. "If his lofty lordship thinks he can disgrace *my* daughter, he'll soon learn his blood isn't so blue—but red as any commoner's."

Stunned by the venom in his words, Elizabeth moved the satchel aside and sank onto the rush-bottomed chair. Never in her life had she seen her father exhibit such violent hatred. He was normally a gentle man, soft-spoken and kindhearted. He shared food with a needy neighbor when their own cupboards were bare. He'd nursed her sick mother when Elizabeth had been too exhausted to stay awake. She had even seen him carry a mouse outside rather than kill another living creature. Only twice since their arrival in England had she glimpsed his dislike for the nobility, once when a duke's passing landau had spattered him with mud and once when reading a newspaper recount of the old scandalous affair between Lord Blandford and Lady Aylesford.

Her father jerked off his cape and hurled it onto the bed. Muttering curses, he paced the room. Somehow she had to reach the tender man she knew and loved.

"Papa?" she said, leaning forward. "Lord Hawkesford meant me no harm. He acted the perfect gentleman." A blush warmed her cheeks at the memory of his ungentlemanly proposal.

"Gentleman, pah!" Angrily her father ruffled his fingers through his sparse gray hair. "This is all my fault. I should have warned you about these lords—scoundrels, every last one of them. Think they have the God-given right to any woman who strikes their fancy."

"You shouldn't condemn an entire class because of a few wicked men."

He shook a stubby finger at her. "They're all cut trom the same cloth, take my word for it. They're snooty and patronizing, don't care a whit for anybody but themselves."

"It's not like you to be so unfair, Papa. Why do you despise the nobility so?"

His cheeks paled beneath his gray whiskers. Or was it just a trick of the wavering light? Before she could decide, he swung away and busied himself making tea over the spirit lamp.

"No particular reason," he said over his shoulder. "Guess it just seems wrong to me after living so long in a country where bloodlines don't limit a man's success."

His vague answer bothered Elizabeth. "You've never said much about our life here in England before we moved to America. Where did we live?"

"Yorkshire."

"Shouldn't we have gone there, then? I thought that's one of the reasons we came, so you could contact old friends."

"I've posted a few letters, but haven't received any replies yet."

His back was turned so that she could not see his expression. Had a clash with a peer prompted their move to New York when she'd been a child of two? "Did you work for a nobleman in Yorkshire?"

Owen's hand tensed around the chipped ironstone teapot; then he laughed heartily. "Of course not, Libby. I've never been one to consort with aristocrats."

"But what about Mama? She came from a genteel family. She gave me her father's ring—"

"All of her relatives are dead," he said dismissively.

"So you see, Libby, there's nothing to tell. You're best off forgetting the whole rotten lot of them."

Elizabeth sighed. She could make no such sweeping denunciation of the nobility. At least Lord Nicholas had the decency to apologize. And he had saved her life when many people would not have bothered with a stranger.

A shudder seized her. Just a few days earlier no one had stopped to help when a fast-moving hansom cab had knocked her into a gutter. Not even the driver had paused to see if she were hurt.

"It's curious, isn't it," she mused aloud. "Tonight was the second time in less than a week that my life was endangered."

Tea leaves scattered as her father jerked around, spoon in hand. "What?"

"Remember the hansom cab that nearly ran me down in the Strand?"

"Bless my soul, yes." The spoon clattered to the floor. "The two incidents can't possibly be related," he said, as if trying to convince himself. "They just can't be."

"Of course not. I wasn't trying to suggest they were —I was only commenting on the peculiarity of the coincidence."

Owen's brow remained furrowed as he stared at the marks on her throat. "Great God, you might have been killed tonight."

Seeing his horror brought a resurgence of that helpless terror, that dreadful panic. Elizabeth quivered, tears pricking her eyes. "Oh, Papa," she cried, rushing into his arms. "I was so frightened. If Lord Nicholas hadn't come along..."

"Hush, little one. Try not to think about it anymore."

Burying her face against the solid warmth of his chest, she breathed in his familiar rye whiskey scent, rubbed her cheek against his rough coat. With the soothing stroke of his hand on her hair, the tide of fear inside her began to ebb. He had always been there to shield her from harm, but her mother's death the previous autumn had ended that. Grief made her father seek solace in drink, and Elizabeth became the strength in the family. When he expressed homesickness for England, she readily agreed to the trip, hoping the change in surroundings would cheer him. Since their arrival a month ago, though, he had sunk into deeper despair.

His arms tightened. "This is all my fault, Libby. I should have been there to protect you, both times."

The anguish in his voice shot to her heart. Elizabeth drew back to study the familiar sad lines on his whiskered face. "Please don't blame yourself, Papa. I should have known better than to stay at Westminster until almost dark."

"Perhaps I shouldn't have brought you here. Perhaps we should have stayed in New York."

"But then I wouldn't have been able to see all the old monuments and churches here, to visit all the art museums. You've given me a wonderful opportunity, Papa."

"I'm glad for that. If only..."

"If only, what?"

Sighing heavily, he shook his head. "If only I had the money to find us lodgings in a safer neighborhood."

Elizabeth had the odd feeling that was not what he'd started to say. "We'll have the money in a few months," she said. "You'll soon secure a teaching position, I'm sure of it. And who knows? Perhaps I shall land a grand commission...to sculpt Gladstone or maybe even Queen Victoria herself."

He smiled with a ghost of his former cheer. "That's my Libby, always full of hope, always looking on the bright side. I'm proud of you, girl."

He left to finish fixing his tea and Elizabeth wandered to the worktable. On the untidy surface her copybook lay open to the sketch she'd started of Lord Nicholas. Even in those few quick strokes, the splendor of his profile was unmistakable. Yet something about him looked not quite right.

Sitting, she took the pencil and began to fill in the

details from memory. His essence evaded her . . . that force of character she had seen from the moment she'd regained consciousness in his arms. Elizabeth flushed, recalling how she'd condemned him as nothing but a handsome face. Now that the heat of anger had passed, she was not so certain of her judgment. It took a strong and sensitive man to tender an apology, didn't it?

Then again, maybe her father was right. Maybe she was too trusting, too ready to believe the best of people.

Absently she reached for the ball of clay lying heavily in her pocket. With a shock Elizabeth saw that unintentionally she'd begun sculpting the earl's face . . . the firm line of his jaw, the haughty tilt of his chin. She moistened the drying clay in a bowl of water and began to refine the rudimentary image. The familiar earthy scent of the clay soothed her.

Hours later, long after her father had retired to his adjacent bedroom, she looked in satisfaction at the likeness of Lord Nicholas. It was unfinished, but at least she could see that elusive spark of life within the clay. She wrapped the bust in a damp rag and covered it with oilcloth, then washed her hands and tumbled into bed.

Despite her weariness Elizabeth found herself staring into the darkness. What if she'd agreed to the earl's proposal? He would have taken her into his arms, held her against that hard body, kissed her. Perhaps at this very moment she would have been lying naked beside him. . . .

The image made her feel strangely warm. Rolling over, she fluffed the pillow into a more comfortable shape, then closed her eyes, willing him out of her mind. It was no use.

Try as she might, she couldn't stop thinking about him.

Chapter 3

He couldn't stop thinking about her.

For the tenth time in as many minutes, Nicholas attempted to concentrate on the speech of a minor lord. The bill under discussion was one he supported: a proposal to expand public education. The debate had drawn a fair-sized crowd to the long, stately Chamber of Lords with its elaborate heraldic designs on the walls and ceiling. A few peers dozed off the effects of luncheon, the other members listening courteously.

Nicholas knew he should be reviewing his own imminent speech. Instead he found himself recalling how soft and vulnerable Elizabeth Hastings had looked upon awakening in his arms, how the rain-dampened fabric of her bodice had outlined her womanly shape. In his mind he unbuttoned her gown and peeled away her chemise, cradled her bare breasts in his hands and put his mouth to her puckered nipple—

A loud exclamation interrupted the fantasy. Murmuring swept the assemblage, but Nicholas had no notion of what point the speaker had made.

To hell with Elizabeth Hastings, he thought, shifting irritably on the red leather bench. He couldn't understand why she obsessed him. She was an artist, for God's sake, too unconventional and independent for his tastes.

The ache in his loins did little to improve his disposition. Remembering how disdainfully she'd rejected his proposal, he scowled. He hadn't felt so humbled since

adolescence, when his father had chastised him for
succumbing to the charms of a pretty parlor maid.
From then on, Nicholas had conducted discreet liaisons
within his own social circle.

Until now.

Too late he'd recognized the innocence inherent in
Elizabeth Hastings's proud bearing and offended dignity. His sense of honor had prompted an apology and
that should end the matter. She had made her contempt unmistakable.

*You have a pleasing face. Beyond that, nothing about you
interests me.*

The words haunted him. Maybe he was too accustomed to fawning women. His pride was bruised; that
must be why he couldn't purge her from his mind. The
acknowledgment of his conceited behavior was a bitter
pill to swallow.

Reaching into the pocket of his morning coat, Nicholas drew forth the signet ring he'd forgotten to return to Elizabeth Hastings. He ran a finger across the
seal; embossed in the silver was a soaring swan on a
shield. Although he didn't recognize the coat of arms,
it clearly belonged to a noble house. If her grandfather
was a peer, then why did she live in poverty? And why
did she have that husky-soft American accent while her
father spoke like a native Englishman?

It was none of his concern, Nicholas told himself. Yet
for four days now he'd kept the ring when the most
logical course of action was to return it by messenger.

So much for logic.

Restlessly he moved on the hard bench, only half
hearing the droning voice of yet another bombastic
bore. Anticipation burned inside Nicholas. He would
stay long enough to say his piece and cast his vote.

Then, using the ring as an excuse, he would call on
Elizabeth Hastings.

"Does your brother know you're here today?"

From her chair at the worktable, Elizabeth gazed suspiciously at the girl standing before a half-finished bust

on a pedestal. Afternoon sunshine poured through the tall windows, setting fire to Cicely's chestnut hair. Her coarse white apron looked incongruous against the turquoise-striped silk of her gown, and clay smeared the lace at her cuff. Unlike the earl, Lady Cicely Ware's appearance was closer to average than perfect. Her features were symmetrical but unremarkable. All that saved her from the ordinary was a mischievous smile and thick-lashed eyes the color of lapis lazuli.

At the moment those eyes were avoiding Elizabeth. "Who, Nicholas?" Cicely said, as if she had a dozen brothers instead of just one. "Oh, pooh, of course he knows I'm here."

She walked quickly to the unkempt boy perched on a wooden box in the center of the room. "Might I bother you to turn a bit to your right, Kipp?"

With ill-concealed boyish awe, the urchin regarded Cicely. His face was filthy beneath a misshapen bowler hat, his feet bare beneath tattered knickers. "Be glad to, yer ladyship, ma'am." Obligingly Kipp Gullidge shifted position.

"Not quite so far, please. There, that's perfect. Thank you."

Cicely returned to the pedestal and studied the bust. "Now perhaps I shall get this right."

Half amused and half exasperated, Elizabeth refused to be distracted. "Back to your brother. If Lord Nicholas knows you're here, he must have changed his way of thinking over the past four days."

Cicely's hands froze on the clay. "Four days? How did you . . . oh." Her voice dropped to an abashed murmur. "He came here to see you, then."

Elizabeth nodded.

Cicely's blue eyes were big with guilt. "Oh, pooh. And I was hoping I'd convinced him I'd given up art."

"You should have told me he disapproved of your working with me, Cicely."

Her lips pursed into a pout. "It's none of his concern. If I'm old enough to come out into society, then I'm old enough to make my own decisions."

"Yet he *is* your brother. Like it or not, that does give him something to say about your behavior."

"All Nicholas wants is to see me married off to some stern-faced prig." Wrinkling her patrician nose in disgust, she added, "He thinks I ought to spend my time snaring a husband, then devote the rest of my life to pleasing him. How terribly tedious!"

Elizabeth agreed, though she kept the opinion to herself. "Regardless, you should have been honest with me."

"I'm sorry," Cicely said in a subdued voice. "If you tell me not to come here any more, I'll understand."

The proud set to her chin brought a stinging reminder of the earl. "No, I won't say that," Elizabeth said. "I couldn't bear seeing your talent wasted."

Cicely dubiously eyed the bust. "Do you really think I have talent? Looks rather out of kilter."

Kipp craned his neck. "Blimey, it looks like me all right."

"Let me see," Elizabeth said.

Setting aside her sketch pad, she rounded the table, her Turkish trousers swishing. Though only roughly shaped, the highlights and hollows of the face were unmistakably Kipp. Yet somehow the impish quality of his personality was missing.

"These lines here are a bit out of proportion," she said, indicating the jaw and chin. "You used a penknife, didn't you? To breathe life into the clay, you're better off relying on your fingers." Elizabeth swept her thumb across the malleable clay. "See how free, long strokes give freshness to the surface? And remember what I told you—you want to create more than a mere likeness. You must look beneath the outer features and express the inner character."

"You always make it look so simple," Cicely said dolefully. "I don't understand . . . I was always good at drawing, yet I don't appear to be making any progress at sculpting."

"It takes lots of time and work. Don't get discouraged."

"But how much time? I want to become as skilled as you."

Laughing, Elizabeth returned to her chair. "Patience, Cicely. I started sculpting when I was younger than you and I've been at it for eight years now."

Cicely arched curious brows. "Where did you learn so much?"

"I attended art school in New York. But most of all, I learned by doing...by making mistakes and trying again, over and over."

"Then I shall do so, too," Cicely declared. "I intend to come as often as possible to study with you."

"What about your brother?"

"Oh, pooh," Cicely said with an airy wave of her hand. "He's off at parliament much of the time. Anyway, I won't let Nicholas stand in my way."

Elizabeth couldn't so easily shrug off the earl. If he were to discover his sister's deception, he would certainly take steps to stop her. What would he do? Put a guard on Cicely? Banish her to the country? Elizabeth doubted he'd come back here after the setdown she'd given him. Somehow that thought sparked a peculiar pang of regret.

Picking up her pencil, she gazed at the copybook. The page contained sketch upon sketch of the earl— studies of his face, his body, his hands. The memory of his finely chiseled features was both bright and elusive. She recalled the suggestion of arrogance in his posture, the hint of superiority in the set of his lips. Yet certain details escaped her.

Frowning, Elizabeth nibbled at the end of her pencil. Were his eyes soft or severe? Did his hair curl just the slightest bit or was it as well disciplined as his personality? She longed to see him again, to examine him from every angle. The thought of viewing him without his clothing especially fascinated her. At the Art Students League of New York, she'd done many drawings of nude models; now she felt the burning desire to see sunlight flowing over Lord Nicholas's strong torso, gleaming on the magnificent curves and planes of mus-

cle, metamorphosing the man into a perfect living
sculpture.

"Bloody 'ell," Kipp muttered.

Elizabeth looked up to see the urchin shifting restlessly on the wooden box. "What's wrong?"

"Cor, Miss Libby, me leg's in a crimp," he said, rubbing a bare, filthy calf. "'Ow much longer you be wantin' me to sit so quiet?"

Her heart went out to the boy. "I'm sorry, Kipp.
You've certainly earned a break."

"Better yet, why don't we stop for the day?" Cicely
suggested. "It's so pretty outside, we could stroll to the
Embankment and make some sketches."

Cicely's eagerness to quit troubled Elizabeth. This
was not the first time the girl had ended the sculpting
session early. Certainly she had talent, but her enthusiasm came in fits and starts. Did she have the interest
and dedication necessary to devote her life to art? Or
was Lord Nicholas right? Was she intrigued by a false
romantic perception of artists?

Glancing at her copybook, Elizabeth decided she
wasn't accomplishing much today, either. She slapped
the pad shut.

"All right, Kipp, that'll be all. If you'll wait a moment, I'll fetch your payment." Rising, she headed toward the ginger jar where she kept her meager stash of
money.

"Oh, do allow me, please." Heedless of her clay-
smeared fingers, Cicely dug into a small frilly reticule
and extracted a sovereign. "Here you are, Kipp."

Eyes round and brown as his bowler hat, the boy
snatched up the gold coin and clutched it to his shabby
checked shirt. "Cor, is this all fer me?"

"Why, of course," Cicely said, eyes sparkling at his
delight. "You may spend it however you like."

"God bless you, yer ladyship, ma'am," he said, bobbing his head.

The wage far exceeded the tuppence Elizabeth had
promised Kipp for acting as model. She wanted to protest, but held her tongue. Cicely meant well by the

grand gesture. Though Elizabeth had told the girl about Kipp's background, Cicely couldn't seem to grasp the fact that the boy's mother would likely squander the money on gin.

Regarding the pair with fondness and frustration, Elizabeth stepped to an open door. The tiny room adjacent to her studio was scrupulously neat and frugally furnished with an iron cot and washstand. Sitting beside the single opened window, glasses perched on his nose and a Bible in his lap, was her father.

"Papa? As soon as I change clothes, Cicely and I are going out."

Smiling, he removed the spectacles. "I'll be right along, then."

"You needn't trouble yourself. I'll be back before dark."

"Regardless, I shan't allow you to go out alone."

"You never objected in New York."

"I won't take any more chances with your life, Libby. First you nearly got run down by a hansom cab, then a criminal tried to choke you." A stark expression on his whiskered face, he laid down the Bible. "I couldn't bear to lose you, too. You're all I have left."

Elizabeth's heart contracted. Her own grief at her mother's death still ached like an unhealed wound. Sometimes she had the feeling that if she turned around, Lucy Templeton Hastings would be standing there, her eyes laughing, her smile tender. How much worse it must be for a husband to lose a beloved wife.

"You'll not lose me, Papa," she said, giving him a quick hug. "But I'd love for you to come with us."

As she left the bedroom Elizabeth wondered if only sorrow had prompted her father's mood. She adjusted the cheap lace fichu covering the fading bruises on her throat. Did he still think the episodes of the cab and the criminal might somehow be connected? Surely not; the notion was absurd.

Why would anyone want to kill her?

* * *

"Kill her," whispered the shadowed figure. Though the afternoon was sunny, heavy curtains on the windows kept the barren room dim and stuffy. "Two weeks already and she's still alive."

"'Tain't my fault the bleedin' gent come along to save 'er," whined the man in the porkpie hat. "'E tried to kill me, that 'e did!"

"So you fled like a frightened rat. And in four days, you've not found another opportunity."

"The trull ain't left 'er rooms. An' that old man o' 'ers been stickin' closer to 'er than a flea to a mongrel. Wot d'you expect me—"

"Expect! I expect you to stop sniveling and earn your pay. You'll not see a tuppence more until the bitch is lying in the morgue. Now get on with you!"

Glowering, the coarse-faced man slunk out the door. For a moment faint noises from the street mingled with the quiet sound of breathing. The room was empty of furnishings; this was not a place to live . . . it was a place to wait and watch.

Footsteps echoing on the filthy wood floor, the figure moved through the shadows. Well-scrubbed fingers parted the tattered curtain; the heel of a hand rubbed a clean spot in the soot-streaked windowpane. Three floors below, the narrow byway teemed with activity. Children played skittle, women gossiped on stoops, a costermonger bawled out his wares, selling vegetables from a barrow.

Disgusting. It was hard to imagine Lucy's daughter living in such squalor.

A quartet of people emerged from the tenement directly opposite. A scruffy boy waved a farewell and darted into the crowd. The remaining three, two young women and a gray-haired man, started down the street toward the Strand.

Fingers tensed around the ragged drapery. There was Lucy's savior, Owen. And beside him . . .

The watcher's eyes focused on the woman in the center of the trio. The cygnet had grown into a beautiful swan. She was petite and lithe and proud of bearing. In the sunlight her loosely gathered hair shone black as a raven's wing.

She looked so like Lucy it was uncanny.

Lucy.

Long-buried grief burned like a draught of bitter medicine. For too many years Lucy had been gone. It was hard to believe the contents of that letter. Lucy couldn't be dead . . . it must be a trick! Yes, that was the answer. They were hiding her, protecting her. The proof that she lived must lie in her daughter's lodgings.

Elizabeth was the disease . . . Elizabeth must die.

Not Lucy.

Chapter 4

Pausing in the open doorway of Elizabeth Hastings's lodgings, Lord Nicholas stared in consternation. What had once been a charming hodgepodge of miscellany was now a chaos of clutter. The soft light of dusk drifted over scattered papers and plundered belongings. The drawers of the table had been pulled out and emptied. Feminine garments lay jumbled before an opened steamer trunk. Even the coverlet had been ripped from the ancient iron bedstead, and the bamboo screen tilted drunkenly against the wall.

Standing amidst the mess, their backs to the door, were Elizabeth and Owen Hastings. The stout, gray-haired man held an arm around his daughter's slim waist. Her head was bowed, her shoulders slumped.

Alarm pulled at Nicholas's heart. Stepping through the debris, he removed his silk top hat and asked, "Are you all right, Elizabeth? What's happened here?"

The pair swung around in unison and stared in surprise. Then Owen's face darkened; Elizabeth's lightened.

"We're fine, thank you," she said. "We came home a few minutes ago to find the place looking like this."

She waved despondently at the turmoil. Nicholas felt the violent urge to throttle the criminal who had ransacked her rooms. Elizabeth Hastings was a proud woman, an independent woman. She had little in the way of material goods, but he could understand her sense of violation.

"We must report this to the police," he said. "They'll question your neighbors, find out if anyone was seen entering or leaving the place."

"Humph," Owen growled. "You'll get little help from that lot of lazy actors and shiftless drunks."

Seemingly oblivious to her father's words, Elizabeth bent to caress the splintered mandolin at her feet. Only then did Nicholas spy the woman perched on an overturned crate beyond.

"Cicely!"

Her blue eyes huge, his sister sprang to her feet. She looked bravely defiant, though her twining fingers betrayed nervousness. "Nicholas," she squeaked, "whatever are you doing here?"

He leveled a stern look at her. "I should ask *you* that."

"I . . . I left my reticule. Last week, I mean . . . before you ordered me not to come here, of course."

"You couldn't have sent a footman?"

She shrugged prettily. "I was out anyway, so I thought I'd fetch it myself."

"I see," he said, his voice heavy with irony. Not for a moment did his sister fool him with those soulful eyes and that blithe smile. "Then you can, of course, explain why your cuffs are smeared with clay?"

"My cuffs?" Guilt stole over Cicely's face as she examined the stains at her wrists. "Oh, pooh. I don't suppose you'd believe I fell into the mud?"

"Hardly. Tell me, how did you manage to escape Miss Eversham's watchful eyes?"

"I slipped out the back door of the milliner's shop." For a moment Cicely looked as proud as a naughty child, then her fair face tightened into familiar rebellious lines. "It serves you right for having her spy on me, Nicholas. I don't need a governess anymore. I'm old enough to know my own mind."

"On the contrary, Cicely, you've yet to prove your maturity. You had express orders not to come here."

Owen bristled like an angry boar. "So, we're not good enough for the likes of you, are we, your lordship? You can't abide knowing your own sister prefers the company of commoners."

Nicholas focused his most icy glare on the older man. "What I can't abide is allowing Cicely to ruin her reputation. Not, of course, that her welfare is any concern of yours."

"You bloody pharisee!" Owen shook his fist. "How dare you imply that associating with my daughter will corrupt Lady Cicely? Libby's a good girl and a fine artist! You ought to be grateful she's willing to teach your sister."

Nicholas controlled a rising resentment. "I mean no insult to your daughter. Nevertheless, I cannot encourage Cicely to consort with bohemians."

"You're just jealous," Cicely burst out. "*You* may have gotten the looks in the family, but *I* was born with the artistic talent."

"Enough, all of you." Elizabeth dropped the broken mandolin and stood, sending Nicholas an unhappy look that sliced straight to his heart. She turned those stunning violet eyes to her father and Cicely. "Can't we discuss this later? So much has happened today; so much has been lost." She gestured at the untidy room.

Owen gathered her into his arms. "I'm sorry, Libby," he said in an abashed tone. "I didn't mean to upset you. We'll find the scoundrel who did this."

"I just don't understand," she murmured. "Why would anyone be so destructive?"

"The Proverbs say, 'The tender mercies of the wicked are cruel,'" said Owen, brushing a hand over the loose cascade of her black hair. "Whoever did this possesses no human compassion. There are many people in this world like that, Libby. Far, far too many."

His eyes held a distant look that struck Nicholas as odd. Something had soured Owen on life, something that colored his views on aristocrats. . . .

His gaze moving to Elizabeth, Nicholas forgot all but the sharp longing to be the one comforting her, kissing away her sadness, fulfilling her every need until she felt no melancholy.

But that was impossible.

"Come along, Cicely," he said brusquely. "You'll wait in the carriage."

"But I—"

"This is not a topic for debate."

At that quiet, chilling tone his sister meekly said her good-byes and collected a clay-soiled reticule from the floor. Silently Nicholas offered her his arm. Taking one last glance at Elizabeth Hastings's forlorn face, he escorted Cicely down the narrow flight of stairs filled with the smells of food and rubbish.

A small crowd gathered around the closed landau with its crest on the polished black door. A cluster of slatternly housewives gossiped behind their hands, several unkempt urchins played tag on the littered sidewalk, a pieman stopped and gawked at the sight of a lord's fine carriage gracing this tumbledown neighborhood. Sitting stiff and regal in the coachman's seat, Greaves held his whip at an angle that clearly discouraged anyone from so much as touching the vehicle.

Pickering leapt from his rear perch, his face impassive as he opened the door. Nicholas gave his sister a hand inside.

"Wait here," he ordered, tossing his top hat beside her as she settled her skirts.

Cicely looked startled. "We're not going home?"

"I'll just be a few moments. And, by God, you'd best stay put until I return."

Leaving her pouting inside the landau, he gave explicit directions to Greaves regarding Cicely; then Nicholas again mounted the five flights of stairs to the Hastings flat.

He found both Owen and Elizabeth digging through the rubble.

"Was anything stolen?"

Owen glowered. Elizabeth looked up, her brow furrowed. "As a matter of fact, yes," she said. "I can't seem to find the sketchbook with all the drawings of my mother. . . ."

"I meant money," Nicholas said. "Or something of

monetary value that would interest a common thief."

"Oh." She waved a hand toward the overturned washstand as she continued to search. "The ginger jar was broken, but our money's still there."

Frowning, he stepped carefully through the clutter to see the appallingly small amount of silver scattered amidst the broken bits of blue and white porcelain.

"Perhaps we frightened the culprit away before he could steal the coins," Owen suggested.

"You would have seen him coming down the staircase, then," Nicholas said. Hands on his hips, he studied the high north windows; one stood open, the cool breeze of dusk stirring the papers on the floor. Outlined against the rose-streaked sky was the flat roof of the next tenement, easily reached by an agile burglar. "Unless, of course, he exited through that window."

Owen followed the earl's gaze. "Bless my soul... Libby, we didn't leave that window ajar, did we?"

Elizabeth glanced up, a sheaf of drawings in her hand, a distracted expression on her face. "I don't remember. All I want is to find that sketchbook. You know the one I mean, Papa. You and Mama gave it to me for my sixteenth birthday—the cover is royal blue with gold embossing."

Owen sifted through the papers, his whiskered face oddly frantic. "It must be here somewhere," he muttered. "It *must!*"

A peculiar intensity underscored his words, an intensity Nicholas might have ascribed to fear had that not been absurd. Surely losing a few drawings of Elizabeth's late mother would be cause for sadness, not alarm. Unless Owen was hiding something? Could he have known what the thief was really after?

Nicholas pushed away the unlikely idea. Owen Hastings's mood was probably based on worry for his daughter's safety. After all, had they surprised the burglar, the episode might have ended in tragedy. . . .

The thought made Nicholas's blood run cold. Not only would Cicely's life have been endangered, but

Elizabeth's as well. He wondered suddenly if her neck were still bruised beneath that lace fichu.

"Miss Hastings."

She glanced up. "Yes?"

In the fading light her eyes were the deep, distinctive hue of damson plums. Her quaint mulberry gown and the flowing hair caught back at her temples lent her an aura of unadorned sensuality. Desire flared in him. Had she any notion of how seductive she looked?

Tersely Nicholas asked, "Did you report that first incident to the police?"

She tilted her head to the side. "The hansom cab? No, should I have?"

"What cab?"

"The one that nearly ran me down—" She paused, confusion clouding her eyes. "I'm sorry, of course you meant that dreadful man who tried to strangle me. Yes, I did draw the police a likeness, but the inspector seemed doubtful he'd be apprehended."

Nicholas wasn't surprised. A criminal could easily vanish into the nearby Seven Dials rookery, a nucleus of crime riddled with dark alleys and winding passageways, a place into which even the police were reluctant to venture.

Feeling taut as an overwound clock, he said, "Tell me about this incident with the cab."

"Now see here," Owen declared, straightening his stout frame and glaring at the earl. "I'll take care of my daughter. There's no need to meddle in our affairs."

"It's all right, Papa. I don't mind telling him. After all, he *did* save my life." Sitting on her heels, Elizabeth plucked a glob of clay from the floor and manipulated it absently as she related the story. "I'm sure it was just an accident," she concluded with a wave of her clay-smudged hand.

But Nicholas wasn't so certain. Deep in thought, he righted a crooked drawing tacked to the wall. It seemed incredible that three times in two weeks calamity could strike Elizabeth Hastings.

Disquieted, he addressed Owen. "This neighborhood is far too dangerous for your daughter. You cannot in all conscience keep her here."

"That's simple for you to say." Owen kicked at a chisel; the tool went rolling through the debris. "Did you ever stop to think some of us can't afford a fancy mansion in Mayfair or Belgravia?"

"Papa will find a job soon," Elizabeth said. "Then we'll move."

"In the meantime," Nicholas said, "don't you have relatives to whom you can turn?" Reaching into the pocket of his morning coat, he drew out the signet ring and held it in the palm of his hand. "What about the owner of this?"

Owen stared, his face paling. "Where did you get that?"

"I gave it to the earl, Papa." Elizabeth rose gracefully, the lump of clay clutched in one hand. "To reimburse him for ruining his coat sleeve when he rescued me."

"Why, you greedy blighter!" Owen spat at Nicholas. "More wealth than the lot of us could ever dream of and you'd still make a lady reward you."

"Think what you will," Nicholas said stiffly. To Elizabeth, he said, "I never meant to keep the ring—when I left the other night, I'd forgotten it was in my pocket. I came here today to return it."

She looked stunned. "Thank you."

He stepped through the litter to gently press the ring into her clay-stained palm. Her hand felt fragile yet strong; her scent was earthy yet appealing. Her bold, beautiful eyes studied him with rapt attention, and he swallowed the bitter knowledge that her interest in him was purely artistic. With dismaying quickness, his body responded to her nearness. How different their relationship would have been had she accepted his proposal. He would have possessed the right to touch more than her hand, to learn the feminine form beneath that flowing gown, to discover the womanly warmth beneath that unconventional facade.

"All right, then," growled Owen. "You've done what

you came here for, your lordship. Now if you'll excuse us, my daughter and I have work to do."

Releasing Elizabeth's hand, Nicholas turned to the older man. "You didn't answer my question about your relations. Why haven't you contacted the owner of that ring?"

"What I do is no affair of yours."

"Papa, please, don't be rude." Fastening the ring to the chain around her neck, Elizabeth told Nicholas, "My grandfather is dead, the rest of the family, too. I'm afraid we have no alternative but to stay here."

Nicholas caught Owen's eyes sliding away from his daughter, and again suspected the man was hiding something. What? Did it have something to do with the former owner of the signet? A stunning thought struck. Was Owen Hastings's secret connected to the purportedly "accidental" threats to Elizabeth's life?

His insides took a sickening plunge; with effort Nicholas held himself steady. The notion seemed preposterous. Why would anyone wish to murder a penniless artist? And why would her father conceal that knowledge when he appeared so devoted to her?

Yet the possibility nagged at Nicholas; he resolved to do some quiet investigating. The urge to protect Elizabeth welled within him, coupled with an inexplicable longing to keep her close. An idea hit with the force of a thunderclap, an idea that seemed the perfect solution. . . .

"You do have an alternative," he said. "You can move into my home and teach Cicely."

Elizabeth stared, her lips parting in astonishment. Live in his house? See him every day? In spite of her dislike for his highbrow manner, excitement sparked inside her and her fingers dug into the modeling clay. She could study his perfection until she knew every line, every angle. . . .

Her father snorted in disgust. "I see you change your opinions to suit your own selfish purposes. A moment ago we weren't good enough to associate with your sister."

The earl arched his dark brows. "Those were your words, Mr. Hastings, not mine."

"Yet you did make it plain you didn't want Cicely to study art," Elizabeth stated.

"I'm beginning to realize how determined she is. Whether that determination arises from sincere interest or from stubborn defiance I cannot yet say." He paused, his cool eyes making her feel curiously warm. "I'm willing to indulge Cicely provided she studies within the confines of her home."

Elizabeth tried to discern the thoughts behind that handsome facade. Perhaps it was the fading light, but her skills of observation seemed to have deserted her. His words sounded reasonable, but she wondered at his abrupt turnabout. Did he still mean to make her his mistress?

Her insides tightened into a delicious knot; the clay felt hot and damp in her fingers. With a shock she realized that a part of her *wanted* him to want her. Yet surely he couldn't still desire her after the angry words she'd flung in his face.

"My daughter is too talented to work as your servant," Owen snapped. "She's a wonderful artist who's managed to flourish without your patronage."

"Indeed?" Lord Nicholas mused. "So you'll let her remain here and risk another accident? I wonder at your lack of concern."

Owen's face paled. An intense look passed between the two men, a look Elizabeth couldn't fathom. Her father opened his mouth, then tightened it to a thin line.

"How dare you imply my father isn't concerned," she snapped.

Owen's shoulders slumped. "It's all right, Libby." To the earl, he added stiffly, "All right, then, you have my consent. Libby will move into your household."

Flabbergasted, Elizabeth stared at her father, her fingers frozen on the clay. "I will?"

He came closer and put his hands on her shoulders. "I must do what's best for you, Libby." Expelling a heavy sigh, he added, "The earl is right. You aren't safe here."

The deep lines of suffering on his face tore at her heart. "Papa, what happened today didn't threaten my life. The thief ran off the moment he heard us returning."

"What about the man who tried to throttle you?"

She shuddered. Recalling Lord Nicholas's protection, she sought his eyes. The memory of that terror retained the power to tighten her throat and hasten her heartbeat.

Looking back at her father, she said, "That incident was a misfortune, Papa, a coincidence. It could have happened to anyone."

"It's settled, Libby." Releasing her, he faced the earl. "I mean to come with her."

Picking up a drawing, Lord Nicholas gave a careless shrug. "As you wish. I'm sure your daughter would be more comfortable with you near."

"You'll pay her a suitable wage, I trust. I'll not live on your charity, either. I'm planning to find a post as a teacher."

"Perhaps I could be of assistance."

"I'll do well enough on my own." Owen narrowed his hazel eyes. "And you'll treat my Libby like the decent girl she is."

The earl set aside the paper and his chilly gray gaze came to rest on Elizabeth. "I wouldn't dream of doing otherwise."

His voice iced over with distaste. Her fingers clenched the clay; her cheeks went hot. Her father couldn't know just how easy a promise that was for the earl to make.

"Just one moment, both of you," she said. "I haven't yet agreed to anything."

"Will you force me to remove my sister from temptation altogether?" Lord Nicholas said. "If you won't consent to my conditions, I shall send her to the country."

The steel in his tone told Elizabeth he meant every word . . . he would banish his vivacious sister. Resentfully Elizabeth knew he was playing upon her sympathies and her friendship with Cicely.

"It's not that I object to teaching your sister. You're asking me to give up the freedom I have here, the freedom to do my own work."

"The freedom to lay yourself open to attack?" Lord Nicholas said dryly. "I rather doubt Cicely would take up all your time. The span of her attention tends to be rather short. You'll have ample time to pursue your own artistic endeavors."

Elizabeth longed to make *him* her artistic endeavor. Each time she looked at the earl she caught some fascinating detail she hadn't noticed before . . . the indomitable set of his shoulders or the softening of his granite gray eyes when he spoke of his sister. She recalled the tender pressure of his hand when he had given her the ring; his skin was not calloused like a common laborer's, but smooth and strong. Her nimble fingers worked at capturing in clay the essence of his energy.

Weakening, she said, "I'd need a studio and space to store all my tools and materials."

"You may use my conservatory. And I will, of course, purchase whatever supplies you and Cicely should need." In the deepening dusk the earl's eyes were dark as graphite. "My primary concern, Miss Hastings, is to keep my sister content and happy within the bounds of propriety."

The gentling of his voice when he spoke of Cicely persuaded Elizabeth. "All right, then."

"Excellent. Gather up whatever you'll need for the night and we'll join my sister in the carriage."

She stared. "I can't leave now. Why, it'll take days to sort this mess—"

"Be sensible, Miss Hastings. You can't stay here." He swept a hand around the chaotic room.

"His lordship is right," her father said in a weighted voice, as if the admission cost him dearly.

Dismayed, Elizabeth accepted the truth. Shadows gathered in the corners, veiling her ruined treasures. Tears stung her eyes. Desolation clutched at her stomach, a sense of violation at knowing a stranger had rifled through her possessions. The item most precious of all was missing. . . .

Lord Nicholas took a step toward her, then stopped, almost as if he'd meant to comfort her and thought better of it. "I'll send my footmen round first thing tomorrow to collect the rest of your belongings."

"The sketchbook with my mother's portraits—"

"I shall instruct my men to take special care to look for it."

"Thank you."

"My pleasure."

His smile took Elizabeth by surprise. Somehow his face looked kinder, less imposing and more approachable. The vestiges of doubt vanished in the delight of studying the masculine dimples on either side of his mouth. She felt a sudden shivery longing to press her lips there. . . .

Her father cleared his throat. "Well, Libby, perhaps we'd best pack a few things while there's still light to see by."

Flustered, she pocketed the clay model of Lord Nicholas's hand; its weight against her thigh made her imagine his skilled fingers caressing her, shaping her like a living sculpture. She wondered wistfully if warmth dwelled within the earl, if the right woman might chip away his stern marble facade and find a tender man beneath.

Confused by her wayward thoughts, she turned her attention to stuffing some personal items into her artist's satchel. As her hands sifted through the chaos, her mind sifted through the changes taking place in her life. She couldn't deny a simmering excitement. Did she desire only to study Lord Nicholas's perfection?

Or had her woman's heart taken precedence over her artist's eye?

Chapter 5

When they emerged into the teeming street, the sky had gone a deep slate gray. Everyone was out enjoying the balmy evening. Laughing children darted through the crowd; housewives clustered to gossip, day laborers hurried home. The ever-present odors of rubbish and smoke and cooking perfumed the air.

One of Elizabeth's neighbors, a large-boned actress from a nearby Covent Garden theatre, gaped at the fine figure of the earl. "'Ey, 'andsome," she called, wriggling her generous hips. "Need a place to lay yer 'ead for the night?"

With haughty disdain Lord Nicholas ignored the woman, though color washed his elegant cheekbones. Elizabeth swallowed a bubble of startled amusement. The arrogant Earl of Hawkesford . . . embarrassed? Somehow he didn't seem capable of such a human emotion.

They headed through the throng of people toward an opened landau at the curb. The twin coach lamps were lit against the thickening darkness.

"What the devil," Lord Nicholas muttered.

Elizabeth spied the reason for his exclamation. Surrounded by curious spectators, Cicely sat in the carriage like a queen holding court.

The earl quickened his pace. As Elizabeth hurried to keep up, she saw Kipp standing alongside the elegant vehicle. From the elevated front seat, the stout coachman brandished his whip.

"Get on with you, lad," he said, his voice booming above the din. "Don't be botherin' 'er ladyship, or the earl'll turn yer filthy 'ide to mincemeat."

Kipp planted his fists on his hips. "I ain't afraid o' no fancy-pants earl."

"Oh, leave off, Greaves," Cicely said. "I tell you I know the boy." Catching sight of her brother, she leaned over the side and lifted a ladylike hand. "Why, hullo, Nick! Will you kindly tell Greaves to cease badgering my friend?"

Ignoring her, Lord Nicholas glared first at the impeccable liveried footman, who stood at rigid attention on his rear perch, then at the coachman, who nervously bobbed his cockaded hat. "Greaves, I trust you have an explanation for why the top has been folded down?"

"'Er ladyship asked me to, m'lord," said the coachman, his tone subdued.

"I see," the earl said in his most chilling voice. "And if she asked you to let her roam the neighborhood unescorted I suppose you'd have agreed to that, as well."

"No, m'lord," the coachman said hastily. "I'll set it to rights immediately."

He started to clamber down, but Lord Nicholas stopped the servant with an imperious wave. "Never mind. The purpose was to protect my sister in my absence. Since we're about to depart, that hardly matters now."

"Oh, Nick, please don't be angry," Cicely said, her smile cajoling. "I threatened to put down the top myself if Greaves refused. It was growing ever so dark and stuffy inside."

"Aye, an' she wanted to talk to me," said Kipp, thrusting out his thin chest. "'Er and me's the best o' mates."

"Indeed." Lifting haughty eyebrows, Lord Nicholas surveyed the unkempt boy, from his misshapen bowler hat to his filthy bare toes. "And who, might I ask, are you?"

Kipp squared his scrawny shoulders and jabbed a thumb at his ragged shirt. "Me name's Kipp Gullidge, yer lordship, sir. 'Er ladyship's been makin' a likeness o' me."

"Kipp is a friend of mine," Elizabeth said. "He sometimes poses for me."

"He's a good boy," her father added with a touch of antagonism. "I wouldn't allow my daughter to associate with just anyone."

The earl's gaze swung to her, his flawless features set into a familiar forbidding expression. It seemed suddenly difficult for her to catch a breath. Despite the lamplight she could not read his thoughts. Unexpectedly he turned away and offered a hand to the boy.

"It's a pleasure to make your acquaintance, Master Gullidge."

Surprise stabbed Elizabeth as Lord Nicholas shook the urchin's grubby hand. The earl looked as grave as if he were greeting Gladstone himself. Kipp's chest puffed out even more, and he glanced around as if to make sure the onlookers had noticed a person of quality singling him out.

Elizabeth's heart went liquid. Lord Nicholas might easily have snubbed the boy, but instead had given him something to swagger about for days to come.

"I was just telling Kipp about the break-in," said Cicely.

"Aye, an' the bugger 'oo done it'll 'ave the devil to pay when I nab 'im!"

Lord Nicholas aimed a stern look at the lad. "I forbid you to involve yourself. You're to leave this matter to the police, do you hear?"

"But 'e tore up Miss Libby's—"

"I'll have your word on this, Master Gullidge."

Abashed, Kipp hung his head; with a grimy toe he traced a crack in the pavement. "Aye, yer lordship, sir."

"We've a gentleman's agreement, then. And a gentleman never breaks his word."

Kipp straightened his drooping shoulders. "Aye, sir."

"Very good." Ignoring the avid-eyed bystanders, Lord Nicholas addressed Elizabeth and her father. "Shall we go, then?"

The footman leapt down to open the door. He extended an impeccable, white-gloved hand. Unused to such deference, Elizabeth felt awkward as she accepted his assistance into the landau and sat down opposite Cicely.

"You're coming with us?" the girl asked. Her puzzled eyes fastened on the straw case and artist's satchel that Owen brought into the carriage and propped at his feet.

Elizabeth smiled. "Your brother has engaged me as your art instructor. Papa and I will be staying at your house."

Cicely let out a squeal of delight. Swiveling as her brother seated himself beside her, she snatched the sleeve of his morning coat and demanded, "Is this true, Nick? You're allowing me to study with Elizabeth? Oh, you're such a wonderful brother!"

Lord Nicholas aimed an austere look at her. "This isn't meant as a lark, Cicely. You must apply yourself and learn, prove to me and to yourself that your interest in art is genuine."

So this was a test, Elizabeth realized in dismay. He meant to establish once and for all that he was right. And he was using her to do it.

"Oh, pooh," the girl said, with a dismissive flutter of her fingers. "You think everything ought to be work. I prefer to seek enjoyment in life."

The earl merely tightened his lips and settled against the seat. Elizabeth waved a good-bye to Kipp, her father and Cicely echoing the farewell. A lump formed in Elizabeth's throat as she realized how lost and lonely the boy looked. Impulsively she leaned over and kissed his dirty cheek, her arms encircling his thin frame. "I'll come back and visit."

"Aye, miss," he said, though she could see the

doubt in his dark eyes. She swallowed a reassurance. Words would mean precious little to a street boy who knew too much about broken promises.

"If you need Miss Hastings," the earl advised, "she'll be staying at Hawkesford House in Berkeley Square."

"Aye, yer lordship, sir."

The carriage started over the cobblestones. One arm hugging the side of the landau, Elizabeth looked at Kipp standing in the street, shoulders hunched. When the darkness had devoured his slight form, she sat back and saw the earl gazing at her. Warmth shone in his expression... or did the glow of the lamps merely soften his handsome features?

Elizabeth turned her warm face to the cool night breeze. Misty eyed, she watched the familiar neighborhood stream past. Lights winked in windows; noises and smells filled the air. It might be commonplace and tumbledown, but this small section of London had been her home for the past month, a place as real in her heart as the crowded avenues and quiet parks of New York.

Misgivings suddenly pricked her. What did she really know of the aristocratic life she was about to enter? Accustomed to the omnibus, she had never before ridden in such luxury. Discreetly she stroked the smooth seat and drew in the faint rich scent of leather. She felt grateful for her father's presence beside her, yet worried, too. How would Owen adjust to living in the household of the Earl of Hawkesford?

Cicely chattered, making excited plans that Elizabeth only half heard. She fingered the ring on its chain around her neck and wondered about her grandfather, her mother's father. Owen refused to speak of him. Even Mother had acted sad and silent whenever Elizabeth had mentioned him. Had Lucy grown up in surroundings as genteel as the earl's?

The landau headed toward Mayfair; dingy shops and dark tenements gave way to splendid stores and stately homes. The clop-clop of hooves and the rattle of wheels created a symphony of sound. The streets glowed with gaslights. Dandies capered on fine horses; magnificently dressed ladies stepped into carriages, aided by footmen in swallow-tailed coats and knee breeches.

At last the landau drew to a halt. A grand, sprawling house stood across from a shadowed park. Surrounded by an ornate wrought iron fence, the oyster gray stone building looked like a country mansion strayed into a London square. Elizabeth stared in awe as the footman helped her from the carriage. Gas sconces lit the entryway; Corinthian columns supported a pediment above the gleaming, brass-fitted door. Adorning the center of the pediment was a stone medallion on which soared a gracefully carved hawk.

"'Mors ante dedecus,'" her father said, craning his neck to read the inscription below the medallion. In a faintly derisive voice, he translated, "'Death before dishonor.'"

Lord Nicholas inquired politely, "You read Latin?"

Her father squared his shoulders. "A word or two," he said curtly.

"Don't be so modest, Papa." Hugging his arm, Elizabeth looked at the earl. "My father is an instructor of Latin, mathematics as well. For many years he taught at a boys' academy in New York."

"What brings you to London, then?" Lord Nicholas asked.

"Papa grew up in England. He wanted me to see all the museums and art treasures here."

"I see."

Lord Nicholas shot her a keen look that made her stomach clench. She was still wondering at the meaning of his scrutiny when he turned and strode up the steps. As they followed his tall, dignified figure, Cicely tipped her pert nose and said, "Well, if I have anything to say on the matter, you'll stay for a long, long time. This household needs some livening up."

At the door stood a beanpole of a man in tails and black tie. "Hello," Elizabeth said, smiling.

The cadaverous butler lifted his graying brows and looked down his long nose at her. Suddenly she saw herself through his critical eyes: the old-fashioned mulberry gown and unstyled hair. She regarded him with a twinge of amusement. Apparently she didn't fit the usual mold of noble guests who entered this hallowed establishment.

Cicely breezed inside and dropped her soiled reticule on the azure silk seat of a chair. "Good evening, Peebles."

"Lady Cicely!" That austerity of countenance dissolved into relief. "Praise heaven, you're here. Her ladyship was about to organize a search party."

"Oh, don't be silly, Peebles."

"Is my aunt at home?" the earl asked, handing his top hat and gloves to the manservant.

"Yes, my lord. In her rooms, I believe. She's been in quite a state since Miss Eversham returned without Lady Cicely."

"Oh, pooh. You needn't carry on so. I was only gone a few hours."

"A few hours too many," Lord Nicholas said, shooting a severe look at his sister.

Cicely meekly ducked her head, but not before Elizabeth caught the twinkle of unrepentant mischief in those lapis lazuli eyes.

To Peebles, he said, "Tell my aunt I wish to have a word with her in the drawing room."

"Very well, my lord." The butler bowed, then stepped stiffly away.

"This way, if you please," said the earl.

Without a backward glance he strode across the vast foyer, Cicely at his heels. Elizabeth accepted her father's arm and followed, their footsteps echoing on the gleaming white marble floor. She marveled at the balanced beauty of the room. Twin stairways curved like a horseshoe, joining at the second floor, then continuing in a dizzying spiral to the third story. She longed to stop and study the gilt-framed paintings that embellished the walls. The few elegant chairs looked as though no one had ever sat in them. Even the air smelled immaculate, redolent of beeswax and brass pol-

ish and linseed oil. Absorbing the luxury, she wondered what the earl had thought of her cramped lodging house.

They entered a long drawing room hung with draperies of pale green brocade. A gentle hiss came from
fan-shaped gas sconces. Furnishings of mahogany and
walnut formed precise groupings atop the Persian car-
pets. Elizabeth's eyes were drawn to the extravagant
ceiling with its garlands and medallions, then down
again, to a stunning mantelpiece of pale marble veined
with gray.

She stroked the smooth stone, tracing the carved
simplicity of the columns. "Lovely," she murmured. "It
looks like a Robert Adam design."

"It is," Lord Nicholas stated, coming to stand alongside her. "He was commissioned by my great-grandfa-
ther to do the interior of the house. That's the second
earl's portrait above the mantel."

Elizabeth lifted her eyes to the aristocratically handsome gentleman clad in old-fashioned knee breeches.
"It's a Reynolds, isn't it?" she asked, reverently studying the fluid elegance of the brush strokes.

"Quite astute, Miss Hastings."

"You see what I told you?" Cicely said, plopping
onto a brocaded Queen Anne sofa. "The men always
inherit the good looks in this family. And if ever you're
bored, Nick can entertain you for hours with the history of every piece in this house."

His jaw tightened, accentuating the perfection of his
cheekbones. "It would do you well to learn your heritage."

"Oh, pooh. I've no interest in dusty relics."

Her casual attitude disturbed Elizabeth. Didn't Cicely appreciate the fortune of birth that had given her
such an extravagant home? Even Owen seemed to have
put aside enmity long enough to be fascinated by the
surroundings; his head was tilted in a study of the titles
inside a glass-fronted bookcase.

The tap of footsteps drew her attention to the doorway. Elizabeth stared, dazzled by the woman who

swept into the room. With her noble beauty, she might have stepped straight off a Gainsborough canvas. She wore an evening gown of ice blue silk that suited her porcelain skin to perfection. Her rich russet hair, beribboned and drawn into a chignon, made her look as stately as Britannia on a ship's prow. Like the earl, this woman had high cheekbones and a straight nose, cool gray eyes, and a haughty bearing. As she drew nearer, Elizabeth detected the fine age lines around the eyes and mouth.

"Cicely, you wicked child," she scolded. "What a fright you gave us! Imagine, abandoning poor Miss Eversham like that. And then going off alone, staying out after dark, like a common shop girl! I pray no one of consequence saw you. Were my dear sister alive, she'd be appalled to witness her daughter's behavior—"

Her thin eyebrows arched at Elizabeth. Pinned by that cool scrutiny, Elizabeth repressed an amused smile.

Swiveling toward the earl, the woman demanded, "What is the meaning of this, Nicholas? What mischief has Cicely wrought now?" In a lowered voice, she added, "And why have you brought this...street woman into our home?"

"Mind your tongue," Owen snapped. "Fancy lady or not, I won't hear you speak ill of my daughter."

Gasping, she whirled toward him. "How dare you address me in that tone."

"My daughter is your equal. The Book of Proverbs says, 'A good name is rather to be chosen than riches.'"

"Enough." The earl's frosty voice ended the exchange. "May I present my aunt, the Lady Beatrice Fairfield. Aunt Beatrice, this is Miss Elizabeth Hastings and her father, Owen. I've engaged Miss Hastings to instruct Cicely in sculpting."

Elizabeth gave Lady Beatrice a sunny smile. "I'm pleased to make your acquaintance."

Lady Beatrice's fine features drew into a deeper grimace. "Nicholas, have you gone mad? A lesson or two in drawing is one thing, but sculpting! All that mud and plaster. Ugh." She shuddered. "We'll be outcast if anyone hears of this. No proper lady would interest herself in such a common profession."

"It's hardly common," Elizabeth said. "The museums are crowded with aristocrats enjoying the artwork."

"We may admire," Lady Beatrice enunciated, "but we do not create."

Cicely sat straight on the sofa. "I don't want to be a lady if it means I can't study art."

Lady Beatrice turned disapproving eyes toward her nephew. "This is insanity! Why, she'll never find a suitable husband if you continue to succumb to her outrageous whims. Not even the temptation of her marriage portion will—"

"That's quite enough," the earl broke in testily. He strode across the room and pulled the gold bell cord. "As Cicely's guardian, I shall decide what's best for her."

"His mind is made up, Aunt Beatrice," Cicely said archly. "There's simply no purpose in arguing about it any longer. We're lucky Elizabeth has consented to be my mentor."

"That's quite enough from you, too, young lady," Lord Nicholas stated. "I haven't forgotten your behavior today. You're not to set foot outside this house for the next fortnight."

"Oh, no!" Cicely exclaimed, eyes wide with dismay. "But the Garforths' ball is a week from Wednesday."

"Behave yourself and I may allow you to attend for a brief time. Otherwise . . ."

Cicely's mouth settled into a pout, but she made no further protest. More and more Elizabeth wondered if there were a kernel of truth in the earl's assessment of his sister's conduct. At times Cicely did seem more rash than reasonable, more capricious than committed.

When a pretty, white-capped parlor maid appeared in the doorway, the earl said to his aunt, "Has the Holland bedroom been aired recently?"

"Why, yes, but—"

"Then Miss Hastings will stay there. Her father is to have the adjoining room."

Lady Beatrice looked shocked to the depths of her patrician soul. "You can't mean to put an *art* instructor on the same floor as the family! I should think the servants' attic—"

"I don't recall soliciting your opinion on the matter."

His quiet tone made his aunt go pale, except for a daub of pink on each cheek. Elizabeth couldn't stop a surge of sympathy. She knew all too well how it felt to be the recipient of the earl's displeasure.

"I trust you haven't forgotten our dinner engagement with Lord and Lady Melton," Lady Beatrice told Cicely. "They're due to arrive shortly."

Cicely pulled a face. "Then I suppose I'd better go, too," she said, rising from the sofa.

Grateful to escape the tension, Elizabeth headed toward the door. Her father looked troubled as he offered her his arm and again she pondered her wisdom in coming here. Hadn't she simply propelled herself into another nest of problems?

Following the parlor maid into the hall, she couldn't resist a backward glance. Her limbs went weak; Lord Nicholas stood gazing after her, one arm resting on the mantelpiece. The elegant pose drew back his morning coat and afforded her a glimpse of his lean waist. A warm, wonderful sensation curled inside her. She longed to spend hours studying the masterpiece of his body, to run her hands over him, to seek out each rib, each rock-hard curve of flesh, to discover if his muscles were as well formed as they looked....

She lifted her eyes to his. He looked displeased, angry almost. Her spirits wilted. Was he already regretting his decision to bring her here? Her inability to discern his thoughts both frustrated and fascinated her.

In a burst of perception, Elizabeth knew why she had agreed to the arrangement. It was not to nurture Cicely's talent; it was not to allay Owen's fears. It was to confront the powerful, perplexing emotions Lord Nicholas aroused in her.

"Really, Nicholas. Must you parade your interest in the chit?"

The earl only half heard the question. Elizabeth's amethyst eyes held him enthralled for a long moment before she turned and vanished down the hall. What was the meaning of that solemn look? Was she already regretting her decision to live here? Restless and impatient, he steeled himself against the unreasonable urge to go after her, to demand an explanation.

He swung his gaze to his aunt and uncomfortably realized she awaited an answer. "Forgive me," he said in pointed confusion. "I miss your meaning."

Aunt Beatrice pursed her lips. "Don't play the simpleton with me, Nicholas. You know I refer to your involvement with that... that *bohemian*." Her rosebud mouth curled around the word. "Have you lost all sense of discretion? Imagine, settling your mistress here in one of London's most respected households—"

"Miss Hastings is not my mistress; she's a talented artist."

The stern statement stopped Lady Beatrice for only a moment. "If she isn't yet, then she soon will be. I've seen that look in a man's eyes before."

"Directed at yourself, perhaps?"

Coloring, Lady Beatrice evaded his gaze. "Perhaps," she allowed, her slim shoulders stiff with pride. "I am not yet so very old, you know."

Nicholas felt instantly ashamed for baiting her. Beneath his aunt's bitterness lay sorrow and fear... sorrow for the beloved husband she had lost three years earlier, and fear that she would never again find a man to match him. Childless, she had focused her attentions on her niece and nephew, and hid her true warmth behind propriety and convention.

He crossed the room to enfold her delicate hands in his. "You're as ravishing as you were at eighteen, Aunt."

A smile wavered on her lips. "How do you know?" she scoffed. "At my coming out, you were still wearing knee breeches and sailor suits."

"Ah, but I remember the only woman whose beauty could rival that of my mother's." He lifted her hand and gallantly kissed its smooth back. "Then, as now, any man would be proud to call you his own."

Her smile deepened into genuine warmth. "You've grown to be quite the flatterer, Nicholas. It's no wonder you're considered such a brilliant catch."

He released her hands and stepped away. "I don't lavish unmerited compliments. If I'm a brilliant catch," he mocked, "it's because those society mamas want a title and wealth for their daughters."

"Ah, but the daughters see your handsome looks," Lady Beatrice said, wagging an elegant finger at him. "Any woman would." Her face tightened. "Even that artist looked at you that way."

Hope flared in him. Denying the absurd longing, Nicholas strode to the sideboard to splash brandy into a glass. "You're mistaken," he said, calming the cadence of his heart. "She isn't interested in me in the least. Her only interest is art."

Lady Beatrice was silent; when he turned, glass in hand, he saw shock rounding her gray eyes. "You mean you've already asked her to become your mistress?" she said slowly. "And she refused you?"

Nicholas cursed his aunt's astuteness . . . and his own carelessness. Taking a burning gulp of brandy, he realized the futility of denial. "Yes. So you see, you've nothing to fear."

Lady Beatrice still looked suspicious. "Then why did you bring her here? Why are you treating her like an honored guest?"

"Because I'm hoping she'll become more than an art instructor to Cicely. My sister needs a companion, someone nearer her own age than you or I."

"A companion!" His aunt's fine features went rigid. "Have you taken leave of your senses? Not only is this woman a bohemian, but judging by her accent, she's an

American as well. She'll turn your sister into a wild
Indian."

Controlling his impatience, Nicholas set his glass on
the mantelpiece. "Your prejudice is showing, Aunt."

She waved a dismissive hand. "Americans know
nothing of the social graces. She probably can't even
carry on a polite conversation. Is that the sort of company you want for your sister?"

"You might consider the fact that neither you nor I
nor Miss Eversham have been successful in altering Cicely's independent behavior. Since she respects Miss
Hastings, I judge this well worth a try."

"Indeed," Lady Beatrice sniffed. "I can think of a
hundred women who would make a more appropriate
companion than an itinerant *artist*. What do you know
of her background? Her breeding?"

"Cicely needs a friend, not a bloodline. Despite
her unusual profession, Miss Hastings is respectable
enough. She'll make a decent chaperon."

"You can't mean to actually send this woman into
society with your sister." Beatrice's look of disapproval
turned to horror. "Why, you do, don't you?"

Stunned by the realization that he wanted Elizabeth
to be accepted by his social circle, Nicholas remained
silent.

"She'll disgrace this family! What will we say when
people inquire about her lineage?"

Nicholas hadn't the foggiest notion. "I'll handle anyone ill-mannered enough to ask."

Beatrice shook her head. "This isn't like you, Nicholas. This isn't like you at all."

Irritated by the truth in her words, he paced to the
door. "I don't know what you mean."

"Yes, you do," his aunt said, following. "You've
been different these past few days. Restless and withdrawn." She paused delicately. "I don't mean to meddle in your affairs."

"Then don't."

In spite of his blunt words, she went on in a softened voice, "You really should marry, you know."

Startled, he swung back. "What has that to do with anything?"

"Everything. You need a wife to keep your interests close to home. To keep you from straying to an improper sort of woman."

Annoyed and amused, Nicholas leaned a shoulder against the door frame. "Having a wife doesn't necessarily stop a man from straying, Aunt."

Color tinted her porcelain cheeks. "I'll grant you, affairs may be quite common for some men. But if you were to make a love match, you would have no need to seek happiness elsewhere."

The wistful look on her face stirred a storm of yearning in Nicholas. He knew with sudden clarity that he wanted the same joy his aunt had once known. Elizabeth Hastings flashed into his mind. Irritated, he banished her image. A woman of her class was for bedding, not wedding. It was unthinkable for a man of his position to marry anyone but a woman whose background and breeding matched his own.

Yes, the more he pondered it, the more appealing the idea of marrying became. He was weary of discreet liaisons with jaded mistresses. And it was long past time to fulfill his duty of producing heirs to carry on the Ware family name. In his mind he pictured a precocious daughter with unruly ebony hair and sparkling violet eyes. . . .

"Perhaps I shall begin to look over the prospects more seriously," he said.

Lady Beatrice smiled in delight. "The Meltons are bringing their daughter tonight. She's the toast of the season, you know."

Nicholas tried to conjure a picture of the girl, but could recall only a vague image of a giggly blonde with watery blue eyes. "What's her name? Marilyn? Maria?"

"Marianne," his aunt said in a scolding tone. "Don't you remember? You sat beside her at Lord Amberley's dinner party last week. Marianne was quite smitten with you. Consider her, Nicholas. She would make you the perfect wife."

But as he went upstairs to dress, the only woman Nicholas could think about had gypsy black hair and amethyst eyes.

Chapter 6

❧❧❧

"**I** can scarcely wait to see everyone's faces when we appear at dinner." Blue eyes merry, Cicely clasped her hands in delight. "I vow no one will recognize you."

"I hardly recognize myself," Elizabeth murmured, staring at her reflection in the dressing room mirror. In a remarkably short time, she had been metamorphosed into a lady, at the sacrifice of comfort. A plethora of pins pressed into her scalp, taming her curls into a sleek chignon. The corset steels pinched her ribs and stole her breath. Her high-necked gown of tissue-thin magenta silk concealed the fading bruises, and the narrow cut of the skirt made her feel as stiff and unwieldy as a statue of dried clay.

She wanted nothing more than to spend the evening exploring the unfamiliar surroundings, seeking out the conservatory and planning her new studio, then perhaps curling up in a corner of her cavernous bedroom and sketching the earl from memory. Instead she was trussed up in a lady's fashionable armor, preparing to pick daintily at her food and make inane conversation with snooty people who would likely regard her as an oddity. And all because Cicely had cajoled her into going down to dinner. On the other hand, she felt a curious compulsion to prove to Nicholas and Beatrice that an American artist could also behave like a lady.

Elizabeth tugged at her lace-edged bodice in a vain

effort to ease the pressure of her corset. "How do you abide this dreadful contraption?"

"Oh, pooh. You'll grow used to it after a while." Turning this way and that, Cicely scrutinized her hourglass figure in the cheval mirror. "Stays do such splendid things for the figure, don't you think?"

"There's nothing ugly about the natural proportions of the human body."

Cicely crinkled her nose. "You wouldn't say that if you had *my* baby fat. Without a corset, I scarcely *have* a waistline."

A tall, plain-featured woman marched in from the bedroom. "Perhaps if my lady would cease indulging her taste for sweets?"

"Oh, shush, Eversham. You're a worse scold than Nick." Twirling about in her Cambridge blue gown, Cicely continued to preen. "I rather fancy wearing my pearls tonight. What do you think?"

Face sober, the governess held out a string of glossy pearls. "I've already taken the liberty of fetching them from your jewelry case."

"Whatever would I do without you, Eversham?"

"You seemed to manage quite well this afternoon," Miss Eversham said gruffly as she fastened the necklace around the girl's neck.

Turning, Cicely threw her arms around the woman. "I'm *so* very sorry," she said in dramatic repentance. "I really and truly am. I promise it'll never, *ever* happen again."

Miss Eversham extracted herself from the girl's embrace. "I should hope not, my lady," she said, smoothing her black bombazine skirt. "It's long past time you put such childish pranks behind you. How many times must I tell you, it's dangerous for a woman to venture forth alone, as well as damaging to her reputation."

Though severity edged the words, Elizabeth detected a flash of fondness on the governess's homespun features. Her fingers itched to capture that emotion on paper. But nothing so prosaic as a pencil existed within this luxurious female domain of gown-filled wardrobes and neatly arranged hatboxes.

Cicely patted Miss Eversham's shoulder. "Well, things shall be quite different now that Elizabeth has come to instruct me in art. There'll be no need for me to steal away to study with her."

"Hmph. I most certainly hope so."

Yet the governess looked downcast, and Elizabeth realized in sympathy that Miss Eversham must fear losing her position if Cicely mended her ways.

"Come, let's go downstairs," Cicely told Elizabeth. "We're late enough already."

Elizabeth wondered at the girl's eagerness, then Miss Eversham raised a forestalling hand. "You are quite certain, my lady, that the earl did request Miss Hastings's presence at dinner?"

"Of course," Cicely said with an airy flutter of her fingers. "He wants my new art instructor to feel at home here. Isn't that so, Elizabeth?"

Mischief gleamed in her eyes. Unsure of Cicely's intent, yet unwilling to plunge her into more trouble, Elizabeth nodded.

"It's a pity we couldn't talk your father into dinner, as well," Cicely said.

Touched by the girl's concern and knowing Owen would feel more comfortable taking a tray in his room, Elizabeth said, "He's rather tired tonight. Besides, he didn't have anyone as generous as you to borrow such finery from." Irony laced her voice as she glided a hand over the cool silk of her gown. In truth, she felt ludicrous in this confining costume.

Cicely's impish smile reappeared. "I can't wait until my brother sees how marvelous you look. I do so like to catch him by surprise."

As they walked into an opulent hall lit by hissing gas jets, Elizabeth felt a breathlessness that she couldn't attribute to the corset. The prospect of seeing Lord Nicholas again turned her insides to soft clay. A quivery anticipation bloomed in her, overshadowing the discomfort of her underpinnings and the unfamiliarity of her wobbly high heels.

As they descended the grand, curving staircase, the rustle of fabrics mingled with the unsteady tap of Elizabeth's shoes. Only half listening to Cicely's chatter, she craned her neck to view the paintings on the walls. A Turner. A Vermeer. A Holbein. Awed, she vowed to study them more closely later. A man who owned such a magnificent art gallery must have good taste.

The murmur of genteel voices floated through the vaulted entry hall. "Aunt Beatrice will be mad as a hornet when she sees you coming down to dinner," Cicely whispered as they approached the drawing room. "But she won't dare say a word, not in front of Lord and Lady Melton. She'd *die* rather than cause a scene."

Elizabeth slowed her steps. So that was Cicely's purpose... to needle her aunt. Although reluctant to be a party to the girl's devilry, Elizabeth couldn't help feeling a prick of amusement. Perhaps the look on Lady Beatrice's face might be entertaining.

Yet as she entered the drawing room Elizabeth found that her eyes sought no one but Lord Nicholas.

He sat facing the door, one arm draped along the back of the Queen Anne sofa. If he looked handsome in day wear, he looked positively stunning in the black suit and white shirt of evening dress. Not a single chestnut hair lay out of place; his nose and mouth and eyes held the elegance of a Donatello marble. Gazing at his fine face and figure made her feel giddy. How she longed to strip away that civilized facade and breathe his warmth and life into clay.

A grave smile curved his lips as he conversed with the blond girl beside him. His expression of indulgent humor died the instant he spied Elizabeth.

His eyes narrowed, traveling the length of her. Her heart vaulted and her palms dampened. She reached for her pocket, only belatedly realizing she carried no clay. Clasping her hands before her, she wondered why he frowned. Had she forgotten some essential of dress? Could he detect her discomfort?

Elizabeth caught herself. Why should she care what the earl thought? If his favor required her to be something she was not, then she wanted no part of him.

The girl at his side had the unnaturally pale hair of a china doll. Only her petulant pout made her look human. Tugging at his sleeve, she regained his attention.

Lord Nicholas bent his head and whispered something that brought a chirp of laughter to her rosy lips. Rising with sinuous grace, he came toward Elizabeth and Cicely.

"I see you deigned to join us," he told his sister.

"Oh, pooh. You know I'm always late. And this evening I had to help Elizabeth dress." Cicely aimed an arch smile at him. "What do you think, isn't she lovely?"

His eyes swept Elizabeth. "Quite acceptable."

Vague disappointment washed over her. Was that the loftiest praise he could manage?

"Our guests have been waiting to see you," he told his sister.

Cicely took his arm; when he offered the other to Elizabeth, she hesitated, then curled her fingers around his hard muscles. His masculine scent enveloped her. With a trace of lusty humor, she decided he smelled as delectable as he looked.

He led them to the small gathering seated across from the blond girl. True to Cicely's expectation, Lady Beatrice tightened her mouth in displeasure. She rose stiffly, the man and woman beside her standing as well.

The man set down his glass of sherry and bowed over Cicely's hand. "Good evening, Lady Cicely," he said, an affable smile twitching his ginger side-whiskers. "Pleasure to see you again."

Demure as a schoolgirl, Cicely dipped a curtsy. "Thank you, Lord Melton."

Elizabeth followed suit, smiling modestly as she swept into an elaborate genuflection.

Lady Melton stepped forward amid a rustle of rose taffeta, bringing to mind an opulent, pink-fleshed

Rubens. "Hello, Cicely. I see you've a houseguest."

Cicely's eyes sparkled in that mischievous manner Elizabeth was beginning to distrust. "May I present Miss Elizabeth Hastings? She's—"

"The daughter of our mother's childhood friend," the earl broke in, slanting a firm look at his sister. Cicely pursed her mouth in disappointment, like a child denied a sweet.

Appalled and angry, Elizabeth glared at Lady Nicholas. How dare he invent a past for her! She had a perfectly respectable background, nothing to be ashamed of, nothing to hide.

"Your mother's childhood friend?" Lady Melton repeated, her plump face wrinkling in curiosity. "Now which friend might that be? I don't recall Sarah ever mentioning anyone by the name of Hastings."

"Hastings was her married name," Lord Nicholas said smoothly. "I rather doubt you knew the girl, anyway. The family moved to America years ago."

"Gracious me," said Lady Melton, lifting her lorgnette to regard Elizabeth with the fascinated disgust one might direct at an insect. "Imagine, growing up so far from civilized society. I cannot conceive that any proper family would allow such a thing."

Before Lord Nicholas could tell any more lies, Elizabeth concocted one of her own. "My family is quite old and respected. Can't you tell by the name? We trace our ancestry back to the Battle of Hastings. My forebears burned and pillaged with the best of them."

Lord Nicholas's elegant mouth quirked with humor, but the sight added fuel to her anger. Her intent was not to amuse him.

"The Battle of Hastings!" Lady Melton looked suitably impressed. "Now, would you be connected to the Huntingdon Hastings? Or to the Hastings of Hastings?"

"Do tell," said Lord Melton, his florid face beaming with curiosity. "Do tell, indeed."

"It's so kind of you to take such an interest, sir," Elizabeth said sweetly.

"'My lord,'" Lady Beatrice corrected. To Lord and Lady Melton, she added, "You must forgive our house-guest. As a foreigner, she isn't familiar with the proper forms of address."

Elizabeth stifled her irritation. She might not have had a privileged upbringing, but her mother had taught her politeness. "If you like, *my lord and lady*, I can regale you for hours with the most fascinating tales of my her-itage. Lord Nicholas would be happy to embellish them, I'm sure."

"Perhaps later," the earl suggested dryly. "Come along, Miss Hastings."

One hand firm at the small of her back, he guided Elizabeth to the girl seated demurely on the sofa. Like her mother, she had the red-and-white coloring of a Rubens, though she was still a rosebud. Her gown's clashing combination of green gauze and pink tulle made Elizabeth feel faintly nauseated. The girl came gracefully to her feet, hands clasped in front of her skirts.

"Marianne," the earl said, "may I present Miss Eliza-beth Hastings? Lady Marianne Yale."

Unable to quell her curiosity, Elizabeth said, "Yale. Would that be your married name?"

"Goodness, no." Marianne's hard blue eyes belied the delicacy of her features. "My father, Lord Edward Yale, is the Marquis of Melton. Did I hear Nicholas say you're an American?"

Intrigued by the contrast of politeness and disdain in the girl's voice, Elizabeth said, "I am."

"You must find our society here in England quite vastly different from what you are accustomed to."

"Actually, I'm learning more and more that people are much the same everywhere. Greed, ambition, and hypocrisy exist in all walks of life. Only the surround-ings are different."

"Really, Miss Hastings!" Marianne looked horrified. "You would compare *us* to the common masses? *We* have standards of behavior, refinement of manners."

Elizabeth didn't know whether to rant or laugh. "So

I'm told. However, a few bad apples can spoil any bushel, English or American."

"What Miss Hastings means," Lord Nicholas said smoothly, "is that one cannot admire a person simply because of the fortune of birth. One must look deeper, to the quality of the character beneath."

His intense stare ignited a vivid curling sensation deep within Elizabeth. Did she detect warmth in those flawless features, or did the artist in her long to paint tender emotion into his haughty expression?

"That is what *I* mean," Marianne said sharply. "The upper class has high moral standards, much higher than commoners." She slipped a hand around the earl's arm and tilted a pretty smile at him. "Don't you agree, my lord?"

Realizing Marianne regarded her as a rival, Elizabeth stifled a bubble of laughter. If only her ladyship knew the earl's true opinion of his houseguest!

Indulgently he patted the pale hand on his black sleeve. "The young ladies of my acquaintance are beyond reproach. I have only the highest regard for their beauty as well as for their behavior."

Marianne emitted a trill of laughter. "Might I include myself in that assessment?"

"I meant for you to do so."

"Thank you, my lord."

Watching them share a smile, Elizabeth felt her spirits sag inexplicably. They made a handsome couple, the earl so powerful and perfect, Lady Marianne so refined and feminine. She thrived on social situations, a woman from his own world, the sort of woman he would eventually marry.

Cicely glided up, her face aglow with familiar devilry. "How charming to visit with you again, Marianne. I see you've met our new houseguest."

Apparently confident she had staked her claim to the earl, Lady Marianne dropped her hand. "Yes, thank you. We've been having a most stimulating discussion of moral behavior."

Cicely arched her eyebrows. "I would have thought you'd be discussing art."

"Art?" Marianne said, as if the word were foreign to her vocabulary.

Lord Nicholas's cheeks tightened as he glanced from his sister to Marianne. "Miss Hastings is an artist."

"Ah, I see," said Marianne, looking appalled and yet smug, as if the news confirmed her opinion.

Elizabeth bit back a smile. So her ladyship of the high moral standards was also a bigot. Well, let her enjoy her world of narrow views and tight corsets! Elizabeth wanted no part of it.

Lady Melton hastened toward them, lorgnette raised, rose taffeta skirts whispering. "Did I hear you properly? You're an artist, Miss Hastings?"

Elizabeth lifted her chin with pride. "Yes, I am."

"Most curious occupation for a woman," said Lord Melton, ambling up behind his wife, a glass of sherry in his beefy hand. "Most curious, indeed."

Lady Beatrice followed, her face grim. "Now, Edward, drawing is perfectly acceptable as part of a young lady's education."

"Even Queen Victoria is an accomplished artist," Elizabeth pointed out.

"Yes," Cicely said with a guileless grin. "Her drawings are often sold to benefit charity."

"You see, it is quite the respectable pastime," Lady Beatrice said smoothly. "Miss Hastings is here to instruct my niece in . . . ah . . . some of the finer aspects of art."

Laughter leapt inside Elizabeth. Of course, Lady Beatrice meant only to preserve her own reputation, yet there was something gratifying in seeing her forced to defend the woman she scorned.

"Speaking of art," she told the earl, "on my way downstairs, I couldn't help admiring your paintings. You have excellent taste."

His finely chiseled lips crooked into a smile. "Regrettably I cannot claim your admiration. My forebears were the collectors, not I."

"You'll do better to stick to more tried and true investments," Lord Melton said, waving his glass of sherry. "Art's too risky, too risky, indeed."

"Collecting brings enjoyment to the investor," Elizabeth said. "Instead of letting your money gather dust in a bank vault, you can take pleasure in gazing at the art in your own home."

"Provided one purchases only the old masters," Lady Melton said, her eyes appearing owllike through the lorgnette. "However can one enjoy these silly aesthetic painters?"

"Quite so," her husband agreed. "Remember the twaddle that fellow Whistler tried to pass off as art? Might as well fling a pot of paint at a wall! Get the same result. The same result, indeed!"

"Whistler." Marianne aimed a sly look at Elizabeth. "He's an American painter, isn't he?"

"By birth, yes," Elizabeth said lightly, "but he's lived in England for so many years he might well consider himself more *your* countryman."

Venom hardened Marianne's face. Before she could reply, Peebles announced dinner. The cadaverous butler led the way into a sumptuous dining room where a pair of liveried footmen waited to serve the meal. Delicious aromas emanated from the silver serving platters on the mahogany sideboards.

Elizabeth found herself seated between Lady Melton and Cicely. Across the snowy damask tablecloth, Marianne lost no time engaging Lord Nicholas in low-pitched dialogue. Lady Beatrice adroitly took charge of the conversation at the other end of the table. Elizabeth soon grew bored with the exchange of social chitchat and the discussion of Queen Victoria's upcoming visit to Balmoral Castle.

She concentrated on her meal, reveling in the asparagus soup, the poached salmon, the veal in cream sauce. Never in her life had she eaten such exquisite food. Lady Beatrice kept a watchful eye out, as if expecting Elizabeth to disgrace the family. Couldn't the woman at least give her guest credit for having the common sense to observe which fork or spoon to use? Irked, Elizabeth felt tempted to line the tiny French peas along her knife blade and eat like a true barbarian.

Her annoyance disintegrated as she stole a sidelong look at Lord Nicholas. Though still angered by his falsification of her past, her admiration for his looks remained undimmed. The light from the ornate silver candelabra set his cheekbones into sharp relief. Generations of privilege and wealth had given him the confidence no amount of tutoring could supply. He fed her starving senses in a way mere food could never satisfy. Her fingers ached to test the texture of his chestnut hair, to examine the whorls of his ears, to undo that formal white necktie and investigate the sinews and muscles beneath.

The chirp of Marianne's laughter distracted Elizabeth; unexpected resentment stabbed her. Whatever did Lord Nicholas see in that silly girl? With the attention he paid her, one would assume she possessed a fine intellect and a charming character. Of course, Elizabeth told herself waspishly, maybe the earl didn't care if a woman were small-minded so long as she were willing to yield to his physical needs.

Heat chased over her skin as she imagined him naked. Her corset seemed to squeeze tighter, forcing the breath from her lungs. Hastily she looked down at her plate as a footman whisked away the remains of dinner and then served dessert. Beset by a fierce longing to escape this stilted setting, she trifled with the gooseberry fool, stirring the fluffy substance until it turned into a pale puddle.

Once the interminable meal ended, she retired with the ladies to the drawing room. She was bored silly by the chitchat and about to plead a headache by the time Lord Melton and the earl rejoined the women. Relieved, Elizabeth decided she'd experienced enough of polite society to last a lifetime.

But Lord Melton sank to the sofa beside his wife. "Play something for us, my dearest Marianne," he said.

"You do that Chopin piece quite well. Quite well, indeed."

"I wouldn't dream of boring all of you," his daughter demurred.

"You could never bore us," Lord Nicholas said, smiling indulgently from his stance by the mantel.

"Well, if you insist." Clearly pleased by his encouragement, Marianne sat at the mahogany pianoforte.

As the girl began to slay a sonata, Elizabeth forced herself to sit still. She resisted yawning by exercising her willpower. Everyone else seemed to listen with well-bred interest... even Cicely. Then the girl caught Elizabeth's glance and winked, and Elizabeth had to swallow a giggle.

She wondered if the earl, too, hid his boredom. He was such an expert at deception that even with her skills of observation she could not detect his true feelings.

The recital ended and Marianne demurely accepted her compliments. Elizabeth managed to maintain a civil smile even as Lord Nicholas kissed the girl's hand. When at last they stood in the marble foyer after saying good night to the Meltons, Elizabeth took a deep breath to ease her trepidation. His false presentation of her background still rankled. She would confront the earl now, before this charade got out of hand.

Squaring her shoulders, she said, "Lord Hawkesford, I wonder if you would be so kind as to show me where I'll be working?"

"Don't bother the earl with trivialities," Lady Beatrice said. "A servant can direct you in the morning. Come along now, Miss Hastings."

"No." Lord Nicholas's quiet voice echoed through the huge room. "You and Cicely go on upstairs. I believe Miss Hastings has something she'd like to discuss with me."

Lady Beatrice had no choice but to obey. Pursing her lips in disapproval, she started up the curving staircase. Cicely, looking mystified and curious, trailed her aunt.

Elizabeth watched until they disappeared through

the opulent doorway at the head of the stairs. Her heart surged as she turned to see the earl gazing at her. Something gleamed in his eyes, something warm and intriguing that she could not quite identify... something that made a delicious shiver scuttle over her skin.

"Shall we?" he said.

He offered her his arm. Forcing a smile, she clasped his hard muscles. Lord Nicholas led her through a dizzying maze of hallways until at last they arrived at a room shrouded in shadows. As he struck a match to light the lamps, Elizabeth breathed in the musky damp scents of earth and plants. That curious combination of alarm and excitement rippled through her again.

They were alone.

Chapter 7

H e had her all to himself.

Lighting the gas jets, Nicholas felt an unexpected rush of elation. Though the muffled chime of the library clock tolled the hour of one, he felt vital and invigorated. The evening had been interminable, the company of his aunt's friends tedious. Weary of acting the gentleman, weary of trying to find something interesting about the giggly Marianne, he'd spent the time comparing her dull personality to Elizabeth's sparkling wit.

With a flick of his wrist Nicholas doused the match and dropped it into an empty clay pot. Turning, he saw Elizabeth gazing intently at him. His blood surged in response to her frank stare. There was nothing coy about her, nothing artificial. Even in that high-necked evening dress, with her black curls tamed into a ladylike chignon, she had a luster of life about her, an irresistible newness that reached out to him.

Seeing the determined look in her eyes, he knew she meant to start another argument. "So, what do you think?" he asked, to delay her.

She blinked. "About what?"

Nicholas made a sweeping gesture. "Does the room meet with your approval?"

"My approval?" Elizabeth looked startled, as if she'd never expected him to seek her opinion.

She twirled to examine the conservatory. Wonderment crept over her face, making her eyes shine and her lips part. Nicholas experienced the curious sensation of seeing the room through the freshness of her gaze: the steep-pitched roof of darkened glass panes, the fanlight windows and Doric columns, the deep shadowy niches overgrown with greenery, the silent fountain topped by a stone satyr.

She clasped a hand to her bosom, drawing his eyes to the fine shape of her breasts. "It's magnificent. Like a Grecian temple."

He felt ridiculously pleased. "My father had the conservatory built for my mother. She raised camellias here."

Elizabeth bent to touch a glossy green leaf. "Does no one care for them anymore?"

"When my mother died not long after Cicely's birth, my father ordered the room closed. The servants keep the plants watered, but . . ." How could he explain the tender devotion the cold and reserved Justin Ware had shown toward his beloved wife?

The moistness in Elizabeth's eyes nonplussed Nicholas. In that soft, exotic voice, she said, "You must have been just a boy when she died."

Long-buried pain stirred inside him. Shifting his gaze to the twining growth of an ivy, he said with a curtness intended to close the subject, "I was ten."

The gas jets hissed into the silence; water plopped faintly from a faucet on the far wall. "Nothing can ever make up for the loss of a mother," Elizabeth said.

The sympathy and sadness in her voice drew his gaze to hers. Remembering her own recent loss, he felt a sudden kinship with her, a bond of shared grief that transcended their differences.

Impulsively he took a step nearer. "Do you know what I regret most? That I never had the chance to know my mother as an adult. That I have only a child's memories of her." His candor surprised him. He'd never before expressed his sorrow to anyone. Never.

"How sad that must make you," Elizabeth said softly. "I'm sorry."

Unlike the mumbled platitudes he'd heard from

others, her words vibrated with sincerity. Again he found himself curious about her past. Her innate refinement, her delicate grace belied her uncommon upbringing. Tonight she had proven herself capable of holding her own in society. Who was she? A peer's poor relation fallen on hard times? Why had she grown up in America? Nicholas renewed his resolve to ferret out the significance of the signet ring, to identify the noble house denoted by the swan coat of arms.

Her shoes tapped on the flagstones as Elizabeth walked to a nook overflowing with vegetation. She sank to her knees before a shadowy bush, the silk of her gown rustling. Walking closer, Nicholas saw her part the waxy leaves to reveal one perfect pink blossom.

"How curious," he mused, crouching beside her. "This isn't the season for camellias to bloom."

Her rapt gaze studied the many-petaled blossom. "In America we'd call it a maverick. Something wild and rare and free."

Like you, Nicholas wanted to say. He felt the sudden fierce desire to shower her with flowers, to see her lying naked in a bed of blooms...

He reached for the stem. "Why don't you take it?"

Her quick fingers caught his wrist. Beseeching and beautiful in the gaslight, her eyes met his. A deluge of desire swamped his senses. Her lush scent mingled with the odors of damp earth and untamed undergrowth. He could think of little else save the nearness of her body, the firmness of the fingers enclosing his wrist... and the need throbbing heavily in him.

His intense physical attraction to her still surprised him. Why did he feel such a powerful longing for an artist, a woman whose way of life was so foreign to his own?

"Please don't," she said, her voice husky. "The camellia belongs here, in its natural setting."

"As you wish," he murmured. "This room belongs to you now, Elizabeth. I promise to do my utmost to give you whatever you need. You have only to ask."

By the look on her face, she must have realized he meant more than material goods. Her lips parted; her fingers tightened on his wrist. For one wild moment he harbored the hope that she felt an answering desire for him.

But her hand dropped to her side, leaving only the imprint of her warmth on his skin. She gazed at him with the same absorbed attention she'd afforded the camellia, the same candid consideration she'd shown him upon first entering the conservatory. Fleetingly he imagined her as a young girl, studying life with bold interest and wide, staring eyes, as if she found the smallest detail awesome and fascinating.

A shy smile wavered on her lips. "There *is* one thing I'd like."

"Name it."

She hesitated. "Once I get my studio set up here," she said slowly, "will you sit for me?"

The question crashed into his passion. Desire drained away, leaving him empty and disappointed. Surging to his feet, he walked off, hearing the echo of her stinging denouncement: *You have a pleasing face. Beyond that, nothing about you interests me.*

"I'm sorry," he said coldly. "That's out of the question."

Forehead furrowed, she cocked her head. "But why?"

Why, indeed? Nicholas wondered. Looks of admiration from other women had never bothered him. The truth struck with galling force. He meant no more to Elizabeth Hastings than the flawless camellia, yet he wanted her interest to be more personal; he wanted her to value the man more than the insignificant shell of physical perfection. The knowledge left him feeling curiously vulnerable, open to the ache of unfulfilled needs.

"Sitting for me wouldn't have to take up much of your time," she hastened to say. "I'm sure you'll find that—"

"No."

The color drained from Elizabeth's face, leaving her

cheeks as pale as lily petals. Hands clasped before her, she remained seated on her heels, the magenta silk of her gown framing her thighs. A most unladylike position . . . and yet somehow it suited her.

Suddenly impatient to escape her dispassionate interest, Nicholas said curtly, "It's growing late, so why don't you tell me the real reason you wished to come here? I'm sure it wasn't to wheedle me into posing for you like a bowl of fruit."

Her mouth tensed and her shoulders squared. "I think you know why," she said. "I resent the deceitful way you introduced me to your friends."

He welcomed her anger, welcomed the opportunity to return to familiar ground. "I'm sorry," he said, his tone formal. "I would have warned you of my intentions earlier had I known you were coming down to dinner."

She slammed her palms against her thighs. "*Warned* me! Do you suppose *that* would have excused your deception? You deliberately misled Lord and Lady Melton, told them a passel of lies, as if I were inadequate."

Nicholas arched his brows. "I don't recall hearing you correct me. You seemed to enjoy the deception."

"Should I have branded you a liar in front of a roomful of your friends? Not I, your lordship. You think me an ill-mannered bohemian, but I know better than to insult my host."

Her indignant attitude aroused the dark urge to laugh. "I never know what to think of you, Elizabeth."

She tossed her chin up. "Don't change the subject. I demand to know why you put me in the position of pretending to be someone I'm not."

"If you were more familiar with society, you'd appreciate what I've done for you. No one will receive you unless you come from an acceptable family."

"Did it ever occur to you that I might not *care* whether or not I'm accepted by your snobbish friends? For that matter, why should *you* care?"

Why, indeed? Wrestling with inner turmoil, Nicholas prowled the stone flags. Why *did* he feel so eager for her to fit into his social circle? Uncertain of the answer, he said, "As Cicely's friend and companion, it's vital that you appear respectable. I'm only trying to make life easier for you."

"Easier for me or easier for yourself?" Elizabeth countered. "You couldn't hold your perfect head up if the news got out that you had a social liability living in your household. Well, I refuse to be a party to your brand of hypocrisy. *I'm* not ashamed of who I am, even if you are."

He felt torn between shaking her and reassuring her. "I never said I was ashamed of you, Elizabeth."

Her dark brows drew into a skeptical line. As proud as a gypsy princess, she knelt on the stone floor, blending beautifully with the wild background of greenery. "I wonder why I find that so hard to believe."

Nicholas let out an exasperated hiss. He would not allow her to be chewed to ribbons by the merciless maws of drawing room harpies. "Comprehend it or not," he stated, "you'll do as I say."

Her lips parted in anger and astonishment. "Is that a command, your lordship?"

"Yes."

Elizabeth scrambled to her feet...and swayed. Alarmed, Nicholas shot to her side to slip a steadying arm around her back. Nestled against him, she felt as precious and delicate as a late-budding camellia.

"Are you all right?" he asked gruffly.

"It's just these silly heels." Bracing a hand on his chest, she kicked off her shoes; each went flying into the shrubbery, landing with a muffled plop. "There, that's where they belong."

Elizabeth tilted her face up. Her eyes shone bright; her smile flashed brilliant. Then she seemed to grow aware of their nearness, the stance that was a mere heartbeat from a lover's embrace. Stockinged toes peeping from under her hem, she retreated a step and glared at him.

"I don't know why women endure such ridiculous clothing."

"Ridiculous, Elizabeth? I happen to find you lovely."

A blush crept over her skin; she looked so sweetly flustered in the gaslight that he wanted to kiss her... and not just on the lips. He wanted to learn the taste and touch and scent of her skin. He wanted to unpin her hair and let the glossy black locks ripple over her bare breasts. He wanted to feel her body next to his, softening and swaying in surrender.

Mischief suddenly curved her lips. She twirled as gracefully as a ballerina, the magenta train of her gown whispering. "Do I pass the test, then? Am I as lovely a lady as the noble Marianne?"

Nicholas couldn't stop a smile. "I wouldn't dream of comparing your vivid beauty to any other woman, titled or not."

For an instant Elizabeth looked inordinately pleased. Then the light left her face and a frown creased her brow. "You're terribly accomplished at flattery, aren't you?" She gestured at herself. "These clothes are a symbol of the false image you've ordered me to assume for society. You want me to hide my true self behind silk and hairpins."

Annoyance pecked at his good humor. "Fine clothing is meant to enhance a woman's beauty, not disguise it."

"Well, I don't happen to care for your standards of beauty." Tugging at her high lace collar, Elizabeth wriggled uncomfortably, drawing his eyes to the adorable shape of her breasts. "Believe me, this is the first and last time I'll ever wear a corset."

Shock at her frank words pierced Nicholas, followed closely by the renewed blaze of desire. She was here under his protection, he reminded himself, yet all he could think about was seducing her.

"You shouldn't speak of such things in front of a gentleman," he snapped.

Her chin shot up. "Another command, my lord? One evening, and already my head is swimming with your silly rules."

"Silly or not, speaking so candidly might induce a man to take advantages you don't intend." Telling himself she needed to be taught a lesson, Nicholas strode to her as his voice dropped to a grim whisper: "He might well think *this* is what you're inviting."

Shedding conscience and judgment, he shaped his palm to the beguiling curve of her breast. He heard the hiss of her indrawn breath, saw her eyes widen to great purple pansies against her glowing skin. Yet she didn't move away, not even when he slid his hand over the silk of her bodice. The stiff corset hid her softness, but her warmth radiated into his fingers, heating his blood to an unbearable degree. She smelled like half-wild herbs and sun-warmed earth. His thumb found the peak of her breast and circled it slowly. Her lashes lowered a little; her slumberous expression hit him like a blow to the solar plexus. He wanted to take her right there on the stone floor, encompassed by a tangle of plants; he wanted to lie with her beneath the night-darkened roof of glass; he wanted to slide his hand under her skirts and caress her—

Something in her gaze froze his fantasy. Her rapt eyes glided over his face, as if memorizing every line and angle. She looked absorbed, spellbound, fascinated . . .

Fascinated by the position of his hand? Or by what she termed his physical perfection?

Despising his uncertainty, Nicholas drew his fingers from temptation, curling them into a fist at his side. "Do you comprehend my meaning, Miss Hastings?" he said coldly. "If you fail to watch your words, you'll soon find your reputation beyond the pale."

Elizabeth shook her head; the dreamy look cleared from her eyes. "I won't live a lie, Lord Nicholas. I'm an artist, first and foremost. Whether society accepts me or not doesn't matter in the least."

Her obstinacy frustrated him. "It matters to me," he said brusquely, "so long as you live under my roof.

Mark my words. If you fail to act like a lady, I won't feel obliged to treat you like one."

Taking one last look at her startled, kissable face, he turned on his heel and strode out of the conservatory.

A curse echoed through the empty room.

At the soot-streaked window, a solitary figure held back the filthy curtain to peer at the mist-drenched street below. Despite the drizzle that hid the midday sun, the byway abounded with people: a wizened old woman selling posies, a knife grinder turning his raucous machine, a young mother trudging along with a swaddled baby in her arms.

But it was not these ordinary folk who attracted the wrathful gaze of the watcher. It was the pair of liveried footmen who carted wooden crates out of the tenement across the street and loaded the boxes into a dray.

Fury cut like a scalpel into the watcher's heart. Lucy had been spirited away again, away from where she belonged.

A knock shattered the emptiness. "'Ey, you in there?" came a muffled shout.

The figure wheeled around, angrily kicked aside the shreds of a newspaper, and flung open the door.

The man in the porkpie hat burst into the room. "She's done moved out," he gasped. "The bitch's run off!"

"Run off! Is that all you came to report?"

The coarse-faced man stared. "Didn't you 'ear wot I said? The trull's gone!" He scurried to the window and pointed. "See 'ere! Them fancy fellows are cartin' off all her things."

"As they have been for the past hour. Where the devil were you?"

The man uneasily shifted his hobnail boots. "I got to catch me a few winks sometime," he grumbled. "Wot d'you expect—"

"I expect you to drink your gin on your own time.

Now get your lazy hide back down there. You're to follow those footmen when they leave."

"Follow 'em? Where to?"

"To Berkeley Square, you dolt! Didn't you see the Hawkesford crest on the landau the other day?"

"Ain't bein' paid to know me letters," the man whined.

"Paid! You're being paid far more than you're worth. You watch that girl and look for an opportunity. You'll not see even a tuppence if you don't hurry."

Scowling, the man adjusted his porkpie hat and scurried out.

The figure moved across the dirty floor to pick up the notebook propped against the wall by the window. Loving fingers brushed off a cobweb clinging to the royal blue cover, then traced the name embossed in gold. *Elizabeth Templeton Hastings*.

Lucy's daughter. Lucy's sin.

No, Lucy could never sin. Lucy was too good, too beautiful. This book was a shrine to her loveliness. A slim-fingered hand, meticulously groomed, turned the vellum pages. Lucy laughing. Lucy smiling. Lucy gazing dreamily into the distance.

Yes, the drawings were proof that she lived. The letter containing the news of her death was nothing but a vile lie, a vicious attempt to keep Lucy from returning home.

But soon she would be free. The knowledge was a soothing balm, the long-awaited healing of a wounded soul.

Yes, her daughter was the cancer. Her daughter must die so that Lucy could live again.

Chapter 8

Whatever could have happened to that notebook?

Releasing a baffled sigh, Elizabeth straightened her weary back after sorting the contents of the last packing crate. She had searched for two days now, but the treasured drawings of her mother were nowhere to be found. Her insides twisted with distress. The notebook was all she had left of her mother . . . that and the ring she wore on the chain beneath her simple blouse. Of course, she could draw her mother from memory, but would the freshness be there? Could she recall every nuance, every detail?

A spatter of raindrops struck the glass roof of the conservatory. Disheartened, Elizabeth sank onto an overturned wooden box. Reaching into the pocket of her Turkish trousers for a lump of clay, she moistened it in a nearby jug of water, then began to absently work the substance. The familiar pliancy beneath her fingers brought a measure of calm, as did the sight of her surroundings.

Even in her dreams she had never imagined such a perfect place to work. The conservatory looked charmingly wild with overgrown camellia bushes, climbing ivy plants, and winding flagstone paths. Yesterday a swarm of workmen had descended upon the room, fixing the dripping faucet, replacing a few broken panes of glass, and repairing the fountain so that water now splashed from the satyr's tilted urn, the musical sound mingling with the tapping of raindrops. Her worktable was already scattered with an array of tools: chisel, mallet, penknife, spatula. Clay-stained cloths draped her sculpting pedestals.

Something crashed behind her, followed by a muttered, "Oh, pooh!"

Swiveling, she saw Cicely gingerly stepping down from a packing crate. The girl stooped to retrieve the book lying on the floor, then climbed back to finish straightening the row of anatomy and art volumes on the wall shelf.

"You haven't come across my sketchbook with the royal blue cover, have you?" Elizabeth asked.

Cicely shook her head. "Maybe it's inside that box you're sitting on."

"No, I've unpacked everything," Elizabeth said, digging her fingers into the clay. "I haven't seen the notebook since the day my lodgings were vandalized."

Cicely gasped and nearly fell off the box. "You don't suppose the thief took it, do you?"

"Of course not. Why would anyone want sketches of my mother?"

Cicely dramatically put a hand over the pleated green silk of her bosom. "Why, don't you see—? He must have known you're a famous artist. He's probably planning to sell the pictures and make a fortune!"

Elizabeth laughed. "Come now, Cicely. I'm hardly Rodin or Millais. I can't imagine the public clamoring for my work."

"Why, you're the finest artist in England. With Nick's patronage, you'll soon have so many commissions you'll hardly know what to do with yourself."

The clay went slick beneath Elizabeth's fingers. Ever since that night here in the conservatory with Lord Nicholas, the mere mention of his name set her heart to racing. She didn't understand why such an annoying, arrogant man could make her feel so weak. Whenever he was near, all she could think about was how much she wanted to touch his strong body, to feel his hand caress her breast again. Thoughts of him kept distracting her from her art.

"Your brother hasn't promised me a single commission," she said. "He won't even let me sculpt *him*."

"Oh, he's such a stuffed shirt." Cicely dusted off her hands, then lifted her skirts and hopped onto the stone floor. "One thing I can say about Nick, he isn't vain in the least. He hates for anyone to make a fuss over his looks."

Wrestling with a jolt of jealousy, Elizabeth studied the clay in her lap. "Lady Marianne was making quite a fuss the other night. He didn't seem to mind *her*."

Cicely grinned. "Didn't Marianne behave like a perfect ninny? Imagine, thinking she could impress us with her piano playing!"

In a gale of giggles, she collapsed onto the box. Recalling Marianne's murderous rendition of the sonata, Elizabeth couldn't help laughing, too.

"Then why do you suppose your brother is interested in her?"

"Oh, he's used to acting the perfect gentleman," Cicely said with a dismissive wave of her hand. Leaning forward, she confided, "Anyway, he's probably just surveying the prospects. I overheard him telling Aunt Beatrice it's time he married. Family duty and all, you know." Cicely imitated his deep voice.

Elizabeth's insides gave an odd squeeze. "Do you think he'll marry Lady Marianne?"

"Good God, I should hope not!" Cicely's fair face screwed into a comic look of horror. "I shudder to think of such a silly twit as my sister-in-law. Thank goodness Nick has looks and money. He has his pick of women—" She stopped abruptly and stared. "What about you?"

Confused, Elizabeth tilted her head. "What *about* me?"

"*You* could marry Nick!"

"Marry—?" she repeated numbly.

"It's the perfect solution! Why didn't I think of it before?" Cicely sprang up and executed an exuberant dance. "If you marry my brother, you'll never go back to America. And I wouldn't have to put up with yet another person blathering at me about my behavior." ·

"Now wait a moment," Elizabeth said sharply, trying to untangle the shocking thrill gripping her insides. "That's the most ridiculous notion I've ever heard. The earl would never want to marry *me*."

Cicely stopped twirling. "Why not? You're pretty and talented and brave. You'd make the perfect match for my straitlaced brother. Why, you'd set society on its ears!"

"I don't want to have anything to do with society. And I rather suspect society doesn't want to have anything to do with me, either."

"Oh, pooh. No one said it would be easy. We'll just have to come up with a scheme to make Nick propose marriage. Hmm... maybe we could arrange a compromising situation—"

"That's out of the question, Cicely." Shooting to her feet, Elizabeth thrust the clay into her pocket. "I'm not marrying *anyone*."

"You're not?" The girl looked baffled. "Why, everyone gets married at some time or another."

"Not me," Elizabeth said firmly. "*I* intend to devote my life to art. I've no time for a husband and children. Even if I *were* interested in marrying, a man as narrow-minded as your brother would be my last choice."

"Don't you ever want to do anything else but sculpt?"

"No."

"Oh. Well." Cicely looked dejected; then she brightened. "Then I'll have to find him someone else who wouldn't badger me. Let me think..." She snapped her fingers. "I know! Phoebe!"

"Phoebe?"

"The Lady Phoebe Garforth, no doubt."

The crisp male voice came from the entrance to the conservatory. Elizabeth whipped around to see the earl standing in the doorway. Warmth flooded her cheeks. How much had Lord Nicholas overheard?

As he strode inside, a few rays of watery sunshine struck the fine planes of his face. His mouth was set in a stern line, his eyes as charcoal gray as rainclouds. The impeccable cut of his morning coat and trousers emphasized his height and breadth. Elizabeth absorbed his presence like dry clay soaking up water.

Nicholas, on the other hand, seemed to have no such admiration for her. Unbidden disappointment swelled inside her. He afforded her scarcely a glance as he headed toward his sister.

"Hullo, Nick," Cicely said, waving gaily. "I thought you were at parliament today."

"I was. Apparently I came home just in time, else I might have been denied a voice in choosing my bride."

His sarcasm seemed to fly straight over his sister's head. "Oh, pooh, don't be silly. You'd have final say, of course. I just meant to steer you in the right direction."

"Ah. And so Lady Phoebe Garforth will be the lucky recipient of my proposal."

"Well, why not?" Cicely said, lifting her slim shoulders in a breezy shrug. "You keep thrusting me at her brother Charles, so I simply thought to keep it all in the family."

A look passed between the two, Cicely merrily defiant and Nicholas patiently exasperated. "You would do well," he said in a low voice, "to pay heed to Charles's feelings. He's an honorable man and he cares deeply for you."

Cicely thrust out her lower lip. "Well, I don't care a fig about him. He's too old and stodgy."

"He's twenty-eight, a year older than I. And just because he doesn't steal away to study art or shock people with bold remarks doesn't make him stodgy."

The earl's unreasonable anger brought out Elizabeth's protective instincts. "Cicely should have the right to choose," she felt compelled to point out, "just as you do."

He swung toward her, his eyes sharp with resentment. "Limit your opinions to art, if you please, Miss Hastings. This discussion does not involve you."

His cutting words hurt less than his contemptuous glance. Elizabeth gritted her teeth to subdue a retort.

Something was clearly bothering the earl, but that didn't excuse his ill-mannered behavior.

Turning his back on Elizabeth, he told his sister, "We'll speak of your future another time."

With stubborn Ware pride, Cicely thrust her chin up. "There's nothing to speak of. My mind is made up about not marrying Charles."

"May I presume, then, that you don't wish to attend the Garforths' ball on Wednesday next?"

Cicely assumed an instant posture of meekness. "I didn't say that. Oh, please, Nick. I haven't been out of the house for two whole days now and I daresay I'm on the verge of going mad!"

"I have your word that you'll behave yourself?"

"Yes, Nick." But Cicely's eyes, Elizabeth noted, shimmered with irrepressible mischief.

Swinging to Elizabeth, the earl said curtly, "Where is your father?"

"I don't know," she said, still mystified by his ill humor. "I haven't seen him since breakfast."

"If you do see him, tell him I wish to speak with him." He paused, his distaste evident as he eyed her Turkish trousers. "The Wallingfords will be here for tea in half an hour. I trust you'll change that outlandish outfit."

Clinging to a thread of temper, Elizabeth folded her arms and matched his haughty tone. "I'm not coming to tea, your lordship. I've far more important things to do."

She took great satisfaction in the way his mouth tightened. At least she'd broken through that chilly disdain.

"Pardon me." He swept her a sardonic bow. "I'd forgotten your devotion to art. I wouldn't dream of demanding your attention, nor of foisting my narrow-minded wishes on you."

The color in her cheeks receded, then flooded hotly back. So he *had* overheard her scathing denunciation of him. She told herself it didn't matter, that it was best he knew her opinion so there could be no misunderstanding between them.

Yet as she watched him stride out of the conservatory, she bit her lip and wished she could call back her words.

Puzzled by her father's tardiness, Elizabeth wandered through the lengthy upstairs corridor with its gilt wallpaper and medallioned plasterwork ceiling. She wanted to pass along Lord Nicholas's message, but Owen wasn't in his bedroom. He wasn't in the library, either. In fact none of the servants she'd questioned could recall seeing him since early that morning. Now it was nearly dinnertime and worry began to prick her.

These past few days Papa had seemed more moody and withdrawn, though he usually found time to visit and inquire about her work. Elizabeth couldn't blame him for not wishing to join the Ware social gatherings. She herself found it difficult to adjust to the pomp and circumstance with which Nicholas conducted his household.

Suddenly she caught sight of her father emerging from the servants' stairwell at the end of the hall. She started to call out, but a peculiar air of furtiveness about him stopped her. He glanced back down the stairs, as if expecting someone to be following. Mystified, she hurried toward him, her shoes making no sound on the plush garnet carpeting, her loose Turkish trousers causing no betraying rustle.

"Papa? Is something wrong?"

He jumped and swung toward her, his hazel eyes glittering in the gaslight. "Bless my soul! It's you, Libby."

His face looked pale beneath his gray side-whiskers, and his hand tightly gripped his walking stick. Glancing down the length of him, she spied mud caking his mist-dampened Inverness cape, his trousers, and shoes. Concern clutched at her. "What's happened, Papa?"

He drew a breath; his husky shoulders squared.

"Happened? What do you mean? You just... startled me, that's all."

But his eyes slid away and again Elizabeth sensed that curious secretiveness. "Something *is* wrong." She stepped closer and ran her fingers over a jagged groove in his walking stick. "This gouge wasn't here before. And where did you get so dirty?"

"Dirty?" Owen looked down at himself as if realizing for the first time the state of his clothing. "Oh... I went for a walk and fell into the mud. Clumsy of me, wasn't it?"

Somehow his jovial laugh didn't ring true. Elizabeth tilted her head at him. What would her father be hiding from her? Could he have gone out seeking a job and felt reluctant to admit failure to her? Elizabeth's heart constricted. Yes, that must be it. He wanted to provide for her; living off the earl's charity must sting her father's pride.

Heedless of the mud, she threw her arms around him and pressed her cheek to the roughness of his whiskers. "Oh, Papa, I'm sorry if you're not happy here."

"Hush now, what's this?" He drew back to look at her, hands on her shoulders, affection softening his eyes. "Who said I'm not happy?"

"I know how you dislike the nobility, Papa, yet you moved into the earl's house for my sake. If you're so uncomfortable here, we can leave, find another place to live."

"No!" Owen burst out. Taking a deep breath, he aimed a frown at the sumptuous corridor, then said in a more controlled tone, "It's true, all this extravagance isn't to my liking. The scriptures say, 'Where your treasure is, there will your heart be also.'" Earnestly he squeezed her shoulders. "You're my riches, Libby. You're safe here and that's all that really matters."

The devotion in his voice brought a fond smile to her lips. She still didn't believe the robbery and the attack were related, yet she couldn't bear to upset him by saying so again. "All right, Papa, I won't speak of leaving anymore."

"Good," Owen said, his craggy face relaxing. "Come, Libby, walk me to my room. I've a mind to wash up before I ruin the earl's priceless carpet."

An arm around her shoulder, he propelled her down the long corridor. Relief poured through Elizabeth. Thank goodness her father didn't want to leave here. In the deepest part of her, she couldn't bear the notion of never again seeing Lord Nicholas. The memory of his hand on her breast made her feel warm and breathless. With a pang, she recalled he had meant only to teach her a lesson. A lesson meant to jolt her into behaving like his vision of a lady.

A door opened at the end of the hall and Lord Nicholas stepped out of his rooms. He paused, his tall and elegant form framed by the glow of gaslight. He wore formal evening attire that fit him to perfection, dark jacket and trousers, and a pristine cravat with a pearl pin. As he started toward them, Elizabeth felt her heart beat faster.

Swiftly she murmured, "I forgot, Papa. The earl wished to have a word with you—that's why I came looking for you."

Her father stiffened. "A summons from his high-and-mighty lordship?" he said, twirling his cane. "I wonder that he would deign to speak to a lowly commoner."

"Please, Papa, he's our host—"

Then Lord Nicholas was standing before them, sketching a brief bow. His smoothly handsome features gave no indication that he'd heard Owen's derogatory words or that he recalled her own caustic comment of that afternoon.

"Good evening," he said. "I trust you both have had a pleasant day?"

"Yes, thank you," Elizabeth replied, determined to match his impeccable manners. "I was just passing along your message."

The earl's sharp eyes took in Owen's disheveled appearance. "Pardon me for intruding, but you haven't suffered an accident, have you?"

"Just a clumsy slip into a puddle, that's all." Her father's taut explanation clearly invited no further inquiry.

"I see," Lord Nicholas said. "I'd like a few moments of your time. If it's not inconvenient, will you join me in the library after dinner?"

"Why don't you tell me what's on your mind right now?"

The earl flicked a cryptic glance at Elizabeth. "I prefer to speak to you in private."

The two men exchanged a long, measuring look that perplexed her. Then her father said tautly, "As you wish."

To Elizabeth, the earl said, "Will we see you at dinner?"

She shook her head. "Thank you, no. I'll take a tray in the conservatory."

His lips tightened, but she told herself she didn't care if he was displeased. The thought of trussing herself up in a corset and petticoats was abhorrent. She wouldn't bow to his presumptuous order to behave like an English gentlewoman.

Affording her a curt nod, Lord Nicholas strode toward the main staircase. Her father uttered a distracted goodbye and vanished into his room, leaving Elizabeth alone in the corridor. Irritated at the way they planned to exclude her from their discussion, she felt scorched by curiosity.

What did the earl mean to say to her father?

"You wish me to do *what*?" Lady Beatrice said, incredulity elevating her usually modulated voice.

Her dumbfounded look made Nicholas repress a smile. Pivoting, he walked to the mahogany sideboard, where he poured brandy into two glasses, then brought one to her.

"Here you are, Aunt," he said, injecting the proper

amount of deference and concern into his words. "You look as though you need this."

The glass clicked sharply as she set it on a marble-topped side table. "Don't try to distract me, Nicholas. You're asking me to turn myself into a tutor, to take that . . . that *artist* and transform her into a lady! Why, it's impossible! She lacks breeding and background. There is simply no foundation on which to build."

"Miss Hastings managed quite well with Lord and Lady Melton."

"Sheer luck," Lady Beatrice said with a sniff. "She did address Lord Melton wrong, but I managed to smooth things over. Imagine how dreadful it would have been if she'd committed a worse gaffe."

Unaffected, Nicholas took a swallow of brandy. "That's all the more reason for doing as I ask. As Cicely's companion, Miss Hastings cannot avoid going out into society from time to time. Would you rather she be unprepared?"

Lady Beatrice pursed her lips in displeasure. "Of course not. Nevertheless, I simply haven't the time. Why, I have calls I must make each afternoon, connections to nurture, people of consequence to visit."

She was weakening, Nicholas judged. "Ah, but you're so perfect for the task," he said. "Can you name a person more suited to taking an untrained girl and molding her into the consummate lady?"

"You're flattering me again, Nicholas. It simply won't work." Though her tone scolded, a smile flirted with the corners of her mouth.

Lifting her hand to his lips, he kissed its satiny back. "Say you'll do it, Aunt. Please."

She drew her fingers away and studied him for a moment, then reached up to pat his cheek as if he were a boy. "Nicholas, you're impossible," she said grudgingly. "I never could refuse you anything."

Elation rose in him, though he guarded his expression. His aunt must never know just how important this was to him. "Thank you," he said with quiet sincerity. "I knew I could depend on you."

Clasping her hands, she gazed pensively at him. "I don't understand this uncommon interest you're taking in that woman. Are you certain there's not something between you two, something...ah...something I should know about?"

His heartbeat surged. "If there were," he lied coolly, "you'd be the first person I'd confide in."

Beatrice still wore a tiny frown. "I wonder," she said, a trace of irony in her voice. "Well, I shall say good night, then. It's not often that energetic sister of yours retires before me."

Nicholas laughed. "We can thank Elizabeth for that. She's been keeping Cicely busy these past few days."

"Indeed." After giving him another long, measuring look, Lady Beatrice sailed out the drawing room door.

Only then did Nicholas understand the source of that scrutiny; he had referred to Elizabeth by her Christian name. His aunt was far too swift not to notice such slips. Draining his brandy, he vowed to be more circumspect in the future. Not a whisper of scandal must touch Elizabeth. Not now, when he was so close to unearthing her past. Already his secretary had discovered the noble house linked to the swan crest; Nicholas made a mental note to reward Thistlewood for such efficient work.

Heading slowly toward the foyer, he recalled his shock of that afternoon when he'd learned the name of Elizabeth's grandsire. He hadn't anticipated her being connected to such a highly placed family. Of course, he couldn't be certain the relationship was legitimate; that was yet another mystery to unravel. Impatience tugged at him. He must find out quickly why someone wished her dead. He'd sent a sharp reprimand to the police commissioner for not having found the man in the porkpie hat. And Thistlewood would depart on the first train to Yorkshire tomorrow to begin discreet inquiries. Though Nicholas burned to conduct the investigation himself, he told himself it was more important that he stay here and protect Elizabeth.

In the meantime, he would do a little digging on his own.

In the foyer a tiny sound drew his eyes. Pickering stood smartly at attention by the front door, though weariness was apparent in the slight sag of his lanky frame. "Lock up for the night," Nicholas said absently. "And get yourself to bed."

A wealth of gratitude on his boyish face, the footman bowed. "Thank you, m'lord."

Pivoting, Nicholas headed down the hall, his footsteps echoing on the marble floor. In the distance he heard the library clock chiming the hour of midnight. Although it was late, he needed to talk to Elizabeth; she might know something that could speed up Thistlewood's search.

Gaslight spilled from the opened doorway of her studio and the faint musky scent of plants and clay drifted to him. Anticipation budded inside Nicholas, a feeling he couldn't deny. Elizabeth stood at the cluttered worktable, her eyes intent on the piece of wood she whittled with a penknife.

A powerful sweep of desire took his breath with the force of a blow. He wanted to sink his fingers into the jet black cascade of her hair, to caress the swanlike curve of her neck, to peel away those ridiculous baggy trousers and find the womanly softness beneath.

He cursed himself. My God, hadn't he learned yet? If he hadn't known her opinion of him already, her candid words this afternoon should have done the trick. Only a royal fool would still crave her. Yet crave her he did; the hot pulsing of his blood gave testimony to that. He wanted all Elizabeth Hastings could offer . . . her body, her tenderness, her smiles, her respect.

Watching as she put down the penknife to wire two bits of wood together, Nicholas felt a tightening in the pit of his stomach, a feeling oddly akin to jealousy. He didn't understand it, this burning passion for a woman devoted to the arts, a woman who found his face far more fascinating than his character.

Yet an inexplicable force drew him to her like a bee to a maverick camellia. Entombing his emotions deep inside himself, he stepped inside the conservatory.

Chapter 9

Blinking weary eyes, Elizabeth whittled absent-mindedly at a bit of wood for the armature she was building. Just moments ago, the muffled tones of a distant clock had tolled the hour of midnight. She had been certain her father would have come by now. Maybe he didn't intend to tell her the outcome of his interview with Nicholas. Irritation nagged at her. What could the earl possibly have to say to Owen that she couldn't hear? And why was she suddenly thinking of his lordship as Nicholas?

Over the gurgling melody of the fountain came the tread of footsteps. Expecting her father, she swung around. And gasped, for it was Nicholas who walked down the stone pathway. The sight of him brought a jolt of joy to her heart; her exhaustion vanished beneath a surge of excitement. Flustered, she let the penknife clatter onto the worktable.

"What are you doing here?" she blurted.

He came beside her and settled into a half-sitting position against the worktable, hands clasping the scarred edge. "I was passing by and saw the lights on," he said. "You're working rather late tonight, aren't you?"

His friendly manner disconcerted her. In the gaslight his eyes were a steady silver gray; his relaxed expression made him seem more approachable and, astonishingly, more handsome. Dazzled by his nearness, Elizabeth felt the urge to smooth her fingers over that firm masculine mouth. Instead she picked up the wood and again wielded the penknife.

"Is working late also something a lady isn't supposed to do?" she said tartly.

He smiled. "I don't dare answer that so long as you have that weapon in your hand."

The fine grooves on either side of his mouth drew her eyes. Realizing how fiercely she stabbed the wood, Elizabeth set down the knife and said lamely, "Oh."

The earl leaned closer to examine the curved lead pipe fastened to a wooden baseboard. His subtle masculine scent made her slightly giddy. "What are you making?"

His look of genuine interest erased her embarrassment and warmed her heart. "An armature. When I do a bust of someone, the armature supports the clay so that it doesn't sag." She deemed it prudent not to tell him the bust she planned was of him.

"I see." Lord Nicholas picked up the small wooden cross. "And what's this?"

"It's called a butterfly. It also helps anchor the clay." Plucking the cross from his palm, she deftly wired it to the loop of pipe. "There, I'm finished."

He straightened, studying her with an absorbed expression that made her blood flow faster. The splashing of the fountain filled the silence; Elizabeth saw a sudden image of the dark and quiet house enfolding them. If she had agreed to become his mistress, she could thread her fingers into the neatness of his chestnut hair, press her mouth to the smooth strength of his jaw...

"What made you want to become a sculptress?" he asked.

Elizabeth blinked, trying to collect her scattered thoughts. "When I was fifteen, a friend of mine died in an accident." As the memory came flooding back, she slowly sank into a chair. "I was shaken, grief stricken for weeks. It was the first time anyone close to me had ever died. Hoping to lift my spirits, my mother bought me some modeling clay. I spent days working out my sorrow, struggling to transfer my feelings to the clay. And when I finished that first sculpture, I did feel better, lighter somehow, as if a burden had been lifted."

She raised her head to look at Nicholas; the tenderness in his eyes made her feel suddenly shy and breathless.

"Do you still have what you made?" he said. "I'd like to see it."

Absurdly gladdened by his interest, Elizabeth shot to her feet. "Come here, then."

He walked with her to a shelf where the small sculpture served as a bookend to her collection of art and anatomy volumes. She touched the polished bronze figure of a weeping woman draped over a gravestone. Seeing the sculpture still made her throat tighten.

"I call it *Desolation*," she murmured.

"It's stunning."

His low tone testified to his sincerity; the praise warmed her heart. "Thank you."

Picking up the statue, he ran his thumb over the tiny tracing of a bird on the base. "The swan. Is that your hallmark?"

Elizabeth nodded. "When I finish a piece, I press the signet into the clay before it dries. Then, if I can manage the money, I have the sculpture cast in bronze."

"Your mother was a wise woman," Nicholas said, setting the figure back on the shelf. "Did she always encourage you in your work?"

"Oh, yes." Awash in bittersweet memories, Elizabeth smiled. "My mother was my greatest champion and my severest critic."

"She had art training, then?"

"Only a little drawing, as a girl. But she had wonderful instincts. I learned so much from her. Things that will be a part of me forever."

"What was her name?"

"Lucy. Lucy Templeton Hastings."

Nicholas studied her intently. "She looked a lot like you. The night we met, I saw a drawing of her in your blue notebook."

"Yes." A troubled pang invaded Elizabeth. "That sketchbook is still missing, by the way."

He lifted an eyebrow. "I'm sure it will turn up."

If only she could be so certain. Then the warm pressure of his hand at her spine distracted Elizabeth as he guided her back to the chair. His candid questions opened a chasm of pleasure inside her. Maybe he wasn't quite so self-centered, after all.

"Tell me more about your mother," he suggested, resuming his informal pose against the table edge. "She was raised here in England, was she not?"

Elizabeth nodded. "Both of my parents grew up here. I was born here, too, but we moved to America when I was two."

"Ah." Nicholas fell silent for a moment, studying her with those disturbing smoke-hued eyes, eyes that possessed the power to make her insides melt. "Do you know why your parents left?"

She lifted a shoulder. "I guess because they wanted all the opportunities America has to offer." An impish impulse made her add, "And freedom from all the rules and regulations people seem to have over here."

The corners of his mouth quirked, deepening his masculine dimples. "Are you saying your mother was a member of the gentry?"

A daub of suspicion colored Elizabeth's thoughts. "I think so, but she never spoke much of her life here. Does it matter?"

"Only if it involves you." His murmured words made her insides flutter; the sensation intensified as his gaze descended to her bosom. "You wear that signet ring on a chain around your neck. It came from your grandfather, did it not?"

Drawing forth the ring, Elizabeth curled her fingers around it like a talisman. "Yes, my mother gave it to me on my thirteenth birthday."

"Did she tell you anything about him? His name, perhaps? What sort of person he was?"

Elizabeth shook her head. "She said he was dead,

that I have no other relations left here." Her eyes narrowed. "Why do you want to know?"

"Because I'm curious about you," he said, his voice as low and liquid as the murmuring fountain. He leaned closer, eyes fixed on her. "I want to know everything about you, Elizabeth. Everything that shaped you into the woman you are."

A fierce flare of yearning heated Elizabeth. Her heart wanted to believe him; her mind told her to mistrust him. The signet bit into her palm as suspicion won out. She had never felt more than a passing interest in the owner of the swan crest; her grandfather was a shadow figure to her, an insubstantial person in a world full of clear, vibrant images. So why was Nicholas so keen on ferreting out her grandfather's identity?

"You can't possibly care about me," she said slowly. "You only care about my lineage. You want to find blue blood in me, to keep you from being ashamed to have me in your house."

"That isn't true."

His words were fervent, but when Nicholas averted his eyes for an instant, Elizabeth knew he was lying.

Disappointment stabbed her spirit; an absurd emptiness touched her heart. Letting the ring drop to her chest, she rose stiffly, hands clenched at her sides.

"Is that why you insisted on speaking to my father? I suppose you tried to pry information out of him, too."

Oddly enough, Nicholas's eyes seemed full of concern. "You're wrong about that, Elizabeth."

"Am I?" Lifting her chin with dignity, she said, "If you'll excuse me, your lordship, I must retire so I can get up early tomorrow. We *common* folk have to work for a living."

Turning her back, she marched out of the conservatory.

As she sat at her worktable the next morning, Elizabeth was still meditating on the encounter. Her pencil swept over the drawing pad, shaping the homespun features of Miss Eversham, while her mind wrestled with the memory of Nicholas's inscrutable expression. The feeling that she'd missed a vital clue last night pestered her like a subtly inaccurate line on a sculpture. She couldn't question her father; he had already gone out for the day.

"You're frowning, Miss Hastings. Is my portrait giving you difficulty?"

Blinking, Elizabeth focused on Miss Eversham, who sat stiff as a statue in a chair beside the burbling fountain. Sunshine warmed the brown hair scraped into a bun and softened the austere angles of her face.

"Oh, no," Elizabeth said hastily. "I was only concentrating. I'm so pleased you agreed to sit for me—you're a compelling subject."

Doubt drew the governess's lips into a lean line. "I don't see why you think so. I'm hardly Helen of Troy."

"You have character. That makes you far more fascinating than some empty-headed society beauty. Just wait and see."

"Hmph," Miss Eversham snorted. Yet pleasure sparkled her plain brown eyes and she sat even straighter.

Smiling to herself, Elizabeth deftly wielded the pencil to shape the woman's hawk nose. The governess truly was an engaging study, so starched and servile, so civilized and straitlaced, so . . . so *British*. And so unlike the laundresses and laborers Elizabeth had sketched in America.

Over the fountain's melody, footsteps tapped and silk rustled. She looked up to see Lady Beatrice sailing down the stone pathway like a privateer in pursuit of quarry. Her sapphire morning gown trimmed with flounces and fringe made her an elegant ship, indeed, Elizabeth decided with irreverent humor.

Lady Beatrice aimed a glare at the governess. "Miss Eversham! What are *you* doing here? And where is my niece?"

Miss Eversham sprang guiltily to her feet and dipped a curtsy. "Good morning, your ladyship," she said, fingers smoothing her skirt of sober black bombazine.

"Forgive me, but Lady Cicely is still abed and I had a few moments free—"

"And thought you would sit for a chat? I'm shocked, Miss Eversham. Surely you have mending to do, lessons to prepare. I've never before known you to desert the duties the earl pays you to perform."

The governess meekly inclined her head. "Yes, your ladyship. It shan't happen again."

Irked, Elizabeth slapped her sketchpad and pencil onto the cluttered table. "We weren't chatting, Lady Beatrice. I persuaded Miss Eversham to sit for me. I assure you, she was most reluctant to do so and agreed only out of the goodness of her heart."

Her ladyship's mouth thinned. "Indeed. How fitting, then, that I am here to discuss your behavior. Miss Eversham, you are excused."

Flustered beneath her ladyship's pointed look, the governess curtsied again and scurried out of the conservatory.

"One does not fraternize with servants, Miss Hastings. You would do well to remember that."

Amused by the imperious words, Elizabeth picked up her pad and turned to a clean page. "I wasn't fraternizing; I was drawing. And why should you be concerned with my behavior? After all, you consider *me* to be on the level of a servant."

Lady Beatrice lifted her chin. "Duty compels me to be here today. My nephew has assigned me the task of instructing you in deportment. The next time you enter polite company, you must be properly prepared."

Elizabeth's fingers tensed around the pencil. So this was the earl's doing, was it? With typical arrogance he clung to the notion of transforming her into an English lady. Hurt stung her insides. Why couldn't he accept her as she was?

"I'm as prepared as I'll ever be," she said, distracting herself with a quick sketch of Lady Beatrice. "I told the earl I had no intention of assuming a false identity simply to please him."

Lady Beatrice looked startled. "You said that to Nicholas?" Recovering herself, she said severely, "Nevertheless, as long as you reside in this household your behavior reflects upon the Ware family. Cicely must not be exposed to a poor example."

"I thought I managed quite admirably with Lord and Lady Melton."

Her ladyship set her chin at a determined angle. "I'll grant you, you fared better than I had anticipated. Still, you must learn a number of critical details. For one, you should have stood up and curtsyed when I came in. A lady must always do so when a person of higher rank enters the room."

"Then I would be rising whenever *any*one walked in. How tiresome!" Elizabeth smothered a smile. "I suppose *you* consider me so lowborn I should show such deference even to the servants."

"Really, Miss Hastings! Flippancy does not become a lady."

"I'm not here to learn a new role. I'm an American and equal to any human being. We have a constitution that says so."

"And I'm not here to discuss foreign policy. You must learn to guard your tongue." Like a schoolmarm, her ladyship shook a manicured finger, a gesture Elizabeth hurried to catch on paper. "Civilized conversation is an art. One must work at it, learn what one can and cannot say in well-bred company."

When she started to lower her arm, Elizabeth said quickly, "Don't move."

Lady Beatrice froze, her eyes round and gray. "What's wrong?" she squeaked. "I haven't an insect on me, have I?"

Laughing, Elizabeth swiftly finished the sketch. "No, I'm just drawing you. There, you can relax now."

Lady Beatrice let her arm fall. "Drawing *me?*" she said, curiosity softening her cultured tone.

"Come and see."

Her ladyship paused as if unsure; then she glided around the worktable to peer at the sketch pad. Silence reigned for a moment. "Oh, dear," she said in a small voice. "Do I really look so . . . so shrewish?"

Elizabeth bit back a grin. "Only when you scold."

"Well. At least drawing is quite a genteel skill for a lady."

"I'm not a lady," Elizabeth said. "I'm an artist."

Lady Beatrice assumed a regal pose. "I see no reason why you can't be both. You seem to have a quick mind, Miss Hastings. Stand up, please; we've work to do."

Humoring her and expecting to be entertained, Elizabeth complied.

A look of comic horror swept her ladyship's patrician face. "Dear St. George, you're wearing trousers! You're in more need of my expertise than I'd dreamed."

"This is my working attire. I won't consider changing it."

As if Elizabeth hadn't spoken, the older woman tapped her lower lip with a finger. "I shall arrange for my dressmaker to take your measurements. We shall see what *he* can do with you."

"I can't afford new clothes, especially at *your* prices."

Her ladyship waved a dismissing hand. "Oh, but Nicholas will see to the cost."

Anger pricked Elizabeth's sense of humor. "I won't allow the earl to drape me in fancy clothes like a kept woman."

A flush tinted Lady Beatrice's porcelain cheeks. "A lady does not speak of such females. And I will not allow you to be an embarrassment to my nephew. Now, we will begin with deportment. I must have your undivided attention, if you please."

"That's impossible," Elizabeth said flatly, sitting back down. "I refuse to stop working just to listen to a long list of pointless rules."

Lady Beatrice pursed her lips. "Then I shall conduct our lessons as you work. That way, you can take notes. We will now discuss the proper terms of address, beginning with a duke and his family."

Pacing with dignified steps, her sapphire skirts swishing, she commenced a complicated inventory of instructions. Half amused and half annoyed, Elizabeth gave in. Single-mindedness was, without a doubt, a family trait.

Resigned, she began a sketch of Nicholas as she listened with half an ear. At the close of an hour her head spun with trying to distinguish the social precedence of dowagers and widows of younger sons and married daughters of peers.

She couldn't resist commenting, "Wouldn't it be simpler to treat everyone equally?"

Lady Beatrice stopped. "We are all born to a specified station, Miss Hastings. To consider everyone alike is absurd. How, for example, could I be like Miss Eversham? We must remember that the common masses look to the aristocracy for leadership."

"Equality works well in America."

"America," her ladyship sniffed. "Now there is a country without culture, without refinement. Imagine, not even a monarch to serve as an example of personal dignity and national pride."

"'Pride goeth before destruction and a haughty spirit before a fall,'" said Owen.

Elizabeth turned to see her father standing in the doorway, framed by trailing ivy plants. Though his words were admonishing, the smile creasing his whiskered face brought a rush of gladness to her. His plain brown suit was meticulously clean, his thinning gray hair neatly combed. This morning he looked vigorous and happy, much like the father she knew when her mother was alive, the father she had missed so much these past months.

"I beg your pardon," Lady Beatrice enunciated in her most snobbish tone. "Your daughter and I are engaged in a private dialogue. If you wish to speak with her, I should be obliged if you would do so at another time."

Owen stepped jauntily closer to give Elizabeth a peck on the cheek. "I should like to speak to my daughter now. Begging your ladyship's pardon, of course." He swept into an elaborate bow.

"Well!" Lady Beatrice looked miffed, though she could hardly refuse. "We shall continue our lessons later, then. We have a great deal of ground yet to cover, Miss Hastings." Head held high, she sailed out on a rustle of sapphire silk.

"Lessons?" Owen asked.

"Oh, she has some silly notion of teaching me the difference between a duke and an earl. Tell me now, what has you smiling so this morning?"

His hazel eyes twinkled in the sunlight. "I've been offered a position."

Elizabeth hugged him. "Oh, Papa, that's wonderful news! Where? When will you start? How long have you known about this?"

Chuckling, he held a hand up. "One question at a time, please, Libby. I went for the interview this morning, but they offered me the post on the spot. I'll be tutoring a boy who's bedridden with a fractured leg. He missed the last month of school, and his brother doesn't want him to fall behind come autumn."

"You've met the boy, then?"

"Oh, yes. We got on quite satisfactorily. For all his high rank, he's a plucky lad, reminds me a bit of Kipp."

"What's his name?"

"Lord Francis Garforth. His elder brother is the Marquess of Sedgemoor."

Surprise rippled through Elizabeth. "Garforth? Cicely mentioned a Garforth family, Lord Charles and his sister, the Lady Phoebe."

"Francis is their younger brother."

"I see." Warm with curiosity, she plucked a lump of clay from a box, dipped it into water, then began kneading it. "How did you find out about this position?"

Owen's expression grew grave. "Lord Nicholas recommended me. That's why he wanted to speak to me yesterday."

The clay hung heavy in her hand as she stared at her father. Nicholas had done such a considerate deed? Arrogant, self-serving *Nicholas*?

Her cheeks burned. She had been offended by his

wish to speak to Owen alone; she had accused the earl of using her father. She recalled the time Nicholas had been so kind to Kipp, shaking the boy's hand instead of snubbing him. Was she wrong to believe Nicholas was so wrapped up in his own autocratic desires?

"Why didn't you come tell me about this last night?" she asked.

Hands clasped behind his back, Owen paced slowly. "Because at first I was angry. I believed Lord Nicholas was patronizing me." His gaze troubled, he looked at Elizabeth. "I came close to ignoring the interview. But I was letting pride rule me; I didn't want to admit that a nobleman might truly want to help me."

"I suppose even an earl can have a spot of goodness in him."

"Perhaps," Owen conceded grudgingly, "Lord Nicholas is the exception to the rule. Although he does act superior too much of the time." His face brightened. "Well, enough of my lectures, Libby. I must be off to prepare my lessons—I start my employment tomorrow." He strode out, whistling.

Elizabeth sat on the edge of the scarred table and stared at the clay in her hands. For a long time she didn't move. She was glad her father finally had a mission to occupy his mind and drive away his grief. Yet she mustn't let Nicholas's generosity sway her. She mustn't let herself go soft and weak because of a single act of kindness.

Her fingers dug into the earthen ball. Lord Nicholas Ware wanted to shape her like this lump of clay, to mold her into his image of a lady. Because in her present natural state she was an embarrassment to him. He likely regretted inviting her into his house to teach his sister.

She would do well to remember his motive.

"You're not coming to tea?" Cicely said in surprise, the orchid pink Parisian dress clutched to her bosom.

"No," Elizabeth said, "I have something else to do this afternoon."

"Oh, pooh. Nick asked that all of us be there, you especially. Aunt Beatrice was most insistent about that."

"I know." Perched on a brocaded hassock in Cicely's sumptuous dressing room, Elizabeth bit back a remark on what the earl could do with his orders. "Your aunt told me this tea was to be the test of every ridiculous rule she's drummed into my head for the past two days. But I'm not going."

"You'll miss all the excitement. Not about the duke, mind you, but his nephew, Mr. Drew Sterling." Cicely twirled dreamily, the pink gown billowing around her, "He's *so* deliciously wicked. I've been simply *pining* for an introduction, but Nick would never let me within a furlong of Drew and his fast crowd. 'An immoral influence,' he said." Her face assumed an amusingly accurate parody of her brother's most stern expression.

Elizabeth swallowed a smile. "I wonder why he relented, then."

"Oh, pooh, Nick probably has some dreary political matter to discuss with the duke. While they're busy, *I* plan to charm Drew." Holding up the frothy gown, Cicely eyed herself in the cheval mirror. "Do you suppose this bodice is cut low enough?"

"It looks appropriately daring."

"Good. Drew Sterling wouldn't want a schoolroom miss." Her eyes soulful, Cicely sighed, looking exactly like a schoolroom miss. "I can scarcely believe I'm going to meet such a worldly man. Someone who's not stuffy like Lord Charles Garforth. Oh, this shall be the best afternoon of my life—"

"Then I'm sorry to miss it," Elizabeth said, before Cicely could launch into another rapturous monologue about the Duke of Rockborough's profligate heir. "But I must visit Kipp. I promised I would when I left nearly a week ago."

"Kipp!" Cicely swung around, negligently tossing

the dress into a heap on the rug. "Oh, but I want to go, too! Why don't you wait until tomorrow?"

"You aren't allowed to leave the house for another week yet," Elizabeth gently reminded her.

Cicely's face drew into a mutinous pout. "Drat Nick and his silly restrictions. I've half a mind to sneak out, anyway."

"But you don't want to miss the big tea party. Besides, it occurred to me that my blue sketchbook might have been left by mistake. I want to check at my old lodgings."

"Oh, pooh. I did *so* want your opinion of Drew Sterling." A crafty gleam entered her eyes. "Would you change your mind if I were to lend you my very best gown?"

"Which one might that be?" Elizabeth asked dryly, glancing around at the numerous wardrobes lining the walls. "You have enough clothes here to wear something different each day of the year."

"Oh, don't be silly. Half a year, perhaps, but no more. And so many of these gowns are horribly outdated."

Her frivolous manner exasperated Elizabeth. In some ways Cicely could be as narrow-minded as her brother. "A family in Seven Dials or the Devil's Acre could live for a year off the money just one of these dresses cost. For once they'd have a decent meal on the table and a fire in the hearth."

"Really?" Cicely looked startled. "You mean those poor people can't even afford food or heat? I never thought about that before." Her eyes turned misty. "Dear me, all those wretched, hungry children . . ."

Elizabeth hadn't meant to touch off tears. Rising hastily, she patted the girl's hand. "It's not your fault, Cicely. We'll speak of this later. Now I must be going or I'll never return before dark."

"Nick will be blazing angry when he finds out you've left the house against his wishes."

"Then do me a favor...don't tell him I've gone. He'd only worry needlessly."

Cicely lifted a negligent shoulder. "As you like. Believe me, I know how he can carry on."

"I'm sure he'll manage to sip his tea quite well without me," Elizabeth said tartly, heading for the door. "And you may certainly tell him I said *that!*"

Chapter 10

"**S**he said *what?*" Nicholas snapped, his voice echoing through the drawing room.

Cicely affected a sullen look. "Well, don't shout at *me*. I haven't done anything except relay what Elizabeth said, that she refuses to come to tea."

She eyed him demurely, but the betraying twinkle in those blue depths told Nicholas his sister relished seeing someone else defy him. For once, he thought, she hadn't an inkling of the upheaval her news had made of his plans. He'd wasted two entire days at Brooks's, seeking the chance to strike up an acquaintance with the aging Duke of Rockborough.

Too impatient to wait for Thistlewood to uncover Elizabeth's link to the Rockborough clan, Nicholas had contrived this tea so he could observe the reaction of the duke and his family to Elizabeth. When they saw the woman who looked so like Lucy Templeton Hastings, he hoped to catch a shocked expression, a guilty shifting of eyes, some clue to the identity of her would-be killer.

Elizabeth's absence would render the effort useless.

Pivoting on his heel, Nicholas strode across the room.

"Where are you going, Nick?"

"To the conservatory," he said, flinging the words over his shoulder. "Elizabeth *will* be here for tea."

"Oh, but Nick, I don't think..." Cicely's voice trailed off, as if she'd reconsidered arguing.

At the doorway, he nearly collided with Lady Beatrice. "My pardon, Aunt."

Her slim fingers waved away the apology. "Has the duke arrived yet?"

"No," he said curtly. "And apparently Miss Hastings will be late."

"Late?" Lady Beatrice said, frowning. "I informed her of your wishes. She had ample time to prepare." She lifted one dainty shoulder beneath her gown of amber India silk. "Ah, well, we'll simply put her manners to the test on another occasion."

Another occasion wouldn't do, Nicholas thought darkly. If Elizabeth failed to cooperate, he'd invite everyone to the conservatory on the pretext of meeting the resident artist.

Peebles entered, his posture as rigid as a lamppost. "His Grace the Duke of Rockborough has arrived, my lord."

Nicholas bit back a curse. Protocol left him no choice but to play host to his guests. "Go to the conservatory and fetch Miss Hastings," he ordered the butler. "Tell her I want to see her here *instantly*. You're to accept no excuses."

Peebles looked faintly dubious. "Yes, my lord."

Nicholas hoped that for once Elizabeth would have the courtesy to obey. Because the person who wanted her dead was most likely one of the quartet filing into the drawing room.

A shrunken man leaning on a cane led the troupe. Beneath a fringe of gray hair, his fossilized face bore traces of youthful handsomeness and his avid eyes attested to a quick wit. Nicholas's stomach clenched. Elizabeth was the only other person he knew with eyes that rare shade of violet.

"Good to see you again, Hawkesford," the duke said, his voice booming for so slight a person. Looking at the two women and man behind him, he let out a cackle of laughter. "Tried to trounce me at the faro table, by Jove, he did. But I won, fair and square. Fair and square! Isn't that so, Hawkesford?"

Unwilling to expose his scheme, Nicholas injected a trace of chagrin into his voice. "You most certainly did, Your Grace."

"Gambling, uncle?" drawled the dark-eyed young man. "Tut, tut. I wouldn't have thought *you* would engage in such an evil pastime."

"Ungrateful wretch." Scowling, the duke shook his silver-topped stick; its swan crest matched Elizabeth's ring. "*I* didn't play for money. *I* played for a suit of armor and I'm here today to collect it."

A storklike woman clad in fussy folds of lime green tulle minced forward. "Now don't be angry, Your Grace. Drew meant no offense, did you, son?" Her skirt shifted slightly as she aimed a discreet kick at his ankle.

"Of course not, Mother," he said in a bland tone. "I'm sorry, Uncle. It was not my intention to liken your vices to my own."

"You'd best be sorry, by Jove!" The duke banged his cane for emphasis. "Unless you want me to tighten my purse strings again."

With keen interest Nicholas observed the exchange, surmising it to be an on-going family argument between the duke and his heir, with Drew's mother acting as arbitrator. The elder woman who looked on silently, her features plain and placid, must be Adelaide, the Duchess of Rockborough. Clad in a dreary dress of brown silk, she looked rather like a heavy draft horse.

Her face betraying a trace of shock at the quarrel, Aunt Beatrice dipped a curtsy to the duke. "I'm pleased to meet you, Your Grace." Hastily she supervised the introductions and ushered their guests into chairs.

Cicely, Nicholas noted as he leaned an elbow on the mantelpiece, adroitly managed to insinuate herself beside Drew Sterling. Already she was tilting a bright-eyed face to him and complimenting the cut of his morning coat.

Unexpectedly Nicholas felt his heart tighten. His sister looked so womanly in that flattering gown of pink Italian silk and Valenciennes lace. Somehow, without his ever noticing when it had happened, the mischievous hoyden had grown up into a pretty lady. But did she have the experience to handle a spoiled ne'er-do-well like Mr. Drew Sterling? As if to endorse the opinion, Drew eyed the low sweep of her bodice.

Nicholas's gaze hardened. If even half the gossip were true, the duke's heir was too slick, too reckless for any decent female. In his late twenties, Drew had a negligent air about him, a sulkiness to his aquiline features. Bloodshot eyes and a slack mouth gave testimony to the rumors. Yet in comparison to his other relations, he was a sleek racehorse in a stable of nags.

Chatting with Cicely, Drew leaned indolently against the sofa. Gossip whispered that in the few short weeks he'd been in town, he had already accrued colossal gambling debts. Could that fact give him cause to want Elizabeth dead? Assuming she was indeed the duke's granddaughter, did Drew wish to keep her from inheriting a portion of his uncle's vast wealth?

Yet how did Drew—or any of them, for that matter—know she was in London?

Smiling graciously, Aunt Beatrice rang for tea. "I was so pleased to hear Nicholas had invited you to meet us, Your Grace."

The duke snorted. "Don't hold with all this visiting back and forth. Lots of dull-witted conversation. I came to London to buy blades."

"Blades?" Beatrice repeated, startled confusion beneath that veil of politeness.

"Yes, blades!" The duke thumped his cane on the carpet. "Collect 'em, I do. Dirks, halberds, pikes, claymores, any kind so long as they're antique. Got two hundred cases of 'em back in Yorkshire. And a collection of old weapons and armor to rival the Tower of London."

"Good gracious. That's quite...amazing," Lady Beatrice said, looking more appalled than impressed.

"Come to visit my agent here twice a year, see what knives he's found me at auction. Always bring the whole family, let 'em gad about town for a few weeks."

Nicholas saw the sudden, ghoulish image of an ancient knife piercing Elizabeth's breast. His blood chilled. What was keeping her? The sooner she arrived, the swifter he could solve the mystery.

Pickering entered, bearing the silver tea service, which he set on the low table before Lady Beatrice. She busied herself pouring the steaming brew into blue and gold porcelain cups while the silent footman passed around a tray of rich pastries and dainty sandwiches.

"Would you care for a dish of tea, Lady Arthur?" his aunt asked.

"Please." With birdlike fingers, Drew's mother took the cup. "And do call me Philippa. I feel almost as though we're old friends since His Grace knows your nephew."

The duchess made a sound suspiciously like a snort.

Looking sharply at her, Nicholas saw her enormous white teeth sink into an eclair. Her broad face lacked expression as she chewed the morsel. He wondered what thoughts lay behind those dull dark eyes. Could she hate Elizabeth enough to concoct a plan to kill her? Did she possess the cold-blooded cunning to hire a cutthroat? She was Elizabeth's grandmother... or perhaps not. Perhaps Lucy Templeton Hastings had been born on the wrong side of the blanket.

Shifting impatiently, Nicholas sipped his hot, fragrant tea. He would find out soon, when he received Thistlewood's next report.

"So, Philippa," Beatrice said brightly, "do you also hail from Yorkshire?"

Philippa nibbled at a slice of cherry cake. "Yes, we— that is, Drew and I—make our home with the duke and duchess at Swanmere Manor. It was built during Queen Anne's reign."

"So was the plumbing, such as it is," drawled Drew.

"Don't like it, then move out, I say!" The duke leaned forward, a calcified grin on his face, his gnarled hand gripping the cane. "Be glad to set you up in trade, selling china plates or India cotton. Earn your own keep for a change." A cackle of laughter erupted from him. "Do you good to experience the sweat of honest labor, by Jove."

Drew's elegant fingers went taut around the teacup, his eyes sharp and dark. "Oh, but I wouldn't dream of leaving my beloved relations," he said smoothly. "Especially you, dear Uncle. I do so wish to be a comfort to you in your old age."

"Old?" bellowed the duke, glaring as he attempted to straighten his stooped frame. "Who are you calling old? I'm as hale as I was twenty years ago!" He drew in a gulp of air. "But you'd like to think—"

He stopped, wheezing.

Philippa's cup clinked into her saucer as she leapt up to grasp the duke's arm. "Are you all right, Your Grace? Lord Hawkesford, we must summon Doctor Marsh— he's waiting with the coachman."

Alarmed, Nicholas strode to the doorway and motioned to Pickering. "Fetch the physician from His Grace's carriage. And be quick about it."

The footman darted off as Nicholas returned to the duke's side. "Is there anything I can do?"

"Perhaps a sip of tea?" Lady Beatrice seconded, worry wrinkling her patrician features.

"Or a glass of water," Cicely said, glancing wide-eyed at Drew.

"Just tell this female . . . to remove her claws." Gasping, the duke shook off Philippa's hand. "I'm fine . . . just need . . . to catch my breath. I'm not an invalid . . . no matter what . . . your son wants to think."

"Drew is most concerned about your health," Philippa protested, hovering over the duke. "Just as we all are."

"Hah," Hugh Sterling spat, his face pale. "He'd love to . . . see me choke . . . by Jove."

Scowling, Drew leaned forward. "Come now, uncle, you're carrying this entirely too far—"

"Excuse me." A slender, fair-haired man scurried into the drawing room. Clad in a plain brown suit, he looked harried and anxious. His blue eyes swept the gathering and stopped on the duke. "How are you feeling, Your Grace?"

"Fit as a damned fiddle . . . only a bit breathless."

Marsh opened his leather satchel. "I'll administer something to calm your nerves."

Lifting his cane, the duke imperiously waved the doctor away. "Your potions put me to sleep. I'll be fine . . . in a moment."

"But Your Grace—"

"Quit your prattling. You fuss more than my wife."

Biting into her second eclair, the duchess chewed and swallowed; then in a surprisingly intelligent, surprisingly deep voice, she asked, "Are you all right, Hugh?"

Good God, Nicholas thought, she *can* speak.

The duke leaned over and patted her sturdy shoulder. "Quite hale now, Addie," he said, his voice steadier, the mockery back. "'Twas just a spot of the asthma. You can set your mind at ease."

"I already have." Turning her brown eyes from him, she concentrated on the pastry again.

Marsh bowed to the duke. "Perhaps I should remain in the room, Your Grace—"

"Oh, botheration," Hugh Sterling snapped, thumping his cane on the rug. "I don't need you smothering me as well. Run along with you."

The doctor's lips tightened, yet he merely bowed again and departed. Sympathy stirred in Nicholas. It must be trying for Marsh to deal with a patient as irascible as the Duke of Rockborough.

"You gave us such a start, Your Grace," Philippa said, fluttering her hands. "Oh, this wretched London weather. All the fog and smoke are enough to make anyone ill."

Nicholas hid a flash of amusement. With those lime green sleeves flapping, she looked like a skinny parrot. He'd love to hear Elizabeth's candid opinion—

He caught himself short. Why should he care what Elizabeth thought? But he did, and that fact fed his irritation. The ormolu clock on the mantelpiece chimed five times. For God's sake, what was taking Peebles so long? Nicholas shifted impatiently. If she failed to arrive soon, he *would* march this party to the conservatory.

Setting his cup on the marble mantelpiece, he strode forward and took Philippa's arm. "Please sit down, my lady," he said, escorting her back to her chair.

"Oh, thank you, your lordship. You're so very kind to think of me." Discreetly she fanned herself with a damask napkin.

"Might I freshen your tea?" Aunt Beatrice asked in concern. "Or perhaps a soothing drink of tisane might refresh you. I can ring for the footman—"

"Thank you, but you needn't bother," Philippa said. "I'll revive in a moment, I'm sure I will."

Nicholas studied her features, wan against the bright green of her gown. She seemed frail, or was that a performance? As the widow of Hugh Sterling's younger brother, she must have been left without monetary resource since she and her son lived with the duke. Did Philippa perceive Elizabeth as a threat? Was she determined to safeguard her son's inheritance? Certain lands would be entailed to Drew, of course, but the duke must have other holdings, which he could will to whomever he pleased. Holdings that might one day sate her son's hunger for card games and flashy mistresses.

A girlish giggle brought his eyes to Cicely, who shared a quiet conversation with Drew. Their heads were close, one chestnut haired, the other black. Displeasure formed a knot inside Nicholas. This tea has gone on long enough, by God.

"Your Grace?" he said. "Are you prepared to inspect your winnings?"

"Yes, by Jove! Thought you'd never ask." Using the cane as leverage, he hauled himself up.

Nicholas yanked the bell rope. When the liveried footman appeared in the doorway, he said, "Fetch the chest, Pickering."

"Aye, m'lord."

A few moments later he and Dobson came in, heft-

ing an ancient, leather-trimmed chest between them
and setting it down on the rug.

Cicely leaned forward, hands gripping the sofa, as if
to restrain herself from leaping up in unladylike curiosity. "That chest is from the attic, isn't it?" Blushing, she
glanced at Drew. "Not that I've been up there recently,
you understand...I remember it from a *very* long time
ago, when I was only a child."

"Open 'er up, Hawkesford." The duke hobbled
closer, his violet eyes alight with greed. "Been cooling
my heels since our game yesterday afternoon. Time to
pay the piper, by Jove."

Obligingly Nicholas flipped open the latch and lifted
the lid, the leather hinges creaking. Inside lay a tar-
nished jumble of armor, the bait he'd used to entice the
duke here, the winnings of the card game Nicholas had
taken such care to lose. And all for nothing...so far.

"Pickering, if you would be so kind as to lift the
armor for His Grace's viewing."

The footman sprang to obey, half-staggering beneath
the weight of the breastplate as he drew it up against
himself.

"By Jove, it's in near perfect condition." The duke
drew an old-fashioned quizzing glass from his pocket
and examined the armor more closely. "Persian...
eighteenth century, I'll hazard. Look at the gold inlay
on the arm guard."

Aunt Beatrice tilted her head in civil interest. "Ah,
that must be one of the relics the third earl, Nicholas's
grandfather, brought back from his travels. I'm sure His
Grace will display it to greater advantage than we ever
have."

She launched into a well-bred discussion of antiquities, while Cicely fidgeted and Drew yawned and Philippa fanned and Adelaide ate. As the duke gleefully
scrutinized his windfall Nicholas wondered, not for the
first time, if Hugh Sterling himself might be the one.
Was Elizabeth an embarrassment to him, perhaps the
offspring of an outcast illegitimate daughter, the reminder of a blemish on the family honor?

Cicely's low voice saying Elizabeth's name caught his ear. ". . . and I'm taking sculpting lessons from her."

"How novel," Drew murmured, looking bored.

"She's quite daringly unconventional," Cicely declared. "You'd have had the chance to meet her today, but she lost her sketchbook—" Her eyes met Nicholas's, widened, then lowered quickly, almost guiltily.

Lost her sketchbook. Suspicion made his blood run cold. Surely Elizabeth wouldn't have ventured out—

"My lord." A frown pinching his gaunt face, Peebles addressed Nicholas from the doorway.

Alarm sent him striding from the group without so much as a polite apology. "Where's Elizabeth?"

The butler swallowed, his Adam's apple bobbing like a cork. "That's why I've come, my lord. I've searched the house, but Miss Hastings isn't here, not anywhere."

Dread clamped around Nicholas's heart. "Send for my carriage." Pivoting sharply, he said, "Cicely, come here. I need a word with you."

She rose, smiling winsomely at Drew before coming to the doorway. "What is it, Nick?" she hissed. "I was engaged in conversation."

"You'll be engaged in having your backside paddled if you don't tell me where Elizabeth has gone."

Biting her lip, Cicely avoided his eyes. "She made me promise not to say."

Tempted to wring his sister's pretty neck, he bit out, "Promise be damned! Has she gone back to her old lodgings?"

Cicely's guilty expression revealed the truth even before she said grudgingly, "I . . . yes. She wanted to see Kipp—"

Brushing past his sister, Nicholas marched to the group at the tea table. The duke gloated over his armor, the duchess consumed yet another eclair, Drew leaned indolently against the sofa, and Philippa looked all simpering attention.

"I've an urgent errand I must attend to," Nicholas said. "If you will excuse me."

Frowning, Lady Beatrice rose. "What is it—"

Heedless of his discourtesy, he strode into the entrance hall. Fear trembled inside him, squeezing his belly. Elizabeth was out there somewhere, vulnerable to attack. By God, when he got his hands on her, he'd leash her free-spirited ways once and for all.

Where the hell was she?

Elizabeth sat on the steps of St. Mary-le-Strand, hugging her knees and marveling at the differences between London and New York. The church occupied a small island in the middle of the busy Strand. Humble drays and fine carriages crammed the cobbled street, liveried coachmen exchanging curses with common tradesmen. London was cramped and crowded, old and unyielding, an elderly maid set in her ways. New York, on the other hand, was brash and bold, with broad avenues and modern buildings, a vigorous young maiden embracing life.

Yet Elizabeth loved the ancient feel of London, the sense of being part of a rich and deeply rooted history. Generations of people had marched up and down the very steps on which she sat. After all the churches and museums she had visited, countless more awaited her, a vast treasure trove of antiquities still to explore and sketch.

A movement beside her drew her gaze; Kipp picked up a pebble and sent it skipping across the tiny courtyard. Clad in his usual dirty checked shirt and tattered knickers, he bent to retrieve another stone. As he aimed, his expression of boyish concentration brought a wave of affection to her heart. The palm-shaped bruise beneath the dirt streaks on his cheek ignited a flare of fury.

"I won't let you go back there," she said, resuming their earlier argument.

He tossed the pebble across the yard before turning

to her, plucky resolution in his dark eyes. "She's me mum. I 'as to 'elp 'er."

"It's wrong to throw your life away, laboring in a workhouse, as she wants you to do." Despising the need to be blunt, Elizabeth gently touched his bruised cheek. "Just so your meager wages can buy her more gin."

"I can take care o' meself," Kipp said stubbornly, pivoting to hurl another stone.

His withdrawal opened a chasm of sympathy inside her. That spunky manner hid a defenseless boy, forced to become a man at too young an age. The thought of Kipp doomed to a life in a dingy factory made her shudder.

"I know you can take care of yourself," she said softly. "But we're friends, and friends are supposed to help each other. The instant I return home, I'll speak to Nicholas about finding you a position."

"'Oo's Nich'las?"

"The earl, Cicely's brother." Confidence hugged Elizabeth's heart; instinct told her she was right. "He'll come up with a better job for you, something decent. I know he will."

"'E's the bloke that shook me 'and." Hope sparked in his eyes, then died. "Bloody 'ell . . . er, beggin' yer pardon, Miss Libby, but why would some fancy-pants earl want to 'elp *me*?"

"He found my father a position as a tutor. I'm certain he'll do just as well for you."

"I ain't smart like yer dad."

"You've got a quick mind, nimble fingers, and a willingness to learn."

When Kipp still looked skeptical, Elizabeth patted his thin shoulder. What else could she say to reassure a boy who fended for himself because no one else cared?

The church bells chimed five times. "We'd best be getting back," she said, rising from the steps and dusting off her violet dress. "I don't want my father to worry."

Elizabeth picked up her sketch pad and tucked it

under her arm. Hands plunged into his trouser pockets, Kipp fell into step beside her. She wished she could erase his gloomy expression. What if she failed him? What if Nicholas aimed those disdainful gray eyes at her and refused to involve himself in the rehabilitation of a street urchin?

Then she would enlist Cicely's aid. Because Nicholas, for all his blustering, seemed unable to resist his sister's whims. In the meantime, she herself would employ Kipp as a model, at least until he could find a job in fresh air and sunshine.

Fondly she watched him roll an empty tobacco tin, nudging it with a dirty bare toe, deftly avoiding the constant stream of passersby. The smell of damp air and sewage crept from the river on a wisp of curling mist. The proliferation of canvas awnings over the shop windows shaded their eyes from the setting sun. The clatter of coach wheels and iron-shod hooves created a din that diminished as they entered the narrow streets beyond the Strand.

Nearing the boardinghouse where she and her father had lived, Elizabeth thought of the royal blue sketchbook. It hadn't been left in their old lodgings. That is, if she could believe the new occupant, a weary woman with three small and dirty children clinging to her tattered skirts. Sighing in mingled frustration and regret, Elizabeth faced the fact that the drawings of her mother were lost; she would have to reproduce them from memory.

"Cor!" Interest on his filthy face, Kipp quit kicking the tobacco tin and stared down the street. "There's yer earl's carriage now, Miss Libby."

Despite his expressed doubts of Lord Nicholas Ware, Kipp started at a trot toward the elegant black landau parked at the curbside of her former boardinghouse. Elizabeth tightened her fingers around the sketch pad as she hurried after the boy. Nicholas . . . here? He should still be at tea. Perhaps he'd sent Miss Eversham or a footman after her.

Then the earl emerged from the tenement and strode

toward the vehicle. Giving way before his tall, lordly form, the crowd of curious onlookers parted like the Red Sea. Her spirits soared, then sank. He looked stern, angry, forbidding. He paused to speak to Greaves, the coachman. As Nicholas turned toward the door held open by a footman, he saw her.

For an instant his handsome face came alive with emotion... relief? He took a step toward her. His eyes were intense, his hair mussed as if he'd raked his fingers through the chestnut strands. Then all sentiment evaporated from his expression, like a slate wiped clean.

Elizabeth trailed Kipp through the small gathering. Had she imagined that flash of concern? Reaching Nicholas, she tilted her head to gaze into his grim gray eyes.

"Hello," she said, feeling foolishly happy.

"Are you all right?" he snapped, sounding distinctly irritated.

"Of course. Why shouldn't I be?"

"Why the devil did you go out without telling me?"

Stung by his gruff manner, she raised her chin a fraction. "I'm a grown woman. Not, of course, that I feel obliged to account for my free time."

"Indeed." Irony weighted his voice. "Get inside, please," he said, inclining his head to the landau.

"In a moment. I have something to talk to you about first."

"Get inside now, Miss Hastings."

His fierce glare made her stomach quake and her willpower rebel. "Only if we take Kipp with us, since what I have to say concerns him."

Lips drawn into a taut line, the earl aimed an impatient look down at Kipp. "For God's sake... all right, he can go."

"Cor!" exclaimed Kipp, his eyes agog as he stared at the fine carriage. "Yer wantin' me to ride in *there*?"

"If you've no objection," Nicholas said, his tone reluctantly indulgent.

"Blimey! I mean, no, yer lordship, sir!"

Kipp glanced around to ascertain that all the on-lookers had witnessed such an astounding invitation delivered by a peer of the realm. Then, as if fearing the earl might withdraw the offer, the boy made a dive for the step of the landau.

Nicholas seized Kipp's grubby sleeve. "Not so fast, Master Gullidge. A gentleman must always allow the lady to precede him."

"Aye, yer lordship, sir." Abashed, Kipp moved aside so the footman could assist Elizabeth into the carriage.

Clutching her sketch pad like a shield, she sat down and collected her wits. He was furious at her for leaving his house unescorted, furious that she refused to con-form to his rigid standard of feminine behavior.

"Blimey!" Kipp said again, as he plopped onto the seat beside her. Experimentally he bounced up and down on the plump leather cushion. "Ain't this grand?"

"Sit tight, lad," Nicholas ordered, as he settled op-posite them. "I'll not tolerate misbehavior."

Instantly Kipp went still, though as the carriage started the swaying ride, he inched to the window and peered out, his eyes alight.

Elizabeth looked at the earl. Her heart did a somer-sault when she caught him staring at her; that hand-some face looked coldly furious. She took a deep, doubting breath. He couldn't be in all that unreason-able a mood . . . after all, he *had* allowed Kipp to come.

"Your lordship?" she said, imbuing the proper note of meekness into her voice. "Might I ask you some-thing?"

He regarded her with icy intolerance. "You would do well to keep silent, Miss Hastings. After obliging me to cut short my visit with the Duke of Rockborough, you're hardly in the position to demand favors."

Elizabeth swallowed a retort. "It's not for me," she said. "It's for Kipp."

"Indeed." Nicholas glanced at the boy, who sat enthralled by the sights, his nose pressed to the glass.

"Might I venture to guess it has something to do with that bruise on his cheek?"

Though his face was expressionless, Elizabeth felt encouraged. Leaning forward, the sketch pad clutched to her bosom, she said in a low voice, "Yes, because he objected when his mother wanted to send him to a workhouse. It would mean laboring long hours in a dank, airless room with a hundred women and children, picking old clothes apart to salvage whatever fabric is still usable. I cannot let him suffer such a fate."

Nicholas looked suddenly weary. "Hundreds of thousands of Londoners are forced to live that way, Elizabeth. I can support bills in parliament to improve working conditions, but I cannot advocate closing all the workhouses. At least they provide a means for decent people to earn a lawful living."

"But you *can* help Kipp get a better position, as you did my father," she murmured, then added judiciously, "please."

A muscle in his jaw tensed; otherwise he might have been carved of stone . . . an exceedingly fine statue, Elizabeth reflected. She yearned to delve into the thoughts behind that perfect countenance.

"I shall see what I can do," he said.

Relief shimmered through her; she hugged her sketch pad when she longed to leap up and embrace him. "Thank you, Nicholas," she said, smiling. "I was so hoping you'd say that."

Those granite gray eyes flicked to her mouth. "That isn't all I intend to say to you, Miss Hastings. However, I shall withhold any further remarks until we may speak in private."

His formal tone chilled her; she felt her smile wilting like a camellia stung by a frost. Of course, he meant to chastise her for her unladylike actions. As if she were a wayward child!

Annoyance swam to the surface of her emotions. She welcomed their coming confrontation. She had a few things to say to him, too!

Chapter 11

"Cor, Miss Libby, I ain't never seen so many gents and ladies before."

Kipp's awed remark gave Elizabeth an excuse to slide beside him and gaze out the window. For the rest of the rolling ride, she chatted with the boy and steadfastly refused to pay any heed to Nicholas. Yet she felt the earl's presence, so superior and angry, an arm's reach away. His tautly controlled emotions rattled her more than an open display of temper.

A curious sense of homecoming warmed her when the landau drew to a halt across from the quiet park in Berkeley Square. As she accepted the footman's white-gloved hand and stepped from the carriage, Kipp scrambled out behind her. He gaped at the grand, gray stone mansion, then shot Elizabeth a suspicious look.

"Is this one of them borin' art places, like the one you dragged me to by Trafalgar?"

"A museum?" Elizabeth laughed. "No, this is where Lord Nicholas and Lady Cicely live."

Kipp tipped his head back, one grubby hand clamped to his crushed bowler hat as his gaze climbed the tall Corinthian columns. "Blimey! It's a bloomin' palace!"

Nicholas looked at the poker-faced coachman. "Greaves, take Master Gullidge to the mews and get him cleaned up." To Kipp he said, "There'll be no fussing over bathing. If you're to be my new tiger, you must learn to dress and act accordingly."

"Tiger? Wot's that?"

"You're to be my groom. Do exactly as Mr. Greaves says and you'll have a place here for as long as you like."

"'Ere?" Kipp stole another wide-eyed peek at the house. "Yer wantin' *me* to work 'ere?"

"I'll pay you a fair wage. Unless you've some objection to the arrangement?"

The boy whipped off his hat and earnestly clasped it to his scrawny chest. "Oh, no, yer lordship, sir. I'll do me very best, that I will. You won't be regrettin' takin' Kipp Gullidge in."

"Very good." Turning to Elizabeth, his eyes fiercely silver in the waning light, the earl offered his arm. "Come along, Miss Hastings."

Hesitating only an instant to say farewell to Kipp, she wrapped her fingers around the smoothness of the earl's elegant coat sleeve. The muscles beneath felt firm and alive; Elizabeth's stomach curled into a delicious knot. A man who displayed such generosity to a lowly street urchin could not be entirely hard-hearted.

Unexpectedly Nicholas leaned closer and plucked the sketch pad from under her arm, handing it to the footman. "See to it this is taken to the conservatory, Dobson."

"Aye, m'lord."

Nicholas started up the steps and Elizabeth hastened to keep pace. One hand lifting her skirt hem so she wouldn't stumble, she felt her heartbeat quicken.

"Where are we going?" she asked, as he marched her swiftly through the foyer and past a curious parlor maid.

"To have our little talk."

"Ah, yes. I'd like to give you an earful."

"Really?" he drawled, leading her unerringly through the labyrinth of corridors. "I suggest you close your mouth and listen, Miss Hastings. Silence is a trait much valued in a lady."

Elizabeth clamped her lips shut, only because the sudden rising steam of anger scalded her throat. A lady! With Lord Nicholas Ware, everything always came back to that.

He turned sharply and hauled her toward the library. The instant they entered the long, book-lined room, she released his arm and her tongue.

"If you've brought me here to lecture me on manners," she said, folding her arms, "you're wasting your time. I've never pretended to have any interest in hobnobbing with your noble cronies, nor in making inane conversation about the weather and the latest fashions."

Nicholas settled onto the edge of a claw-footed writing desk. Though the pose was casual, she sensed his seething emotions in the way his eyes raked her. "I'm amazed at you, Miss Hastings. Even you should be familiar with simple courtesy. You ought to have told me beforehand you had no intention of accepting my invitation to tea."

Disregarding a prick of guilt, she elevated her chin. "An invitation or a royal summons?"

"Call it what you like, by God, but I wanted you there. Is that so much to ask, that you tear yourself from your own selfish pursuits long enough to drink a cup of tea?"

"To simper and smile like one of your empty-headed society ladies? No, thank you, your lordship."

He moved his hand in an impatient gesture. "No one is asking you to change what you are, Elizabeth. There's a vast difference between exercising prudence and acting the fool."

Annoyed, Elizabeth drew in a breath scented by leather book bindings and a heady trace of the earl. "I don't understand why you're carrying on so. Why should it matter to you whether or not I socialize with a duke and his family?"

For an instant she had the impression of violent emotions stewing within Nicholas; then a closed look banished all expression. "I've told you before, as long as you live in this household, Miss Hastings, I expect you to know the proper mode of behavior for a lady. It's for your own good."

His sudden formal manner frustrated her. Oddly, she preferred the infuriated man over this unfeeling stranger.

"Really, your lordship? Or can't you bear to associate with a woman who refuses to conform to your rigid standards? A woman capable of independent thought?"

"Independent!" Nicholas uttered a scathing laugh. "I suppose that's your excuse for going off unchaperoned into one of the roughest areas of the city."

"I was never in any danger."

"How can you be so sure of that? After two attempts on your life—and possibly a third, when your lodgings were ransacked?" Nicholas slammed his palm onto the leather-topped desk. "My God, and you label society women fools."

He cheeks heated. "Those episodes were all coincidences. Today ought to have proven I'm perfectly capable of taking care of myself."

"It proves nothing. From now on, you're to remain in this house and out of trouble. Do I make myself clear?"

Without flinching, she met his icy eyes. "I do not take orders from you unless they pertain to my role as art instructor."

A moment of charged silence flashed between them. The anger on his face sparked a wild flare of satisfaction inside her.

"I'll not allow you to put your life in peril," he said with quiet menace, "even if I must assign you a twenty-four hour guard."

The color faded from her cheeks. "You wouldn't dare." But the unfaltering chill of his gaze told her otherwise. "I'll do as I please. You forget, your lordship, I'm not yours to command."

Head held high, she marched toward the door of the library. No more than two steps past the desk, she felt his hand clamp around her upper arm. He swung her to face him, blazing anger melting the frost from his eyes.

"I warned you once before, Elizabeth," he said in a low voice. "If you refuse to behave the lady, I won't feel obliged to treat you like one."

Yanking her against him, he pressed his mouth to hers in a punishing kiss that caught her by surprise. For one wild moment Elizabeth stood immobile within the hard embrace of his arms. She parted her lips to protest and his tongue invaded her mouth. A shocking thrill sped through her, a sudden sweeping magic that wove an irresistible spell over her raw senses. The intimate assault robbed her of reason and she abandoned herself to his rough, arousing kiss. If this was Nicholas's idea of discipline, she wanted more.

She steadied her trembling hands on the warm wall of his chest. His tangy taste and male scent pleased her, she who had always regarded sight and touch as the most vital of the senses. Gliding from pectorals to biceps, her fingertips absorbed his classically carved strength. She longed to see the drama of his body without the barrier of clothing, to feel the artistry of his bare flesh beneath her palms, to depict the strength of his muscles in bronze. When he rubbed his hips to hers, a small sound of delight burst in her throat. His lips gentled, yet the softening sparked an even more turbulent fire inside her.

His hand moved in slow circles over the base of her spine; the other stroked her nape beneath the thick fall of her hair. Mesmerized by the intensity of his kiss, Elizabeth felt the hunger for artistic creation ebbing. In its place a new appetite awakened, the need to feel his hands tracing the curves and valleys of her body, as if he were the sculptor and she the clay.

Seeking to bind them closer, she wound her arms around his neck and explored the texture of his hair, the perfection of his face. His heart beat a strong, swift rhythm against her breasts. He smoothed his palms up her back and down again, shaping her to his firm form until she felt like clay in his hands, ready to be molded into vibrant life. Dear God, how could she ever have thought him cold?

A fever gripped Elizabeth, filling her with more energy and excitement than even sculpting could ignite. The warmth seemed centered in her belly, slowly spreading outward to her breasts and thighs, swelling into a heavy throbbing ache. Time and place whirled away; all that mattered were the heady sensations curling inside her and the sweet pleasure of sliding her body against his.

Nicholas lifted his mouth and rested the shaven sleekness of his cheek against hers. His hands tensed around her shoulders as he exhaled a deep breath that stirred her hair and disturbed her blood.

"God!" he muttered hoarsely, his voice sounding strained, desperate almost. . . . if she could trust her scattered senses. "My God, Elizabeth."

Abruptly he thrust her away. His eyes dark and turbulent, he snapped, "Can't you ever react the way you're supposed to?"

Pivoting on his heel, he strode out of the library.

Elizabeth winced as the door slammed shut. Knees wobbly, she sank onto a velvet hassock and gazed numbly at the shelves of leather-spined books, the scattered sofas and twin-globed gas lights. Astounding, how she could feel so lightning struck, yet nothing around her looked singed.

She skimmed an unsteady finger over her lips. A kiss. Such a tiny word could never encompass the flood of wild emotion ebbing within her body. She'd wanted Nicholas to go on kissing her, forever and ever, teaching her where the restless yearning within her could lead.

Can't you ever react the way you're supposed to?

A knot swelled inside her throat. Nicholas had meant to chastise her, not reward her. He had been angry and appalled by her response; a lady wouldn't have exhibited such passion. Why couldn't he accept her for herself ?

For a moment her shoulders bowed, then Elizabeth

sat straight on the hassock. Curse Nicholas Ware and his inflexible standards. First he'd wanted her to be his mistress. Then he'd wanted to make her a lady. Now he wanted her to be dishonest. To veil her feelings and douse her passion. Stoicism might be something *he* excelled at, but it was not a skill *she* aspired to attain!

Had Nicholas indeed been so unaffected? For a short time he had seemed as enraptured as she, lost to the turbulent sensations in their bodies and soaring emotions in their souls. Of course, Elizabeth thought crossly, a *gentleman* was permitted to feel erotic pleasure. Only the lady was supposed to stand there like a cold marble stature.

Resolution firmed her chin. *She* would not hide behind prim femininity and polite manners. She would accept the role Nicholas had once offered her. One kiss was not enough; she longed to unlock the rest of the mystery.

And Nicholas would be her key.

"Oh, pooh!"

Turning to look at Cicely, Elizabeth ceased kneading the mass of clay on the worktable. "What's wrong?"

"I simply can't get this ear right," Cicely said, frowning at the half-formed bust of Kipp on the pedestal. "It's driving me mad."

"Blimey," Kipp said, craning his head to see. "You mean I been sittin' 'ere so long fer nothin'?"

Elizabeth smiled as she wiped her clay-smeared hands on her apron. Though Kipp grumbled, he was a changed lad compared to the hapless urchin Nicholas had rescued two days ago. The afternoon sunlight flowing through the conservatory's glass roof burnished Kipp's clean black hair. She still felt a faint shock of amazement to view him as a well-scrubbed youth clad in smart blue and gold livery with buckskin trousers.

Cicely made a face. "Oh, do hold still, Kipp. I'm having a difficult enough time without you wriggling all over that chair."

Walking over to examine the bust, Elizabeth immediately spied the problem. "The whorls of the ear should be shallower than in real life," she said. "Remember, clay doesn't have the luminosity of living flesh. The ear needs only the hint of a hollow, otherwise it ends up looking like a chasm."

"Keep it simple . . . why can't I remember that?" Absently swiping at a strand of chestnut hair, Cicely left a clay streak across her cheek. "So what do I do now?"

"Fill in those hollows and rework the ear."

Cicely dolefully eyed the bust. "Do you really think it's worth the effort?"

"Of course. You're preserving Master Kipp for posterity."

Kipp scratched his hair. "Fer wot?"

"For the future," Elizabeth said.

The boy jabbed a thumb at his lapel. "I got me a future 'ere, workin' fer the earl."

"And for me," Cicely chided. "So just sit quietly until I correct what I've done wrong."

"Don't get discouraged," Elizabeth said, giving the girl a quick hug, mindful of her own clay-stained hands. "You can't expect perfection on your first try."

Kipp restlessly swung his shiny top boots. "Mr. Greaves'll tan me 'ide if I ain't back to the mews on time."

"He'll do nothing of the sort," Cicely said, arching an aristocratic brow. "I persuaded him to spare you for an hour, and you've still fifteen minutes left."

"Aw, 'urry it up . . . please, yer ladyship, ma'am." Clasping his tidy blue lapels, Kipp thrust out his thin chest. "I got grander things to do these days than sit 'ere like a lump."

Smiling, Elizabeth returned to the worktable. As she kneaded the clay in preparation for sculpting, she felt her insides go as soft and supple as the substance in her hands. Kipp's newfound sense of importance was due to Nicholas's generosity. The more she reflected, the more she could see that hidden beneath the earl's cold mien lay a tender heart the right woman could nurture.

Ever since that shattering kiss two days ago, she'd felt the burning urge to reform his rigid beliefs, to find more chinks in the armor of his indifference. But to her frustration she hadn't seen him, not even when she'd made a special effort to attend dinner. The earl was busy, Lady Beatrice said, involved in affairs at parliament and in his own business interests.

That he hadn't sought her out left Elizabeth uncertain and disappointed. Maybe he hadn't been as affected by the kiss as she. Maybe his breath didn't catch and his blood didn't warm when he remembered holding her in his arms. Maybe he didn't think about her at all.

Firmly she quelled the doubts swarming her mind. She had made her resolution and she would stick to it.

Closing her eyes, she drew in the loamy odor of the clay and thought of the clean scent of Nicholas's skin. Feeling the smooth earthen texture beneath her fingers, she imagined stroking the sleek strength of his muscles. Hearing the harmony of the fountain, she recalled the beat of his heart, the swiftness of his breathing. An ache awakened deep within her belly. What if he did more than kiss her? What if he undressed her, touched her naked breasts—

"There you are, young lady," he snapped. "Your behavior this time is reprehensible."

Startled, Elizabeth opened her eyes to see the earl striding down the flagstone path. Her fingers froze on the clay; her heart leapt with joy. Sunlight polished the perfect planes of his cheekbones and warmed his well-groomed chestnut hair. Yet even those hot rays could not melt the frosty fury on his face.

For one disconcerting moment, Elizabeth wondered if he'd read her lusty thoughts. Then she realized he was addressing his sister.

"I'd hoped you'd outgrown your childish behavior," he said. "Sometimes you exhibit all the sense of a peahen."

Cicely cheerfully met his ferocious gaze. "I can't imagine what you're talking about, Nick."

"Then allow me to enlighten you. As I was preparing to go riding this afternoon, I discovered a rather curious fact. My favorite pair of boots was gone. Further inquiry revealed a great number of other items missing from my wardrobe. Quinn admitted you'd cleaned out my dressing room, that you'd said I'd granted you permission to donate my old clothing to charity."

Amusement flashed through Elizabeth; she'd never dreamed her tirade about London's poor would bring *this* about.

"I didn't know your valet was the sort to tell tales," Cicely said lightly, though her gaze dropped to the front of Nicholas's charcoal morning coat.

"Don't equivocate, Cicely," he said in a voice as hard as bronze. "You lied to him."

She made a show of wiping her clay-smudged fingers on the apron protecting her dress of sea green faille. "Oh, pooh. That prissy Quinn wouldn't have let me into your hallowed chambers otherwise."

"Wisely so, it would seem. I should confine you to the house for another two weeks."

Worry swept Cicely's face. "Please, Nick, don't be angry. It was for a good cause."

"Ah, so that excuses your rash conduct," he said, his voice weighted with sarcasm. "How did you accomplish this heartwarming act of generosity without leaving home?"

Kipp slid off his chair by the fountain. "Er . . . 'scuse me, yer lordship, yer ladyship. I 'as to get meself back to work."

"One moment, lad," Nicholas commanded.

Kipp froze as if caught in stone like the satyr atop the fountain.

"I suspect my sister had an accomplice," Nicholas said, shooting the boy a look. "Would you happen to know anything about this 'good cause'?"

The boy hung his head and traced a crack in the

flagstones with the toe of his topboot. "Aye, yer lord-ship, sir," he mumbled. "'Twas me, I 'as to say, wot took the clothes to the poor'ouse."

Blue eyes blazing, Cicely took a step toward Nicho-las. "Don't you dare scold Kipp. I accept full blame in this matter."

Nicholas arched his brows. "At least you're showing a sense of responsibility. A shame you didn't do so *be-fore* you gave away my most comfortable pair of boots."

Kipp edged toward the ivy-draped door. "Mr. Greaves'll be lookin' fer me."

"Go on, then," Nicholas said, without removing his glare from Cicely. "And in the future be cautious about involving yourself in my sister's pranks."

"Aye, yer lordship, sir."

As the boy darted from the conservatory, Cicely thrust out her lower lip. "I don't see why you're carry-ing on so, Nick. I just wanted to help those starving people in Seven Dials and the Devil's Acre."

For the first time Nicholas aimed those glacial eyes at Elizabeth. "Seven Dials? Have you been filling my sis-ter's head with radical ideas?"

Elizabeth refused to flinch. "That was not my intent. I only meant for Cicely to learn something of the real world. You've kept her insulated like a hothouse camel-lia."

"I thought you were only interested in art; you've told me so often enough. Since when have you decided to change the world?"

Resentment rose in her; before she could give voice to her feelings, Cicely spoke.

"You needn't blame Elizabeth, either. I acted on my own. I didn't think you'd mind me giving away a few old rags."

"It would seem we've arrived at your problem, Cice-ly. *You don't think.*"

"I'm sorry about the boots, Nick," she said, looking genuinely contrite. "I didn't realize they were so dear to you."

"Never mind." Furrowing his fingers through his

hair, he let out an exasperated hiss. "But the next time you feel so driven to philanthropy, you might stop to consider all the charitable institutions our family already supports."

Cicely's eyes were big and blue. "What do you mean?"

"Ware funds provide income for the Stanhope Hospice for Women as well as for the Whitechapel School for Orphans. So you see, there's no need to contribute the clothes off our backs as well."

"Oh, my . . . I didn't realize." Cicely looked surprised and pleased; then she tilted an uncharacteristically meek face at her brother. "You're not still angry at me, are you?"

The stern lines of his face relaxed. "Not as long as you remember to ask next time before you act."

"I will, I promise," she declared, untying her apron and flinging it over a chair. "But please don't forbid me to attend the Garforths' ball tonight."

Fondness mellowed his expression. "I ran into Charles at parliament yesterday. He's most anxious to see you again."

"Oh, Lord Charles." She fluttered a dismissive hand. "It's Mr. Drew Sterling *I* hope to impress."

The fine edges of Nicholas's mouth turned down. "Forget Sterling. He's not for you."

"You're not being fair," Cicely said, her eyes shining with irrepressible excitement. "As heir to a dukedom, he's perfectly acceptable."

"As a profligate gambler, he's eminently unacceptable. If he's present at the Garforths, you're not to get within ten feet of him. Is that clear?"

"Whatever you say, Nick." She airily waved a hand. "Excuse me, I must make sure Eversham has seen to the pressing of my gown." Twirling, Cicely darted from the room.

As Nicholas gazed suspiciously after his sister, Elizabeth felt her blood quicken. This was the moment she'd been awaiting . . . the chance to be alone with him, to pour out all the needs aching inside her. Yet her tongue felt cloven, her feet glued to the floor. Here he stood, the model of pristine perfection while her hands were caked with clay, her apron dirty, her hair tumbling in an untidy mass down her back. Generations of privilege and wealth had given him an inbred air of assurance; in contrast, she felt gauche and uncertain, her emotions simmering too close to the surface.

He swung abruptly to her. "Has my sister spoken to you of Drew Sterling?"

"A little," Elizabeth admitted, unwilling to get Cicely into more trouble yet grateful for a distraction. "Cicely said she met him at tea the other day, that he was most attentive."

"Did she discuss his family with you?"

The watchfulness on Nicholas's face puzzled her. "The duke and duchess? No, she spoke only of Drew —he seemed to have made a deeper impression on her."

"I see," he muttered. For a moment Nicholas gazed down at an overgrown camellia bush; then he focused an aloof look at her. "I know how you disdain social events, Elizabeth, but I wondered if you might come to the Garforths tonight, for my sister's sake. I'd like you to help me watch her around Sterling."

His formal manner stung; they might never have shared that fevered kiss. She bit back the confession that she planned to attend the ball; she wanted to meet Lady Phoebe Garforth, the paragon Cicely had singled out for Nicholas's future wife.

"Why should I interfere with Cicely's right to choose her own friends?"

"Because Sterling has been involved in more than one scandal. I will not tolerate scandal in *this* family."

Elizabeth busied her hands with the clay. Would he consider *her* proposal scandalous?

His face candid with concern, Nicholas took a step closer. "For all her womanly airs, Cicely is still young and foolish enough to let Sterling entice her into going off alone with him. No doubt a single kiss would set the naive girl to swooning."

Elizabeth nibbled her lip in consternation. Was *she* setting too much store by a kiss? She wanted Nicholas to want her; he wanted a chaperon for his sister. "I suppose I must pose as the daughter of your mother's long-lost friend," she said dryly.

"The ruse is necessary, a small price to pay for preserving Cicely's reputation."

Elizabeth lifted her chin. "I won't hide the fact that I'm a sculptress, that I work for a living."

"Fine. Just come with us . . . please."

His earnest expression made him appear less godlike and infinitely more approachable. The constraint around her emotions melted like wax in a casting mold. "All right, Nicholas, I will."

"Excellent."

Something beyond satisfaction warmed his handsome face, a hint of hunger that made her go soft and yielding inside. Her hands stilled, the clay heating beneath her palms, her heart blazing with hope. He did want her . . . she hadn't been mistaken. His eyes flicked over her; then he turned to the half-finished bust of Kipp.

"Is this my sister's work?"

She forced herself to be patient. "Yes, it's her first attempt. She's doing quite well for a beginner."

Hands clasped behind his back, his heels clicking on the stone floor, Nicholas circled the pedestal. "I don't pretend to be an expert, but the bust seems a trifle askew."

"Cicely needs to make mistakes and learn how to correct them. Sculpting is more than copying a skeletal structure and facial features. She's learning to capture the individuality of the subject's character."

"I see."

He prowled the conservatory, pausing to pick up first a chisel, then an art volume from the shelf. Her hands kneaded the pliant clay; her eyes followed his tall form. Elizabeth imagined him naked, sunshine pouring over his sculpted body. He would stand much like Michelangelo's *David*, one hand at his side, the other lifted carelessly to his shoulder. His pose vibrant with energy, his eyes warm with need, he would gaze at her, challenge her artistic talent and invite her woman's passion—

". . . are you listening, Elizabeth?"

Blinking, she caught his cool stare. Embarrassment heated her cheeks. "What?"

"I said, did Cicely construct her own armature?"

"Yes," she said, absurdly pleased that he'd remembered the term. "With help from me, of course."

"How many hours a day do you spend instructing her?"

"Two or three . . . more if she doesn't have letters to write or calls to make with your aunt."

"What do you do the rest of the time?"

"I work on my own projects." The bust of *you*, she thought.

"How many hours a day does that comprise?"

"I don't know . . . I never thought much about it. Twelve hours, perhaps more."

He stopped pacing to quirk a dark eyebrow. "What else do you do?"

The intensity of his gaze rattled her. "I eat, I sleep, I read," she said tartly. "Why the inquisition? I didn't realize when I accepted this post that I would have to give an accounting of my free time."

The sun-burnished skin over his cheeks tightened. "I'm merely trying to ascertain whether or not my sister shares your devotion to art. It would seem she does not."

The implication of his words chilled her heart. Now she understood his remote demeanor, his probing questions. Distractedly Elizabeth dipped a cloth into a basin of water and wrung it out, then walked toward him and draped the damp rag over the bust.

"It's true," she said, wiping her fingers on her apron. "Cicely does have other interests. Yet she has talent as well, a talent I am doing my best to nurture." Feeling an unreasonable depth of hurt, Elizabeth met his eyes squarely. "I won't deny her the chance to develop her gift, Nicholas. If you force me to leave here, I will simply resume teaching her elsewhere."

He started visibly, his hand lifting as if to touch her. "Ask you to leave? I would never—" A trace of color etched his strong cheekbones . . . or was it just a trick of the sunlight? His arm dropped to his side. "You mistake my meaning," he said coolly. "I'm concerned with my sister's progress, nothing more. You're certainly welcome to stay for as long as Cicely wishes to study art."

Relieved and frustrated, she stared at him. Just when she caught a glimpse of his true self, he exasperated her with that flawless composure.

"If you will excuse me, Elizabeth."

He politely inclined his head before turning away. A bolt of distress shot through her.

"Nicholas, don't go, please!"

He swung back, eyes alert. "What's wrong?"

Feeling suddenly foolish and shy, Elizabeth stepped to the worktable. "I . . . I want to apologize. For assuming you were too indifferent to care about the plight of London's poor."

He made an impatient, almost embarrassed gesture with his hand. "It isn't something I publicize."

"I imagine there are lots of things about you I don't know."

"Look beneath the surface, then. Isn't that what you've been trying to teach my sister?"

He sounded brusque to the point of rudeness. Again he started toward the door. He was leaving because she lacked the pluck to open her soul.

The words tumbled out in a wild surge: "Do you still want me to be your mistress?"

He halted. His elegant figure stood rigid; the burbling of the fountain filled the silence. Then Nicholas jerked back around. "What did you say?" he asked hoarsely.

Elizabeth took heart from his stunned expression, from the yearning softening his mouth. Her fingers dug into the clay as need throbbed inside her, leaving her shaken and aching. Breathlessly she said, "When we first met . . . you asked me to be your mistress . . . but I told you—"

"I recall your answer," he said, the bite back in his speech. "I have a 'pleasing face.' Beyond that, nothing about me interests you."

"That was before I knew you . . . before I came here to live . . ." Her voice dropped to a husky murmur. "Before you kissed me."

A curious stillness wrapped him. "So one kiss changed your mind. Or was it perhaps touching my 'pleasing body'?"

"Well, of course I admire your body," she said, and felt dismayed by his sudden scowl. "I know you think a lady shouldn't be so bold, but I believe in honesty."

He laughed, a harsh sound. "I wouldn't dream of stopping you from speaking your mind, Elizabeth. You do so with tedious regularity."

His ill-tempered response daunted her, but it was too late to turn back now, too late to stop the need for him that billowed around her heart. She stepped to him and stopped, her clay-soiled fingers twining in her apron.

"You haven't answered me," she said in a small but determined voice. "Will you take me as your mistress?"

Something flickered across the dazzling handsomeness of his face, a fleeting impression of longing that vanished into a stark frown. Hands clenched at his sides, he stared at her, as if wrestling with an inner turmoil. "I'm sorry, Elizabeth," he said, his words dropping like stones, "but my feelings have changed since then."

Disconcerted, she gaped at him. Her cheeks heated with mortification. "Your feelings!" she snapped. "You haven't any feelings, Nicholas Ware."

Marching to a large wooden tub, Elizabeth started to drag it toward the worktable. The bottom scraped the stone flags. She gave the tub a reckless tug and her fingers slipped, grazing her knuckles. Tears sprang to her eyes. With a cry of angry frustration, she sat back on her heels and sucked on the injured area.

Nicholas appeared beside her. She glanced at him through blurry eyes, then looked quickly away. He was tall, far too tall. His nearness sent an agonizing shaft of longing through her. She felt the stupid urge to lay her smudged cheek against his pristine shirt and cry.

He put his hands on the rim of the tub. "Where do you want this?"

She took her knuckles out of her mouth. "You needn't bother. I can manage on my own."

"I'm sure you can," he said, a trace of tender humor in that precise, British voice. "Nevertheless, why don't you tell me where you want it."

"Beside the worktable."

In one fluid motion he picked up the tub and transported it the few necessary yards, ignoring the fact that it dirtied his clothing. Elizabeth rose, blotting her eyes with a clean corner of her apron.

"Thank you," she said stiffly, wishing he would go away yet wanting him to stay.

He stayed.

She couldn't bear to look at him, to face the glitter of disdain in his eyes. Head lowered, battling the bitter taste of humiliation, she walked past him to the table. Plunging her fingers into the clay, she rolled a hunk into a loaf and dropped it into the tub; it landed with a dull plop.

"What are you doing?" he asked, his voice subdued.

"The clay was too mushy. I let it dry a little overnight."

"Oh."

Another awkward silence ensued, punctuated by the occasional plop of clay into the tub. Concentrating on the task, Elizabeth told herself it was ridiculous to feel such a fierce yearning to be the woman of his heart. Nicholas Ware didn't possess anything as human as a heart.

From beneath her lashes she glanced at him. Why was he still standing there? To gloat? To savor the satisfaction of adding yet another admiring woman to his stable of conquests?

Abruptly he strode to the table. He plucked the loaf from her hand and flung it aside. Planting his palms on the heap of damp clay, he leaned over the table. He stood so close she caught his arousing scent over the pervasive earthen smell. "Elizabeth, look at me."

Feeling defensive, yet unable to ignore him, she lifted her gaze. His face wore a frank expression of longing, his eyes a desolate look of regret.

"Elizabeth," he whispered, gently wiping a tear from her cheek. "Please try to understand what you're asking of me. We can't tumble into bed like a pair of lusty peasants."

"Why not?" she said, swallowing a telltale lump of pain. "You think *me* no better than a peasant."

"That isn't true," he murmured. "You're a fine woman; I admire your integrity, your pride . . . God help me, even your independence."

The sincerity in his voice swirled around her heart. Yet could she believe him? "Then why don't you want to make love to me?"

"Because you're under my protection, Elizabeth. Don't you see—? When I first met you, I wasn't constrained by any promise to protect you. But now everything's changed. I can't take advantage of your innocence."

"Take advantage?" she scoffed. "I'd hardly call it that, considering you have my consent."

"Your reputation would be destroyed."

She rolled her gaze heavenward. "For goodness sake, Nicholas, you of all people should know I don't care Boston beans about what other people think."

"And what if you bore a child out of wedlock?" he said, his voice low. "Have you considered that?"

She stared uncertainly; he stood so close she could see each dark lash shading his silver eyes. Warmth melted her at the thought of holding his baby; cold nipped her at the knowledge that he'd never marry out of his class. The pain vanished under the force of a revelation. She wanted Nicholas for far more than the physical; she yearned to share tender moments, to make him smile, to understand all the perplexing and powerful feelings he aroused within her.

"I'm willing to take that risk," she whispered. "Are you?"

His eyes blazed with emotion. He leaned forward, his mouth vulnerable, his expression soft . . . so soft that her heart pounded with hope and her lips parted in expectation.

Abruptly he jerked back; his first slammed into the soft clay. "God, why can't you understand? Maybe you care nothing for honor, but I do."

Disappointment clogged her throat. Swallowing hard, she said, "Honesty is a part of honor. At least I listen to my feelings instead of hiding them inside starched collars and stiff stays."

He straightened, thrusting a clay-smudged hand through his hair and mussing its natural perfection. "An affair with you is impossible," he said through gritted teeth. "Do you hear me? Impossible! I wish to God it weren't so—" Uttering a growl of frustration, he spun around and strode from the conservatory.

Her emotions careening between despair and delight, Elizabeth wilted into a chair. Nicholas did desire her . . . yet his principles overrode his passion. How was she to convince him to act on his feelings?

Determination firmed her spine. At tonight's ball, she would begin chipping at the marble of his resistance. She would show him that an eccentric artist *could* fit into his world, if she so chose.

Whatever else might happen, Nicholas Ware would not ignore her.

Chapter 12

Try as he might, he couldn't ignore her.

As he guided yet another demure debutante around the crowded dance floor, Nicholas had eyes only for Elizabeth. She was waltzing with that damned rake, Lord Buckstone, her head tilted at him in fascination, her face alight with flirtatious charm. She looked ravishingly attractive in a gown of wisteria satin, the décolletage daring yet fashionable. The bodice hugged the curve of her breasts; the color enhanced the unusual hue of her eyes. That opulent mass of black hair had been drawn into a chignon of curls secured by a jeweled comb. Circling her throat was a splendid necklace of Egyptian design, a filigree of silver around a single moonstone. He stared, bemused and proud. Who would have thought a bohemian artist could outshine every noblewoman at the ball?

Her graceful movements gave him the pleasure of viewing the swanlike curve of her neck and the purity of her profile. Leaning forward, Elizabeth spoke to her dance partner. Buckstone threw back his blond head and laughed, then bent closer to reply; she smiled brilliantly. Nicholas gritted his teeth. Widowed and wealthy, Buckstone was a renowned connoisseur of the ladies. He and Nicholas had often vied for the same woman, with Nicholas's good looks giving him the edge. But he wouldn't win this time. Because he had too damnably much respect for Elizabeth to engage in a discreet liaison.

". . . if you please, my lord."

The trilling voice pulled his eyes back to his dance partner. Lady Marianne gazed at him expectantly, and he realized she awaited an answer.

"I beg your pardon?" he said, years of discipline keeping the impatience from his voice. "I must have been distracted by the music."

Marianne batted her lashes. "I said only that you might loosen your fingers a trifle. I promise I shan't run away from you, Nicholas."

With effort he relaxed his grip on her hand, but the tension strangling the rest of his body refused to ease. At one time he would have found Marianne a pleasant diversion from the schemes of politics and the monotony of society. She was attractive enough, with that fair hair and pink complexion. But now he found her manner dull compared to the vivacity of Elizabeth Hastings. As the waltz came to a close, he felt a sense of relief at the fulfillment of duty.

Marianne fluttered a black satin fan at her flushed cheeks. "The breeze from the gardens feels wonderful. I vow I'm positively wilting from the heat in here."

Her coyness irked Nicholas. If she wished him to invite her out onto the darkened loggia, then why the devil didn't she say so? Elizabeth certainly would. . . .

"I'll fetch you some punch," he snapped.

Ignoring Marianne's startled expression, he strode off without her. He brought back the drink, then excused himself at the first possible instant.

Lifting a glass of brandy from the tray carried by a passing footman, Nicholas strolled through the crowd. Guests crammed the elegant town house. The tinkle of feminine laughter and the rumble of masculine voices vied with the sprightly tune played by the orchestra at the far end of the ballroom. With a brief nod he acknowledged the greetings of friends and acquaintances. Tonight he felt too keyed up for idle conversation, too restless for well-bred blandishments.

Like a drowning man seeking air, he pursued but one goal. Near the opened French doors, he found her.

Elizabeth stood surrounded by a bevy of swains, Cicely at her side. His heart clenched. Unlike him, Elizabeth hadn't forgotten to keep an eye on his wayward sister. Drew Sterling was nowhere in sight, thank God; most likely he was engaged at one of the gaming tables in the drawing room.

The cool evening breeze fluttered wisps of black hair around Elizabeth's face. A familiar hot longing squeezed his loins. With serious interest she listened to the fair-haired man standing before her, his back to Nicholas. Only when the man turned slightly to speak to Cicely did Nicholas recognize his aesthetic profile.

That damned Buckstone again!

Scowling, Nicholas leaned a shoulder against the nearest pillar, half hidden by a huge fern on a pedestal. He took a burning gulp of brandy. Integrity and duty be damned! He had to be this century's biggest fool to turn down the chance to share her bed. But for his misbegotten scruples he and Elizabeth might have slipped home early tonight. Right now he could be sliding his hands up the silken length of her legs, seeking the curve of her bare bottom, sinking himself into the snug velvet of her—

Stop it, for Christ's sake! His hand gripped the glass so hard his knuckles turned white. Was he so selfish he could steal her innocence, ruin her future, risk getting her with child? Elizabeth deserved the honor of his protection, not the infamy of his misuse.

Besides, if he entertained any doubt that her interest in him was purely superficial, tonight supplied the proof. His rejection hadn't hurt her. On the contrary, she laughed and flirted as if she hadn't a care in the world. He had awakened passion in her, nothing more. Or had he? Suddenly remembering her tears, her eyes as brilliant as the petals of a dew-drenched pansy, he felt a rush of tenderness and an aching emptiness which he ruthlessly vanquished. Her pride had been bruised, he told himself, and even that seemed to have healed quickly enough.

"So she's the reason you've been so tied in knots lately."

Nicholas jumped, turning a jaundiced eye on his friend, Charles Garforth, the Marquess of Sedgemoor. For once Nicholas didn't appreciate Charles's keen brown eyes, nor his shrewd ability to see straight to the core of a problem.

"To whom are you referring?" Nicholas asked coolly.

"Your resident artist, who else? She must be the reason you're hiding here, sulking."

He drained his glass. "Just because I choose to spend a few moments alone hardly means I'm sulking."

"Mmm," said Charles, looking unconvinced. Brushing aside the leafy fronds of the fern, he leaned against the green papered wall, his copper hair gleaming in the gaslight. "She's made quite the impression on everyone tonight. The belle of the ball, so to speak."

"Really," Nicholas drawled, his gaze pulled irresistibly to Elizabeth. She smiled dazzlingly as Buckstone whisked her off for another waltz. Glowering, Nicholas lifted the brandy glass to his lips.

Charles laughed. "That's empty," he observed, taking the glass and setting it on a footman's tray. "You're lovesick but good, old chap. Never thought I'd see the day when you'd fall for a decent woman."

"Never thought I'd see the day when you'd pry into my private affairs," Nicholas said.

A grin lit Charles's boyishly freckled face. "Affairs, Nick? Come, you can tell all to your blood brother. Have you forgotten the pact we made at Eton? No secrets."

"Back then I didn't know about matters of the heart."

"Ah, so you do admit your heart is involved."

Nicholas's stomach took a painful plunge. It was true; somehow his affections had gotten all tangled up in his desire for Elizabeth until he could no longer say which tormented him the more, passion or . . .

No, it was impossible; he could not term what he felt for her "love." That was a gentler emotion, something poets wrote sonnets about, not this agony twisting inside, this turbulent yearning to absorb her body and soul.

Charles fetched fresh drinks. "You look like you need this . . . and a friend."

Somehow Nicholas found himself pouring out the frustrating story, from their first meeting in a dank, dark street to Elizabeth's relation to the Rockborough clan. He omitted only the invitation into her bed; he had no wish to taint her reputation, not even to his most trusted friend.

"What's your next move?" Charles asked.

"I can only wait. So far Thistlewood's been able to turn up damnably little."

"Curiouser and curiouser," Charles remarked. "A pity the duke and duchess aren't here tonight. We might have done a bit of sleuthing, observed their reaction to seeing Elizabeth."

"I know," Nicholas said, taking a swallow of brandy. "I feel so damned frustrated. How can I protect her when I don't even know who I'm up against?"

Charles looked thoughtful. "I've never seen you so taken with a woman, old chap. You haven't been thinking of marriage, have you?"

"Marriage?" The notion stunned Nicholas, swept him into fantasy. To lie beside her each night, to have the right to possess her beautiful body—

"For God's sake, be sure of yourself," Charles urged. "You'd be throwing her to the wolves. Society might accept an artist as a novelty, but they'll turn on her if she weds one of their own."

"Don't worry." Nicholas laughed to cover a stab of pain. "Elizabeth Hastings is interested only in art. She views me as a model, not a man."

"Quite the novel predicament for you. A lady who chooses to pursue art instead of England's most sought-after bachelor." Charles's gaze drifted to the crowd of dancers. "If it's any consolation, Nick, you haven't the patent on unrequited love."

Nicholas didn't need to look to know the focus of

that moody gaze. "For God's sake," he said in an ami-
ably chastising tone, "if you'd just relax enough around
my sister to carry on a decent conversation, she might
see you in a different light."

"I know, it defies all logic. I tell myself that, but..."
Charles shrugged, his expression like that of an anxious
youth. "Then I take one look at her lovely face and clam
up."

"I've precisely the opposite problem with Elizabeth.
Whenever I'm with her all I seem to do is rant and
rave."

Charles wore a crooked grin. "Women bring out the
worst in a man. So why the devil do we need them so
much?"

Nicholas chuckled. "Let me know if your logical
brain ever deduces the answer to that."

Charles frowned suddenly, his eyes narrowing as he
peered through the press of people. "I say, isn't that
Drew Sterling speaking to Cicely? Phoebe must have
put his name on the invitation list—I certainly wouldn't
have." He cast an indignant look at Nicholas. "Since
when do you allow that bounder near your sister?"

"Unfortunately he gained an introduction when he
came to tea with the duke and duchess." Nicholas decided a dash of jealousy mightn't hurt Charles. "Cicely
seems quite taken with Sterling...and you know her,"
he said, lifting his shoulders in a shrug. "It's damned
difficult to keep her from going after what she wants."

"She can't possibly want that reprobate. All he cares
about is squandering an inheritance he hasn't yet received. He's probably after her marriage portion."

"Most probably," Nicholas agreed, sipping his
brandy and relishing his friend's quandary.

Then he caught sight of Elizabeth gliding off the
dance floor, her arm entwined with Buckstone's, her
face flushed and shining. His amusement went sour.
That acquaintance had gone on long enough. Turning,
he set his brandy glass in the fern pot for want of a
better place.

"Oh, there you are, Nicholas!"

Resplendent in a gown of sumptuous saffron taffeta, Lady Beatrice swooped toward them like a ship at full sail. She nodded briskly to Charles, then focused a frown at her nephew.

"Have you seen the spectacle our houseguest is making?" she hissed. "Imagine! After all my careful instructions, she's had the gaucherie to dance with the same man three times. And with Lord Buckstone, no less! People are beginning to talk."

"No doubt," Nicholas said. "I had just determined to have a word with her."

"Thank goodness you've recalled your duty." Swinging toward Charles, she added in a scolding undertone, "And you! You should be diverting Cicely from that gambler, Drew Sterling. You must be firm with her if you ever expect her to encourage your suit."

"With all due respect, my lady, she won't listen—"

"No excuses," Lady Beatrice said, tapping his lapel with her fan. "I shall expect results from the both of you, and quickly!" Her beribboned russet hair held regally, she sailed away.

"Why do I feel like a chastened schoolboy?" Charles asked.

Nicholas laughed. "Admiral Beatrice does make her opinions known. Come along, let's bowl the ladies over with our charm and wit."

"That's easy for you to say. Cicely will probably freeze me out, as she always does."

"So don't let her. Compliment her. Ask her to dance, then invite her into the garden for a romantic look at the stars."

"Spoken like a true rakehell," Charles said with a wry grin. "I envy you your knack of winning the ladies."

"At present," Nicholas murmured, "I'd hardly call myself a winner at amorous encounters."

Straightening his shoulders, Charles brushed a hand over the black lapels of his evening coat. "All right. After you, old chap."

They set off through the tightly packed assemblage,

Nicholas in the lead. As they neared the French doors where Elizabeth stood, he felt that familiar charge of excitement disturbing his heart. Resolutely he tamped down his rising emotions. His sole purpose in approaching her was to steer her clear of Buckstone.

Serene and ladylike, she sipped a cup of punch and chatted with a cluster of people. A peculiar pang invaded Nicholas. Somehow he preferred her unadorned, smelling of clay, wearing those ridiculous trousers, her hair tumbling down her back.

Cicely stood with Drew, apart from the group. Lady Phoebe stood at Elizabeth's side, but Nicholas's eyes focused on the thin, aesthetic features of Peter Tate, the Viscount Buckstone.

Nicholas gave the man a terse nod. "Buckstone."

"Hawkesford." Buckstone inclined his neatly groomed fair head. "I say, I've been meaning to have a word with you all evening. You deserve to be boiled in oil for keeping such a lovely woman hidden away at Berkeley Square."

Elizabeth playfully slapped his arm. "You exaggerate, Lord Buckstone. There must be a hundred women here more lovely than I."

"None that interest me," he declared. "You possess more than outer beauty; you have intelligence and talent, as well. No other lady here could have created such a stunning necklace."

Buckstone gazed at the silver-filigreed moonstone resting on the milky sweep of her bosom. Digging his fingers into his palms, Nicholas fought to contain a jolt of anger and chagrin. *He* hadn't known the necklace was her own design.

"Do you truly make your own jewelry?" Lady Phoebe asked, her blue eyes bright with admiration.

Elizabeth smiled. "I'm afraid you're looking at my one and only effort. I created it in an art class."

"You American women are so lucky." Phoebe sighed. "To make one's own life, to come and go as one pleases must be wonderful."

Charles chuckled. "Yes, your ogre of a brother does

keep you chained in the attic, eh, Phebes?"

She made a face at him. "Yesterday I missed riding in Hyde Park, all because you returned home late from parliament. Had I been a man, I could have gone alone."

"Were you a man, you wouldn't have been clamoring to show off your latest dress, so there'd have been no point in going, anyway."

"Male logic," Phoebe said, disgust wrinkling her dainty nose. "Who can understand it?"

"Not you, Phebes," her brother said good-naturedly. "Logic is something you can't even begin to—"

His mouth clamped shut, his shoulders stiffening. Following the direction of Charles's gaze, Nicholas saw Cicely approaching, Drew Sterling sauntering alongside her.

Nicholas felt his own body tense. Sterling looked more indolent than ever and far too self-satisfied.

Clinging to his elegant arm, his sister brought Sterling into the group. "Hullo, everyone."

"A pleasure to see you, Cicely," Charles said, his voice rigidly proper. Disapproval hardening his boyish face, he glanced at Sterling without acknowledging him.

As Cicely caught Charles's look, a shadow dimmed her radiant smile; then she tipped her chin to a rebellious angle. "I brought Drew to meet you, Elizabeth," she said gaily. "I've been telling him all about my art lessons. Drew, this is Miss Elizabeth Hastings."

"So you're the sculptress," he drawled. His dark eyes dipped to her décolletage. "Pretty necklace you're wearing."

"Thank you."

Nicholas gritted his teeth. Was every man here staring at her breasts? He forced himself to concentrate on Sterling's face. If he were the one who wanted her dead, surely he would show some betrayal in his expression, a sign of recognition. . . .

A faint frown marred those aquiline features. "You

look rather familiar, Miss Hastings. Have we met before?"

"I doubt it," Elizabeth said, smiling. "I grew up in New York."

"Ah, yes, I must be mistaken, then." Sterling glanced away, already losing interest, his eyes raking the assemblage as if in search of entertainment.

Indecision tugged at Nicholas. Sterling's reference to familiarity could be a flawless performance, a cover for vicious, cold-blooded emotions. Or it could be genuine. Drew Sterling would have been perhaps eight or nine years old when Owen and Lucy Templeton Hastings had left England with their young daughter. Since Elizabeth looked so much like her mother, that could account for Sterling's reaction.

"I hope His Grace is enjoying good health?" Nicholas said.

Sterling shrugged. "What he enjoys is poor health. Gives him an excuse to hound everyone."

Cicely gave Drew a sympathetic look. "He was too ill to attend tonight?"

"Sleeping off one of Dr. Marsh's potions, I suppose. Nothing to worry your pretty head over."

He patted her hand; Nicholas clenched his jaw.

Buckstone cleared his throat. "Since we're all gathered here, I should like to make an announcement. I plan to erect a monument to my father's memory at the place he loved best, our estate in Ireland." He flashed an admiring look at Elizabeth. "I mean to have a competition to select the sculptor. Elizabeth has done me the great honor of agreeing to submit a design."

Shock paralyzed Nicholas. Buckstone's pale blue eyes glittered with triumph and his lips arched into a smile. For the first time in his life, Nicholas felt the savage urge to bury his fist in another man's face.

"How wonderful!" Cicely cried, clapping her hands.

"You make it sound as though *I'm* doing *you* a favor," Elizabeth chided the viscount, "when in truth it's the other way around. Designing a monument is a marvelous opportunity to build my reputation as an artist."

"I'm so pleased you view it that way," Buckstone said.

His false modesty infuriated Nicholas all the more. That damn conniving philanderer! He didn't care a whit about any monument; he wanted to get Elizabeth alone on his Irish estate.

Suddenly Nicholas went numb, jolted by lightning. God! What if she were willing? Fresh from his own rejection, she might offer herself to Buckstone.

The viscount bowed to her. "May I have the pleasure of another dance?" he inquired. "We have plans to discuss, and we might as well enjoy ourselves as we talk."

Buckstone twirled her onto the dance floor before Nicholas could collect his devastated emotions. What could he do anyway? he thought bitterly. By enticing Elizabeth with what she loved best, Buckstone had scored his most brilliant stratagem ever.

Drew made a restive movement. "I believe I'll return to the drawing room. I'm missing the card games."

"Oh, please stay," Cicely said, presenting him with a brilliant smile. "The music is so lovely."

Charles glanced at Nicholas; apparently misinterpreting his friend's scowl, Charles made a stiff bow toward Cicely. "Er . . . would you care to dance?"

Clearly vexed that the wrong man had responded to her hint, Cicely pursed her lips. Drew seized the chance to slip away, leaving her no recourse but to accept the offer. She flounced toward the dancers, Charles trailing her.

"They make a lovely couple," said Phoebe.

"Yes." Nicholas spared them no more than a cursory glance; he was too obsessed with searching the crowd for Elizabeth and Buckstone.

"If you ask me to dance, you'll get a better view of your artist."

Nicholas felt heat rise from under his starched collar. Turning to Phoebe, he saw a wise look in her youthful blue eyes. "Is my interest so obvious?" he asked.

"Only to someone who's known you for so long." She held out her arm. "Shall we?"

Nicholas dutifully led her into the swarm of dancers. Holding Phoebe close, he listened with half an ear to her witty discourse about the other guests. Her undemanding chatter was a balm to his bruised pride. For so long he'd thought of Phoebe simply as Charles's baby sister; now he saw her as a woman, kind and gentle, her figure slim and pleasing. Perhaps Cicely was right; perhaps he should court Phoebe. Such a tractable lady would make a far more suitable wife than a willful woman like Elizabeth.

Wife. He slammed the lid on the tenderness lifting his heart. She was not the woman for him; she was already wed to her work.

Yet over and over his eyes strayed to Elizabeth, each time the waltz steps swung him in her direction. The numbness left him at the sight of her in Buckstone's arms. With rising fury Nicholas glared at her. Didn't she know she was playing with fire? Did she truly not care a whit for her reputation? Or his feelings?

By the time the last strains of music faded, Nicholas had worked himself up into a justifiable rage. Pausing only to give Phoebe a sincere thanks, he cut a determined path through the throng and found Elizabeth alone by a pillar. No one could guess by looking at her that she hadn't been born a lady. Her lustrous black hair shone in the gaslight, her high cheekbones and full mouth giving her an aristocratic air. An aura of mystery enveloped her, an aura as exotic as a hothouse camellia. He had the impression he could never learn everything about her, even if he were to love her for a hundred years.

The thought fired his anger anew. Without even trying she could reduce him to another of her panting admirers.

"I see your devoted lapdog has deserted you," he said.

She turned, looking not the least bit surprised. "Lord Buckstone didn't desert me. He's fetching punch."

"A pity, since you shan't be here to drink it."

Elizabeth's heart tripped in alarm as his strong hand closed around hers. Yet she far preferred to face hot fury than cold indifference. As he hauled her through the multitude of lords and ladies, the evening took on a sudden sparkle, the gaslit chandeliers twinkling, the colors of gowns turning rich and vivid, the aromas of fine perfumes caressing her heightened senses. A delicious chill of anticipation leapt up her arm and into her heart. She loved the warmth and firmness of his fingers, the masculine power inherent in his clasp, the feel of his life and energy flowing into her.

"If you want to dance," she said, "you might ask me in a civilized manner."

His eyes raked her. "You've danced enough tonight."

She went willingly as he pulled her through the opened French doors and onto the loggia, a long roofed porch that ran the length of the town house. Moonlight silvered the formal gardens. Here and there, couples strolled arm in arm along the winding paths. The scent of roses hung heavy in the summer night air.

Instead of leading her down the steps, Nicholas drew her deeper into the shadows. The trill of feminine laughter drifted from the garden. The prospect of stealing a moment alone with him warmed her blood and quickened her heartbeat. This was why she had endured the prissy company of Lord Buckstone, to force Nicholas to notice her.

"Why are you so angry?" she asked in her most innocent voice.

He let loose her hand so abruptly she stumbled backward; her fingers met the rough stone balustrade.

"Because you're making a fool of yourself," he growled. "You can't spend all evening with one man and expect people not to talk."

"Let them talk if it busies their small minds. Peter is a charming man. *He* appreciates me for what I am—an artist."

She could scarcely make out Nicholas's face in the

darkness, but she heard his harsh bark of laughter.

"You're a babe in the woods when it comes to playing society's games, Elizabeth. Buckstone doesn't care about any commission. He wants to seduce you."

She had suspected that, but the thrill of designing the monument made her forgive the viscount's motives. "I can manage him," she said. "And I plan to win that commission for the monument on his Irish estate."

Nicholas stepped closer, emerging from the shadows of a pillar. Moonlight gilded his classic features, the chiseled planes of his cheekbones, the slash of his lowered brow.

"What else do you have planned?" he bit out. "To share his Irish bed?"

Nicholas was jealous! Swallowing a bubble of exuberance, she kept her voice steady. "My plans are no concern of yours, Lord Hawkesford."

"I see. I'm supposed to look the other way while my sister's mentor cavorts with a notorious philanderer."

"From what the ladies were whispering, *you're* far worse than he is. By dragging me out here, you've probably done more damage to my reputation than he did."

"I'm surprised at you, Elizabeth. I didn't think you were the type to pay heed to gossips."

Vexation pricked her. Why didn't he deny the rumors about his prowess with women? "Oh, but in this case it's more than idle chatter. I saw how close you were holding Lady Phoebe on the dance floor. I saw you whispering in her ear, no doubt arranging an assignation."

She stopped short, afraid at the hardening of his face. Her fingers curled around the cool stone railing. From the garden came the rumble of a man's voice; then the lilt of music masked the sound.

Nicholas stood as silent as a masterpiece of moon-dappled marble. "I do believe," he said softly, "that you're jealous."

"I am not." But inside Elizabeth knew the heart-wrenching truth. The gentle Lady Phoebe had been bred to make the ideal wife for a man of Nicholas's rank. Elizabeth genuinely liked Phoebe, which made watching them together far more hurtful than seeing him pay court to that silly Marianne.

Nicholas's eyes blazed silver in the moonlight. "You are jealous, by God!" he whispered in triumph. "Your behavior tonight has been a blatant invitation."

"For what?" she scoffed.

"For this."

His hands latched hard onto her shoulders, pulling her to him with a force that should have hurt but somehow didn't. His mouth closed over hers, his urgent kiss draining any thought of protest. The skillful sweep of his tongue brought a moan of longing to her throat. Pliant and willing, Elizabeth felt her body turn to warm wax, ready to be molded by his clever hands.

She adored his taste and scent, the richness of brandy and the tang of soap. The intensity of his kiss tilted her head back against the hard muscles of his upper arm. Against her breasts she felt the impassioned thud of his heart. Her own blood beat hotly in her ears. Obeying the urges inside her, she slid her hands over his smooth coat. One of her fingers stole between the buttons of his shirt, encountering the rough silk of his chest hair.

His arms went taut around her, his mouth moving to nip the tender lobe of her ear. Trembly and weak with wanting, she reached for a shirt button and worked it free, then another. When her hand slipped inside to caress the carved strength of his chest, his breath came out in a hiss.

"God! Elizabeth . . ."

The knowledge of his passion filled her with heady excitement. His thumb brushed across her nipple, and it tightened with a sweetness that made her shiver. The response coursed through her like a sterling silver thread, coming to rest deep within her belly. Her insides clamored for more and she moved her hips restlessly. He groaned, then took her lips in another shattering kiss, his hand tracking lightly over her breast, tracing its shape and softness.

Driven by the desire to explore him, she finished unbuttoning his shirt to the waistband of his trousers. She parted the fine linen and skimmed her hands over his bare chest. The curling pelt of hair pleased her; the sleek, hard muscles entranced her. No work of art could surpass his male splendor, the breadth of his shoulders, the tautness of his belly, the slimness of his waist.

"You're magnificent," she breathed, pressing her lips to the heat of his skin. "I wish I could see you in the moonlight... I wish I could sculpt you in marble."

His muscles tensed beneath her cheek; his hands tightened around her upper arms. Abruptly Nicholas thrust her away. "A shame you won't get your wish," he said.

His arctic drawl chased the warmth from her being. His eyes were slitted, his anger a noxious presence in the fragrant summer night. Bewildered, Elizabeth leaned weakly against the pillar as he rebuttoned his shirt. She felt bereft, abandoned. A keen ache of loss wrapped around her heart. Why had he turned cold?

The sight of him so casually straightening his clothing aroused a fierce fury inside her. "You can't bear for a woman to speak her mind, can you?" she snapped. "You pushed me away because I don't play frivolous games like your other women."

"Like hell you don't play games," he said, shoving his shirt into his trousers. "No doubt you expected a commission to sculpt me in exchange for your favors. Isn't that the way you plan to win the commission from Buckstone?"

The insult made her gasp. Without thinking, Elizabeth slapped him hard across the cheek. His head snapped back under the force of the blow. For a moment he stood there, glaring at her, his hands clenched at his sides, the rasp of his breathing blending with the backdrop of music.

"Damn you," he said in a savage whisper.

Pivoting sharply, Nicholas strode down the shadowed loggia, his tall form vanishing around the corner of the town house.

Elizabeth felt the urge to run after him, to apologize for losing her temper, to do anything that would wipe the look of freezing contempt off his handsome face. Yet he richly deserved that slap!

Racked by confusion, she leaned against a pillar and blinked against the sting of tears. She had driven Nicholas away by behaving like a common hussy. How could she ever hope to earn his love and respect if she could not act the lady?

Love. Awe sparkled inside her like the lilting notes of music drifting through the French doors. She loved Nicholas. How or when or why such a powerful emotion had been born within her, she could not say, yet it shimmered in her soul, radiating through her like a warm and tender presence.

But beneath the glitter and glow, pain clasped her heart. Her impetuous actions and rash tongue had extinguished any spark of affection Nicholas might have felt for her. Perhaps it was for the best. Their lives were like warm bronze and cold marble, elements too diverse to ever mesh into one.

Chapter 13

"I say," Lord Buckstone remarked as he strolled through the conservatory a week later, "have you seen the latest exhibition at the Royal Academy?"

"Aye, guv'ner, that I did," said Kipp, sitting proudly in the chair by the burbling fountain. "Miss Libby took me."

Buckstone stopped pacing to aim a cold look at the boy. "I beg your pardon?"

Apparently assuming the viscount was slightly deaf, Kipp shouted, "I said, *Miss Libby took me.*"

Stifling a smile at Buckstone's appalled look, Elizabeth glanced swiftly at the lead wire in her hands. Out of the corner of her eye, she saw Cicely whip a handkerchief over her mouth and utter a strangled cough.

"Miss Libby?" Buckstone said. "Are you referring to Miss Hastings?"

"Aye, guv'ner." Thoughtfully Kipp lifted a hand as if to adjust the battered bowler hat that no longer rested on his combed black hair. He scratched his ear instead. "Don't rightly know why she wanted to take me there. Just a lot of snooty folks gapin' at a bunch of paintin's."

A spatter of raindrops struck the glass roof. "Indeed," Buckstone said in a chillingly sarcastic tone. "Then you'll be pleased to know I was addressing the ladies."

"That's all, Kipp," Elizabeth said, rounding the corner of the worktable. "You may return to Mr. Greaves now."

"Thank Gawd Almighty!" The boy surged up, then darted her an abashed look before walking sedately out the vine-draped door.

Buckstone shifted irritated blue eyes to Elizabeth. "I cannot conceive why Hawkesford tolerates such insolence and tale-telling in his servants. Imagine, expecting me to believe a lady of quality would take a member of the staff to the academy!"

Elizabeth hid her annoyance. Snapping at Peter Tate could accomplish nothing and harm much. She had no wish to antagonize the man who would soon award the commission that would, she hoped, distract her mind and her heart from Nicholas.

"I'm sure Kipp didn't mean to be rude." She couldn't resist adding, "And he didn't lie; I did take him to the exhibit. I believe in encouraging everyone to develop a love of art."

Buckstone appeared taken aback; then his thin face assumed a conciliatory expression. "Pray accept my apology, Elizabeth. It truly is admirable of you Americans to take such a benevolent interest in educating the common masses."

She smiled serenely. "Why, thank you, Peter."

"You are indeed an original," he said, bestowing an admiring look on her as he resumed his promenade. "I daresay you made quite the impact at the Garforths' last week."

"Did I?" The image of Nicholas's coldly furious face sprang to her mind. Swiftly she glanced down, concealing a wrench of heartache as she nonchalantly twisted the wire with a pair of pliers. "Why do you say that?"

"Because I heard many a favorable comment about you," Buckstone said. "People were discussing that marvelous Egyptian necklace you were wearing. When I described it to my jeweler, he said three women had come in this week to order a similar design."

With startled pleasure, Elizabeth stared at him. "Truly?"

"Yes. I myself ordered one for my mother's birthday. You've sparked quite the rage, my dear."

"I never expected anyone to appreciate my attempt at jewelry designing."

"It was more than the necklace," he murmured. "Your charm won over everyone. They're calling you the jewel in Hawkesford's coronet."

The viscount strolled closer. He cut a fine figure in his wine-colored morning coat, though Elizabeth privately preferred Nicholas's muscular beauty and sincere wit to Buckstone's svelte form and phony blandishments. That poetic intensity must explain the viscount's appeal to women, she surmised. And, of course, his wealth and title attracted as well.

Buckstone stopped beside her, his eyes probing. "You and Hawkesford disappeared from the ball. I trust he hasn't turned your pretty head."

Her breath caught as she recalled that steamy kiss, that shocking slap. Bending a length of wire in half, she lied, "Of course not. I . . . didn't feel well and Nicholas was kind enough to escort me to the carriage."

Suspicion still narrowed the viscount's eyes. "Perhaps you'll forgive me a friendly word of advice. Hawkesford's had a string of mistresses; he has no interest in permanent attachments."

Elizabeth's heart squeezed tight. Swallowing hard, she said, "I didn't think a gentleman discussed such topics with a lady."

"Pardon my boldness. I mean only to save you heartache." Buckstone kissed her hand. "You're a lovely woman, Elizabeth. Until you left the ball, I was the envy of every man there."

"You exaggerate," she said lightly, rescuing her fingers from his damp clutches.

"You're too modest. My dear, you are a fragrant rose in a field of noxious weeds."

"Oh, pooh," Cicely said, her eyes twinkling. "I'm no raving beauty, but I never likened myself to a weed, either. Really, Bucky, where have your manners gotten to?"

Stiffening, Buckstone swung toward her. "A thousand pardons, my lady. Of course, I wasn't including *you* in my assessment."

"Of course." With a dramatic sweep of her scratch tool, Cicely added texture to the bust's hair. "We lady artists are attractive to men because we're so original. Is that not so, Bucky?"

Annoyance flitted over the viscount's features. "I admire a woman who has the pluck to shed the constraints of society."

He started to turn back to Elizabeth, but Cicely's guileless voice stopped him. "You mean a woman who'll forget her scruples and have an affair with you?"

Elizabeth bit her lip to restrain a giggle. Buckstone's normally pale face had gone scarlet.

"That is not what I meant at all!" he blustered. "I would never dream of misusing a lady."

Elizabeth aimed a hard-won frown at Cicely, who smiled mischievously before returning to her work.

"Of course not, Peter," Elizabeth said. "You're the finest of gentlemen."

"Thank you." The rigid set of his shoulders relaxed. He stared as she attached the long piece of wire to a supporting pipe. "I say, isn't that a human form you're making there? A rather curious piece of art," he added, gazing askance at it.

She smiled. "This is only the supporting armature—I'll build the clay figure around it."

"I see." Unlike Nicholas, Buckstone's interest in her work seemed perfunctory, for he consulted a gold pocketwatch and said, "I'm afraid I must go. I've an engagement for tea at White's. But I'll be back to visit again . . . if I'm not intruding."

His frank gaze scalded Elizabeth; discomfited, she shifted her position. "Certainly I welcome your company," she said, forcing a courtesy even Lady Beatrice would have praised. "Especially if you don't mind that I work as we talk."

"Never, my dear. I am your most ardent admirer."

"Don't forget my design," she said, handing him the

sketch pad containing her plan for the memorial. Palms damp with anxiety, she asked, "When might I expect a decision?"

"The other two sculptors haven't been as swift in submitting their proposals. Perhaps within a week or two?"

She swallowed her impatience. "Of course."

As he walked out the door, Elizabeth touched the sterling ring for luck. Such a brilliant appointment, her first big commission in England, would likely lead to other opportunities. She would be flooded with projects. . . . For a moment she lost herself in dreams of grandeur, dreams of leaving her mark on the art world.

And what of Nicholas? A storm of pain drenched her happiness. A future without him seemed dark and bleak. Yet he didn't fit into her life, nor she into his. This week the monument design had torn her from sleep, from meals, from company. When could she have spared the time for a man? If her career flourished as she hoped, she'd be even busier.

She eyed the fabric-covered shape half hidden by a camellia bush. Beneath the cloth lay the lovingly rendered bust of Nicholas. Yet even while pressing the swan trademark into the base, she'd felt vaguely dissatisfied. Turning to the worktable, she studied the armature. Perhaps a life-sized study would appease the emptiness gnawing her. She couldn't forget the feel of his chest beneath her fingers, the trimness of his waist, the span of his shoulders. She imagined the perfection of his naked body. He would reach for her, his tender hands caressing her, his hungry mouth arousing her, his low voice whispering words of love—

". . . don't you think?" Cicely said.

A blush scorched Elizabeth's cheeks. "What did you say?"

Cicely studied the bust of Kipp. "I'm nearly finished, don't you agree?"

Elizabeth walked closer to examine the sculpture. "You've done well—his personality comes through. Once the clay dries we'll have it cast in bronze."

Cicely sighed dreamily. "Drew would look marvelous in bronze. I shall do him next."

The girl's obsession with the rake worried Elizabeth. Drew Sterling had come to call this past week; in the midst of the visit, Nicholas had arrived home, his chilly disapproval putting a damper on the meeting.

"Didn't you say Drew was leaving London soon?"

"Yes, he has to kowtow to his uncle, the duke. But Drew intends to return at the first possible moment. . . . Can you keep a secret?" Starry-eyed, she said, "He kissed my cheek!"

"He does seem to know how to charm a lady," Elizabeth said dryly. "But isn't he keen on gambling?"

"Only because he hasn't yet found the right woman," Cicely declared. "He'll change, you'll see. Then Nick will approve of him, too." In a whisper of peach silk, she swept to the water faucet and stooped to wash the clay from her hands.

Frowning, Elizabeth walked slowly to the worktable. She could tell Cicely that Drew wouldn't change his stripes so easily, but wouldn't it be best for the girl to learn that hard lesson on her own? No matter what happened, she wouldn't alter her brother's feelings; the earl was too set in his ways.

Elizabeth sighed. She could well understand Cicely's desire to transform Drew. She herself longed to change Nicholas's strict opinions, to make him accept her as she was, to let go of his scruples. Such a tangled web they'd woven. Nicholas, too, was bent on metamorphosis, to make her fit his mold of a lady.

Or had he given up?

Her mouth went dry. For most of the week he'd been out, tending to business or political matters. As the days crept by she felt more and more certain that her slap had killed his interest in her. Nicholas respected logical thought, not rash outbursts; by acting on her emotions she had relinquished his respect. Yet how could she be anything but herself?

Restless, Elizabeth picked up her sketch pad. "I'm going for a walk," she told Cicely, who was browsing through the small library of art books on the shelf. "Would you like to come?"

"Actually I'd rather read for a while. Do you mind?"

Pleased at the girl's diligence, Elizabeth picked up her shawl. "Of course not."

"You should take along a footman," Cicely said. "You know how Nick feels about us venturing out alone."

The memory of his imperious order pricked Elizabeth's anger. "Nonsense. I'm only going across to the square. He'll never even know I was gone."

Heading down the overgrown pathway, she found a door half hidden by the bushes, which she unlocked with a key from a nearby hook. The hinges creaked as she slipped outside. The cool, gray afternoon suited her mood. Tendrils of vapor wreathed the formal garden, coiling around the trimmed topiary and meandering over the fragrant rosebushes.

She passed a craggy-faced gardener clipping a box-wood; he tipped his cap and nodded. Ignoring his inquisitive gaze at her Turkish trousers, she found a wooden gate in the stone wall. The iron handle, slick with mist, wouldn't budge. Locked. Retracing her steps, she asked the gardener's assistance.

Obligingly he fished inside his pocket, produced a large key, and fumbled with the lock. "'Is lordship, 'e keeps the place battened up tight these days, 'e does. Too many thieves and murderers about. Asked me to keep a sharp eye out, 'e did."

Thieves and murderers...a convenient tale, Elizabeth thought resentfully. Nicholas wished only to keep her under his thumb. Her heart lifted a little as she set off across the street. In spite of his orders she had escaped his domain.

A wrought iron fence surrounded the square, and the park was nearly deserted on this dismal day. A starched nanny wheeled a pram along the winding pathways; the hunched figure of an old man strolled beneath the spreading branches of plane trees; two boys played tag near the Chinese-roofed pumphouse in the center of the square.

Elizabeth sat on a hard bench and idly sketched the nanny. The air smelled thick and damp, and the distant rattle of hansom cabs and carriages drifted from the street. The children darted away, heading toward one of the elegant town houses lining the square. Her eyes idly followed them. Her father would be returning soon from his tutoring post at the Garforths; he usually arrived home in time to take tea with her in the conservatory. That was their special time together, a time she treasured, when they shared the happenings of the day.

The old man shuffled to a bench a short distance away, easing himself down. Or was it a man? The dark hood of the cloak shielded the face from her view. She could see trouser cuffs peeping beneath the hem, but perhaps there were other women who affected her own unconventional style. Or who were too poor to be choosy about clothing.

Lifting the sketch pad, she began to draw the ancient form, the stooped shoulders, the head bent as if in woe. Sympathy welled within her. What did an elderly person reflect upon? Lost dreams? Memories of a happy past? Would she someday sit on a park bench and meditate on bygone glories? Would she think back on the English earl she had once loved and wonder what had become of him? Swallowing her sudden sorrow, she let her pencil glide over the paper, capturing the pale hand slipping inside the cloak, perhaps to rub an aching belly or to reach for a bottle of gin. . . .

Inside the cloak, slim fingers caressed the carved wooden hilt of a Scottish dirk. The single-edged blade had been honed to the sharpness of a scalpel. Two hundred years ago the dagger had been used to kill rival highlanders.

Today it would serve a higher purpose . . . to heal the malady afflicting Lucy, to cleanse her of sin and set her free.

Keen eyes watched the nanny wheel the pram out of the park. Impatient fingers tightened around the barrel-shaped grip of the knife. So much time had been wasted; so little time remained. There had been too many days of waiting . . . waiting for Lucy's daughter to venture forth alone.

The square was empty now. The wind whispered through the trees . . . whispered that the chance had come at last. In a few moments the bitter scent of blood would rise into the misty air.

Blood that would bring Lucy back.

With creaky movements, the figure rose from the bench and started slowly down the path.

His black mood lifted as Nicholas strode down the corridor, the heels of his riding boots ringing on the marble floor. Cicely wasn't in her rooms, nor was she out making calls with Aunt Beatrice. That meant his sister must be in the conservatory with Elizabeth.

Anticipation rose sharp and sweet within him. He tried to shove the feeling away, but it crept back, defying all logic. God help him, he wanted Elizabeth. He wanted to gaze into her vivid eyes. He wanted to watch her lithe movements and hear her merry laughter. Most of all he wanted to touch her, to sift the silk of her hair through his fingers, to taste the softness of her lips, to wrap her in his embrace and absorb her passion, her vitality.

I wish I could sculpt you in marble.

The memory of her words stung more hotly than her slap. Despite her passionate response to his kisses, he meant nothing to her beyond the physical. He was a model for her to sculpt; Elizabeth had space in her busy life only for her work.

The knowledge frustrated and embittered him. For the first time he craved more than a physical joining, more than a brief, loveless liaison. Damn her for stealing his heart without bestowing her own in return!

Yet, as he neared the conservatory, a thrilling surge of impatience filled Nicholas. Already he could detect the damp scent of vegetation, the arousing hint of herbs and clay he associated with Elizabeth. Reining in his quixotic emotions, he stepped through the opened door.

Warm, humid air enveloped him as he walked down the pathway, through the jungle of glossy-leafed camellia bushes. He glanced eagerly around the glass-enclosed room. Amid the clutter on the worktable stood an armature for what looked like a human figure. The splashing of the fountain mingled with the tap of his footsteps on the stone flags and the occasional patter of raindrops. Disappointment left a sour taste in his mouth.

Elizabeth wasn't here. Her absence felt like a physical pain.

Turning to go, he caught sight of Cicely near the ivy-covered wall. She was engrossed in reading, and her chair was partially hidden by the tangle of foliage. His initial purpose in coming here rushed back.

Heading toward her, he wondered what could so snare her attention that she would fail to hear his footsteps. "Good afternoon, Cicely."

She jumped. A pencil slipped from her fingers and pinged to the floor. Whipping toward him, she slammed the book shut. Her blue eyes were wide, her cheeks flushed. "What are you doing here?" she squeaked.

He knew that expression of guilt. Spurred by suspicion, he lifted the book from her lap. She made a move as if to snatch back the thick volume, then sank into her chair and watched him with an air of rebellious resignation.

He looked at the book. *Gray's Anatomy.* A sheet of paper stuck out of the middle; Nicholas opened to the marked page. His eyes narrowed on the illustration of male genitals. The loose paper contained a shockingly accurate rendering of a man's nude body, right down to his—

Lips taut, Nicholas clapped the book shut. The

thought of his sister making such an immodest sketch appalled and angered him.

"What the devil do you think you're about?"

Cicely tilted her chin stubbornly. "I'm studying. All artists have to learn human anatomy—just ask Elizabeth."

"I'll speak to her, believe me, I will." He jabbed the book into the air for emphasis. "To inform her this is totally inappropriate subject matter for a young lady."

"Oh, pooh, they're only pictures. You're carrying on like the queen's minister of protocol." Despite her brazen words, Cicely blushed crimson.

"I'm carrying on out of concern for your welfare. You're not to consult this book again, do you hear?"

Her lower lip jutted out. "You never let me do anything the least bit daring or amusing."

"On the contrary, Cicely, you may do whatever you like . . . within the bounds of proper behavior. Speaking of which, Charles and Phoebe are coming to dinner tonight. I shall expect you to conduct yourself as a lady."

"I will as long as you don't thrust me at Charles. I prefer to choose my own men."

Her undaunted spirit ignited a spark of darkly affectionate humor in Nicholas. "I know you do, Cicely. You've made that eminently clear. Now where is Elizabeth?"

Cicely regarded him sulkily. "She went out for a walk."

Alarm dried his throat. "Out?" he said hoarsely. "Where?"

"Just across the street, to the square."

"Alone?"

"Well, yes," Cicely said, shrugging. "I told her to take a footman, but she said—"

Nicholas didn't hear the rest because he was already sprinting out the door. The speed of his footsteps on the marble floor matched the pounding rhythm of his heart. If Thistlewood's latest report was correct, Elizabeth could be in grave danger.

Rounding a corner, he startled a parlor maid; squealing, she dropped a stack of linen. Nicholas rushed past her, down the echoing corridor. He felt sick with fear ... fear for Elizabeth and for himself. Fear that he would be too late ... fear that he would lose all that had become most precious to him.

In the entrance hall Aunt Beatrice descended the grand staircase. "You're home early, Nicholas," she said, smiling. "Shall I ring for tea—"

"Later," he snapped.

"But Nicholas—"

He ignored her startled face. Long strides carried him toward the door, where Peebles stood at rigid attention. Only then did Nicholas realize he still held the anatomy book.

He thrust it at the butler. "Burn it."

"Yes, my lord." Clutching the book against his cadaverous, black-clad chest, Peebles sprang to open the door.

Nicholas strode out into the vaporous air and leapt down the steps, two at a time. His keen eyes surveyed the fog-shrouded square; it looked deserted. So intent was his inspection that a hansom cab nearly ran him down. He dodged the horse's hooves and ignored the driver's curse. God, where was Elizabeth?

His gaze swept the plane trees, the small pump-house, the nymph fountain near the far railing. A gust of wind spattered raindrops against his face. Half running, he shot through the opened, wrought iron gate, his shoes crunching on the path.

Then he spied her bent over a sketch pad, sitting on a bench beneath the trees. His heart did a wild leap of relief. Praise God, she was unharmed. No murderer stalked this quiet park; only an old man, cloaked against the mist, strolled the path toward her.

Nicholas's fears melted beneath the heat of a colossal anger. She might be safe this time, but she'd damned well never again take such an idiotic risk!

He marched swiftly past the stooped figure. Elizabeth remained absorbed in her sketch. An ebony veil of hair hid her features, but he recognized the total concentration on her task. As she swung her head toward him, a succession of emotions flitted over her face: artistic curiosity, startled pleasure, guarded interest.

"Hello, Nicholas."

Her melodic voice stirred a softness within him which he squelched. Taking hold of her arm, he dragged her from the bench. The sketch pad tumbled to the wet ground.

"You deserve to be thrashed," he said fiercely. "What the devil are you doing out here alone?"

"Drawing. In my own free time, I might add."

"Freedom be damned! If you set so much as one toe outside my doors, you're to have a footman escort you."

She didn't flinch under his furious gaze. "More orders, your lordship? I'm an American, in case you've forgotten, and an independent woman."

Her proud manner incensed Nicholas. Gripping her arms tighter, he gave her a shake. "You might have been killed! By God, I really will have to lock you up!"

"You are hurting my arms," she said coldly.

"Good," he snapped, though he loosened his hold a fraction. "Perhaps bruises will convince you where mere words have failed." He had to make her understand without revealing what he knew of her past, the secrets only Owen had the right to tell her. "The maniac who attacked you has never been caught. He could be out here anywhere, waiting for a chance to catch you alone!"

"Don't be absurd. That was an isolated incident. No one else is going to bother me."

"Perhaps you should ask your father about that."

Nicholas regretted the words the moment they slipped out. Elizabeth looked startled, and her eyes widened to pansies, huge and purple. Suddenly he felt drowned by the violent urge to make love to her, to demonstrate his domination of her right here, on the damp lush grass of the square, in full view of a hundred watching windows.

She tilted her head warily. "My father? What do you mean?"

"Never mind." Nicholas picked up her sketch pad and thrust it at her. "Come along," he said, seizing her hand and pulling her down the path.

She stepped smartly to match his pace. "I want to know what you mean, Nicholas."

"Forget it." He searched for a distraction. "There's something else we need to discuss. My sister's behavior."

"If you're referring to her interest in Drew Sterling, Cicely has acted with admirable discretion."

"Discretion," he stated with black humor, "is hardly the word I'd use to describe her most recent lapse in conduct."

He sensed her irritation in the stiff set of her shoulders. A protective hand at her back, he guided her across the busy street. Entering Hawkesford House, he drew her into the sumptuous confines of the drawing room, shutting the double doors.

Elizabeth set down her sketch pad and folded her hands, gazing at him with cool expectation. "Well, Nicholas?"

Walking to the mantelpiece, he struggled to regain his fury toward Cicely; in light of the danger to Elizabeth that matter now seemed trivial.

"My sister has been making sketches from your anatomy book," he said. "Did she have your permission to do so?"

"I told her she could borrow any of my books, if that's what you mean."

Her offhand manner made him speak more bluntly. "Did you know she was drawing unclothed men?"

Elizabeth didn't look shocked in the least. "No, I didn't. But I must admire her initiative."

"Admire?" Anger leapt inside him. "I might have guessed *you* would see nothing wrong with such indecent behavior."

She laughed. "Oh, please, Nicholas. Surely you're not embarrassed by the human body!"

To his utter chagrin, he felt a dull heat rise from under his starched collar. Pivoting sharply, he paced the room. "That's neither here nor there. Praise God *I* caught Cicely, that her lascivious pictures weren't found by one of my aunt's friends."

Elizabeth continued to smile. "Are you saying Cicely would be shunned for drawing a man?"

"It isn't amusing. A few maliciously whispered words can taint a woman's reputation forever. It's hardly a practice I condone, but one we must all live with."

"But copying a picture out of a book? Imagine how the tongues would wag if people knew that in art school I studied anatomy by drawing naked male models!"

Nicholas hadn't thought Elizabeth could still shock him. Yet the image of her sitting in a classroom, casually sketching a man's private parts, staggered him. Her free-spirited upbringing had been so radically different from the rigid rules of his youth. How could they ever hope to find a middle ground?

Something in her face changed, a softening, a yearning. She bit her lip, then took a step toward him, fingers twisting in the loose folds of her trousers. "Nicholas, I know you'll think me bold . . . but I'd be dishonest if I didn't say you're far more attractive than any of those men were."

His body reacted with hot desire; his mind responded with cold anger. Her admiration both gratified and infuriated him. Only a fool would want a woman to scorn his good looks, but God! Couldn't she exhibit any regard for his character as well?

"We have a saying here in England," he said icily. " 'Save your breath to cool your porridge.' Don't bother suggesting again that I pose for one of your sculptures."

The light went out in her eyes, yet she held herself with a noble bearing. "Believe me, your lordship, I wouldn't dream of broaching that topic. I wouldn't want you to think I was fishing for a commission."

"Excellent. We're in agreement." He walked to the door and paused, assaulted by an uneasy memory. "By the way, if you're looking for your copy of *Gray's Anatomy*, I had Peebles burn it."

"Burn it!"

Staring at his lordly figure, Elizabeth stood riveted, too stunned to move. How could Nicholas stand there with such calm hauteur and announce he'd destroyed her property? Yet why was she surprised? It was precisely the sort of domineering tactic the earl took as his right.

Bitterly she said, "I suppose that's another example of governing my life, your lordship. And all because I can't ever react the way I'm supposed to."

His brooding gray eyes studied her. "I'll admit I was angry when I gave the order, but I'll still not have such material available to my sister. My secretary, Thistlewood, is out of town. When he returns, he'll reimburse you the cost of the book."

As the door slammed shut behind Nicholas, Elizabeth wilted into a brocaded armchair. She wondered if he even understood the significance of the burned book, that it symbolized his inability to accept her life, her dreams. If he'd been furious enough to incinerate such a minor detail, how he must despise her most precious vocation, her sculpting.

Perhaps she should leave Hawkesford House. Her heart plunged to her feet. Then the memory of Nicholas's concern for her safety bolstered her spirits. Somewhere inside him flickered a tiny flame of caring, a flame that drew her, a flame she longed to fan into an inferno. But how? If she were to act on her feelings, he'd be repelled by her forwardness.

Unable to resolve the dilemma, she fled to the conservatory. If she couldn't reach out to Nicholas, she could at least satisfy the restless yearning inside her. Working feverishly, she began winding sausages of clay around the armature. By gaslight night after night, she draped the wire until it assumed the rough proportions of a man.

On the third evening, Elizabeth stared wearily at the sculpture. The rugged contours resembled Nicholas, but how could she fill in the details? She could only guess at the shape of the leg muscles, the curve of the buttocks, the sinews of the arms.

Frowning, she turned her gaze to the deepening twilight. A flicker of movement at one of the windows caught her eye. Horror seized her heart. Pressed against the glass was a bristly face. A face with the features of a bulldog.

The man in the porkpie hat!

Chapter 14

The lantern cast a wavering circle of light over the darkened garden. The scent of roses perfumed the cool night air. Looking through the glass panes of the conservatory, Nicholas saw the shadowy tangle of camellia bushes rimming the center of the room, where the pale glow of gaslight illuminated the scattering of work tools and shrouded pedestals. Beside the fountain stood the rough sculpture of a man, the sculpture Elizabeth must have been working on only an hour ago, believing herself to be secure within the walls of Hawkesford House.

He imagined someone standing here, peering at her graceful figure, reveling in the knowledge that she was alone and vulnerable, plotting to creep inside and clamp
his crude hands around her swanlike neck. . . .

A nauseating mix of fear and anger choked Nicholas. Dropping to his haunches beside the policeman, he demanded, "Well? What do you think?"

Detective Inspector Mulvey motioned to Kipp, who stood gravely at attention. "Bring that lantern a mite closer."

The boy briskly obeyed. "Aye, guv'ner."

Mulvey scrutinized the pair of footprints embedded in the soft earth of the rose bed. "Hobnailed boots, your lordship." He glanced up, lamplight illuminating the spiderweb of veins on his face and the bulging eyes that reminded Nicholas of a trout. "Belonged to a

191

rather big man, or so I'd guess by the size of the prints."

"We already know that much," Nicholas said, hard-pressed to restrain his impatience. "After the first incident nearly a month ago, Miss Hastings sketched a likeness of the man. I, too, gave a concise description to your chief superintendent at Scotland Yard."

Mulvey's pale fish eyes lowered deferentially. "Ahem. Yes, your lordship. I recollect the episode."

"Shall we proceed with the investigation, then?" Nicholas surged to his feet, a thorn catching briefly at his trousers as he started down the crushed stone path. "The intruder went this way," he said, the inspector trotting to keep up. "One of my men found another footprint over there."

He pointed to an area beside a shadowy clump of boxwoods, and Kipp scurried ahead with the light.

"No one else saw the man?" Mulvey asked.

"He must have escaped in the time it took Miss Hastings to run to the dining room to fetch me. We searched the grounds immediately, but he was already gone."

"I see. Must've slipped through a gate, I'd guess."

"The gates were locked."

"Just takes one careless gardener—"

"I checked the locks myself," Nicholas said curtly. "Judging by the direction of that last footprint, the man likely climbed over the wall up ahead."

In a few quick strides he reached the shoulder-high stone wall which enclosed the formal gardens. Half running, the lantern swinging in his hand, Kipp drew alongside Nicholas. The swaying light briefly illuminated a small, dark lump beneath one of the rose bushes. Bending, Nicholas picked up a battered, flat-crowned hat with a turned-up brim.

"Here's something our trespasser dropped," he said, flipping the hat to Mulvey.

The inspector rotated it in his rawboned hands. "Porkpie hat, no distinguishing marks. Venture into Petticoat Lane or Seven Dials and you'll see a half a hundred of 'em in the space of an hour." He stuck the hat under his arm. "I'll take it along just the same. Evidence, you know."

Mulvey's casual attitude grated on Nicholas's nerves. "Your confidence overwhelms me," he said icily. "I trust you'll at least *try* to find the man."

"Oh, yes, your lordship," the inspector hastened to say. "Didn't mean we wouldn't do a systematic search. Just want you to know what we're up against. Hundreds of places to hide in them rookeries. Places even the police daren't go. Fine gentleman like yourself couldn't know about such rat holes—"

"I'm acquainted with the rookeries."

"Oh?" Mulvey's protuberant eyes stared for a moment, then dropped beneath Nicholas's glacial glare. "Ahem. Guess I'd best proceed, then. Need to question the others . . . if I might, your lordship?"

"Follow me."

Turning, Nicholas marched toward the house, Kipp trotting ahead to light the way. Without slowing, the boy swung his scrubbed face around. "You'll catch 'im, yer lordship, sir," he said, his brown eyes shining with worshipful trust.

He pulled open the massive door and Nicholas strode into the gaslit entrance hall. He wished to God he shared Kipp's confidence. His throat felt clogged with fury and frustration and fear. He hated this damned feeling of helplessness. He wanted to *do* something. Anything. To track down that blackguard and throttle him. To squeeze out the truth about who had hired him.

Fists clenched, emotions under rigid restraint, he walked into the drawing room, Mulvey following. Nicholas's eyes sought Elizabeth; she sat on the Queen Anne sofa between a white-faced Owen and a frowning Aunt Beatrice.

Elizabeth appeared calm but pale. She still wore a soiled apron over her blouse and voluminous trousers. In her hands she absently turned a ball of clay. When she saw Nicholas, a small smile bloomed on her lips.

With total neglect of logic, his insides went as soft as pudding. He recalled her frightened face as she'd burst into the dining room and rushed to him, her hands clinging to his, her eyes large with alarm, her words halting and breathless. A fierce thrill sped through Nicholas. In her moment of need, she had come to him. Dare he hope her actions bespoke trust in him? That deep inside, she thought of him as more than simply a model of physical perfection?

Lady Beatrice aimed a glare at Mulvey. "Have you apprehended that vile man?"

The inspector shifted, clearly ill at ease with both the luxurious setting and the wrath of a gentlewoman. "Not yet, m'lady. My sergeant is in the kitchen, questioning the servants. Checking for anyone who might've seen the man—"

"Indeed," Lady Beatrice said, her fine eyebrows arching. "Elizabeth saw the intruder. Or do you doubt her word?"

"Ahem. No, m'lady. But we mustn't leave any stone unturned. Somebody might've noticed something, a detail that could help in our search."

"Of course we'll cooperate with the police," Owen said. " 'The wicked flee when no man pursueth.' This cowardly devil must be brought to justice."

"Who might you be, sir?" asked Mulvey.

"Owen Hastings, Libby's father." He placed an arm around Elizabeth's shoulders.

"Were you also with the family when the incident occurred?" the inspector asked.

"No, I was upstairs in my room, reading."

Licking the lead of a stubby pencil, Mulvey jotted a note on his pad. "Did you see or hear anything unusual?"

Owen shook his head. "No, but by God above, if I could get my hands on the villain who would frighten my Libby so . . ."

He tightened his arm around her slim shoulders; Elizabeth tilted her head and smiled at him. Their closeness touched Nicholas's heart. Turning away, he went to a window and stared into the darkness. How could he ever convince Owen to tell her the truth? Yet Owen must tell her.

"My lord?"

Nicholas swung toward Mulvey. "Yes?"

"Was anyone else in the house at the time?" the inspector asked. "Anyone other than the servants?"

"My sister, Lady Cicely. She was at dinner with my aunt and me."

"And where might the lady be?"

"Upstairs." Nicholas recalled her vehement protests at being denied all the excitement, but he had no wish to involve her in this sordid matter. "I assure you, she cannot add anything to what we've already told you."

His flatly uncompromising tone must have convinced Mulvey, for the inspector focused his trout eyes on Elizabeth. "Miss Hastings, can you describe to me precisely what happened?"

"There isn't much to tell," she said slowly. "I was working in the conservatory. Something caught my eye . . . a movement at the window, I think. Then I looked over and saw him, peering at me." She shuddered visibly, fingernails digging into the ball of clay in her lap. "I recognized him immediately, of course. He was the same man who'd attacked me before."

"Before?" Aunt Beatrice echoed, gray eyes widening. Whipping her attention to the earl, she demanded, "What is going on here, Nicholas? Did you know of this other attempt?"

He gazed steadily at his aunt. "I was aware of it, yes."

"He saved my life," Elizabeth said softly. "It happened near Covent Garden, where my father and I used to live. That awful man in the porkpie hat tried to strangle me, but Nicholas rescued me just in time."

The admiration lighting her lavender eyes made Nicholas unreasonably warm. He told himself to look away, but couldn't tear his gaze from her. He felt like a callow youth, enraptured by a girl for the first time, unable to control his intense reaction.

Aunt Beatrice shifted shrewd eyes from Elizabeth to him. "Oh? I'm beginning to see," she said with a note of dryness. Directing a regal look at Mulvey, she said crisply, "Are you quite through with us, Inspector?"

"Yes, m'lady." He bent into an awkward, lumbering bow. "Thank you for your time."

"Come along, Elizabeth," Aunt Beatrice said, rising fluidly from the sofa. "Nicholas can handle the rest of this matter. You've had quite the fright."

"Yes, my lady," she murmured.

Like a dainty schooner trailing in the wake of an elegant yacht, Elizabeth followed Beatrice out the door. Elizabeth's preoccupied expression caught at Nicholas's heart. He wanted to go after her, to hold her close and soothe her fears. But the strictures of society and his own uncertainty denied him that satisfaction. Thank God his aunt had unbent enough to take Elizabeth in hand.

Mulvey shifted uncomfortably. "Ahem. Must run along now, your lordship. Got to check on my sergeant in the kitchen."

"I want that man found—and quickly," Nicholas stated, his glare pinning the inspector. "I'll take up this matter with the commissioner if necessary."

Mulvey's fish eyes bugged out further. "We'll do our best, your lordship. Indeed we will." Swinging around, the porkpie hat still jammed under his arm, he scurried out.

Owen cleared his throat. "I wish to thank you, your lordship," he said stiffly, "for taking such a personal interest in this case."

He stood by the sofa, his stocky shoulders rigid beneath the rough tweed coat, as if the words of gratitude did not come easily. In spite of his anger, Nicholas felt a grudging respect. The response annoyed him; he could not forget Owen's indirect role in this appalling turn of events.

"If I take a personal interest," Nicholas said coldly, "it's because I do not tolerate intruders trespassing on my land and threatening my guests."

Owen's hazel eyes clouded as he glanced away. "And rightly so, your lordship." Hesitating a mere fraction of a second, he added, "If you would excuse me, I shall retire now." Head bowed, he started toward the door.

"I know of Elizabeth's relation to the Duke of Rockborough," Nicholas said.

Owen froze. With the jerky movements of a puppet, he wheeled around. "I don't know what you mean," he said hoarsely.

"Don't you?" Nicholas walked toward Owen, eyes fixed on the older man's whitened, whiskered face. "My secretary, Thistlewood, has just returned from a fortnight's stay in Yorkshire. He unearthed quite an interesting old scandal."

Owen stared for a moment; then he crumpled into a chair, hands supporting his head. "So the duke coming here for tea wasn't happenstance."

"No. I wanted to see if he would recognize Elizabeth since she looks so much like her mother. Unfortunately she went out that afternoon."

"God forgive me," Owen choked out. "I dreaded this day. For so long, I hoped and prayed to somehow spare Libby. . . ."

Compassion stirred in Nicholas, a compassion he ruthlessly squelched. "Hoping and praying," he snapped, "will not alter the fact that someone is determined to kill her. She deserves to know why."

Owen raised his head, his eyes beseeching. "I meant to tell her when we arrived here in London. Truly I did. But when the time came, I couldn't bring myself to speak the words. Libby's always set such store on honesty. She'll never forgive me."

Giving vent to anger, Nicholas slammed his palm onto a rosewood side table. "Would you rather she died? Time and again she's placed herself in danger because she refuses to believe someone would want to hurt her."

"I'll take Libby away from here, then," Owen said wildly. "Home to New York, where she'll be safe. I should never have brought her back to England in the first place. Never!"

Cold fingers of dismay squeezed around Nicholas. God! How could he bear for Elizabeth to leave?

"The killer could follow her," he argued. "At least here Elizabeth has my protection. If she knew the truth, she could be on her guard until the culprit is apprehended."

Closing his eyes, Owen kneaded his forehead. The lines of worry deepened on his face, making him look years older. "I know you're right," he muttered. "But I'm so afraid to lose her . . . my precious daughter."

Reluctant sympathy welled within Nicholas. Yet first and foremost he must protect Elizabeth. "If you don't tell her," he said with quiet firmness, "I will."

Straightening his back, Owen raised bleak eyes to Nicholas. "All right, your lordship," he said heavily. "Tomorrow is my day off. I'll tell her the entire story first thing in the morning."

Elizabeth absently ran a finger over the polished Holland tiles of the mantelpiece. An embroidered fire screen concealed the grate; the cool summer night didn't require a coal blaze. Like the rest of the house, her bedroom had been designed with tasteful elegance. Exquisite plasterwork adorned the ceiling and magnolia satin draperies hung from the windows and four-poster bed. It seemed a sinful luxury to retire each evening to an immaculate room, to sleep on a mattress without lumps, to have a maid deliver warm bathwater each morning, to wear clothes of the finest quality.

But tonight Elizabeth felt too restless to take more than passing pleasure in her sumptuous surroundings.

Wandering to a window, she parted the curtains and peered into the darkness. Was that hideous man out there somewhere? Hiding in the shadows, staring up at her room, biding his time until everyone slept? Planning to steal inside the house and come searching for her?

Horrified, she remembered the brawny fingers

closed around her neck, cutting off her air, the pain searing her lungs, the tide of darkness rushing over her. . . .

She drew back sharply. Hands shaking, Elizabeth tugged the draperies shut and took a deep breath to quiet her racing heart. It was absurd let her imagination run wild. Nicholas would make certain the house was locked and guarded. He would keep her safe.

Dear God. Nicholas had been right from the start. No longer could she believe those other incidents had been unfortunate coincidences: the hansom cab nearly running her down, that man trying to strangle her, her lodgings ransacked. Incredible as it seemed, someone wished to kill her.

But why? *Why?*

Clutching the sterling ring as a talisman, she paced the soft Axminster carpet, her white lawn nightdress swishing around her ankles. Nicholas had warned her to stay close to home, that the throttling incident had been no chance encounter.

Perhaps you should ask your father about that.

Nicholas's cryptic statement in the park came back to haunt her. At the time she'd let him distract her, sure he'd only been making groundless talk to keep her from disobeying him. Now she knew her mistake. But what could her father possibly know about that disgusting man in the porkpie hat? Papa never kept secrets from her—

A crash of glass came from the next room; her father must have dropped something. Tossing a white cambric wrapper over her nightdress, Elizabeth tied the lace sash and then tapped on the adjoining door.

After a long moment she knocked again. The door opened and Owen Hastings stood framed against the yellow gaslight. He'd discarded his coat and rolled up his shirt sleeves.

"Yes, Libby?"

"I'd like to talk with you, Papa."

His eyes slid away from hers. "Can't it wait until morning?"

He sounded so unwelcoming, so unlike himself. Curious . . . after that frightening incident in the conservatory, she had expected him to be anxious to offer solace.

The scent of rye whiskey drifted to her. Peering past him, she saw on the jade marble hearth the splintered remains of a decanter lying in a pool of amber liquid.

"Papa! You've been drinking again."

"Just a nip," he said, but he didn't meet her eyes.

The despondency she sensed in him aroused a twist of compassion. Not since he'd gotten his post at the Garforths had she seen him touch alcohol. Determined to comfort her father, she slipped into the bedroom.

"What's wrong?" she murmured. "Have you been thinking about Mama again?"

He followed slowly and sank into an armchair, burying his face in his hands. "Yes," he said, his words muffled, "I suppose I have."

Saddened, Elizabeth gazed at his bowed, despairing figure. Nine months had passed since the death of Lucy Templeton Hastings, yet grief still overwhelmed him. Elizabeth's own sorrow ached within her, but the passage of time had dulled the pain. She tried to imagine the loss of a beloved mate after so many happy years of marriage. How would she feel if she were to never again see Nicholas? A wintry wave of distress iced her insides.

Kneeling, she hugged her father. For an instant his back felt rigid beneath her fingers. Then he uttered a hoarse cry and his arms went around her, drawing her fiercely against him. His faint scent of rye whiskey surrounded her like a comforting blanket.

"I love you, Libby," he whispered. "I don't ever want you to forget that."

Elizabeth drew back and smiled, surveying his familiar hazel eyes, the unhappy grooves on his whiskered face. "Of course I won't forget," she chided softly. "I love you, too."

Owen gripped her hands tightly. "'Where your treasure is, there will your heart be also,'" he quoted.

"You're my treasure, Libby, all I have left of your mother. I couldn't bear to lose you, too."

"You won't, Papa." His melancholy mood troubled her. Giving his hand a reassuring pat, she straightened. "I came in here to talk about what happened tonight. That man must have tracked me here somehow. It sounds absurd, but Nicholas said you might know something."

Her father regarded her with a strange, alarmed look; then he shot from the chair and paced the bedroom. "I don't know his name, if that's what you mean."

His agitated manner disturbed Elizabeth. "What's bothering you, Papa? From both you and Nicholas, I get the impression something is going on that I don't know about."

"I'm sorry, Libby," Owen said, the words sounding dragged from his lips. "I'd planned to tell you all about it in the morning."

"All about what?"

Hands balled into fists, he swung to face her, the harsh glow from a twin-globed gas lamp throwing his craggy face into sharp relief. He sucked in a breath, then said quietly, "I'm not your natural father, Libby."

Sure she'd misheard him, Elizabeth blinked in bewilderment. "What are you saying?"

"Before we were married, your mother was companion to the Duchess of Rockborough. The duke seduced Lucy, and you are the result of that brief union."

Elizabeth stood absolutely still, unable to credit his shocking statement, unable to think past a fog of disbelief. Her mouth felt like parched clay. "This can't be true. It can't be."

"It is, Libby. I wish to heaven it weren't so. . . ."

"Why didn't Mama ever say anything?"

"Because she wanted to forget the past, to leave behind the heartache she'd found in England."

"The . . . affair she'd had?"

Owen nodded. "When His Grace learned of Lucy's pregnancy, he set her up in her own household. And when you were born, he acted the proud father, even gave Lucy that ring you always wear."

Elizabeth numbly touched the lump beneath her cambric wrapper, the sterling silver ring hanging from its chain. "This belonged to my..." She faltered, the word "father" sticking in her throat.

Owen's lips curled into a sneer. "To your blood father, who pretended to care so much about you, until the duchess presented him with a son and heir. Then the duke dismissed you in favor of his legitimate child. He no longer had a place in his life for a two-year-old girl born on the wrong side of the blanket."

"And you?" Elizabeth whispered. "How did you become my father?"

"I was the vicar at a nearby church...and I loved both Lucy and you with all my heart." Owen's expression softened for an instant, as if he were recalling some deep, abiding emotion; then his stony look returned. "When I saw how Lucy had been hurt, I convinced her to marry me, to start a new life in America, where the duke couldn't track you down and take you away. That's just the sort of depraved thing he'd do."

Swallowing a nauseating knot of pain, Elizabeth tried to convince herself the story was fabricated, a fairytale like the ones he used to tell her at bedtime. Yet it would explain so much...Owen's moodiness, his hatred of the nobility.

"But you did bring me back to England."

Owen nodded gloomily. "On her deathbed Lucy made me vow to do so. She was so proud of your artistic talent, but we lacked the money and the connections to help you. She had a wild notion the duke would act as your patron.

"I told her it was useless, that His high-and-mighty Grace of Rockborough didn't care a fig about you. But she was adamant and so I promised her. When we arrived in London, I felt honor bound to post a letter to the duke, arranging a meeting." His eyes were brilliant with tears. "But I couldn't go to the meeting, Libby. I couldn't hand you back to that rotten scoundrel."

Staring at Owen, she tried to reconcile his familiar image with the stranger who had shaken her belief in her own identity and in his honesty. Something inside Elizabeth shifted, shattering her life like an earthquake and leaving an agonizing emptiness within her breast.

"How could you have lied to me for so long?" she choked out.

"I was afraid, Libby," he said in a low voice. "Afraid I'd lose my only daughter."

"But you suspected my relationship to this duke had something to do with these attempts on my life."

"I've been afraid of that, yes. It was only after I wrote to the duke that someone tried to kill you. The duke would have known where we were living because the address was on my letter. That's why I agreed to move in here with Lord Nicholas, to keep you safe—"

"Keep me safe!" Uttering a cry of disbelief, she shook her head slowly, trying to think past the haze of hurt. "A man tried to *kill* me and you never once warned me it had to do with my past. I thought you always did the right thing, like the perfect father—" Her voice caught on the bitterness in her throat. "I considered you to be a great man."

"'Great men are not always wise.'" Hands outstretched, Owen took a step closer. "Can you ever forgive me, Libby? As God is my witness, everything I did, I did out of love for you."

"Out of love for me?" she said, her voice ragged with doubt. "Or out of hatred of my true father?"

"Never mind that villain. The duke doesn't matter . . . he doesn't care about you, not the way I do."

Owen walked toward her, his steps tentative, his eyes imploring her understanding. Elizabeth stiffened; she couldn't forgive him, not yet. The wound inside her was too raw. . . .

"I need time to think," she whispered. Pivoting, she fled to the sanctuary of her bedroom and slammed the door.

Pressing her flushed cheek against the cool wall, she ignored her father's knocking. No, she corrected herself, Owen Hastings was not her father. She no longer knew what to call him.

The rapping ceased abruptly. Only the rasp of her breathing disturbed the silence. Her heart felt like a throbbing ball of pain. The gaslit room blurred before her eyes. Feeling the splash of hot moisture on her hand, Elizabeth looked down, uncomprehending, until she realized she was crying.

Her fingers lifted to the ring; it hung like a leaden weight around her neck. Her real father had once owned the ring, not her grandfather, as Mama had told her. Dear God! Even her own mother had lied to her.

Elizabeth felt lacerated, her emotions cut to the bone. In the space of a few words, the image of her beloved father had altered; the memory of her perfect mother had changed. If she could no longer believe in her parents, who *could* she trust?

Nicholas.

Half stumbling in her haste, she darted across the bedroom and wrenched open the door into the hall.

Chapter 15

Nicholas sat before the Hepplewhite rolltop desk in his bedroom. Flicking back the sleeve of his burgundy silk dressing gown, he concentrated on checking the production figures for his farmland in Sussex and meticulously reckoning each sum on the list. Over the scratching of the fountain pen, he could hear Quinn tidying the dressing room, the clothes being brushed, the boots being polished. Normally the familiar sounds of the valet's movements blended into the background. Tonight they grated on his nerves.

The image of Elizabeth's gypsy beauty intruded as well. Instead of numbers, Nicholas kept seeing the terrified lavender of her eyes, the trembling curve of her lips, the milky paleness of her complexion. Tonight's incident had brought home to him how precious she had become. He wanted to hold her close and keep her safe. How fulfilling it would be to find her waiting and willing in his bed each night.

But that wasn't what Elizabeth wanted, Nicholas bitterly reminded himself. The vow he'd overheard her say weeks earlier echoed in his mind: *I intend to devote my life to art . . . I've no time for a husband and children.*

Subduing a wave of deep desolation, he forced his attention to the ledger before him. When he'd added the same column three times and arrived at three different sums, Nicholas flung down the pen in disgust. He couldn't work, he couldn't sleep, he couldn't do anything but dream about an unconventional sculptress who wouldn't spare the time to fall in love with a besotted English earl.

Thrusting back his mahogany armchair, he got up and stalked to a marble-topped side table. Crystal clinked as he splashed brandy from a decanter into a glass. As he took a swallow, Quinn appeared in the doorway.

"Your pardon, my lord. Shall you be requiring my services any further tonight?"

"That will be all."

Bowing, the valet departed, the door closing quietly.

Silence hung heavy around Nicholas. Draining the brandy glass, he set it down sharply. He went to a window and parted the curtain to stare moodily outside. Clouds drifted over the sliver of moon and the scattering of stars. The gardens lay in an abyss of shadows. He half hoped the cutthroat would sneak back tonight, for Dobson and Pickering were armed and patrolling the grounds.

Nicholas yanked tight the sash of his dressing gown, wishing it were that villain's neck. By God, if the police failed to work fast, he'd have to take further steps, perhaps confront the duke and his family. He must be damned careful, though, because he might end up frightening the would-be killer into taking rash action, action that could have dire consequences to Elizabeth.

Tomorrow morning Owen would tell her the truth. Leaning against the window frame, Nicholas wondered how she would react when she learned her beloved father was not her blood kin after all. It was difficult to imagine; Nicholas's own father, the fourth earl, had been a cold and reserved man, hardly the model of a loving parent. His death ten years earlier had been a somber experience, but more like the passing of a distant relative. The sadness had receded quickly as Nicholas had shouldered the myriad duties of the earldom.

What if Elizabeth hated him for instigating the confession? The possibility struck him with the force of a blow. Would she leave here, never want to see him again? No, he wouldn't let her go. He couldn't. He was committed to preserving her safety. She didn't yet know it, but his heart was committed as well.

A sudden rapping on the door invaded the painful thoughts. No one in the household disturbed him once he'd retired. Unless one of the footmen had seen something outside . . .

Nicholas hastened across the plush Persian rug and yanked open the door. To his utter surprise, Elizabeth stood there, her fragile figure limned by the low-lit gas jets in the hall. With a glance he took in her appearance, the charmingly feminine curves revealed by her lace and cambric robe, the hair tumbling to her hips in gleaming, jet black waves. Her face arrested his attention. Her eyes were great pools of sorrow, tears dampening her long inky lashes. His blood chilled with shock and warmed with compassion. *She knew.*

"Nicholas, I need . . . to speak to you."

Her voice was hesitant, quavering. Emotion stormed his better judgment. He reached out to her, drew her to his side, unable to stop himself from tunneling a hand into the heavy silk of her hair. He shoved the door shut as Elizabeth burrowed her face against his chest and wept, her body trembling. Nicholas felt helpless to comfort her. The only feminine crying he'd encountered before had been the childhood tantrums of Cicely and the crocodile tears of a jilted paramour. Elizabeth's grief evoked a melting tenderness, a profound sympathy.

"It's all right," he murmured, gently stroking her hair. "I'm here, love . . . I'm here."

He didn't know what else to say. How could mere platitudes ease her pain? Because she was always so strong, her vulnerability moved him deeply. Bending his head, he kissed the sweet-scented crown of her hair. At least she had come to him. The knowledge chased the darkness from his spirit. It was a beginning, the first step in winning her love.

It seemed the most natural move in the world to draw her to a wing chair by the hearth, to nestle her small body in his lap, to tuck her face into the cradle of his shoulder. The curve of her waist scorched his palm and her herbal aroma entranced him. His heart ached with the need to console her; his loins burned with the desire to possess her.

He slid his hand upward, over her arm, feeling muscles that were dainty yet firm beneath her smooth cambric sleeve. Unspoken love words crowded his throat... words he clamped his lips tight against voicing. Taking half-guilty joy in holding her close, he listened to her sobs, wanting to absorb her pain and resisting the powerful urge to touch her breasts. By God, he should protect her, not take advantage of her weakened state.

Her hair rippled loose over her shoulders. Moving his hand beneath the heavy curtain, he gently massaged her nape until her weeping lessened. Elizabeth shifted in his lap, her thigh brushing his groin. Fire shot through his veins. Lifting her head, she gazed at him with eyes like misty lavender blue velvet.

"You know about my—" Her voice broke and she wiped her wet cheeks with the sash of her robe. "About Owen, don't you?"

"Yes," Nicholas admitted quietly.

"I've lost him. I haven't a father anymore."

Compassion tightened his chest. "That's not true," he said, sweeping a stray tear from her lashes. "Owen is as much your father as he ever was."

Like a kitten seeking affection, she pressed her cheek into his palm. "Then why do I feel so numb, so lost?"

"Give yourself time, love," he murmured, stroking the satin skin of her face. "As soon as the shock passes, you'll see that he meant only the best for you." Recalling his own father, Nicholas added, "Owen's been a far more loving parent than most."

"I know that in my mind, but somehow I can't feel it here." Clasping his hand, she pressed it to her heart.

Their eyes locked; his longing leapt. Beneath his palm, Nicholas felt the beating of her heart. Did the pace quicken, or was it only a trick of his fancy? When

Elizabeth lowered her gaze, he reluctantly drew his hand away.

"I've soaked your lapel," she said, touching a dampened spot on his dressing gown.

Winding unsteady fingers into the hair at her temple, he said, "It'll dry."

"I didn't mean to pour all my troubles on you."

Soft as the sweep of a feather, tenderness touched him. "I'm glad you came to me, Elizabeth. I hope you'll always feel you can turn to me."

Her lips parted; she seemed about to speak. His pulse pounded with hope. Would she finally admit her need for him was emotional as well as physical? To his immense disappointment she glanced away and withdrew her hand. A faint flush tinted her cheeks; if it hadn't been absurd he would have thought her gripped by shyness. But timidity was not a trait he associated with Elizabeth Hastings.

After a moment she cautiously met his gaze. "You've known about my past for a long time," she said. "That's why you invited the duke to tea, why you've been warning me to be careful."

To his relief she didn't seem angry at his interference. Absently he ran his thumb along the inside of her wrist. "Yes."

"How did you find out?"

"I traced your ring through the coat of arms."

"The sterling swan," she murmured, drawing the silver chain from beneath her nightdress. Cradling the ring in her palm, she touched the crest with the tip of one finger. "I've always thought of this as my trademark, my talisman." Her eyes grew bitter and sad; the ring slipped from her hand and nestled in the valley between her breasts. "But it certainly hasn't brought me much luck, has it?"

"Most people would be thrilled to learn of a connection to the nobility."

Her dainty brows drew into a frown. "But someone's been trying to kill me. Who? Who was that awful man peering in the window at me?"

"A hired minion, no doubt." Nicholas tensed with anger. "If only I'd caught him, I would have found out who's paying him, you can be sure of that."

"But why would anyone want me dead?"

"Both of the duke's sons died in childhood. That makes you his only surviving offspring. Should he choose to acknowledge your relationship, you stand to inherit a great deal of wealth."

"But I'm only his bastard."

Her voice was low and raw with pain. Helpless to soothe her distress, Nicholas burrowed his fingers into her hair. "It's not uncommon for a man to endow a child born out of wedlock."

She shook her head, the cloud of coal-black hair brushing the back of his hand. "I would never ask this duke for anything. I've always made my own way in the world."

"It isn't a question of asking. He may decide to recognize you in his will regardless of your wishes."

"But I don't want him to—especially not if his present heirs would murder me over the matter." Determination firmed her chin. "I shall inform the duke that I will refuse any inheritance. Then they'll leave me in peace."

Tender humor flooded Nicholas. "You really are as rare as that maverick camellia bloom," he murmured, unable to resist sliding his hand down to the swell of her hip. "You never react the way you're supposed to."

Elizabeth went taut in his arms. A parade of emotions flitted across her features: dismay, longing, remorse. "Oh, Nicholas," she said on a sigh. "I wish I could be the lady you want me to be, but I wonder if you and I will ever find a common ground."

His amusement evaporated. "Don't say that."

He spoke gruffly, unwilling to believe her, unwilling to imagine a future without her. He was intensely aware of the closeness of their bodies and the rising heat of his desire. His hand rubbed circles at the base of her spine. Her lashes dipped slightly as she relaxed against him. She was slender and soft, very much a woman. It had been madness to hold her in his lap. Madness to invite her into his room, when the quiet night bestowed them with time and opportunity. And yet...her uptilted face invited his kiss, a kiss he wanted with savage desperation.

A flood tide of desire swept away his scruples; the knot of emotion inside him loosened. He kissed her with all the raw passion churning in his heart and burning in his loins. She quivered, her body yielding, arching to him. Her fervid response was both knowing and naive. Demanding more, his mouth slanted over hers, delving deeper, bending her against his arm.

He shaped his hand to the curve of her breast; her softness filled his palm to perfection. His thumb circled the peak, its arousal apparent despite the sheltering cambric robe. Her purr of delight brought a surge of exultation to him. He wanted to please her, to make this kiss a mere prelude, to release all the powerful emotions wracking his body. Lifting his head, he gazed into her eyes, searching for doubt, for some sign of reluctance. He saw only an open ardor, a willing warmth.

Yet he could not forget that Elizabeth had no room in her life for his child. The knowledge cut deeply into him; resolutely he buried the pain. If he were a discreet and careful lover, pregnancy need not compromise her plans.

"I want you, Elizabeth," he said quietly. "I want to make love to you. Now."

His declaration ignited a flame of joy inside Elizabeth. Could it be true Nicholas felt the same as she? She longed to believe him and yet...

Unsteadily she said, "You told me once that you had too much honor to take advantage of my innocence."

"And you told me to be honest about my feelings." Lifting her hand, he kissed the delicate skin of her wrist, then the work-roughened calluses of her fingers. "I'm doing that now, Elizabeth." His voice lowered to a husky murmur. "I love you."

Sincerity blazed in his eyes; no longer did he wear an expression of cool composure. Her ravaged spirit felt whole again, restored and ready to give. Words seemed inadequate to express her feelings; she wanted to tender her body into his skilled hands and her heart into his cherished keeping.

"Nicholas, I love you, too. Without you I feel incomplete."

His arms tightened convulsively; then he reached around to her nape to unclasp the sterling chain, letting the ring fall with a metallic clatter onto a side table. "We shan't have this between us." He parted her wrapper and began to unbutton her nightdress. "Tonight you'll wear nothing at all."

The erotic promise made Elizabeth quake. She, too, wanted to forget the past, to forget everything but this precious night. In the shadows cast by the gas lamp his hair looked almost black, yet his eyes gleamed like sterling silver. Lowering her gaze, she watched him work at the row of tiny buttons. He muttered a curse as the last one snagged in the fine lace. The cambric whispered as he drew back the folds of cloth, exposing her breasts to the cool air.

Wrapped in the seductive quiet and the intensity of his eyes, she sat still in his lap, her heart tripping, her desire mounting. Then the heat of his hand covered her breast. Pleasure lapped within her as she saw the duskiness of his skin against her milky paleness, felt the texture of his palm graze her soft rounded flesh. His head descended, his mouth closing over her breast, his tongue washing the nipple. The voluptuous sensation astounded her. Uttering a low velvety sound deep in her throat, she arched to him and twined her fingers in the dense dark strands of his hair.

His hand dipped past the cloth bunched about her rib cage, seeking the flare of her hips, the beauty of her thighs. His lips still provoking her breast, he glided his fingers over her robe-clad abdomen, settling possessively at the valley between her legs. A delicious urgency unfurled within her; Elizabeth moved restlessly, impatient for something she sensed only he could give her.

Grasping her waist, he swung her onto her feet. The gaslight etched stark shadows across the perfection of his face.

"Nicholas . . . ?" she said in a confused protest.

"Patience, love," came his soft reply, his eyes equally soft. "I want to look at you."

His hand gave a swift tug; her nightdress and wrapper dropped to the floor, baring her body. A shocking thrill flashed through Elizabeth. She held her breath as his warm hands surged up, thumbs turned inward to graze the globes of her breasts, before moving downward again, passing over her waist to brush the silken black tuft above her thighs. His eyes followed the same path, lingered a long moment, then lifted to her face.

"You're everything I've ever wanted." Nicholas drew her onto his lap again, anointing her face with kisses. "Let me make you mine . . . it'll be perfect, I promise you that."

Sighing in satisfaction, Elizabeth snuggled her cheek against his lapel. "How could anything be more perfect than this?"

A chuckle vibrated in his chest. "My sweet little artist, I intend to show you things you could never learn from one of your anatomy books."

His mouth subjected her to a lengthy, luxurious kiss that left her giddy, delirious for more. She slipped her palms inside his dressing gown. How broad his shoulders were, how solid and smooth. His skin felt warm and alive, contoured by hard muscles and crisp hair.

His hand skimmed over her breasts on a slow descent to her belly, then moved in maddening circles over her hips and legs. When his touch drifted to the soft fleece between her legs, a pulsing grew within her body, a quivering expectation. His eyes smoldering, Nicholas smiled at her in the instant before his finger slid into her sleek satin depths.

His hand began a rhythmic stroking that made her muscles contract. She drew in a sharp breath, tilting her head back against his arm as she abandoned herself to the irresistible pull of excitement. In all her artistic study of the body, she had never dreamed a man's touch could create such compelling sensations, that she could feel so drugged with passion. His mouth adored her temples, her throat, her breasts as the lazy, measured movements of his fingers drove her wild. Panting whimpers clogged her throat. She writhed in his lap, unable to get enough, unable to satisfy the ache leaping inside her.

Frantic for something she could not define, she heard his low urgent voice caressing her like rough velvet. "Give yourself to me, Elizabeth . . . give me everything . . . I want you . . . I love you."

Hot chills wracked her limbs; blissful spasms flooded her belly. She cried out his name, her entire being focused on the rapturous waves breaking within her. The shuddering delight slowly ebbed, leaving her limp and stunned. When she lifted her lashes, Nicholas was gazing down at her, his eyes aglow, his mouth tilted into a crooked smile.

"I'm glad you liked that," he said, his usual clipped speech blurred and raspy. "Because there's more to come."

Feeling the tension in his enfolding arms, seeing the rapid rise and fall of his chest, Elizabeth felt a blush sear her cheeks. Of course, his own passion must still be unslaked. In her utter naiveté, she had succumbed to the exquisite joy and neglected to give him any in return.

"I . . . I'm sorry, Nicholas," she said, sitting straight in his lap and laying a hand on his cheek in apology. "I didn't mean to be so selfish, so—"

His kiss silenced her. Her head swam and her heart soared. Against her lips, he murmured, "I wanted you to be selfish, Elizabeth. I take pleasure in your pleasure."

His words touched a place deep inside her. Pressing her palms to his chest, she said, "I want to give to you as you've given to me."

His smile deepened. "Then move your hands a bit lower, love."

Elizabeth willingly obeyed, her palms coasting downward over hot skin sheened with sweat. The barrier of his sash halted her descent; her fingers fumbled with the tie and parted the garment. With the appreciation of an artist and the admiration of a woman, she let her gaze wander over his shoulders and chest. Nicholas was a model of masculinity . . . perfection of form, symmetry of shape.

She shifted on his steely thighs to give herself room to trace the tapering leanness of his waist, the flat muscles of his abdomen, the center ribbon of hair that led downward to his groin. She halted there, her eyes widening. His male part was full and erect, magnificent beyond any she had glimpsed in a textbook or classroom.

Consumed with curiosity, she tentatively touched him; the heat and hardness startled her, making her snatch back her hand. Her pulse surged and her gaze leapt to his face. "You're so large."

His husky chuckle warmed her. "Only because I want you so very much."

Her loosened mass of hair brushed her shoulders as Elizabeth's eyes were inexorably drawn downward. Entranced, she curled her fingers around him; he more than filled her hand. Experimentally she stroked him as he had stroked her.

He sucked in a harsh breath. His eyes squeezed shut and his head tipped back against the chair, exposing the strong column of his throat. "Ah . . . Elizabeth . . ."

His voice was hoarse and his fingers pressed into her thigh. His ardent response told her more than words could ever express, that the powerful Earl of Hawkesford had placed himself, body and soul, into her hands. He wanted her, needed her, loved her. In a glorious rush, tenderness flowed into her heart and desire into her loins. Still caressing him, she kissed the damp warm skin of his chest.

Abruptly he snared her wrist in his long fingers. She

saw him take a deep breath, felt his muscles strain, as if he were striving to regain control. "I do believe," he said unsteadily, "that it's time we moved to the bed."

Scooping her into his arms, he carried her to the four-poster and laid her down on the cool coverlet. She had a dizzying glimpse of a massive headboard and sapphire satin hangings, then her gaze focused on Nicholas removing his burgundy robe. Gaslight bathed his body, naked as Adam in paradise, all sculpted male grace and hot blatant need.

Bending over her, he tucked the dressing gown beneath her. "What are you doing?" she asked.

He brushed a kiss against her shoulder. "A woman bleeds a little her first time. I'll not have the housemaids speculating that you shared my bed."

Elizabeth felt both pleased by his protectiveness and exasperated by his misplaced sense of propriety. "I don't care who knows. I'm not ashamed of our love."

"Neither am I," he growled. "Yet I'll not hear your good name bandied about."

She meant to voice the hurtful notion that sprang into her mind, to ask if he meant to cloak their relationship in secrecy. But his body came down on hers and all lucid thought spun away. The weight of him felt solid and right. His smooth hard flesh slid over her, his furred chest deliciously abrading her nipples, the heavy heat of his maleness pressing into her thigh.

Lowering his head, he suckled her breast. The erotic ache he had assuaged earlier built with irreversible force. Her breath emerged in quick puffs as she ran her hands down his muscled arms and across his back. Their lips met in a long impassioned kiss, a kiss that tasted of brandy and Nicholas and wonders to come. She arched her hips, seeking to ease the sweet agony inside her.

His leg nudged her thighs wider. Feeling the hot tip of him probing her softness, she strained upward and felt the plunging pressure of his entry and a burning flash of pain. Her muscles stiffened in reflex; she uttered a cry more of surprise than discomfort.

Nicholas went still, his breathing swift and harsh in her ear. "Forgive me," he muttered, stroking her hair. "I didn't mean to be so rough . . . I've wanted you for so long . . . too long."

Her throat tightened. The feel of him embedded within her body made the vestiges of pain dissolve into a wondrous sensation of fullness. "I've longed for this, too," she said softly. "To be in your arms, sharing your bed, receiving your love."

Her words washed over Nicholas in a warm wave. Easing more deeply into her, he gazed down at her, watching for a sign of pain. Her face was flushed and radiant. Her body enclosed him like a satiny fist, unbelievably perfect and supremely right. As he moved slowly within her, her eyes grew slumbrous, her lips parted, her fingers splayed over his back.

When her hips lifted to meet his thrusts, he teetered on the edge of exploding. He fought desperately to restrain his ardor, wanting her pleasure before his, and his limbs shook with the effort of holding back.

Her black hair spilled in a glorious tangle over the white linen pillow. He nestled his lips there, chanting love words, strewing kisses over the salt-tanged skin of her temples and throat. Their bodies rocked together in harmony, the tempo ever rising. He felt a convulsive shudder run through her; she clutched at his shoulders, her head moving back and forth on the pillow. The breath left her lungs in a low moan of fulfillment and the throaty whisper of his name.

Fierce joy surged in Nicholas. He felt himself swell and throb with the relentless approach of his own climax. The moment to withdraw had come. Yet still he delved into her, unable to stop himself, unable to part from her. A primal urge washed over him, the urge to bind her to him with the essence of life. It was more potent than his resolution, more powerful than his will. They were man and woman, one body and soul united in an age-old act of creation. Crying out her name in ecstasy, he poured his seed into her fertile womb.

His breath came in searing gusts. His heart pounded

in exhausted passion. His weight settled over her small body.

Only then did Nicholas realize what he'd done: he, who had always approached life with logic, had lost control of all reason. He felt shaken to the core. He'd acted dishonorably, exposing Elizabeth to an unconscionable risk. In his mind he saw the vivid image of her body blossoming with his child. Yet when he searched himself for remorse, he found only a deep, abiding satisfaction.

Sighing, she stirred beneath him. He shifted slightly, pillowing her head on his shoulder, shaping her silken body to his long length. "Precious, precious Elizabeth," he murmured into her hair.

Against his throat, he felt her smile. "I used to think you were cold and haughty," she said.

"And now?"

She tilted her face to gaze at him, a saucy sparkle in her eyes. "I believe, my lord, that beneath all that noble arrogance beats the heart of a lusty peasant."

He laughed, his hand sliding down skin as smooth and flawless as a camellia bloom. "My words come back to haunt me."

"As well they should," she retorted. "You ought to have let me become your mistress weeks ago. Think of all the time we've wasted."

His heart chilled. *Mistress:* that was the role of her choice. So often lately, he'd thought about marrying her. Their lovemaking had solidified his feelings on the matter, made him certain he wanted Elizabeth as his wife, to share his life and bear his children.

Doubts choked him. Would she be content with an affair if she truly loved him? Was her interest in him more physical than emotional?

She frowned, her lovely eyes full of concern. "Nicholas? What's wrong?"

Suddenly he didn't want reality to intrude on the magic of this night. Tomorrow was soon enough to discuss the future.

"I was thinking," he said huskily, his fingers drifting

along the curve of her breast, "about how much I love you, and there's nothing wrong in that."

Her breath came out on a sigh, a sound he captured with his lips. They touched, kissed, caressed. The world dissolved into a perfect blend of emotion and sensation. Sure and strong, he pressed her against the bed. Like a camellia bud unfurling its petals to the sun, she opened for him, soft and moist and ready. They came together once more, in a sweet, surging rhythm that sent him soaring to the heavens, that set her crying out his name.

The aftermath left him drowsy with contentment. Elizabeth uttered a serene purr as she molded herself to the hard curve of his body. The glow of the gas lamp enclosed them in a private island, a place of beauty and softness. From somewhere intruded the faint sound of a clock chiming the hour of three. Nicholas felt a reluctant stirring of duty. Soon he must escort her back to her own room. At dawn the servants would be up and about, and he would not take the chance of anyone seeing Elizabeth leaving his quarters. Her reputation was more important than his own pleasure.

There was no need to hurry yet, though.

He drew in a breath of air scented with the musk of their lovemaking and the entrancing essence of Elizabeth. Her eyes were closed, her breasts lifting and falling in slow rhythm. He watched, fascinated. He had never seen a woman sleep before, had never before felt any inclination to linger after fulfilling his physical needs. Now he ached to remain entangled in Elizabeth's arms, meshed with every part of her life.

Closing his eyes, he rested his cheek against the silken strands of her hair. A boundless sense of well-being enfolded him. No harm could come of indulging himself for a few more moments.

Chapter 16

Elizabeth awoke to the pearl gray of dawn. With sleepy eyes, she blinked up at the sapphire bed hangings; her leg brushed against something firm and warm. *Nicholas.*

The fine linen bed sheets whispered as she turned to gaze lovingly at him. He slept on his back, one arm flung across the pillow, the other at his side. Watery light seeped through a chink in the curtains to wash him in silver. His rich brown hair lay in charming disarray, his cheeks sculpted in shadow by the bristly growth of beard. He looked as imposing in slumber as he did awake. Yet his sternly classical features were gentled by the same dreamy quality she had seen in him last night, a softening that made her wonder if he, too, had undergone the same mystical change she felt deep within herself, the feeling that her life had shifted onto a new course.

A welter of emotions awakened inside her. She felt an excitement akin to starting a new sculpture and speculating how the finished piece would look. She also felt uncertain and scared, uncertain of where to go from here and scared at her inability to see the pattern of her future.

How much of the change could she attribute to Nicholas and how much to the shocking revelation Owen had thrust upon her?

Restless, Elizabeth slipped out of bed, and burgundy silk slithered to the opulent blue rug. Picking up Nicholas's robe, she noted the small darkened spot of blood. Strange how people carried on so about a woman losing her virginity. She didn't feel she'd lost anything, but gained something precious.

She clutched the dressing gown to her bare breasts. Did Nicholas really mean to hide their relationship beneath a cloak of propriety? The possibility troubled her. Though she didn't wish to flaunt their intimacy, she felt proud of their love, proud enough not to care about the whisperings of a few busybodies.

Obeying impulse, she slipped on the robe; the garment was ridiculously large, the hem brushing the floor. She tied the fringed sash around her waist and folded back the sleeves. The silk embraced her like a lover, its faint masculine aroma reminding her of Nicholas.

Turning to the bed, Elizabeth's eyes absorbed the splendor of his naked body. He said he loved her. Those cherished words shimmered in her mind like newly cast bronze. His image was sketched upon her soul; now the urge to duplicate his beauty on paper burned inside her, stronger than ever before.

In glancing around for paper and pencil, she spied a gold-framed photograph on a table. Curiosity made her step closer and pick up the picture. A stiff-looking older man stared balefully at her; at his side stood a prim, pretty lady. Nicholas's parents, no doubt. In their faces she could see echoes of Nicholas, the noble hauteur of his father, the fine features of his mother. Sympathy tugged at Elizabeth. From the little she knew of his childhood, he had been raised by nannies and then shipped off to the stern taskmasters of boarding school. Her upbringing had been radically different, nurtured by two loving parents. . . .

With a pang, she remembered Owen telling her tales at bedtime, cuddling her close during a thunderstorm, admiring her first attempts at art. Her heart felt torn between pain and understanding. *Give yourself time.* Nicholas's advice comforted her.

She set down the picture and resumed her search. The bedroom was much like the man who lived here: elegant and austere, yet with a subtle warmth. The distinctly masculine decor included a sumptuous marble fireplace, navy wallpaper with thin gold stripes, a discreet scattering of vases and lamps.

Over a fine rolltop desk, a gas lamp still flickered, shedding light over an opened ledger and the pen that lay across the neat columns of figures. A sheaf of paper filled a cranny inside the desk. She drew out a piece, heavy cream stock embossed with the gold seal of a soaring hawk.

Quietly Elizabeth angled the mahogany chair toward the bed, then sat down, curling her bare feet beneath her. She searched the desk for an inkwell, but found none. In dawning delight she realized she held a fountain pen, a pen that carried its own supply of ink within the slim gold barrel. Trust the Earl of Hawkesford to possess the latest invention.

His handsome form lay dark against the tangle of white linens. In smooth strokes she sketched the flowing line of his flanks, the perfect proportions of his biceps and pectorals, the sleek refinement of his head and face. Her thighs tingled as she recalled the supple strength of his arms around her, the snug feel of him inside her, his groans of gratification, his whispered words of love. Her mother had told Elizabeth of the sex act, had wistfully hinted at the happiness a man and a woman could share. Yet Elizabeth had never imagined such supreme ecstasy, such remarkable closeness.

Emotion glowed within her. She applied herself to the drawing, pouring her heart into each movement of the pen. The nib scratched quietly across the paper. From time to time she glanced at Nicholas, checking details, the shape of his thigh or the pattern of his hair. The sketch came alive as her love gave her the ability to depict him with stunning accuracy.

One moment he lay sleeping. The next he was gazing at her, his powerful body poised on an elbow. Her hand went still and her pulse jumped.

"Good morning, love," he said.

His husky voice caressed her. His eyes were laden with affection, dark silver in the dawn light. With lazy grace, he slid off the bed and walked toward Elizabeth. Her throat went dry. His naked body was the personification of proud male glory. No drawing, no sculpture, could do him justice. Yet she felt compelled to try.

The tenderness on his face entranced her. Robbed of speech, she watched him stop beside her, brace one hand on the arm of the chair and lean closer until their warm breath mingled. His free hand cupped her jaw. The pen slipped from her fingers and rolled to the floor as her arms lifted to encircle his neck. His lips parted, playing over hers for an eternal moment, his tongue slow and sure. Elizabeth felt lost, lost in the promise of his kiss, lost to the need overwhelming her senses.

"You should have awakened me," he murmured against her mouth.

"You looked so peaceful . . . I didn't want to disturb you."

He chuckled. "You disturb me without even trying. Feel how my heart is racing."

Taking hold of her wrist, Nicholas splayed her fingers over his chest. Through the tangle of dark hair she felt his wild pulse beat, looked down and saw the swelling proof of his passion. Heat sizzled through her.

"We could always go back to bed," she said breathlessly.

"My sentiments precisely." He sighed against her temple, his hand seeking her breast, then reluctantly drawing back. "Yet we mustn't delay. I should have returned you to your room hours ago."

After pressing another kiss on her mouth, he straightened. His eyes flicked across her lap, started to lift, then fell again. He snatched up the drawing and stared at it. His body stiffened and his features hardened, like gently flowing water freezing under a sudden chill.

"What the hell is the meaning of this?" he asked, his voice ominously quiet, his fingers taut around the paper.

His aristocratic coldness baffled her. "I was drawing you—"

"For what purpose?"

"Purpose? I...I wanted to. I haven't any other reason—"

"Don't you?" Pain glittered in his eyes, a pain that bewildered her. "'I wish I could sculpt you in marble.' You said that to me, remember? Last night, when I stood outside the conservatory with the police inspector, I saw the sculpture you'd begun of a nude man. That statue is of me, isn't it?"

She felt a half-guilty start. "I've been meaning to tell you about that."

"When?" His voice was an anguished rasp. "After you'd used our lovemaking to study my body?"

"That isn't true!" she said, hastening to reassure him. "If I didn't tell you about the sculpture, it was only because I knew you would have forbidden me to do it."

"So you slept with me instead." In naked splendor, he paced before her chair, the drawing in his hand. "So you could examine all the physical details of your subject before you proceeded."

His unjust accusation hurt. "You're wrong, Nicholas. That isn't why I came to you last night."

"Then tell me this," he said hoarsely. "Why was recording those details the first thing you did on leaving my bed?"

"I'm an artist." She held out her palms in supplication. "I'm not always good with words. Drawing is my way of expressing myself, of showing you how I feel."

He stood still as a stone carving; the starkness in his eyes stung her heart. "How *do* you feel, Elizabeth? Will you be content as my mistress?"

Her insides clenched into a miserable ball of confusion. He was giving her all an English earl could offer a woman of her class. Why did she find herself wishing for more?

She took a deep breath. "Yes, I'll be happy. More than anything, I want to spend my nights in your bed."

Unlike the ardor she had expected her declaration to elicit, he looked violently furious. His mouth compressed into a taut line. "And what about the days?" he demanded. "Will you forget me in favor of art? Is love-making all you want from me?"

He savagely ripped the paper. Stunned, she watched his hands reduce the sketch to tiny bits that fluttered downward to lie pale against the blue rug.

Though her heart felt as shredded as the drawing, she lifted her chin. "Do you scorn my work so much that you would destroy it?"

"All I scorn," he said in a low voice, "is your free-spirited brand of love."

Pivoting on his heel, Nicholas strode away. Perplexed by his tormented words and provoked by his icy manner, Elizabeth sat still long enough to watch his magnificent naked back vanish through a doorway. Then she scrambled from the chair to follow him. She found herself in his dressing room, a vast masculine domain lined with elegant wardrobes and tidy rows of footwear, a marble fireplace and mahogany side chairs. The masculine smells of leather and clean linen tinged the air. In front of an opened cabinet, Nicholas was thrusting his leg into a pair of trousers.

Unthinkingly she blurted, "Don't you wear under-drawers?"

Yanking the pants over his lean buttocks, he shot her a dark look. "Why should you care? You don't concern yourself with clothing, only with the flesh that lies beneath."

The ribbon of pain in his voice wrapped around her soul. Understanding shimmered inside her. "Nicholas?" she asked cautiously. "You aren't still thinking I see you only as a pleasing face, are you?"

Ignoring her, he applied himself to buttoning his fly.

"You do think that." Elizabeth hurried to his side and took hold of his arm. "Nicholas, I scarcely knew you when I said that. Everything's changed since then—"

"Nothing's changed. You're obsessed with your art, with physical appearances, just as you've always been."

Snatching a white shirt from a wardrobe, he brushed

past her and marched stiffly back into the bedroom. Elizabeth rushed after him, the dressing gown flapping around her ankles. Frustration strangled her as she watched him plunge his arms into the starched shirt.

"Will you kindly stand still long enough to let me speak?"

Nicholas set his hands on his hips, the shirt parted to expose his broad, bare chest. His arctic eyes traveled up and down the length of her. "Go on."

In lieu of a comforting lump of clay, her nervous fingers twisted the fringed sash. "I know we've had our differences, Nicholas, but I've always admired your character. You're a man of honor, a man who truly cares about others." Her voice dropped to a whisper; her eyes searched his. "The more I've come to know you, the deeper I've fallen in love with you. I don't mean just your body or how you made me feel last night. I love you for the man you are."

He held himself rigid, though his expression gentled a little. "Then why are you satisfied with being my mistress?"

She swallowed to ease the treacherous tightening in her throat. "What else *can* I be? You can hardly offer to marry me. I understand that...and I accept it."

The frost melted from his face. His eyes gleaming with tenderness, he took a step closer. "Elizabeth, you're mistaken about what I can and cannot do. I—"

The door vibrated with furious knocking. Nicholas swore under his breath. "Go into the dressing room. I'll get rid of whoever it is."

"I don't care if anyone sees me here."

"Do as I say. Now."

Seeing the futility of another protest, she moved to obey. She was halfway inside when the hall door burst open. Owen surged into the bedroom, his whiskered face gray with alarm, his hazel eyes focused on Nicholas.

"Pardon, your lordship," he said in a rush. "Libby's missing! Her bed hasn't been slept in. God forgive me, she must have run off! And with someone out there trying to kill her—"

"I'm right here." Elizabeth stepped back into the bedroom.

Owen's head whipped toward her. His eyes widened with shock. He stared at the oversized dressing gown she wore, then glanced at the rumpled bed. Guilt gripped her, but she held her chin high. Her love for Nicholas was no cause for shame.

"Bless my soul—" Owen sputtered. Wheeling toward Nicholas, he spat, "You bloody lecher! What have you done to my Libby?"

Fists brandished, he sprang at the earl. Nicholas made no move to prevent the attack. Owen's fist met the earl's jaw in a sickening crunch. The force of the blow sent Nicholas staggering backward against the bedpost.

Gasping, Elizabeth darted across the room to seize Owen's arm. "Papa, stop! You've no right to hurt him."

"The scoundrel deserves to have his bloody teeth crammed down his lying throat! I was a fool to believe his noble claptrap. He's no different than that lecherous duke."

"I'm here of my own free will."

His arm tensed beneath her fingers. He swung toward her, his face stark with pain. "You don't mean that," he said hoarsely. "You can't make the same mistake Lucy did."

Gathering her dignity, Elizabeth took a step back. "It isn't a mistake. Nicholas and I love each other."

"Love!" Owen shook his gray head. "He has you mesmerized, made you pretty promises, that's all. Good God, Libby, don't you see? He's used you, ruined you—"

"I intend to marry Elizabeth."

Her mouth dropped open. Her eyes veered to Nicholas, who stood massaging his reddened jaw. She tried to calm the wild beating of her heart. He couldn't mean what he said; he must be trying to pacify Owen. An English nobleman might amuse himself with an artist and an oddity, but he would never wed her.

"An earl...marry my Libby?" Suspicion colored Owen's voice. "Why would you do that?"

Nicholas gazed squarely at the older man. "I love her. The ceremony will take place as soon as arrangements can be made."

A long, appraising look passed between the two men.

"I have your word on that?" Owen asked.

"Absolutely."

"All right, then," said Owen, nodding in satisfaction. "You have my consent—so long as you promise to give Libby the freedom to pursue her art. She must have a private allowance to use in her work, money she needn't answer to you about. A thousand pounds a year."

"I agree."

As they deliberated over the terms of payment, Elizabeth's agitated emotions converged into seething resentment. They were settling her life as if she had no opinion in the matter. Didn't either of them—Nicholas, in particular—see fit to ask her if she *wanted* to marry him? Hurt rolled through her, engulfing her in a sea of bitterness. Though he claimed to love her, he'd made no marriage offer until he'd been caught with her in a compromising situation. As much as she loved him, she couldn't marry for the wrong reasons.

"Excuse me," she said.

Both men looked at her. Owen appeared pleased. Nicholas seemed...wary. As well he should be, she thought tartly.

"I won't take your money, Nicholas."

Owen patted the back of her hand. "Now don't let pride get the best of you, Libby. Once you've had time to consider it, you'll see the advantage of having funds at your disposal—"

She yanked her fingers away. "I make my own decisions. You forget...you haven't the right to approve or disapprove the man I choose to marry."

As if stung by a slap, Owen's smile vanished. Elizabeth felt only a twinge of sympathy and regret; the emotional turmoil of the past twelve hours had left her too drained for more.

Looking at Nicholas, she said stiffly, "I'll not marry for the sake of my reputation. Save your chivalrous arrangements for one of your society ladies."

Before he could see the sparkle of tears in her eyes, she spun on her bare heel and stalked to the door.

"Elizabeth!"

She ignored the command in his voice. Her hand grasped the ornate handle, but his fingers closed over her wrist before she could open the door. Ready to do battle, she flung back her head. The torment twisting his handsome face arrested her.

"I've made a muddle of this," he murmured. "Stay, won't you? Let me have the chance to do things properly."

She almost succumbed to his humble tone and imploring eyes. Almost. "You always do what's proper," she said bitterly. "That's your problem."

As she swung away, the gleam of silver on a side table caught her tear-blurred eyes. Pushing past him, she snatched up the chain and ring; the sterling swan felt warm inside her icy palm. At least she had something to hold on to, something to fill the void inside her. She felt the burning desire to unravel the mysteries of her past, to escape her emotional turmoil here and seek out her future.

"Libby?" Owen said hesitantly. "I can't blame you for despising me, but listen to the earl, please."

Feeling pressured and bruised, Elizabeth clutched the ring to her breast. "I'll listen to no one but myself. I intend to pay a visit to the Duke of Rockborough. Perhaps both of you have painted too dark a picture of him."

Owen's face paled with horror. "No!" he choked out. "You can't go alone. It's too dangerous."

"He won't murder me in broad daylight."

"Owen's right," Nicholas said. "You'll not set foot outside this house without me at your side."

"More of your orders, my lord?"

"I mean to protect you, Elizabeth. Believe it or not, I do care whether you live or die."

Through the haze of her anger, she could see the concern shining within those steely gray eyes. So why did she feel so resentful and panicked, as if she'd been pushed into a corner?

"All right, then, come with me if you must," she conceded, walking to the door. "I'm leaving as soon as I dress."

"His Grace is unavailable, my lord," intoned the butler, polite despite the unfashionably early hour.

Beside her on the doorstep, Elizabeth felt Nicholas shift impatiently. "We'll await his return, then," he said.

"I'm afraid that's impossible," the butler said. "His Grace is no longer in residence. He and the family departed on the morning train to Yorkshire."

"To Yorkshire?" Elizabeth exclaimed.

Her dismay must have shown on her face, for the butler's formal manner unbent a bit. "Should you care to pen a note, ma'am, I will send it on to His Grace."

What could she say in a letter? *My Lord Duke, I am your long-lost daughter, the bastard you spurned some twenty years past.*

"No, thank you," Elizabeth said. "That won't be necessary."

Shoulders slumped, she started back down the massive marble steps. Over the past hour, her emotions had careened from curiosity to fear to determination. She wanted to discover who wished her dead. She wanted to see the face of the man who had fathered her. Most of all, she wanted to know why he had rejected her and her mother.

Nicholas's fingers pressed gently into her arm as he handed her into the waiting brougham. He seated himself at her side, and the carriage started the rolling ride down the cobbled street.

After a moment, he said, "What will you do now?"

Staring down at her reticule, she fingered the signet

ring through the brocaded fabric. "Go to Yorkshire, I suppose. As soon as I can gather up my things."

"You'll go only as my wife."

She whipped her chin up. "I told you before," she said in a voice more shaky than certain, "I won't marry you."

A shaft of morning sunlight warmed his resolute face. "You might be carrying my child, Elizabeth."

Her insides curled with shock and pleasure as she pictured herself cuddling his baby. In all the upheaval of the past hours she had never considered pregnancy.

Nicholas took her hand in his. "There'll be no counting of months when my heir is born," he said firmly. "You'll marry me now."

The fear that he'd someday regret his decision gave Elizabeth the courage to argue against what she wanted most. "Child or not, a marriage between us wouldn't work. Our lives are too different, Nicholas. What will society say about you marrying an American artist? You're an earl, a nobleman, and I'm only a bastard—"

"Hush," he said fiercely, his fingers clamping tighter on hers. "I won't hear you denigrate yourself. What happened to the proud woman who swore she was my equal? The independent woman I've grown to love so much?"

His declaration weakened her; yet he must feel he owed her this proposal. "I wasn't meant to be a countess. I've no interest in planning menus for dinner parties or interviewing prospective parlor maids."

"Aunt Beatrice will be happy to continue those duties."

Elizabeth shook her head emphatically. "But you don't appreciate my art, Nicholas. For heaven's sake, you even burned my anatomy book!"

"In a fit of anger for which I apologized. Thistlewood reimbursed you, didn't he?"

"The cost isn't the point. What is, is that you don't understand my need to create, to spend long hours working at my art. You want me to be a lady, to waste my life fluttering a fan and flattering men."

"I admit to feeling that way at first, only because I wanted people to accept you." He kissed the back of her hand. "I've changed my mind. I no longer care what anyone else thinks. What really matters is that we love each other."

Honesty rang in his voice. She wanted desperately to believe in him. . . . "You feel obligated to marry me because of your principles. It isn't necessary, Nicholas. I'd sooner be your mistress than live with the knowledge that I'd forced you into a commitment you didn't want in your heart."

He smiled tenderly. "My dearest Elizabeth, when Owen burst into my chambers, I was about to ask you to marry me."

She stared. The rattle of carriage wheels and the clip-clop of horse hooves filled the silence. "How can I know that for sure?" she whispered.

"You'll have to trust me."

She touched the bruise on his jaw. "But you just stood there and let Owen strike you. You felt guilty for compromising me."

"I deserved Owen's anger, because I should have married you before I took you to bed. He acted as any good father would."

Regret stirred in her; she thrust it away, promising herself she would think about Owen later. Uncertainly she gazed at Nicholas. "I want to believe you. . . ."

"And I want you for my wife, Elizabeth. I won't settle for less, ever again."

She caught her breath. "Are you saying we won't sleep together again unless I agree to your proposal?"

His eyes went dark with determination. "Precisely."

"That's unfair. You're manipulating me."

"I can't be fair when it comes to you." He molded her to his long body, his lips feathering her cheek. "Do you truly want to give up what we shared last night?"

His silvery eyes mesmerized her. Half dazed by his nearness, she shook her head.

His hand curved around her breast. "Neither do I."

Through the layers of bodice and chemise she felt

the sweep of his thumb over the fullness of her flesh. Her nipple leapt to life; her body responded like pliant clay in the hands of a skillful sculptor.

"Was I too rough last night?" he murmured.

"No . . . no, of course not." Unable to resist, she slid her fingers over his shirtfront, delving inside his dark blue morning coat. "You were tender, wonderful."

"Then you enjoyed making love with me?"

The moans of fulfillment echoed in her memory. Closing her eyes, she rested her spinning head on the firm pillow of his shoulder. "You know I did."

His mouth kissed a path to the soft skin of her ear. "Have you ever felt that way with any other man?"

"Never," she whispered.

"And I've never needed a woman the way I need you. Feel how much I want you."

He guided her fingers to his groin; through the tightened fabric of his trousers, he was long and hard and hot. A sigh shuddered from her as she ran her fingers lightly over the bulge, rediscovering the shape of his arousal. He groaned, and she gloried in the sound of his pleasure. His body was so exciting, so male. Desire drizzled through her veins like heated honey. She put her mouth to his throat, breathing in his scent, tasting the tang of his skin.

His hand shifted to her thigh, kneading her soft flesh just tantalizing inches from the place between her legs. "Don't you want to feel me moving inside you again?" he said huskily.

"Yes," she moaned. "Yes, yes, yes."

"Then say you'll marry me, Elizabeth. Say yes, and we'll spend the rest of our lives making love. We'll raise a family, share our joys, all our hopes and dreams. . . ."

She lost herself in the fantasy spun by his words; then all rational thought vanished like a wisp of smoke as his fingers pressed against her mound. Despite the barrier of petticoats and skirts, his touch ignited fire. Restless and aching, she angled to him, lifting a knee onto his thigh.

"What's your answer?" he muttered hoarsely.

Her hips arched toward his questing fingers. "I can't think when you do that."

"Don't think. Just say yes."

"Yes," she breathed. "Yes."

His mouth came down hard on hers. He kissed her possessively, passionately. She parted her lips to the sensual sweep of his tongue. Her arms slipped around his lean waist, caressing the rippling muscles of his back, reaching up to stroke the strong column of his throat.

"I knew I could convince you," he murmured against her mouth. "I'll secure the special license straightaway."

She opened her eyes to his triumphant smile. "Special—?" she said, collecting her scattered senses. "What are you talking about?"

"My dearest love, you've just agreed to become my wife."

The carriage swayed as it turned a corner. She clung to his waist for support. "I did?"

His eyes gleamed. "Yes, and I'm afraid there's no getting out of it. You gave your word of honor."

Elizabeth felt dazed, unable to think, swept along on a rising tide. "A promise extracted under duress."

"Then I shall have to make the arrangements swiftly, before you can change your mind." His thumbs circled gently over her temples. "We can even be married this afternoon."

His expression was tender yet taut, as if he expected her to protest. An unfathomable place inside her glowed at the knowledge of his love. She searched her heart for doubts and found only a deep, abiding warmth. Nicholas was her anchor in the confusing currents, her armature on which to build a new life.

"Yes," she said softly, brushing her cheek against his smoothly shaven face. "I'd like that very much."

Chapter 17

Was he wrong to press Elizabeth into marriage so quickly?

Frowning at the sun-washed rose garden, Nicholas leaned a shoulder against the window frame. Behind him, dishes clinked as a footman discreetly cleared the dining table. He hadn't seen Elizabeth since midmorning, when he'd left to procure the license from the bishop. The women had taken their luncheon upstairs, Cicely agog with excitement, Aunt Beatrice in a flurry of preparations. He'd used considerable tact and judicious flattery to smooth his aunt's ruffled feathers. Despite his assurance to the contrary, he knew she believed pregnancy to be the catalyst for the hasty nuptials. One day his aunt would accept Elizabeth, he told himself. Already he'd seen dislike change to grudging admiration that was fast becoming real affection.

Fierce joy blazed in his heart, a joy tempered by disquiet. Should he have granted Elizabeth a lengthy betrothal and a grandiose wedding?

No, she was not a woman to care for social frivolities. And he dared not wait. It might be damned selfish, but he must move now, before she decided she couldn't fit both him and art into her life.

Intending to clear his desk of business matters, he strode into the corridor and headed for the staircase. After today he wanted nothing to distract him from settling the mystery in Yorkshire . . . and nothing to interfere with the loving he intended to shower on his wife.

In the entrance hall a team of housemaids busily polished the brasswork and scrubbed the acre of white marble floor. Dobson stood at the opened front door and accepted a calling card from a man. A man with fair hair and aesthetic features.

Peter Tate, the Viscount Buckstone.

Nicholas felt every muscle in his body tense. Pivoting sharply, he strode to the door. "Buckstone," he said, acknowledging the viscount with a curt nod. "Might I be of assistance? It's rather early to be out making calls."

Buckstone brushed a white-gloved hand over his Nile green morning coat. Like a preening peacock, Nicholas thought in disgust.

"My business is with Miss Hastings. She doesn't keep conventional hours."

"I'm afraid you've wasted your time," Nicholas said, savoring his news. "Elizabeth is too busy to bother with you today."

"Indeed?" Buckstone drawled. "I think she'll spare a moment to hear me out. It's about the commission."

A cold knot formed inside Nicholas. Looking into Buckstone's triumphant eyes, he knew the viscount held the bait that could entice Elizabeth from marriage. Never before had Nicholas contemplated underhanded action to win a woman from a rival; he had always shrugged and left the choice to the lady.

Until now.

"Come along," he said abruptly.

Turning, he strode into the drawing room. He drew sour satisfaction from forcing Buckstone to trail behind like a faithful hound. Carefully Nicholas closed the double doors. Inside, a pair of gardeners filled vases with great bunches of roses, no doubt acting on Lady Beatrice's efficient orders. Spying the earl, the men tipped their caps and scuttled outside.

"Holding a soiree this evening?" the viscount asked, eyeing a basket of fragrant blooms.

"A wedding reception."

Buckstone's thin features drew into a frown. "I say,

did I hear you correctly? Someone is getting married?"

"Yes. I am."

"You?" the viscount scoffed. "I've seen no banns published. Who is the bride?"

"Elizabeth."

Buckstone's mouth sagged open. His hands froze in the act of peeling off his pristine gloves. His eyes widened until they bugged out like a frog's.

"So you see," Nicholas continued in grim delight, "you truly are wasting your time."

"I don't believe it," the viscount sputtered. "You, marrying a common American artist? No, you must be bluffing. You want to keep her to yourself, as your mistress."

Anger surged in Nicholas. "She's too fine a lady to fill the role of mistress."

"You've dishonored her, then, gotten her with child. That can be the only reason for such undue haste."

The grain of truth in the wild accusation brought a flash of guilt, guilt that made Nicholas want to smash his fist into Buckstone's pale face.

"I'll pretend you didn't say that," Nicholas snapped. "You will not voice a single, damning word to anyone about Elizabeth's character. If I hear you have . . ." His voice trailed off menacingly.

"But people will talk—"

"You won't. And you'll not be courting my bride's favor today, nor ever again."

"But I'm awarding her the commission for my father's memorial. We'll be working together for months in Ireland."

Nicholas's blood chilled. If presented with the choice between the appointment and their marriage, which would Elizabeth select? Willing his fingers not to shake, he picked up a long-stemmed pink rose and casually examined it.

"Perhaps I should make myself more clear," he said icily. "On her behalf, I am refusing your commission."

"You can't do that—"

"Can't I?" he returned softly. "Elizabeth has accepted

me as her intended husband, which affords me the right to speak for her."

Buckstone stiffened. He opened his mouth, then closed it. Scowling, he yanked his gloves back on. "She knows nothing of being a countess. She'll grow bored within the year."

The possibility paralyzed Nicholas. Was he wrong to cage her free spirit? "I'll take my chances."

"You can't stifle her yearning to be an artist. You'll lose her if you try. And when that happens, I'll be there to put the first bit of clay into her lovely hands." Pivoting, the viscount marched jerkily toward the door.

Nicholas subdued a surge of violence. "In case you're still planning to approach her, Elizabeth and I are leaving in the morning for an extended honeymoon trip. By the time we return, I doubt she'll even recall your name."

Only the faintest pause in Buckstone's stride signaled that he'd heard. He banged open the polished oak panel and stalked out, his angry footsteps clicking on the marble floor. Going to the doorway, Nicholas glanced around the entrance hall. He had to make certain Elizabeth was nowhere in sight. One of the maids darted him a curious look as she industriously polished the banister.

Guilt ripped through him as the slamming door echoed through the vast room. If Elizabeth learned what he'd done...

A thorn pricked his thumb. Glancing down, he saw a bead of blood on his skin. Nothing remained on the bloomstalk; shredded pink petals scattered the crimson Turkish rug.

He flung the stem into a cloisonné vase. There would be other commissions, commissions that would not tear Elizabeth from home. Commissions that would allow her to sculpt during the day and lie in his arms at night.

He would make her happy, Nicholas vowed. So deliriously happy he need never again fear losing her.

* * *

"This is preposterous," Lady Beatrice muttered under her breath, as she adjusted a pin cinching Elizabeth's waist. "A ridiculous state of affairs."

"Oh, pooh, *I* think it's splendid!" Hugging a frothy aqua ball gown like an imaginary dance partner, Cicely whirled around, her chestnut hair flying. "Elizabeth is going to be my sister. What fun we shall have!"

"Such indecent haste." Beatrice sniffed. "I don't understand what's come over my nephew."

Her disapproval made Elizabeth's heart throb in dismay. She could scarcely believe that in a few short hours she would marry Nicholas. Staring at her reflection in the cheval glass, she saw happiness and apprehension mirrored in her huge violet eyes. Could she adjust to being the wife of an English earl? Was she committing a colossal mistake by plunging into this marriage? For an instant Elizabeth wished fervently that she were in the conservatory, immersed in the familiar joy of sculpting instead of being the object of so much fussing, instead of standing on the threshold of a new life. Was all this pomp and circumstance a glimpse of the future?

Then she thought of Nicholas, his warm loving smile and his long powerful body, and knew that no fear was strong enough to sway her decision.

For all her opposition, Lady Beatrice had taken charge of the preparations like an admiral directing a fleet. Already the cook had come in to check the menu and the housekeeper to verify the guest list. Several maids, along with Miss Eversham and Cicely, scurried in and out of the dressing room, readying every detail of Elizabeth's toilette, shoes and stockings, petticoats and kid gloves. At present the troupe of women was engaged in altering one of Lady Beatrice's own evening gowns for Elizabeth, since she possessed nothing suitable.

The dress was made of tissue-thin silver gauze draped over an underskirt of magenta satin. Off-the-shoulder sleeves and a deep-cut bodice framed her bosom in lacy splendor, and a wide silver sash wrapped her tiny waist. Tasseled loops of Venetian pearl beads caught up the silver gauze at the sides. The dress made Elizabeth feel radiant, although she had to breathe shallowly. Lady Beatrice had insisted on a corset, and for once Elizabeth had deemed it prudent not to argue.

Critically eyeing the gown, Beatrice tilted her regal head. "Miss Eversham, the hem drags a bit on this side."

"Yes, my lady." As the homely governess knelt to repin the hem, she darted Elizabeth a look of proud satisfaction. Elizabeth smiled warmly back. Clearly Miss Eversham delighted in seeing a woman her social equal snare a man of the earl's stature.

Hugging her knees, Cicely sat on a velvet hassock. "I never imagined my brother could be such a romantic. He's always been so starched and proper."

Elizabeth swiveled for the governess. "I thought so, too," she murmured, "until I came to know him better."

"He must be madly in love," Cicely said.

"We at least half agree, then," Beatrice said dryly. "He must be mad."

Ignoring her aunt, Cicely leaned forward. "Do tell us everything, Elizabeth. Has Nick written you any love poems? Taken you for walks in the moonlight? Why didn't you even hint that you were falling in love with him?"

"Your head is in the clouds," Beatrice said, taking her sharp eyes from Miss Eversham's progress long enough to send the girl a severe look. "Run along now and see to your own toilette."

"But—"

"No arguments, please. We've scarcely three hours before we leave for church. I've my hands full without your disobedience."

"Yes, aunt." Cicely trudged meekly away, then turned back, a mischievous sparkle in her lapis lazuli eyes. "Imagine, my art instructor a countess. Won't that set society on its ears!"

As the girl vanished out the door, Beatrice's fine features formed a scowl. Mingled amusement and trepidation trembled inside Elizabeth. Though she cared little for what people thought of her, she could understand Beatrice's concern, because that concern rose out of love for Nicholas.

"Come, Miss Eversham," said Beatrice, with a clap of her hands. "Time is wasting."

"Yes, my lady." Aided by a wide-eyed maid, the governess deftly drew the skirts over Elizabeth's head, then departed. Left alone in the dressing room with her ladyship, Elizabeth stood uncertainly in chemise and petticoats, and wished there were some way to make amends with Nicholas's aunt. The fragile truce they'd woven during the past weeks lay in tatters today.

Pursing her rosebud mouth, Beatrice studied Elizabeth. "You'll bathe now. I suppose I shall have to help you since the staff is engaged."

"I can manage."

"Nonsense. The earl asked me to oversee this wedding, and it is my duty to obey. Left to your own devices, you'd probably wear those dreadful trousers."

"I won't disgrace his lordship."

"Humph." Circling Elizabeth, Beatrice began to unlace the tight corset. "These relations of yours in Yorkshire. What sort of people are they?"

Not yet ready to tell anyone about the duke, Elizabeth chose her words carefully. "You needn't worry about Nicholas humbling himself. My mother's family is wellborn."

"Oh?" Her ladyship tugged sharply on the lacing. "I spent hours educating you. Why did you never once mention them to me?"

"I've only just found out. When we return, I hope to tell you more." On impulse Elizabeth turned and grasped the older woman's smooth hand. "Please try to understand, your ladyship. I want Nicholas to be happy as much as you do."

"Then call off this unsuitable match."

"I can't. I love him too much."

"Love!" Beatrice drew her elegant fingers free. "No doubt you lured my nephew into compromising you and then took advantage of his sense of honor."

If only she knew the irony of that statement! With quiet dignity, Elizabeth said, "Do you truly believe I would do that?"

Beatrice's gaze wavered; then she narrowed her eyes. "Any woman can be compelled to sacrifice her principles for the chance to acquire a title and wealth, not to mention a handsome husband."

"Not I." On the single occasion she'd been in Beatrice's bedroom, Elizabeth had seen on the bedside table the framed photograph of a kind-eyed man, the husband who had died some three years earlier. "Your ladyship, do you know what it's like to love a man so much you feel empty without him?"

Beatrice's stony expression eased a fraction. "Of course. Mine was an arranged marriage, but Trevor and I grew to love each other. *That* is what I want for my nephew."

"Love is what I wish for him, also."

Beatrice stared at Elizabeth for a long, measuring moment. "I can't approve of this haste. . . ."

"I have reasons to visit my relations, and Nicholas wishes to go with me. Be happy for us, please," Elizabeth added softly. "Nicholas thinks the world of you. He would want your blessing."

She touched Beatrice's hands again and this time her ladyship didn't pull away. A succession of expressions flickered across her fine-boned features: obstinance, indecision, acquiescence.

With a sigh she pressed her polished, fragrant cheek to Elizabeth's. "My dear girl, you're too charming to resist. Perhaps Nicholas has at last met his match."

Standing before the altar in St. George's Church, Hanover Square, Elizabeth hugged a spray of roses and marveled at her sense of blissful unreality. How curious that she could be so vibrantly aware of her surroundings yet feel so cloaked in fantasy. This moment would be stamped on her memory forever: the jeweled light filtered by the stained glass windows, the chilly air sending goose bumps over her skin, the solid warmth of the man standing beside her. She felt dazzling and alive, beautiful for the man she loved.

Without conscious thought she slipped a hand into Nicholas's. His fingers squeezed gently, reassuringly. She glanced up to see him smiling at her, his fiercely handsome face soft with affection, his silver eyes gleaming with love. His impeccable claret suit emphasized the wide breadth of his shoulders and the long length of his legs. In a moment he would be hers. The thought thrilled and frightened and confused her, all at once.

His voice rang rich and clear through the church.

She spoke her own vows breathlessly.

Then it was too late to change her mind; Nicholas was sliding a dainty, diamond-studded band onto her finger. Their lips brushed in a brief, stirring kiss. The swelling notes of organ music echoed her soaring spirits. As they went to sign the register, along with Cicely and Lord Charles as witnesses, she clung tightly to her husband's arm.

The galleries were empty, the few guests scattered in the front pews. Her throat squeezed as she saw Owen standing alone, dressed in his Sunday best. He looked satisfied and proud, yet sadness shadowed his hazel eyes. A palette of conflicting emotions colored her spirits. She could not simply walk past him. No matter that he had kept the truth from her all those years, she longed to share this moment with him. Eyes blurred, she hugged him, his familiar and comforting scent enveloping her as tightly as his arms.

"You'll always be my little girl," he said in a rough whisper. "Always."

Her heart wrenched. Yes, a part of her would always belong to Owen. Yet somehow she could not work the words of reconciliation past the knot in her throat.

Drawing back, she leaned heavily on Nicholas's arm as he guided her out of the church. Cicely joined the newlyweds at the columned portico. Eyes sparkling, she embraced first Elizabeth, then her brother.

"Thank heavens, Nick, that you finally came to your senses. For a while I was afraid you'd wed that prissy Marianne."

Smiling, Nicholas slid an arm around his wife. "Sometimes you don't acknowledge what's right in front of your face. Let that be a lesson to you, Cicely."

He glanced at Lord Charles, who stood a short distance away, addressing Lady Phoebe. Cicely's cheeks colored. Jerking her eyes back to her brother, she elevated her pert chin.

"Oh, pooh," she said with a wave of her kid-gloved hand. "Love hasn't anything to do with lessons. When I marry, *I* shall be swept off my feet by a dashing rake."

As Cicely and Lord Charles accompanied them in the landau back home, Elizabeth wondered at the relationship between the two. His feelings shone clear in the way his brown eyes hungrily absorbed her every gesture. But what did Cicely feel? She chattered gaily, seemingly indifferent to the quiet man sitting beside her. Yet a sense of high-strung awareness hovered about her, a rigidity to her posture, a veiled glance directed his way, a muffled gasp when a bump made their legs brush.

Elizabeth smiled. Perhaps there would soon be another wedding in the Ware household. She hoped so. She wanted the whole world to experience her joy.

"Happy, love?" Nicholas murmured.

"Very much."

Mere words seemed inadequate to express her feelings, and she snuggled her cheek against his coat. When they arrived at Hawkesford House, he stayed by her side, touching her cheek, holding her hand, gazing at her. For once, she knew his thoughts. She knew, because she felt the same burning need inside.

At dinner her new status dictated that she sit at the opposite end of the table from Nicholas. Automatically she sipped her wine and ate what the footmen placed on her plate. Veal with truffles, tender fillet of beef, lobster in a creamy béchamel sauce...the courses seemed to last forever. From time to time, Nicholas caught her eye and his slow smoldering smile left her light-headed and flushed. Somehow she managed to hold a rational conversation with Lady Phoebe to her left and the jovial lord to her right.

Afterward the ladies glided into the drawing room while the gentlemen lingered over port. Nicholas followed Elizabeth into the hall. His knuckles drifted down her arm, leaving her skin hot and her limbs weak.

"Go on upstairs, love," he murmured.

"But our guests are still here."

"Go on upstairs."

The silver-dark intensity of his eyes thrilled her. She found herself obeying willingly.

When she entered her bedroom, a white-capped maid sprang up from the hearth chair. "Oh! Didn't expect you so soon, mum." A blush stained her pretty face as she bobbed a hasty curtsy. "Your ladyship, I mean."

The title still caught Elizabeth by surprise. She was a lady now, after all. Smiling wryly, she asked, "Who are you?"

"Janet, my lady." The girl dipped another curtsy. "His lordship said I was to attend you from now on."

"Attend me?"

"As your lady's maid." Shyly she stepped forward, hands worrying her white apron. "Shall I help you undress?"

Undoing the row of tiny buttons down the back of the gown, Janet chattered freely, apparently forgetting her nervousness as she busied herself at familiar tasks. Elizabeth found an unexpected pleasure in letting someone else put away the clothing, in relaxing before the dressing table instead of tumbling into bed too tired to do more than wash her clay-soiled hands.

"Such lovely hair, my lady," Janet said, combing out the long tresses with a silver-backed brush. "Pure black as a raven's wing. His lordship will be most pleased."

Elizabeth felt her cheeks burn. That was the purpose of all this fussing—not for her own gratification, but to prepare her for the earl's enjoyment. And she was to humbly wait here like an offering on a platter.

Seized by a strange, restless panic, she stood. "Excuse me. I . . . I need a breath of fresh air."

Janet looked startled. "But what will I tell his lordship?"

"That I'll return when it pleases me."

The fine linen robe swishing around her ankles, Elizabeth walked out the door. The instant the latch clicked shut, she stopped uncertainly in the gaslit hall. From the grand staircase drifted the tinkle of laughter and the rumble of voices. Her brief spurt of rebellion died. Where had she thought to go? To the conservatory?

Drawn by the unspoken command of her heart, she headed slowly toward Nicholas's suite. She hesitated before the imposing walnut panel, then knocked decisively.

The door opened. The thin-featured man named Quinn eyed her in surprise. "Miss . . . er, my lady. Might I be of assistance?"

"I'd like to see my husband."

The valet opened his mouth as if to protest, but she angled past him and entered the bedroom. Nicholas stepped from the dressing room, his shirt unbuttoned to his bare chest, the white tails hanging out of his trousers. His attention was focused at his wrist. "Damned cuff link," he muttered. "Quinn—!"

He glanced at her and stopped. The impatience slid from his face. Heat flared in his eyes, drying her throat.

On liquid legs, she moved toward him. "Let me help you," she said, bending to unfasten the heavy gold link from his starched cuff.

Straightening, she saw the shadow of a smile on his lips. Then he aimed a haughty glare at the valet, and Quinn scurried out of the bedroom.

The exchange vaguely disturbed Elizabeth. With a look Nicholas could make servants obey; with a look he could make her melt. Had she been wrong to give herself into his power?

Then his arms enfolded her and she knew nothing could be more right. Their mouths met in an impassioned kiss, full of promise, ripe with love. She parted her lips and his tongue explored her with a fierce sweetness that left her quivering. Her hands slipped inside his shirt to follow the muscled shape of his shoulders. Breathing hard, he moved his mouth downward, kissing her cheeks, her jaw, her throat. Through the nightgown, his palms weighed the fullness of her breasts.

"I'm glad you came to me," he murmured.

"I gather it wasn't proper behavior for a lady."

"Proper be damned," he said, and his silken-hot glance made her shiver. "The Countess of Hawkesford may do as she desires."

"Nicholas..." She gasped as his fingers found the tender joining of her legs. The flimsy nightdress was no barrier to the invasion of his caress. Dissolving against him, she felt the world slide away, leaving nothing but the two of them, nothing but the beating of his heart against her palms, nothing but the fever flaming inside her.

"I love you," she breathed into the salt-scented skin of his neck.

His arms crushed her close, lifting her to him as he carried her to the bed. "I love you, too, Elizabeth," he muttered. "I'll make you happy. You belong to me now, forever, for always."

She gloried in his possessiveness. The hot pressure of his arousal against her belly spoke more of his hunger for her than mere words could express. In a storm of urgency they made love, celebrating their new life. She opened herself to him, heart and body and soul, giving and receiving. The magic in his touch aroused her, building her need to a height so dizzying Elizabeth teetered on the brink of falling. She heard the hoarse rasp of his breathing, smelled the musky scent of his sweat, felt the straining muscles in his back.

"Nicholas ... Nicholas." Again and again she moaned his name as the ecstasy bore her higher and higher. She could think of nothing beyond the spiraling urgency to kiss and caress, nothing but the powerful rhythm of his hips, until at last the shuddering release burst upon them.

Sated, they lay together as their breathing eased and their heartbeats slowed. He rolled to the side, bringing her with him so that she lay half draped over his body, her cheek resting against his chest, her hair cloaking his shoulder.

"Elizabeth," he whispered, his hand seeking the gentle curves of her back. "We needn't go to Yorkshire tomorrow. We could travel to the Continent instead, lease a villa in Nice, make love all day and all night."

Temptation wrenched her willpower. She tilted her head to gaze at him; his face was darkly handsome against the white linen pillows, his hair charmingly ruffled. Reluctantly she said, "I'd rather go off alone with you, Nicholas, you know I would. But first I need to learn why someone wants me dead."

He gathered her hard against him. "That's precisely why we shouldn't go. It's far too dangerous."

"Shall I sit back and wait for him to strike again?"

"We don't know for certain that it's a 'him.' That's what bothers me. We know so little."

She brushed a kiss across the shadowy bruise on his jaw. "Please understand, Nicholas. Meeting my real father is something I need to do, for my own peace of mind."

Eyes half lidded, he stared at her. She felt the force of his thoughts, sensed the battle waged within him. At length he said, "I intend to stay by your side every moment."

"Yes."

"I mean it, Elizabeth. You'll grow weary of me dogging your heels."

"I doubt that, my husband." Smiling, she shifted over him, relishing the roughness of his body hair against her breasts and thighs. "I doubt that very much, indeed."

They left the next morning from King's Cross Station. Settling into the plush confines of a first class compartment, Elizabeth felt excited and pleasantly worried. Fog swirled around the people who scurried along the platform. A man paused to peer into their window and Nicholas imperiously waved him on.

"That's rude," she chided.

His fingers circled her wrist, his thumb caressing the delicate inner skin. "If we've a stranger staring at us for the next nine hours, I can't kiss you as I please."

The rough velvet promise in his voice sent a ripple of longing through her. "You mean the proper Earl of Hawkesford would seduce a woman on a train?"

"Not just any woman... my wife. Since the moment we met, I've had the very devil of a time behaving properly."

She caught her breath at the look in his eyes—soft yet scorching, warm yet wicked. A small shock vibrated inside her. She belonged to him now. The thought left her blissfully happy, yet dizzily confused, as if she were hurtling headlong into unknown territory.

A whistle blew. Grateful for the distraction, Elizabeth pressed her face to the window as the train chugged slowly away. Mist enveloped the cramped brick houses with dark, sagging roofs, the drab factories with chimneys belching forth smoke. The train stopped several times to take on more passengers, and gradually the rows of tenements thinned and the fog began to lift. The buildings of London gave way to grassy meadows and woodland parks.

Turning to remark on the scenery, she saw Nicholas's head rolled back against the leather seat, his eyes closed, his long legs stretched out. She pulled a pad from her traveling bag and began to sketch. The scratching of her pencil was barely audible over the noise of the engine and the clack of the wheels. She felt at peace, rocked by the rhythm of the train, content in the presence of her husband.

After a time he shifted, his firm shoulder brushing hers. "Where do you find the energy to work?" he grumbled. "You exhausted me last night."

She laughed. "Perhaps you inspire my creativity."

"What are you drawing?" He plucked the pad from her lap and stared at the sketch. "Your mother," he said softly. "Lucy Templeton Hastings was a beautiful woman—it's uncanny how closely you resemble her."

"Whenever I've had a spare moment, I've been trying to reproduce the pictures in the sketchbook that was stolen."

He flipped through the pages. "You seem to have had great success. What was she like?"

"Gentle, kind, never lost her temper... unlike me." Elizabeth smiled wryly, then nibbled on the end of the pencil. "Nicholas, do you suppose the same person who's after me also took that sketchbook?"

His face hardened. "It's too big a coincidence to think otherwise."

"But why? Why would someone want sketches of my mother?"

"I've wondered that myself," he said slowly, flicking a glance at the pad. "Perhaps this person mistook her for you. You do have the same luxurious black hair, the high cheekbones, the delicate nose."

As he caressed each part he named, his touch made her shiver deliciously. "You've met the duke and his family," she said. "Who do you think is the likely suspect?"

Setting aside the sketch pad, he seemed to hesitate. "It isn't for me to prejudice you against your relations."

"Then how am I to find the culprit?"

His mouth drew into a strict line. "You're to find nothing, Elizabeth. Enjoy your visit with the duke and leave the detecting to me."

She bit back an indignant remark. "Be reasonable, Nicholas. I might catch something you miss. Don't you want to identify this person as swiftly as possible?"

His dark brows drew together in a frown. Gradually the stern set of his face softened. "Very well, then. You've already met Drew. He's a self-indulgent womanizer. That's why I didn't want Cicely within a mile of him. During the six weeks he was in town, he ran up gambling debts all over London."

"Do you suppose he thinks I might lay claim to part of his inheritance?"

"Precisely. Philippa, his mother, might think so, too. She's an ingratiating sort, hovers around the duke, anxious to please him." He grinned. "I remember thinking you would have laughed. When she flapped her arms she looked rather like a skinny bird."

"I'm sorrier and sorrier that I missed that tea."

"Serves you right for gallivanting all over London without me." His fingers twined with hers. "The Duchess Adelaide was harder to read. She didn't say much, just sat there placid as a plow horse. But it stands to reason she might resent you. After all," he said, his voice gentling, "her husband had an affair with your mother... I'm glad to say."

Troubled, Elizabeth studied him. "But that was over twenty years ago."

"Some people have long memories. Until we know more about the sort of person she is, we have to assume she could be cold-blooded enough to hire someone to hurt you."

"But why now? If she hated me, why wouldn't she have acted when I was born?"

"I don't know. Perhaps she resents you because you've grown up to look so much like your mother."

Elizabeth shivered. "She would have to be mad."

His hand tensed on hers. "The more I think on this, Countess, the less I like it. As soon as you satisfy your need to make the duke's acquaintance, we're returning to London."

She had no intention of agreeing to *that*. "We'll see," she hedged. "Now tell me about the duke, please."

He shot her a piercing look. "The first thing I noticed about Rockborough was his eyes." Nicholas touched her cheek. "They're the same rare shade of violet as yours. He seems rather old and frail, in body if not in spirit. Never travels anywhere without his doctor. In fact the duke had a mild asthma attack at tea and the doctor had to attend to him."

"And his character?" Seeing his hesitation, she pressed, "The truth, please. He may be my father in blood, but I've no other attachment to him, at least not yet."

Nicholas studied her pensively. "His enjoyment in life seemed to come from baiting his relations. And from collecting knives."

"Knives?"

He nodded. "Hugh Sterling is a connoisseur of medieval weaponry. Ostensibly that's why he was in London, to visit an agent who buys for him at auctions."

"Does the duke have a reason to wish me ill?" she asked in a low voice. "Would he resent the sudden reappearance of a bastard daughter?"

"A daughter who is now the Countess of Hawkesford." Gathering her close, Nicholas pressed his cheek to her hair. "I can't answer your question, love, but your appearance certainly changed *my* life."

Elizabeth drew comfort from his warm strength. Closing her eyes, she breathed in his subtle masculine tang. Nothing could happen to her in his embrace. Life took on a glow that drove away dark motives and hidden resentments.

After a time his arms loosened. She shifted, turning her face to the window and her mind to the passing landscape. Alternately flat and rolling, the countryside was lushly green with farms and forests. The motion of the train lulled her as the scenery flashed past. What a change this was from the cramped and crowded streets of London and New York.

"Is the view more fascinating than your husband, Countess?"

She swiveled toward Nicholas. "Not at all . . . it's just that I've never ridden on a train before."

His brows lifted in surprise. "Never?"

"When I was growing up, we hadn't the money to travel. Owen and I had to scrape to pay passage to England."

He brought her hand to his lips. "Those times are over now, Elizabeth. You'll never want for anything again."

She tenderly touched his cheek. "I don't need money to make me happy, Nicholas. Only you."

Suddenly he bent to rummage inside the covered luncheon hamper. "Perhaps this will make you happy, as well." He handed her a heavy, string-wrapped parcel.

"What is it?" she asked, her fingers sliding off the twine. The snowy paper fell away to reveal a thick, leather-bound book. "*Gray's Anatomy*," she whispered, flabbergasted yet rejoicing to the depths of her soul.

Clasping the volume to her bosom, she raised misty eyes to Nicholas. He loved her enough to give her something she so dearly valued and he so clearly scorned. He was lounging in the seat, watching her, an anxious smile on his lips.

Her knees went weak. "Nicholas, thank you." Hugging the book in one arm and him in the other, she brushed a kiss across his mouth.

His hands rubbed stirringly over her shoulders. "Just keep the damned thing away from my sister," he growled. "She isn't quite ready for it."

Elizabeth couldn't take offense; her heart felt too full. "You really do accept my work, then?"

"I want you to do whatever makes you happy."

She searched his face. "And you won't mind if I win the commission from Lord Buckstone?"

His grip on her tensed. Something flared in his gaze; his dark lashes lowered for a moment. When he looked up, his eyes were a cool, banked gray. "Buckstone is only leading you on, Elizabeth. I doubt there really is a commission."

The brooding edge to his voice gave her the impression he wasn't being honest. "I don't believe that. And neither do you."

"I believe what I saw the night of the ball. This is all he wanted." Nicholas shaped his palm to the fullness of her breast, then slid his hand downward, over her lilac silk traveling gown, to the delta of her thighs. "And this."

The blunt gesture both aroused and annoyed her. Stiffening, she pushed away his hand and set aside the book, her pleasure in the gift dwindling. "That isn't fair. Peter never once made an indecent suggestion to me."

"Of course not. He wanted to lull your suspicions until he had you trapped on his remote Irish estate."

"You haven't any proof of that," she flung back. "You just want to have things your own way, because you're used to people doing as you wish."

"Am I supposed to be thrilled that my wife wants to leave me for months on end? To spend her time with a notorious rake?"

Elizabeth swallowed a swell of anger. Trying to understand him, she studied the implacable planes of his face, the set of his jaw and the tautness of his cheekbones. He could be all tender warmth and blazing passion, or as now, all merciless power and chilling control.

"Then come with me to Ireland, Nicholas," she said evenly. "See for yourself that I'm not going to leap into an affair with another man."

He looked at her sharply. "I'm not worried about you having an affair."

"Then why *are* you carrying on so?"

"Why is this so important to you?" he shot back. "I can get you scores of commissions, commissions that will let you work at home."

How could she explain to him her need for the freedom to choose? "But this is a chance I was offered on my own merits, not because I'm wife to the Earl of Hawkesford."

He favored her with a cold stare. "Merits! The only merits Buckstone cares about are the ones beneath your clothing."

Her anger flared. "You're jealous, Nicholas Ware. Jealous because Peter is offering me an opportunity I want with all my heart and soul."

His face looked carved from ice. Only his eyes were expressive, unveiled and vulnerable. Quietly he said, "Do you regret giving yourself to me instead of to him?"

His haunted gaze burned through her resentment. Why were they arguing, anyway? Better to wait . . . wait until she learned if she'd won the commission.

She lay her cheek against the warm wall of his chest. "No, Nicholas, never. I love you."

"Then show me," he said, his voice raspy. "Show me."

His fingers roughly tilted up her chin. His lips pinned hers in a hard, hungry kiss that shook Elizabeth with its intensity. The feel of his tongue plunging into her mouth brought a searing burst of excitement. She pressed herself to him, her arms wending around his neck, her fingers mussing the thick perfection of his hair.

Abruptly Nicholas pulled away. Leaning to the window, he yanked down the tassled black shade, plunging the private compartment into shadows.

She blinked. "What are you doing?"

"Shutting out the world," he said silkily. "Shutting out everything but you."

His hands surrounded her waist. In one swift movement he lifted her onto his lap so that her legs straddled him and her skirts billowed around them. Her breasts yielded to his chest; her calves hugged his hard thighs. Pressing into her most intimate place she felt the telltale swell of his passion.

"But . . . here?" she said breathlessly.

He consulted his pocketwatch. "We've half an hour before the train stops in Huntingdon." His eyes gleamed through the dimness; his hand delved beneath her skirt and petticoats to slide slowly up her silk-stockinged leg. "Half an hour of paradise."

His skilled fingers found the parting in her lace

drawers. Her breath caught and her head fell back as he stroked her dewy warmth. Desire rose sharp and sweet inside her. She wanted him to love her; she wanted to love him. Shifting slightly to give herself space, she reached with quivering hands to unbutton his trousers until no cloth separated their flesh. He lay hot and heavy in her hand and as she caressed him, he closed his eyes and groaned, his head tilting against the leather cushion.

"Elizabeth," he muttered. "This is why I love you . . . this is what you've taught me . . . to be open and free."

Lifting her again, he filled the empty ache inside her with his surging heat. The rocking of the train matched the rhythm of their pleasure, the sway of their bodies seeking, reaching, giving. Elizabeth gloried in the freedom of straddling him, the freedom to stoke the fires of his passion with the movements of her hips. She reveled in his whispered words of encouragement, gloried in the excitement of his kisses, the sensuality of his touch, the headiness of his scent and taste. Clinging to him, she moaned his name over and over on the steadily building ride that plunged her headlong into ecstatic oblivion. . . .

The train chugged slowly into Huntingdon Station, the wheels squealing metallically on the rails. Nicholas gave Elizabeth one last lingering kiss, then helped her back to her seat. Swiftly she smoothed her wrinkled skirts. He repaired his own dishevelment before snapping up the window shade.

Just in time. Heedless of Nicholas's noble glower, a portly matron and her rosy-cheeked daughter entered the compartment and settled themselves in the seat opposite.

Elizabeth glanced at him and caught the wry tilt of his lips, the faint shrug of his shoulders. Save for the glow in his eyes, she couldn't have guessed from his impeccable facade the intimate joy they had shared just moments earlier. He looked as coolly perfect as ever.

He's a master at appearances, she thought, doubts

creeping into her contentment. Was that why he'd given her *Gray's Anatomy*, to lull her into believing he supported her sculpting?

No, she had to trust him. If she didn't, their love might crumble like unfired clay.

Chapter 18

❦

They found lodging at an ancient posting inn near the duke's estate, which bordered the wild Yorkshire moors. Elizabeth acknowledged a secret relief at stealing one more night alone with her husband before facing the truth of her past. As they lay sated in each other's arms, surrounded by the musky scent of their lovemaking and the lonely sough of the wind around the eaves, Nicholas quietly outlined their plans for the morrow.

"We'll leave our things here," he said, his hand absently rubbing up and down her arm. "We can't be certain Rockborough will invite us to stay."

She tipped her head back against his hard shoulder; his eyes shone dark as charcoal in the faint flickering light of a lone candle. "Should we have sent a note to the duke?"

Nicholas shook his head. "I'd sooner catch him off guard. His reaction to seeing you might tell me something."

She noted his lordly *I*, but vowed he would not stop her from aiding him. Her trained powers of observation might find a clue.

His deep sigh stirred the tendrils along her temples. "I hate like the very devil to put you through this," he muttered.

"It's what I want, Nicholas. I won't live the rest of my life in fear."

He made no reply but clasped her tightly, as if he

could shield her from harm by imbuing her with his strength. He had indeed taken every precaution. Upon their arrival, she had been astounded by the entourage that had emerged from the second class railcar. Dobson and Pickering unloaded the luggage under Quinn's sharp directives; Janet and Kipp scurried to find transport to the inn. If they were to stay with the duke, Nicholas declared, he would surround her with people he could trust.

In the dusty inn yard the next morning, Kipp seemed to take her new marital status for granted, his boyish interest focused on the upcoming visit. "I'm to keep me ear to the ground," he told her, jabbing a thumb at his liveried chest. "Ain't nobody goin' to 'urt you with me an' 'is lordship around."

Nicholas helped her into the leased cabriolet, then climbed in beside her, Kipp riding on the tiny pageboard behind. The other servants would wait at the inn. Handling the reins with competent ease, Nicholas guided the open carriage out of the yard. The ancient vehicle creaked and groaned over the rutted road, the swaybacked dun horse looking more suited to pull a plow.

Morning sunshine warmed Elizabeth. Farms stretched over rolling hills, the fields separated by stone walls. The patches of cultivation gradually gave way to a primeval landscape untamed by human influence, save for an occasional cluster of grazing sheep. A cool wind tugged at Elizabeth's plume-trimmed bonnet. Nowhere in New York had she seen anything so barbarously beautiful, so ruggedly remote. Clumps of bushes dotted the countryside and she drew in a deep breath of tangy air.

Nicholas smiled at her. "Heather will be blooming soon," he said over the rattle of the wheels. "And that's the sea you smell. We're not far from the coast."

He pointed out the purple moor grass, bilberry and crowberry shrubs, and the tough-stemmed bracken, the bane of farmers. Kipp leaned over the back of their seat, unabashedly listening. Against the clear sky a

kestrel soared and circled in search of prey. The lonely
vista touched a chord deep within Elizabeth.

"Look familiar, love?" Nicholas said.

Was it her fancy or did the scenery stir long-dormant
memories? She shook her head. "I'm not sure."

He touched her hand. "Give yourself time."

At length he turned the cabriolet onto a bumpy side
road leading to an arched gate in the distance. Connected to either side of the massive entryway stood
twin stone buildings glinting with mullioned windows.
The place looked empty, imposing, and somehow forlorn.

A horseman appeared over the rise, galloping toward them in a thunder of hooves and a cloud of dust.
Nicholas drew the dun to a halt just shy of the gate-
house. Elizabeth tensed as the rider hurtled headlong
at them, as if the carriage were invisible. At the last
possible moment he reined in and his majestic black
stallion halted within an arm's length of the vehicle.

"Cor!" muttered Kipp.

A thickset man, his face broad and plain beneath a
battered felt cap, sat erect in the saddle. Elizabeth was
struck by the contrast between unkempt man and sleek
horse. Yet despite his baggy clothing, he aimed an arrogant glare at Nicholas.

"What business have you here?" he demanded, his
deep voice not servile in the least.

"We've come to see the duke," Nicholas said.

"His Grace is indisposed. We've no visitors sched-
uled. Go away."

Nicholas studied the horseman. "We've come a long
distance," he said in a tone as smooth as cream. "I'd
hoped you would show us more hospitality, Your
Grace."

The brown eyes narrowed, then with a braying
laugh that sent the stallion dancing sideways, the rider
whipped off his cap. A thin mass of graying brown hair
tumbled downward. With a shock Elizabeth realized
she must be gazing at the Duchess Adelaide.

The duchess's pale lips parted in amusement, revealing an enormous set of white teeth. "Should have known I couldn't pull the wool over your eyes, Hawkesford."

He merely smiled. "My wife and I are on our honeymoon trip. We were in the vicinity and thought to pay our respects to you and the duke."

The duchess flicked a disinterested glance at Elizabeth; then her gaze sharpened. "You weren't present at tea," she stated, "yet we've met."

Elizabeth's heart jumped, and she felt Nicholas's strong fingers interlock with hers. "No, I'm afraid we haven't met," she said.

"Elizabeth is an American," he added, "but her mother lived near here many years ago. Their close resemblance might explain why my wife looks familiar."

Elizabeth held her breath under the duchess's piercing stare. The ebony stallion blew gently into the silence, and Kipp shifted on his rear perch.

Abruptly those dark eyes turned back to Nicholas. "Perhaps so," she said, her tone bland.

"I'd like to speak to the duke," he said.

The duchess's homely face drew into a grimace. "Oh, very well. Hugh's likely still abed, but we'll rouse the old bugger."

Wheeling around, she dug her boot heels into her mount and the stallion bounded away. Nicholas snapped the reins; the dun started at a trot, following in the duchess's dust. Elizabeth slowly relaxed her fingers on the sapphire-and-silver stripes of her skirt.

She tilted her head at Nicholas; morning sunlight glinted off his flawless chestnut hair. "Do you suppose she remembered my mother?"

He lifted the broad shoulders beneath his dove-gray coat. "I'm not sure. We'll just have to wait and see."

An avenue of elms lined the winding drive to Swanmere Manor. In contrast to the harshly drawn moors, streams were overgrown with oaks and sycamores, and clumps of wild rhododendron promised a brilliant springtime palette. An occasional tumbledown temple or Palladian bridge embellished the carved hills. A sudden turn in the road revealed the great, green sweep of a lawn, where a few sheep grazed like gray boulders and a circular drive led to a stark, sprawling mansion.

Colossal columns and tall windows broke the harsh gray stone facade, while urns and chimneys dotted the straight roofline at uninspired intervals. The sheer enormity of the dwelling overwhelmed the architectural attempt at classical simplicity; the place looked as stately and unapproachable as Queen Victoria.

A vague discomfort stirred inside Elizabeth. She wasn't sure if the feeling arose from anticipation at meeting her blood father or from a buried recognition. As she studied the house, her fingers reached into her pocket to touch the swan signet, the ring she hadn't been able to bring herself to wear around her neck since Owen's revelation.

Nicholas drew the cabriolet to a halt in front of a huge portico, then leapt lithely out and tossed the reins to Kipp when no retainer or footman came forth to assist them. The duchess was nowhere in sight. Nicholas helped Elizabeth climb down, then their footsteps echoed on the massive marble steps leading to the arched entryway, where a soaring swan adorned the pediment above the door. Feeling dwarfed and ill at ease, she clung to the warmth of his arm. The house appeared deserted, from the dullness of the door brass to the crumbling of the stone mortar.

"Chin up, Countess," Nicholas whispered, flashing her a wink and a smile.

His imperious knock resounded on the great door. He, at least, Elizabeth thought wryly, felt unthreatened by the imminent encounter. After a moment he pounded harder. They waited for what seemed like ages before the intricate knob rattled and the brass hinges squealed and a surprised face poked out.

A white mobcap covered the woman's hair, and eyes black as mica peered out of doughy features. "What d'ye want?" she said in a voice that sounded more wondering than rude. "If ye're lost, go 'round t' the stables an' Black Pete'll gi' ye direction."

"We've come to see the duke," Nicholas said. "The Duchess Adelaide met us in the drive and gave us leave to visit."

"The duchess invited ye?" the woman said, clearly staggered by the notion. She stared from Nicholas to Elizabeth and back again. Hastily she retreated, swinging the door wide. "Coom in, then, if ye will, an' welcome t' ye."

Nicholas's hand at her waist, Elizabeth stepped inside a vast entry hall. The room seemed chilly and dim after the bright sunshine. The shadowed shape of a staircase climbed to the second floor; on either side of the carved newel posts stood identical suits of chunky armor, like silent sentries from another age. Elizabeth gazed askance from the closed visors to the hodgepodge of shields and swords displayed against the dark paneling.

"I'm Mrs. Drabble, th' housekeeper. I'll be puttin' ye t' wait in th' saloon."

She spun, her faded black skirts twitching as she marched off, moving swiftly despite her broad girth. Elizabeth hastened to keep up, Nicholas striding easily beside her. The tap of their footsteps echoed in the dark hall.

Upon entering the saloon, Elizabeth felt as if she'd stepped back centuries. The walls were wainscoted in aged English oak and draped in tapestries, the mullioned windows painted with heraldic scenes. Numerous glass cases displayed more weaponry, maces and dirks and guns. A musty scent pervaded the air and a thin coating of dust dulled the bulky chairs and tables.

At the end of the long room stood the only concession to modernity, a billiards table over which Drew Sterling bent, stick in hand. The crack of balls rang out. Straightening, he saw the visitors and an expression of pleasured surprise spread over his aquiline features. Lifting a hand in greeting, he ambled toward them.

"I say, Hawkesford, what are you doing in the wild, woolly north country?"

"I've business with the duke."

Drew didn't appear to notice Nicholas's coolness. "Glad you've come, old chap. Hope you can stay awhile. We're starved for decent company around here, you know."

"Some of us has plenty t' do," Mrs. Drabble sniffed.

"Don't scold, Drabbie," Drew said, patting her pudgy shoulder. "Be a good old girl and dust off a bottle of that French brandy my uncle keeps stashed under lock and key."

The housekeeper shook her many chins. "Oh, fiddle, it's yer mother I'll be fetchin'." To Nicholas, she added, "Ye've coom t' see His Grace, you say, but he's still abed, wi' the doctor tendin' him."

Elizabeth felt a start of dismay. "He isn't ill, I hope."

"He's only sleeping late," Drew said. "Dozing off the effect of those quackish potions Gilbert Marsh feeds him."

"Here now, Master Drew, don't ye be speakin' ill of th' good doctor." Mrs. Drabble looked at Nicholas. "Who should I say is callin'?"

"Lord and Lady Hawkesford."

As the housekeeper departed, Drew gave Elizabeth a piercing stare. "Lady Hawkesford, you say? We met at the Garforths' ball. Aren't you Cicely's art tutor?"

"Not anymore," Nicholas said curtly. "Elizabeth and I were married two days ago."

Piqued at his presumption, Elizabeth said, "But I will still be teaching Cicely. She has a strong interest in sculpting, an interest I intend to nurture."

Nicholas aimed that lordly look at her, and she stared back without flinching. She knew what he was thinking . . . she knew and felt annoyed. He would *allow* her to instruct Cicely as long as it suited his plans.

Drew waved them into chairs. "Your sister's well, I trust."

Elizabeth saw Nicholas's jaw tense slightly as he sat down. "Perfectly so," he said.

"A pretty thing, Cicely is. A pity she didn't come, too."

"We hardly wanted my sister tagging along on our honeymoon trip."

Drew laughed, his knowing dark eyes flitting over Elizabeth in a way that made her flush. He might not realize, she reminded herself, that they were cousins.

"I don't imagine you would," he said. Strolling to the billiards table, he bent to aim and shoot; the ball careened off the side and rolled to a rest in the center of the green baize. "Drat," he said languidly, before raising his eyes to Nicholas. "Could I interest you in a game, old chap? Low stakes, until you get the feel of the table."

"Perhaps another time."

Drew shrugged. "Cursed table's warped, anyhow, like everything else in this dungeon. Still, it beats twiddling my thumbs, I suppose."

Suppressing a shudder, Elizabeth glanced around the saloon. *Dungeon* was an apt description for the cache of knives and crossbows gleaming dully from their nests of dark velvet inside the glass case. Politely she asked, "Do you share your uncle's interest in weaponry?"

"Gad, no." Tossing down the billiards stick, Drew walked to the fireplace and plucked a slim dueling sword from a display above the carved wooden mantel. "Perhaps I should, though. Might prove amusing to take up fencing. *En garde!*"

He struck a pose, feet planted wide, arm stretched out to point the sword at her chest. Aware of Nicholas tensing in the chair opposite her, Elizabeth sat on the edge of her seat. Her heart tripped a wild dance. For an instant Drew's world-weary expression altered into a look so ferocious she could believe him capable of cold-blooded murder. . . .

"Dear me, whatever is going on here?"

The feminine voice trilled from the doorway. Nicholas stood up, and Elizabeth's widened eyes swung to a woman clad in garish turquoise, the gown adorned with too many flounces and frills, as if she were trying to compensate for her gaunt figure. Her bony fingers fluttered in distress as she swooped forward like a vulture in search of prey.

"Put that dreadful thing away, Drew."

Pulling a face, he lowered the sword. "Don't fret, Mother. I was merely showing off Uncle's infamous weapon collection."

She grimaced. "How morbid. You'll frighten our guests away."

"Perhaps you're right," Drew muttered, stretching up to replace the sword on its wall hooks. "God knows we've few enough visitors to this dismal pile."

"I'm sorry to hear more people don't come calling out here in the country," Elizabeth said pleasantly. "We had quite the enjoyable drive across the moors."

"Our remote locale isn't what keeps company away," Drew said, his sulky expression returning. "It's my dear uncle's penchant for making their visits miserable. He never could bear to see anyone else have any fun."

"That's quite enough." The sourness on her thin lips sweetened into a syrupy smile as Philippa took Nicholas's proferred hand. "My dear Lord Hawkesford, how very marvelous to see you again."

"The pleasure is all mine."

Turning, she said graciously, "And you must be the new countess. When we came to tea at Hawkesford House, that close-mouthed husband of yours never breathed a word of his imminent marital intentions."

"Please, call me Elizabeth. And I'm sorry I missed that tea. I was . . . indisposed."

"Dear me." Philippa's arms flapped like bird wings, and Elizabeth stifled a smile. "All that wretched fog and smoke in London can make a person quite ill. We've a resident doctor who can provide you with a tonic should you need one. But a few days of this fine country air should restore you."

"And bore you," Drew mumbled from his stance near the fireplace.

Philippa drilled a glare at him, but her face dripped honey as she shifted her brown eyes back. "Now, you must promise to stay for luncheon; we've so much to talk about. Tell me, your lordship, what brings you so far from London?"

As Nicholas spun the story of paying their respects to the duke, Elizabeth itched to capture Philippa's expressions on paper. In a flash her lean features could go from ingratiating to shrewish and back again. Could such mood swings signify a fickle temperament, someone who might kill in a fit of passion?

Yet she'd exhibited no sign of recognition. Or was she hiding her reaction?

In the antiquated dining room, Elizabeth chewed a tough cut of mutton and listened to Philippa rattle on about the history of Swanmere Manor and the duke's illustrious forebears. The subject both fascinated and disturbed Elizabeth; it was difficult to accept that her own ancestry lay so deeply rooted in this house.

The Duchess Adelaide had joined them, and sat silently at one end of the lengthy table, her dull-eyed attention focused on her plate. Elizabeth studied the woman with veiled interest. The lively horsewoman of that morning might never have existed. Nicholas had said the duchess's two children were dead. Could Adelaide resent Elizabeth for being the duke's only surviving child?

Finishing his lumpy damson cobbler, Nicholas leaned back in his carved armchair and said conversationally, "Did any of you know that Elizabeth's mother once lived in this house?"

Elizabeth's heart faltered. Drew turned to stare at her. The Duchess Adelaide stopped chewing. Philippa's spoon halted in midair.

"I don't understand," Philippa murmured. "I thought you were an American, Elizabeth."

Nicholas spoke before Elizabeth could. "She moved there as a young girl, some twenty years past. But she was born here." He paused, looking around the table. "Perhaps some of you remember her mother? Your Grace, she was your companion for a time. Her name was Lucy Templeton."

The duchess said nothing, her brown eyes exhibiting no emotion, no trace of her thoughts.

A slice of cobbler quivered on Philippa's spoon. The silver implement clattered to the table, its cream and plum contents spattering the white cloth.

"Lucy Templeton?" she repeated, her voice high and thready. "I don't believe you."

"Then look at my wife," Nicholas said softly. "Look at her and tell me she's not Lucy's daughter."

Elizabeth felt the bite of Philippa's sharp scrutiny. The corners of her thin lips turned downward and her pale cheeks drew inward, as if she'd tasted something sour.

"Then you're . . . you're . . ." she sputtered.

"My uncle's by-blow," Drew said, his eyes intent on Elizabeth. "I was only nine when you left, but you're the very image of your mother. I remember you toddling after me—" He shot a hooded glance at the duchess. "Whenever, of course, my uncle would allow his bastard brat to visit."

Nicholas stood, flattening his palms on the table and directing an icy glare at Drew. "You are speaking of the Countess of Hawkesford."

Drew had the good grace to mumble an apology. Hands damp, Elizabeth twisted the fraying damask napkin in her lap. Hostility hung like a tangible presence in the air. Everyone was staring at her and she wanted to crawl beneath the threadbare Persian carpet. Behind which of these faces lay the mind that plotted her death? Only Nicholas's eyes regarded her with tender warmth, embuing her with the courage to square her shoulders and gaze around at the gathering.

Mrs. Drabble marched in like a sweep of fresh air. "The duke's ready t' receive yer lordship now. An' I'll thank'ee t' make haste. His Grace don't like t' be kept waitin'."

"Then, by all means, let's go," Nicholas said easily.

Philippa shot up, her napkin tumbling to the floor. "What will you say to the duke?" she shrieked.

"Sit down," said the duchess. "You're making a spectacle."

Philippa turned, her eyes spiteful. "A spectacle, am I, Adelaide? Will you welcome the duke's bastard into this house? She must have come here to wheedle an inheritance out of him."

"Hawkesford can support his wife, I'm sure," the duchess said. "And he might not take kindly to your name-calling. So sit down . . . before you make a more ridiculous ass of yourself."

Like a clay figure formed without a supporting armature, Philippa drooped into her chair. Her dark eyes retained a spark of belligerence that belied the benevolent hostess of moments earlier.

"Do pardon us," Nicholas blandly told the others, while holding out a hand to Elizabeth.

She stood on wobbly legs. Holding tight to his arm, she followed Mrs. Drabble out the door and up the flight of stairs dominating the entrance hall. The duchess's defense had been unexpected. Was she really so indifferent to her husband's illegitimate child?

Suits of armor lined the shadowy corridor; the closed visors gave Elizabeth an eerie prickling sensation, as if she were being watched. Apparently oblivious to the display, Mrs. Drabble marched straight past. She halted before a door at the end of the hall and rapped firmly.

You're about to meet your father, Elizabeth thought.

Her throat felt as dry as the dust that hung in the air. Her fingers tightened on Nicholas's arm; his hand brushed over hers in a comforting caress. Then the time for panic ended as the door clicked quietly open.

A slender man stood there, his fair hair burnished by the dim light beyond. Judging by the fine lines around his eyes and mouth, he looked to be a decade older than Nicholas, yet something about the stranger reminded Elizabeth of a choirboy.

"My Lord and Lady of Hawkesford, Doctor Marsh," Mrs. Drabble announced.

His pleasant smile dwindled as his blue eyes moved from Nicholas to her. He started visibly, his scrubbed features paling to ash. Clearly here was yet another person who had known Lucy Templeton.

Gilbert Marsh moved back, motioning them inside. "Good afternoon," he murmured. "The duke has been awaiting you."

Elizabeth stepped into a bedroom glutted with medieval bric-a-brac—swords and shields, arrows and pikes, spears and clubs, and a host of other implements of murder. A horned helmet sat atop the cluttered dressing table; a collection of spurs dangled from the mantelpiece. A wicked-looking trident stood propped in a corner. The presence of so many weapons gave her the shivers, yet the simple carved beauty of a few articles appealed to her artist's eye.

The curtains were drawn, rendering the room dim and stuffy. A medicinal scent pervaded the air. A faint movement drew her gaze to the shrunken figure of a man seated in a wingback chair by the fireplace. His stooped frame was angled forward as he stared intently at her. Stomach tied into a knot, Elizabeth walked slowly toward him. Leaning heavily on a silver-topped cane, he hauled himself halfway to his feet.

"Lucy?" he whispered.

The quavering note in his voice pierced her heart. Without pausing to think, she swept forward and knelt before him, her hand covering the gnarled fingers atop the cane. "Not Lucy," she said gently. "Elizabeth."

Eyes of a familiar violet hue scrutinized her. In the ancient lines of his face she could see traces of rugged handsomeness, though now his cheeks were sunken and his skin puckered. A feeble echo of hurt and confusion curled inside her, the flashing ribbon of memory vanishing so swiftly she could not catch hold of it.

The tension seemed to leach from his chilly fingers. "Elizabeth," he repeated hoarsely. "My little Sterling swan."

She had but a moment to wonder at the watery sheen in his eyes before Gilbert Marsh hurried to take the duke's arm. "Please, Your Grace, do sit down. You're putting undue strain on yourself."

"Oh, botheration." The duke tried to shake off the doctor's assisting hand. "I'm not an invalid."

Unperturbed, Marsh firmly pressed his patient back into the chair. "There now. You're still weary from our journey here. If you're not careful, you'll bring on another of your spells."

"You'd like that, eh? Keeps you on the payroll."

Lips tightening, the doctor plumped a few pillows behind the duke's shriveled figure.

Hugh Sterling gestured at a frayed maroon couch. "Sit down, girl. No sense in hovering too. You, too, Hawkesford."

Pushing aside an elaborately decorated sword sheath, Elizabeth sank onto the lumpy sofa. She couldn't quite fathom this gruff man who had fathered her. When Nicholas's hand sought hers on the cushion, she turned her palm up gratefully.

The duke pulled an old-fashioned quizzing glass from his pocket and studied her. "By Jove, you're the spitting image of Lucy. Though Lucy had green eyes . . . green as grass." Turning to the doctor, who sat on the dressing table stool, the duke bellowed, "What do you think, Marsh? You were a youth back when Lucy was here. Don't you find the resemblance amazing?"

"Resemblance?" The doctor seemed to hesitate. "Indeed, Your Grace. Though you, of course, knew Miss Templeton far better than I."

"Ah, Lucy," the duke said, his eyes gone misty soft. "Finest woman a man could ever hope to meet. Hard to believe she's gone now."

Elizabeth felt Nicholas's fingers go rigid. "How did you know she's dead?" he asked.

Hugh Sterling's gaze turned to ice. "That Bible-spouting Owen came to see me. Accused me of wanting to hurt Elizabeth. Hah! When I hadn't seen hide nor hair of her in twenty years!"

"He came here?" Elizabeth said faintly.

"No, no. Happened back in London. Weeks ago." He brandished his cane angrily. "Damned upstart warned me to stay clear of his daughter. The nerve of him, when he stole you from me in the first place. I wanted to throttle him, but he got away. Even the footman couldn't catch him."

"I recall," Gilbert Marsh chided, "you suffered quite the attack that day."

Shock eddying through her, Elizabeth barely heard the doctor. She remembered the time she had seen Owen sneaking up the servant's staircase at Hawkesford House, his clothing caked with mud and his walking stick gouged. He must have just come from the duke's town house. Why had he never breathed a word to her, even when she had accused him of failing to protect her?

"I thought he'd only sent you a letter," she said.

"Letter? I never received any letter. The wretch must be lying. Always pretended to be so pious, by Jove. Then he took Lucy and my daughter out from under my nose!"

Had someone intercepted that letter? Or was the duke lying? Elizabeth yearned to chip away at the fossilized marble and find the true man beneath. Surely even a curmudgeon like Hugh Sterling wasn't capable of plotting the murder of his own daughter. . . .

"Did you ever come looking for me?" she asked.

The duke spread his palms wide. "Didn't know where to begin. Footman lost Owen in the alleyways off the Strand."

"I meant before, when I disappeared as a child."

Hugh Sterling's gaze dropped to the top of his cane. When he lifted his eyes again, sadness haunted the violet depths. "I wanted to, by Jove. I swear, I did. But Lucy asked me not to." Turning his head, he barked, "Fetch me that mother-of-pearl box, Marsh. There, on the dressing table."

The doctor dutifully delivered the square container. Shooting Elizabeth an intense glance, as if he resented her upsetting his patient, he returned to his stool.

The lid gleamed dully as the duke rummaged inside the box. "Here, read this," he said, holding out a bit of paper.

She unfolded the fragile note. Her eyes blurred as she recognized her mother's handwriting. Blinking, she scanned the brief, faded message, then looked at the duke.

Emotion throbbed inside her. "She loved you, but she wanted me to have a real home. And so you never tried to trace us."

"Yes." The ill-tempered spunk seemed to drain out of Hugh Sterling. He slumped over his cane and stared at her. "Did she ever mention me?"

Elizabeth slowly shook her head. "On her deathbed she made Owen promise to bring me back here, to visit you. I'm a sculptress, you see, and she wanted you to act as my patron."

"An artist, you say?" Surprise and pride shone in his eyes. "Knew you'd make something of yourself, by Jove. Always were a spunky girl."

Drawing the swan signet from her pocket, she knelt before him, holding out the ring in the palm of her hand. "When I turned thirteen, Mama gave me this."

"The Sterling swan," he muttered, rotating the ring in his knobby fingers. "That's what I used to call you. A beautiful name for a beautiful child." The duke dropped the ring back into her hand. "And now you've come back to me. Married to an earl, by Jove." His eyes sharpened on Nicholas and he let out a cackle of laughter. "Makes you my son-in-law, eh, Hawkesford?"

Nicholas smiled. "It would seem so, Your Grace."

"Fine piece of Persian armor I won off you, by Jove."

"Is that it, over there?" Nicholas inclined his head toward the far wall, where a shiny suit of armor stood, the visor closed, the gauntleted hand clutching a pike.

"Got keen eyes," the duke said, grinning. "That card game was no accident, eh? You knew I was Elizabeth's father. Why didn't you say something?"

"It's a long story. I'll tell it to you sometime."

"You'll stay for a visit, then," the duke said, thumping his cane for emphasis. "I won't take no for an answer."

Nicholas coolly inclined his head. "As you wish. Is that agreeable to you, love?"

Throat dry, Elizabeth nodded. An invitation was what they'd counted on, so why did she feel this sudden urge to refuse?

Hugh Sterling cocked his grizzled head at her. "You met the rest of the family yet? Wonder if Addie would recognize you."

The wily expression in his eyes disturbed her. She straightened, pocketing the ring. "We had luncheon together. And yes, everyone knows who I am."

"Wish I'd been there, by Jove! Wouldn't miss dinner tonight for Henry VIII's favorite suit of armor."

"Then you must rest now, Your Grace." Gilbert Marsh came to stand beside the duke's chair.

"You fuss more than an old woman," the duke grumbled. "Come to think of it, you ought to find yourself a woman. You'd make her a good wife."

The doctor said nothing, his features scrubbed clean of emotion, except for a faint tightening of the lips.

Elizabeth felt a twinge of sympathy. How trying for Marsh to be cooped up here with such an ill-tempered patient. But perhaps he had learned to take the duke's disparaging comments in stride.

She and Nicholas went downstairs to find the luncheon party had dispersed. According to Mrs. Drabble, the duchess had gone to the stables, and Drew and his mother had withdrawn to Philippa's rooms. The housekeeper dispatched a man to fetch the earl's servants and luggage from the inn.

Nicholas touched Elizabeth's cheek. "You look troubled, Countess. Let's go out into the sunshine."

The gloomy decor made her subdue a shiver. "Yes, I'd like that."

As they walked down the front steps, he said gently, "Tell me what you're thinking, love."

Elizabeth tried to sort through the confusing mix of impressions. "The duke seemed to have truly loved me and my mother. And yet . . ."

"What?"

She bit her lip and said, "According to Owen, Hugh Sterling shunned me when his son was born."

Their footsteps tapped over the stone path. "Perhaps there's an element of truth in that," Nicholas said. "It's understandable that a man would dote on his heir. Yet the duke kept your mother's letter all these years. That says something for the depth of his feelings."

The thought cheered Elizabeth. Had the duke been the focus of Lucy's youthful passion and Owen the recipient of her deep, abiding love? "My mother must have felt strongly for Hugh Sterling," she said slowly. "I can't imagine she would have betrayed her values for any other reason."

Hand clasped in Nicholas's, Elizabeth wandered toward an herb garden overrun with weeds. Hugh Sterling intrigued her; he had been alternately crotchety and kind, sly and sincere.

"Why do you suppose he's let the place get so shabby?" she wondered aloud. "He must be wealthy if he spends so much on his collection."

Nicholas shrugged. "He seems to relish annoying his nephew. At the same time, it's hard to second-guess Hugh Sterling."

A chill slithered down her spine. "I'd best make sure everyone understands I've no interest in his money."

His fingers tensed; Nicholas, too, must be recalling the attempts on her life. Her throat tightened at the memory of that villain choking her.

Was the person who wanted her dead exulting that she'd come here?

She'd come home.

With a hand that trembled in exultation, the figure at the window rubbed at the glass pane, the better to view her. Lithe and lovely, Elizabeth strolled the uncultivated gardens. Her hair was caught in a lustrous black chignon that enhanced her swanlike neck. When she tilted her head to smile up at the man beside her, her face shone as pure and radiant as the sunshine.

The clean fingers went rigid on the curtain. Elizabeth

was married now. The shock of that disclosure throbbed like a raw wound. She had no right to look so happy.

Because she was the sin that tainted Lucy.

Reaching to a nearby bookshelf, the figure plucked out a sketchbook. A reverent hand opened the royal blue cover and traced a drawing of Lucy smiling. Just like her daughter, Lucy looked so alive. . . .

Fate had brought her home to Yorkshire. Soon she would be chaste again, cured of the ugly blemish on her soul.

The fingers closed around the Moroccan pistol that lay atop the bookcase. The stock felt cool to the touch, inlaid with scrolls of silver wire. A worthy piece for a worthy purpose.

This time there would be no mistakes, no lost opportunities, no hireling to bumble matters.

This time Lucy would live again.

And Elizabeth would die.

Chapter 19

~~~ OG ~~~

"**Y**ou aren't really going to use that gun, are you?" Elizabeth grimaced at the derringer lying on the stone step, within easy reach of Nicholas.

"Only if I must."

The chiseled hardness of his face belied his untroubled tone. Wrenching her gaze from the gun, she looked around. They were sitting on the crumbling steps of an open domed rotunda. A lake matted with lily pads glimmered in the afternoon sunlight. The shore was overgrown with oaks and sycamores, laurels and rhododendrons, brambles and blackberries. No scythe had touched the grasses in years, and the charming woodland setting was alive with the peaceful summer sounds of squirrels chattering, grasshoppers fiddling, and bees droning.

Out here, she could almost believe she was safe. Almost. Since their arrival the day before, she had observed everyone closely, yet she and Nicholas were no nearer to identifying the culprit.

"Do you suppose Philippa assigned us separate bedrooms on purpose?" she asked.

"Certainly." Nicholas reached down to pluck a long stem of grass sprouting from a crack, then ran the blade along Elizabeth's exposed ankle. "She can't bear to see two people so in love."

Her sketch pad slipped to the step as Elizabeth adjusted her hyacinth blue skirts to escape the tickling grass. "That's not what I meant. Perhaps she's the one.

277

Perhaps she wanted us to sleep apart so that she could catch me unprotected."

"Then she failed miserably. I won't let you out of my sight." He picked up the pad and chuckled at the drawing. "Philippa, the stork. Flighty as a bird, that woman is. You've captured her very soul, Countess."

Elizabeth smiled at his effort to distract her. "We should be discussing motives."

Slipping off her shoe, he began to massage her stockinged foot. "I'd rather discuss you," he murmured. "Or rather, us."

"But, Nicholas, I really think—"

"Don't think." He shifted his compelling hand to her ankle. "I just want to steal a few moments alone with my bride."

The gleam in his eyes reminded her of the pleasure they'd shared last night. "Quinn looked positively scandalized when he found out we intended to share a room."

"His opinion is of no consequence," Nicholas said without a shred of sympathy.

"But it's customary, isn't it, for the gentry to keep separate rooms? So that husbands and wives can carry on discreet affairs."

"I don't intend to ever sleep in any bed other than yours."

His declaration thrilled her as much as the feel of his fingers sliding up to her calf, continuing their soft, arousing friction. Through the tangle of trees, she caught a flash of blue livery. "Nicholas, please," she said breathlessly. "The footmen . . ."

"Pickering and Dobson aren't watching us. They're keeping their eyes peeled for intruders."

"What if they come this way to report something?"

"All right, love, have it your way," he said in a silken grumble. "But I can certainly tell you what I'd do if we were alone."

Settling against a pillar dark with leaf mold, he rested an elbow on his bent knee. "First I'd dispense with that lovely gown. . . ." He proceeded to describe in explicit detail how and where he wanted to kiss and caress her. Desire lapped at her composure until she felt as sultry as the summer day. His quiet words washed over her in warm waves; his smoldering silver eyes beckoned to her in ardent invitation.

"Nicholas, have mercy," she said in a voice breathy with laughter. "How am I to finish this drawing?"

"Don't." A wicked grin slanted his mouth. "My desire for you doesn't end with the light of day, Countess."

"You demonstrated *that* on the train." A flicker of white rounded a bend in the lake. Her back straightened. "Oh, look at the swans!"

Nicholas turned. The sleek snowy pair glided gracefully through a patchwork of lily pads, pausing now and again to bend their long necks below the surface of the water, seeking the succulent weeds. In their wake, ever-widening ripples spread over the still pond. Seizing her pad, Elizabeth quickly sketched the two onto a corner of the page.

"I thought only one swan was your trademark," he said. "Dare I hope you're planning to change that since we've married?"

With the end of her pencil, she traced the strong line of his jaw. "Would that please you, m'lord?"

"Perhaps it would make you think of me while you've locked yourself in the conservatory."

"Are you already jealous of the hours I'll spend sculpting?"

Lifting her hand, he kissed the back. "Only if you can't find time for me."

Despite the lightness of his words, she sensed an underlying tension. Would he understand if she was awarded the commission from Lord Buckstone?

Leaning closer, she kissed him. "I'll always find time for you, Nicholas."

With leashed power, his hand enfolded her wrist. "You'd better," he said softly. "You're the Sterling swan. And swans mate for life."

"The Sterling swan." Elizabeth felt the relentless tug

of reality. "The duke said he used to call me that. I wish I could remember him back then. . . ."

"How could you, love? You were only two years old when you left here."

"I know." She sighed, using her pencil to nudge a bit of fallen plaster. "Still, I had the half-formed hope that some childish affection for him would awaken inside me, or at least a few happy memories. Instead he seems like a stranger."

"Perhaps because Owen was the man who nurtured you."

"Oh, Nicholas, I treated Owen so badly. The moment we return to London, I'll make amends."

"I'm glad."

His softly spoken approval galvanized her. Suddenly she yearned for Hawkesford House, for her sculpting and her new life with Nicholas. Getting up, she brushed the dried leaves from her skirts, then picked up her sketch pad. "I shouldn't have dragged you out here. We'll never solve this mystery if we lollygag all afternoon."

"I suppose you're right," he said, pocketing the derringer and falling into step beside her. "I'd like to speak to the duchess. She scarcely uttered a word at dinner last night, even when the duke baited her."

"I'm curious about her, too. More than anyone else here, she seems to keep her feelings close to the heart."

As they rounded a bend, Elizabeth spied the manor house in the distance. Her contentment withered. How much more pleasant to laze by the lake with Nicholas than to navigate the undercurrents of hatred within those walls.

"There's the duchess," he said, "in the paddock."

Shading her eyes, Elizabeth studied the quadrangle of red brick buildings. Situated on rising ground beyond the house and half concealed by a thicket of untrimmed yews, the stables formed a substantial complex, like a miniature village. In a fenced meadow nearby, the duchess stood beside a cream colored horse. She looked more like a groom than a lady; as yesterday, she wore trousers and a baggy white shirt, with a dark cap hiding her hair.

She must have seen their approach, for she straightened as they neared the fence. Her features were as plain and unrevealing as a slab of granite. She gave the horse a light slap on the rump and he trotted off, mane and tail swinging like fine floss, haunches rippling with powerful muscles.

"What a beautiful animal," Elizabeth said, leaning against the weathered gray slats, the sketch pad tucked under her arm.

A spark of life flared in the duchess's brown eyes. "His name's Starfire," she said, tucking her riding crop beneath her arm and coming to the fence slowly, almost reluctantly.

"Was that a poultice on his withers?" Nicholas asked.

She nodded. "He had a small ulcer. It's healing quite nicely."

"Did you use comfrey?"

"Yes, as a matter of fact." Adelaide gave him a sharp glance. "Are you a breeder, Hawkesford? I've never seen you at any of the auctions."

"I keep a stable of hunters in Sussex."

They launched into a discussion of the merits of race horses versus hunters. Unqualified to do much more than distinguish a flank from a forelock, Elizabeth silently studied the duchess. At a glance the broad, flat lines of her face created a dull, almost simple appearance. She must deliberately cultivate an aura of stupidity. But why? To maintain a distance from people she didn't wish to be bothered with? Or to hide a clever criminal mind?

"Would you care to see my new stables?" she asked Nicholas. "We've only just finished putting in the mangers."

He inclined his head. "It would be a pleasure, Your Grace."

Clomping to the gate, the riding crop held stiffly under her arm, Adelaide let herself out of the paddock.

Nicholas placed a hand at Elizabeth's waist as they headed toward the carriage entrance. Crowning the archway was a clock tower and a cupola with tiny windows, the cooing of doves drifting through the summer air.

One glance around the stable yard revealed a different world from the manor house. Here the brick buildings were bright and new, the trim painted, the windows sparkling. Even the large, square dirt yard was raked clean.

"Business must be prospering," Nicholas remarked, as the duchess escorted them past a covered area, where a stable lad wielded a long-handled broom to scrub a horse rug.

"If you raise good horseflesh, buyers will come back time and time again." Adelaide's pale lips curled into a smile of pride. "It took a long while, but I built this place with my own profits."

Tilting her face, Elizabeth studied the elaborate carving at the top of a rainpipe. "I see you've used the swan crest."

"Of course. *I* am a Sterling."

The faint chilly inflection of her voice was like unveiling a statue. So the resentment did run deep, Elizabeth thought. But deep enough to impel the duchess to murder?

Turning, Adelaide flung open a whitewashed door. "Here's the harness room," she said as they entered a tidy area smelling of leather and hung with tack. She marched through another doorway and pointed with her riding crop down a long corridor.

"And the stable block."

Behind the half doors, Elizabeth saw a row of horses' rumps, tails swishing lazily. The sweet scent of hay mingled with the odor of sweat and droppings. Farther down, a man forked straw into a stall.

"You've an excellent drainage system," Nicholas said, stopping to examine the grated channel in the bricked floor.

"I'll permit only the best for my horses—teak for the

walls, wrought iron for the mangers. It's taken months to get things furnished to my specifications."

The dry discussion of stable architecture made Elizabeth impatient. Perhaps, she thought as they walked into yet another palatial block of stalls, she could prick the duchess into revealing something vital. . . .

"Had you no financial help?" Elizabeth asked.

Adelaide gave a sideways look down her long nose. "I've never asked a soul for a penny. Perhaps that's difficult to understand, why a woman would wish to make her own way in the world."

"Oh, I can understand." Half smiling, Elizabeth glanced at Adelaide's mannish garb. "I can understand very well, indeed."

The duchess snapped the riding crop against her palm. "I suppose you find my choice of clothing vulgar."

Nicholas roared with laughter. "Don't let Elizabeth's appearance fool you, Duchess. She's as fond of wearing trousers as you are."

Adelaide stared. "Do you ride, Lady Hawkesford?"

Elizabeth shook her head. "I grew up in the city, and I've scarcely ever sat a horse. I'm a sculptress. I've found trousers give me more freedom of movement while I work."

"An artist, you say?" Adelaide's eyes sought the sketch pad beneath Elizabeth's arm. "I suppose I shouldn't be surprised since my grandmother painted. . . ."

"Your grandmother?" Elizabeth said in confusion. "What has she to do with me?"

The duchess's eyes narrowed to chips of bronze; she slapped the crop against her thigh. "She was your great-grandmother. Lucy was my cousin."

For one long pulse beat everything stopped; the quiet munching of the horses, the shifting of hooves, the rhythm of blood and breath in Elizabeth's body. Beside her, Nicholas tensed. It was difficult enough to imagine her sweet-natured mother having an affair with a married man. To do so with her cousin's husband was unthinkable. . . .

Adelaide swung away, shoulders rigid and regal beneath the white linen shirt. Her departure poured strength back into Elizabeth's limbs. She hurried after the duchess, Nicholas close behind.

"Your Grace, wait!" Elizabeth said.

As if she hadn't heard, Adelaide marched down the corridor of stalls, boots clumping on the brick floor.

"Please, I know so little of my mother's relations. Won't you at least answer a few questions?"

The duchess paused in the doorway to the yard, sunlight gilding her granite features. "What?"

The word was abrupt, yet not entirely unkind. Elizabeth swallowed. "Why did my mother come here to live? Was she really your companion?"

"Lucy was orphaned at seventeen, left penniless. I was all she had left . . . she was all *I* had left of my family."

"So you and Elizabeth are first cousins, once removed," Nicholas said quietly.

"It would seem so."

Questions tumbled through Elizabeth's mind. Knowing she was overstepping the bounds of propriety, yet itching to chisel into that stonelike facade, she said, "Then my mother had an affair . . . with your husband."

Adelaide stared, her face etched in unrevealing lines. "Lucy was always the pretty one, more womanly than I." It was a flat statement of fact, the only betrayal of emotion the way her fingers fiddled with the riding crop. "I can't blame her for that."

Could she believe the duchess? Elizabeth wondered. Or was Adelaide the one?

The duchess pursed her lips. "I've something of your mother's," she said abruptly. "Come with me."

She walked briskly across the bright stable yard and through the arched carriage entrance. Not once did she look behind. Seeing Nicholas wryly lift his brows, Elizabeth felt an answering tickle of humor; Her Grace of

Rockborough was accustomed to obedience.

Elizabeth followed the duchess through the paddock gate, Nicholas at her side. Near the untrimmed yew hedge that formed the far side of the fenced area, several horses grazed. Putting two fingers to her lips, Adelaide gave a shrill whistle. A dappled gray lifted her head, ears pricked. The mare cantered toward them, mane tossing like the rippling of a wave. Elizabeth caught her breath. Sculpture in motion, she thought; marble come to life.

Slowing to a dainty walk, the horse whickered a greeting to the duchess and nuzzled her hand. Adelaide produced a sugar lump from her pant pocket. "There you are, my greedy darling. Now come along and meet someone."

Beautiful gray head bobbing in rhythm to her steps, the horse followed the duchess. Delighted, Elizabeth glided a hand down the animal's swan-curved neck and admired the well-set shoulders and long graceful legs. Dark and liquid, the mare's eyes studied her.

"She's lovely," Elizabeth murmured. "All youth and exuberance."

"Caprice still thinks she's a filly even though she's ten years old." Affection softening her voice, Adelaide paused. "Her dam belonged to Lucy."

Elizabeth's hand froze on the silken mane. "But didn't you say, Your Grace, that my mother had no money...?" Her voice trailed off, and she felt an embarrassed flush heat her cheeks.

"Yes, Hugh gave the mare to Lucy," the duchess said evenly. "Though in all fairness, Lucy did refuse the gift. Nevertheless, Hugh had the papers made out in her name. Her dam is dead now, but Caprice is rightfully yours."

"I can't accept her," Elizabeth protested. "You've cared for her all these years. I don't even ride—"

Adelaide set her chin. "I insist. I'll fetch her papers from the office."

With that peculiar royal dignity so at odds with her mannish appearance, the duchess tramped out the paddock gate and disappeared into the stable complex.

Dismayed, Elizabeth turned to Nicholas, who stood on the other side of the horse. "Now how am I to get out of this?"

He shrugged as Caprice tipped her head down to crop the sun-warmed grasses. "You could accept the mare. She certainly is a beauty."

"Beauty or not, she doesn't belong to me. I wouldn't feel right taking her."

He absently rubbed the animal's sleek gray flank. "The duchess strikes me as a woman who honors her debts to the letter. But perhaps we could breed Caprice and take her foal."

It was the perfect solution. Yet she couldn't resist saying tartly, "Perhaps we could breed her to one of the hunters you keep stabled in Sussex . . . on your estate, I presume?"

Nicholas's hand stilled; an abashed look stole over his handsome face. "Have I never mentioned my . . . our country house?"

She shook her head.

"Well, Countess," he said, reaching across the horse's withers to lace his fingers with hers, "we must rectify that. As soon as this is all over, I'll take you there, introduce you to the beauty of the Downs, show you enough old castles and ruined abbeys to satisfy your artistic soul."

As soon as this is all over. . . .

Elizabeth shivered despite the hot afternoon. "I can't stop feeling uneasy about the duchess, Nicholas. Isn't it peculiar that she's never sold Caprice? I wonder if Adelaide's attachment has something to do with the fact that Caprice's dam belonged to my mother?"

"I can't answer that." Smiling, he squeezed her hand. "I don't suppose it would do any good to tell you to leave the worrying to me."

The impact of his smile tunneled deep within her. Elizabeth felt her spirits lighten, shedding the darkness of doubts, accepting the balm of love.

"I guess you know me too well," she admitted.

A corner of his mouth lifted rakishly higher. "I'm always ready to enlarge my intimate knowledge of you."

She pretended shock. "Always? I hardly consider a pasture appropriate for a romantic interlude with an English earl."

"This English earl isn't as priggish as he used to be," he murmured, his thumb brushing her wrist. "I'd like to take you in the grass, to see the sunshine gild your naked skin...."

"With a score of prying eyes watching me as well."

Nicholas grinned. "The horses won't mind."

"You're impossible."

"You're irresistible."

"Whatever happened to all that iron willpower you had just a few days ago?"

His fingers grazed her breast. "One taste of you and I lost all strength of character."

"Behave yourself." Flushed and aroused, Elizabeth extracted her hand and stepped shakily back. Taking the sketch pad from beneath her arm, she quickly penciled the proud curve of Caprice's neck, the clean lines of her body. "I've never sculpted a horse before. But I may have to start with you."

Nicholas leaned lazily against the weathered fence. "Watch out, Caprice," he advised the mare. "Once she gets an artistic notion into her head she won't let off. She'll have you posing like a damned basket of fruit."

At the sound of her name, the mare tossed her head, then resumed cropping the meadow grass.

"Hah," Elizabeth told him. "You've nothing to complain about, Nicholas Ware. You've yet to pose for me."

He smiled. "I'll disrobe if you'll do the same. I intend to devote my life to studying your lovely curves."

The sultry promise in his eyes robbed her of breath. Sunlight illuminated his flawless features, the chiseled sweep of his cheekbones, the firm jut of his jaw, the powerful muscles of the body she knew as intimately as her own. Her heart throbbed with love. How precious he was to her, how happy he made her.

Suddenly he peered beyond her, toward the row of scraggly yews bordering the far end of the paddock. His gaze sharpened and his spine straightened.

"Get down!" he snapped.

She ducked. A sharp *crack* rent the air.

Caprice squealed and reared, front hooves flailing. A red slash bloomed on her silken mane. Blood!

A heavy weight slammed into Elizabeth, knocking her sideways. Her head struck the ground.

The world went black.

Chapter 20

❧❧❧❧

Gripped by hideous panic, Nicholas feared she was dead.

Shielding Elizabeth's limp form with his body, he braced himself for the slash of hooves on his back. Caprice's hooves slammed to the grass so close the ground quaked. Snorting, the wounded mare galloped away.

Nicholas ran frantic hands over Elizabeth. Her slender body bore no sign of injury, no bloody gunshot wound. Relief poured through him as he spied the faint rise and fall of her breasts.

Trembling with shock, he grasped her shoulders. "Elizabeth!"

She lay still, her eyes closed, the black lashes stark against her white cheeks. The scent of crushed grass tickled his nose. An arm's length away, a bee droned in the clover. So peaceful.

Yet a killer lurked somewhere nearby.

Kipp pounded into the paddock. "Blimey! I 'eard a shot! She ain't dead, is she?"

"No, she's unconscious." Nicholas spared only a glance at the boy's stricken face. "Elizabeth!" he said again, gently shaking her.

She stirred and moaned. Her hand lifted as if to bat him away. Her lashes fluttered.

"Nicholas?" she said, her voice a wisp of sound.

"I'm here, love."

She blinked. "What happened?"

"You fell. Lie still now."

"Saw a bloke running away from them bushes, yer lordship, sir." Kipp pointed to the line of yews. "Don't see 'im no more, though."

Dobson ran up in time to hear Kipp's words. "I'll nab the bugger, m'lord." Brandishing his pistol, the footman raced across the pasture, heading for the wilderness of trees.

" 'Ey, wait fer me."

"Kipp, get back here!"

But the boy either didn't hear the command or chose to ignore it. Swiveling back to his wife, Nicholas clenched his jaw against a swamping wave of guilt. Elizabeth needed his protection; he couldn't leave her alone. If he hadn't looked up and seen the glint of the sun on metal, a glint in the yews where no one ought to be—

She struggled to sit. "Caprice! Is she—"

"She'll be fine, love. The wound was only a graze." Sliding his arms beneath her, he surged to his feet.

"What are you doing?" she asked.

"Taking you into the house."

She wriggled against his chest. "I can walk."

He tightened his hold. "Hush. You'll do as I say."

A group of muttering onlookers had gathered, stable lads and scullery maids, grooms and dairy maids. Clutching a paper in her hand, the Duchess Adelaide marched through the throng.

"What's going on here? I heard a shot." She stopped, her eyes widening on Elizabeth. "Dear God! Has she been injured?"

"She struck her head."

Gilbert Marsh elbowed past the horde. "I'd best have a look at her. Bring her into my office."

"There's nothing wrong with me," Elizabeth said. "Really."

"The doctor's right," Nicholas stated. "Lead the way, Marsh."

When Adelaide made a move to follow, he added, "You'll want to tend to Caprice, Your Grace." He nodded toward the far end of the paddock, where a pair of grooms were trying to calm the agitated mare.

The duchess hesitated; then she stuffed the paper into her pocket and started slowly toward Caprice. Was her concern for Elizabeth genuine? Carrying his precious burden, Nicholas could spare only an instant's speculation before striding after Marsh.

"Put me down, Nicholas."

"No."

"I feel ridiculous—"

His raw nerves exploded into anger. "For God's sake, Elizabeth! Can't you for once let me take care of you?"

She pursed her lips as if to suppress a retort. Resentment flared in her beautiful eyes before she lowered her lashes to stare at his shirt. His arms tensed; he needed to cradle her sweet, warm life, he needed the doctor to assure him she was unharmed. Didn't she realize how close to death she'd come? How furious and guilty he felt at failing to safeguard her again? That bullet might have pierced her heart. He might now be carrying her corpse. . . .

Swallowing the knot in his throat, Nicholas followed Marsh through a door at the rear of the manor house and into a small, neat room. The faint disinfectant scent of carbolic pervaded the air. Rows of bottles and jars filled a glass-fronted cabinet, and medical tomes crammed a bookshelf. The decor was surprisingly homey for a doctor's office, with a pair of chintz chairs by the hearth and a vase of wild roses atop a tidy desk.

"Over here," Marsh said, indicating an examining table.

Nicholas gently settled her on the green leather surface.

"I don't need to lie down," Elizabeth said, bobbing up. "I'm perfectly healthy."

He glared. "You'll do as the doctor says."

"It's all right. Let her sit if she feels more comfortable." Marsh glanced at Nicholas. "If you'll leave us, your lordship."

"I'm staying with my wife."

"It'll only be for a few moments. She'll be more at ease."

"I'm staying," Nicholas repeated, his voice steely.

"As you wish, then."

Nicholas caught a glint of displeasure in those blue eyes before the doctor turned away. Too damned bad if Marsh preferred privacy in which to examine his patients. Under no circumstances did Nicholas intend to let Elizabeth out of his sight.

Prowling the office, he watched as Marsh gingerly felt her scalp.

"Any dizziness?" the doctor asked.

"No."

"Can you recall what happened?"

"Of course. Why do you ask?"

He lifted her lids to peer into her eyes. "Loss of memory can be a sign of concussion."

"I was standing beside Caprice when my husband yelled to me to get down. No sooner did I do so when I heard a shot." Her eyes soft with emotion, she glanced at Nicholas. "He knocked me out of the way of the horse's hooves just in time."

"I heard that shot all the way in here." Marsh waved a hand at the opened medical encyclopedia on his desk, as if to indicate he'd been reading. "Did you see who fired at you?"

"She couldn't have," Nicholas broke in, picking up an illustrated drug catalogue and flipping the pages. "The shot came from beyond the yews. I imagine it was a hunter who'd strayed too close to the house."

Glancing from under his lashes, Marsh nodded. "Undoubtedly."

Was the doctor revealing all he knew? Feigning an interest in the catalogue, Nicholas watched as Marsh turned back to Elizabeth. Could madness lie behind that mild, boyish face? It wouldn't hurt to do a little digging. . . .

"Have you a headache, your ladyship?" Marsh asked.

She hesitated. "Only a slight one."

"I'll fetch you a bromide to ease the pain and steady your nerves."

"You needn't bother yourself—"

"It's my duty as a doctor. The duke would send me packing if I failed to treat you."

Taking a key from his pocket, Marsh walked across the office to unlock the medicine cabinet. He looked like the consummate country doctor in his tidy, untailored brown suit.

"That's quite the dispensary you have there," Nicholas said, strolling behind the shorter man to study the array of containers.

"Saves me from making a trip into Wrefton each time I need something."

"Do you use all those potions to treat the duke?"

The doctor aimed an oblique glance over his shoulder. "Of course not, my lord. Besides the estate folk, I administer to the local farm families as well."

"Do you live here in the house?" Nicholas asked, setting the catalogue on top of the cabinet.

Marsh inclined his head toward a closed door. "I've a room through there. There's a bellpull by His Grace's bedside so he can call whenever he needs me."

Elizabeth's brow furrowed. "Is the duke so ill that he needs a physician close by?"

The doctor slid a look at her. "I mean no insult, your ladyship, but I shouldn't discuss one patient with another."

"Hugh Sterling is my father. I've a right to know what's ailing him."

Marsh's hand stilled on a cobalt bottle. His face was averted so that Nicholas could not see the expression.

Picking up the vessel, the doctor walked to the desk. "All right, then. I don't suppose it's any great secret." He reached into a drawer and withdrew an empty vial. "As you must have already seen, His Grace suffers from arthritis, as well as cardiac asthma. In layman's terms, his heart is weak and he's prone to spells of breathlessness, especially at night."

Elizabeth slipped down from the examining table. "Is there anything you can do for him?"

Uncorking the large blue bottle, Marsh used a paper cone to transfer white powder into the smaller vial. "Make sure he avoids excitement and gets plenty of rest."

"How long have you been his physician?" Nicholas asked.

Marsh darted a glance from beneath his pale lashes. "For nigh on twelve years now, since I completed my studies in Edinburgh."

"Twelve years," Nicholas mused. "Then you must have grown up around here. You knew Lucy Templeton and it's been twenty years since she left."

The paper cone dropped to the desk, spilling a few granules of powder. Compressing his lips in annoyance, Marsh meticulously brushed the white dust into a waste bin. In a flash of humor, Nicholas imagined the doctor, apron around his middle and feather duster in hand, cleaning the tidy office.

"Why the inquisition, your lordship? Do you doubt my ability to administer to the duke?"

"I'm sure my husband means no slight." Elizabeth sent Nicholas a warning frown, then crossed the room to stand before the desk. "Please, Dr. Marsh, don't be affronted. I'm interested in anything I can learn about my mother's life here."

Marsh lifted guarded eyes. "There isn't much I can tell you. I was only a lad of sixteen when she left. At the time, my father was gamekeeper for the estate, so we hardly moved in the same social circle."

"But you saw her, perhaps spoke to her occasionally?"

The doctor shook his fair head. "We shared nothing more than a greeting or a pleasantry. She was too busy with the duke to have time for a mere boy."

"Was she happy here?" Elizabeth persisted.

He bent his head and opened a drawer. "I'm sorry, your ladyship. Anything I say would be pure conjecture. I'd suggest you ask your questions of the duke or duchess." Finding a cork, he plugged the vial. "But do be careful with His Grace. As I've said, his heart is weak."

"I'd never do anything to upset him," Elizabeth said.

The doctor nodded, then pushed back his chair. "I'd advise bed rest for the next day or so, your ladyship. Let me know if you experience dizziness. To relieve any pain, take a teaspoon of this bromide mixed in water."

As Marsh held out the bottle, Nicholas saw Elizabeth open her mouth to protest. Quickly he took the vial and said, "Thank you, doctor. How much do we owe you?"

Marsh held up a well-manicured hand. "Nothing, please. His Grace pays me amply."

"Then thank you again."

Taking firm hold of Elizabeth's arm, Nicholas drew her out into the sunshine. As the door clicked shut behind them and they walked slowly through the uncultivated gardens, she tilted her face up, her chin set stubbornly.

"I'm warning you right now, Nicholas Ware, don't get any notions about me languishing in bed for the next few days."

Despite his black mood, he couldn't help a grin. "Not even if I offer to attend you personally?"

"Hah. I can imagine how much rest I'd get." She plucked the vial from his hand and held it to the sunlight. "Do you suppose it's poison?"

The flare of humor died, leaving the bitter ash of fear in his mouth. "If Gilbert Marsh is the killer, I doubt he'd be so blatant. Nevertheless," Nicholas said, pocketing the vial, "just to be on the safe side, I'll send this to Thistlewood. He can have a chemist test it."

She sighed. "I don't suppose Dr. Marsh has a motive, anyway. He barely knew my mother. In fact, he sounded rather indifferent to her."

"So he says," Nicholas mused. "The question remains, can we believe him or anyone else around here?"

Suddenly Dobson rounded the ivy-draped garden wall, Kipp close behind. By the frustration on the footman's ruddy face, Nicholas knew the assailant had gotten away.

"Beggin' your pardon, m'lord," Dobson said. "We looked all over, me and Kipp and Pickering, but all we found was this, beneath the yew hedge."

He held out a long-barreled pistol. Nicholas took the gun and turned it in his hands. Sleek but heavy, the antique weapon had a stock inlaid with gypsylike silver designs.

"Is that from the duke's collection?" Elizabeth asked.

"It would seem a logical assumption," Nicholas said grimly.

"The weapons cabinets aren't locked. Anyone could have taken the gun."

The disquiet on her fine-boned face cut straight to his heart. For one enraged moment he shook with the need to fire this pistol at the person who would do her harm.

Curbing his anger, he said to Dobson, "Did you find anything else?"

"Miss . . . er, Lady Libby's sketch pad," Kipp said. "I gave it to Mrs. Drabble."

"I meant a clue. A scrap of cloth? A footprint?"

"Just a crushed place on the grass, m'lord," Dobson said. "Shall we continue looking?"

"Yes. Comb the woods. Don't leave a stone unturned."

"Aye, m'lord." Dobson loped off toward the paddock.

Nicholas caught Kipp by the arm. "Hold up, lad. You said you saw a bloke running away. Are you sure it was a man?"

"Aye . . . I guess . . ." Frowning, the boy lifted his cap and scratched his black hair. "Blimey, yer lordship, it could've been a lady, I s'pose."

Nicholas tucked the pistol into his waistband. "Did you get a look at the person's face? See anything that might help us identify him?"

Kipp shook his head. "Couldn't make out more'n 'is shape with them bushes in the way."

"Which direction did he go?"

"Toward the stables . . . I guess. I was watchin' 'er ladyship."

Kipp looked so crestfallen that Nicholas placed a hand on the boy's thin shoulder. "Don't fret, Master Gullidge. I didn't see any more than you did."

Kipp widened worshipful brown eyes. "I'll find a clue, yer lordship, sir. We won't let nothin' 'appen to Lady Libby."

Nicholas gritted his teeth against a flood of fear and guilt. "Indeed we won't."

Elizabeth bent to hug the boy. "Thank you, Kipp. You're wonderful."

Red cheeked, he wriggled out of her embrace. "'Scuse me," he mumbled. "Got to go 'elp the men."

"Just be careful, for God's sake," Nicholas called.

As the boy bolted down the path, Nicholas saw the curtain twitch in Marsh's office. How long had the doctor been watching them? And why? Out of simple curiosity? Or a darker motive?

In the distant paddock Nicholas could see the duchess dressing Caprice's wound. His fingers caressed the ornately scrolled pistol. Had Adelaide concealed herself behind the yew hedge instead of going into the stable office? Or perhaps Philippa or Drew had fired the weapon? Or even the duke himself?

Frustration choked Nicholas. God, there were too many secrets in this house, too much hidden hatred. He had arrogantly walked into this viper's nest, had foolishly delivered the quarry to the hunter. In his vast conceit he had believed himself capable of protecting Elizabeth. Today had almost proven him wrong. Dead wrong. His hand tensed around the pistol stock. He wanted to smash something, to discharge the terrible fury and fear weighing his soul.

Elizabeth's precious face was tipped up to him, her brow drawn into an absentminded frown so familiar that his chest squeezed with tenderness and his heart throbbed with terror. If he were to lose her. . . .

"I've been thinking," she said, tapping her lower lip

with a forefinger. "Perhaps we ought to find out where Philippa and Drew were when that shot was fired."

"Later." Nicholas seized her arm and pulled her down the weedy flagstone path. "Right now, you're coming with me."

She blinked in bewilderment. "Where are we going?"

"Upstairs."

She tugged ineffectively at his iron grip. "But I told you, Nicholas, I feel fine. Just the slightest headache. There's no need to coddle me."

"Coddling be damned. I've something to say to you."

His forbidding expression alarmed Elizabeth. Half stumbling in an effort to keep up with his long strides, she glanced at his face, so furious and so resolute. The rigid set of his jaw told her that any attempt to dissuade him would prove fruitless. She could understand his reaction. Her own heart still pounded with the remnants of panic, the weakness of fright. She would go willingly to the bedroom, to hear him out and then give him comfort.

He hauled her through the massive portico. The entrance hall was dim and dingy after the bright sunlight, and she felt a chill crawl over her skin. Would she always feel such a sense of uneasiness on entering this house?

With the mincing steps of a crane, Philippa descended the grand staircase. Her gaunt features drew into a grimace of concern. "Lady Hawkesford! My maid just informed me that someone fired a gun at you!"

"Yes, but I'm sure it was only an accident," Elizabeth said, as Nicholas propelled her forward.

Philippa waved her skinny fingers. "Such a frightful shock! Do come into the saloon and tell me—"

"Not now," Nicholas said curtly.

They swept up the steps, leaving Philippa with her pale mouth agape and her white-sleeved arms flapping like the wings of a goose. Biting back a smile, Elizabeth glanced up at Nicholas. Judging by the thunderous slash of his brows and the tautness of skin over his cheekbones, he didn't share her amusement.

A quiver of foreboding skittered up her spine as he pulled her into their bedroom. In a patch of sunlight by the crimson-curtained window, Janet sat mending one of Elizabeth's gown.

"Out," Nicholas ordered.

Eyes round, the maid leapt up, smoothing her skirts. The sewing basket tipped and a spool rolled across the worn Turkish carpet. Janet scrambled to catch the spool; it vanished under the bed. Getting to her knees, she stretched an arm beneath the four-poster and brought forth a handful of dust balls.

"Leave it," Nicholas snapped.

"Aye, m'lord." Casting him an awed look, she scurried out and closed the door.

He tugged the long-barreled pistol from his waistband and slammed the gun onto a writing table, then continued without pause to the corner. Yanking Elizabeth's leather trunk into the center of the rug, he flung back the lid. He stalked to the ancient wardrobe and jerked open a drawer, the warped walnut runners screeching.

Elizabeth stared in amazement as he grabbed a cobalt evening gown and stuffed it into the trunk. "Nicholas? What are you doing?"

"Packing. You're going back to London."

Her heart jolted. "I am not."

Lines of tension bracketed his mouth as he wadded a silk petticoat and tossed it at the trunk. "Yes, you are," he said in a voice as hard as bronze. "Today."

"Don't be absurd. We can't leave now. We have to find the killer."

"I'll find the killer. It was a mistake to bring you here in the first place."

Her breath huffed out in angry disbelief; her head began to pound with renewed pain. So he meant to send her off, did he, without so much as discussing the situation?

"I'm not leaving without you, Nicholas."

He stopped, his hands full of frilly underwear, his face full of harsh determination. "You'll do as I say if I have to tie you to that train."

Fists planted on her hips, she faced him squarely. "You're trying to control my life again, without giving me any voice in the decision."

He dumped the lingerie into the trunk. "I'm doing what's best for you."

"Did it ever occur to you to consult me? To ask my opinion?"

"There's no room for opinion in this matter. You're in danger and my duty is to protect you."

"But we haven't any idea who the killer is. He could follow me to London."

"I'd know if anyone left the estate."

"Can you keep track of everyone here?" she said, trailing him to the wardrobe. "Besides, the man in the porkpie hat is still at large."

"Then I'll send you to Sussex."

"And what if the murderer is someone we don't suspect? For heaven's sake, it could even be Quinn or Dobson or Pickering!"

Clutching a heap of silk stockings to his chest, he swung to glare at her. "Now who's being absurd? You're letting stubbornness get in the way of your own safety."

She rubbed her throbbing temple. "I'm safer with you! Why can't you see that?"

The harshness slipped from his handsome face, leaving his eyes haunted and his mouth vulnerable. "No, you're not," he said quietly. "I failed you today, Elizabeth. If I hadn't happened to look up when I did, you could have died."

Horror and shame weighted his words. Understanding drenched the flame of her anger. Lifting a hand to the smooth perfection of his cheek, she said, "Nicholas, don't blame yourself. You've cared about my safety since the night we met. It's what brought us together."

"And it could tear us apart... permanently. I should have been keeping a better watch instead of staring at you. I should have made certain the footmen were patrolling the area."

She gently stroked his rigid jaw. "You'll know better next time, darling. Don't berate yourself over one mistake."

A muscle clenched beneath her fingers; in one swift motion he dropped the stack of stockings and caught her in the circle of his arms. His mouth pinned hers in a bruising kiss. "I could have lost you," he muttered. "My God, I could have lost you!"

Her throat thickened with tenderness; her body heated with passion. "But you didn't, Nicholas," she said, molding herself to him. "I'm here. I want to stay with you, where I belong, where I feel safe."

His breath came out in a harsh hiss and her heart soared with the knowledge of victory. She stood on tiptoe, cupping her hands around the warm marble of his cheeks to draw his lips back to hers. Uttering a low growl of excitement, he kissed her until she trembled, until his hands peeled away their clothing. Elizabeth tried to take the lead, wanting to do all the giving and erase the darkness from his soul. Instead, she found herself yielding to his caresses like clay in the hands of a master.

Pressing her to the tester bed, he joined himself to her, driving hard and deep until the world dissolved into radiant light and erotic sensation. As they swept toward shared ecstasy, they were one living sculpture, one joyous body, the affirmation of life and the exultation of love.

"Did you catch the look on Janet's face when she saw my clothes scattered over the trunk?"

Nicholas grinned as he led Elizabeth down the hall. "I never claimed to have any talent at packing."

"Perhaps, my lord," she said, slanting a sultry look at him, "your talents lie in other areas."

"You inspire me, Countess." Pressing her into a shadowed niche between two suits of armor, he kissed her, long and slow. When he lifted his lips, she felt giddy and flushed and happy. "Have I ever told you," he said, his palms cradling her breasts, "how pleased I am that you don't wear a corset?"

Smiling, she shook her head. "I'm glad because there's enough armor in this place without me adding to it."

His brow drew into a troubled frown. "I don't know how you managed to talk me into letting you stay here. You ought to at least be resting after that knock on the head you took."

"Any more of your brand of rest and I'll be exhausted." When he didn't smile at her teasing, she said gently, "Try not to worry, Nicholas. Come now, or we'll be late for dinner."

Still, he hesitated. "A word of caution, Elizabeth. Eat and drink only what's served to everyone else."

The somberness of his voice chilled her. "Poison?" she whispered.

Nodding, he brushed back a wisp of her hair. "You'll be safe so long as you follow my lead. I'm sorry to frighten you, but I had to warn you."

She forced a smile. "This countess doesn't frighten easily, my lord."

As they headed downstairs, Elizabeth didn't feel half so brave as her words. Someone here had tried to kill her this afternoon. Someone who hated her enough to take such a tremendous risk, the same someone who had tried to arrange her murder in London. Fear and frustration soured her stomach. Not until they solved the mystery would she and Nicholas be able to live in peace.

In the saloon Philippa swooped forward, hands outstretched like talons. "My dear Lady Hawkesford, you've come down for dinner! Are you quite sure you're feeling well enough?"

The woman's syrupy concern bothered Elizabeth. Did Philippa mother everyone? "Yes, I am," she said politely. "Thank you for your interest, though."

"After all you've been through, you must be a bundle of nerves," Philippa said, plucking at her frilly tangerine skirts. "Perhaps you should take a tray in your room. I can ring for Mrs. Drabble—"

"Leave off, Mother. Lady Hawkesford looks in the pink of health." Drew sauntered closer, his lean body impeccably clad in a double-breasted coat and stiff white collar. "Lovely shade of lavender you're wearing, my lady. Matches your eyes."

With the grace of a courtier, he took her hand and kissed the back. Elizabeth felt Nicholas stir restlessly. She discreetly drew back her hand. "Thank you. And do call me Elizabeth. Since we're cousins, it seems silly to be so formal."

"Here's to the absence of formality."

Drew smiled lazily, and Elizabeth saw the appeal that attracted women to him. His aquiline features held the promise of reckless sport, the suggestion of sinful seduction. Why had he decided to be so charming tonight?

Taking firm hold of her arm, Nicholas escorted Elizabeth to the duchess, who sat by the hearth. In contrast to her image in the stables, Adelaide looked majestically feminine in a gown of Lincoln green silk. At the back of her head, black netting held the coil of sparse graying hair. She wore emerald drop earrings and a magnificent necklace of matching cabochon gems that glowed in the light from the setting sun.

"Good evening, Your Grace," Nicholas said. "How is Caprice faring?"

"Tolerably well, thank you. It was merely a flesh wound."

"That reminds me," Elizabeth said. "I don't feel right taking Caprice from you. Why don't you give me her next foal instead?"

The duchess stared; her granite features seemed to soften. "As you like, then. Hawkesford and I will make the arrangements." She paused. "I trust you're feeling better."

"Yes."

Brown eyes hooded, the duchess tapped her fingers

on the chair arm. "Someone shot at you, Lady Elizabeth. You didn't see who?"

"No, I—"

"What's all this about a shooting?" said the duke.

Elizabeth turned to see him hobbling into the saloon. Leaning heavily on his cane, he wore an old-fashioned braided jacket with a large, knotted cravat. With the dusk light smoothing his fossilized features, his face bore a trace of faded handsomeness.

"Oh, Your Grace," Philippa said, rushing to take his arm, "it's nothing to excite yourself over. Let me help you—"

"Take your claws off me." Yanking his sleeve away, the duke glared at the circle of faces. "Somebody shot at my daughter?" he said, wheezing. "Nobody saw fit to inform me. By Jove, I'm the master around here!"

"Please," Elizabeth said anxiously, "don't excite yourself. No one meant to keep the incident a secret."

He arched his grizzled brows. "I trust you, girl, you and Hawkesford. Don't know about the rest of these blighters, though. Have to start listening at keyholes, eh?"

"The shooting happened only this afternoon, Your Grace," Nicholas said. "I'm sure it was merely a stray bullet from a hunter's gun."

"Hunter, bah!" Hugh Sterling banged his cane on the carpet, raising a puff of dust. "Poacher's more the word. Ought to be strung from his bloody thumbs for venturing so close to the house."

"If you'd spare the few pounds to hire a gamekeeper," Drew said, "perhaps you wouldn't have poachers."

"Muttonhead," snapped the duke. "You're the one to give counsel on money. Left debts all over London. Gambling dens! Jewelers! Tailors!" His face reddened. "And who had to honor the bills, else besmirch the family name? Me, by Jove, me!"

"Please, Your Grace," Philippa said, hovering at his elbow. "Arthur left us such a small stipend. Surely you'll not begrudge my son the life of a gentleman. He spends so many long months here in Yorkshire."

"Languishing in this musty rubbish heap," Drew murmured.

"That's all the thanks I get? Should've let the bailiffs haul you off to Newgate." A cackle of laughter erupted from the duke. "That would've taught you some appreciation—"

"Dinner," announced Mrs. Drabble, from the doorway.

Drew leapt to offer his arm to Elizabeth. "May I have the honor, my lady?"

The duke elbowed in front of his nephew. "You'll come with me, girl. This flock of greedy vultures won't prey on my Sterling swan."

"If you don't mind," Nicholas said easily, stepping beside her, "I'll escort my wife."

Elizabeth gratefully clutched his smooth sleeve. Already her head had begun to throb again. The last thing she wanted was to be the cause of more dissension between Drew and Hugh Sterling, to be forced to favor one relative over the other.

The duke looked disgruntled; then his lips formed a sly grin. "Honeymooners, eh? Can't bear to see another man touch her, not even her own papa, by Jove." He aimed a wily look at the duchess, who sat stone-faced by the hearth. "Brings back fond memories, eh, Addie?"

The Duchess Adelaide stared back with blank brown eyes.

"Get off your rump, dearest," the duke added. "You wouldn't want your dinner to get cold."

The party trouped into the ancient dining room, where pale dusk light drifted through the tall windows. On the long, white-draped table stood a pair of candelabrum, each supported by an ornate but unpolished silver swan. Candlelight flickered over the tapestried walls.

The duke insisted on placing Elizabeth to his right; Nicholas sat beside her. Throughout the meal Hugh Sterling doted on Elizabeth, passing her the most select tidbits, refilling her wineglass, and singing her praises. He had a look about him tonight that disturbed her, an expression of secret glee, as though he had something up his sleeve.

He lifted his wineglass. "You're a lucky man, Hawkesford. My daughter's quite the beauty."

"I can't argue that," Nicholas said, flashing her a smile as he sawed at the ubiquitous mutton.

"Strong constitution, too, I'll warrant. She'll give you sturdy sons." For an instant the joviality left Hugh Sterling's face, his eyes darkening with memories. "Had two sons myself. Both died of lung disease. Caught it from each other."

Compassion wrenched Elizabeth. Would the duke be pleased to have a grandchild someday? "I'm so sorry, Your Grace."

"Save your sentiment—it won't bring 'em back." Stretching forth gnarled fingers, the duke patted her hand. "But you came back to me, little swan. It'd make me happy to hear you call me papa."

Elizabeth took a swallow of wine to ease her dry mouth. Somehow she could not bring herself to address him by the name she reserved for Owen. "Yes . . . Father. I'm glad we were able to meet at last."

The duke looked pleased. "That's my girl. So pretty and an accomplished artist, as well. Your pictures'll hang in the National Gallery if I've any say in the matter."

"I'm a sculptress," she said, uneasy with his blandishments. "And I'm hardly well known enough to have my work displayed in a museum." Thinking of Lord Buckstone, she added, "But I'm close to obtaining an important commission, I hope."

"Be glad to help you any way I can. You've Sterling blood in you, by Jove." He looked at Drew, who sat silently eating, his expression morose. "Though the family's been known to sprout an occasional bad seed."

"Root rot in the family tree?" Drew drawled, dropping his fork in melodramatic horror. "'Tisn't I who wastes hundreds of pounds on suits of armor, while the estate goes to wrack and ruin."

"At least I have something to show for my money."

"A collection of dusty relics that'll end up being sold someday to the highest bidder."

The duke's lips drew back into a malevolent smile. "Sold, eh?" Drawing a quizzing glass from his pocket, he peered down the table at his nephew. "Can't wait for me to kick off, can you, boy? Ten to one, you're off to frolic in London the instant I'm laid in the grave."

"Please, Your Grace," Philippa said, the candlelight painting haggard shadows onto her cheeks. "My son means you no ill will."

"Hah," spat the duke. "Spends his days planning how he'll waste the rest of my money. Deny it, Drew. Go on, let's hear another lie."

"It doesn't matter what I say. You'll believe what you like."

Drew slouched in his chair and toyed with the remains of his dinner. Elizabeth felt a flash of pity. Profligate or not, he didn't deserve to be flayed in front of everyone.

She was casting around for another topic when the duchess said calmly, "That's enough, Hugh. This baiting is bad for the digestion."

The duke chortled. "You—trouble with your digestion? You're as hale as those horses of yours."

She gazed back, stone faced. "I was referring to our guests."

"They're not guests, by Jove. They're family. No need to whitewash what we're really like."

Nicholas cleared his throat. "In light of that thought, I've a matter to place before the lot of you." He scrutinized each person in turn. "Despite what I said earlier, I don't believe the incident this afternoon was an accident. Someone deliberately shot at Elizabeth. I suspect that 'someone' may be living in this house."

Silence lay as thickly as the dust on the sideboards. A candle sputtered; a daub of hot wax plopped onto the tablecloth. Dismayed, Elizabeth tried to catch Nicholas's eye, but he was looking around the table. Why hadn't he warned her of his plan to confront everyone?

Philippa's spoon clattered to her plate. "Deliberately, your lordship? By one of us? That's outrageous!"

"Outrageous, bah!" Hugh Sterling wagged a lumpy finger at her. "Hawkesford's a sharp one. If he says one of you tried to murder Elizabeth, then it must be so."

"But why—?" Philippa said stupidly.

"For the money, you dunce," the duke said, his breathing growing labored. "I'll wager you've thought long and hard about that these past few days."

Her jaw dropped. "Your Grace! Surely you don't think I . . ."

"Who else here would see Elizabeth as a threat?" He sucked in a gulp of air. "You . . . you and that no-good son of yours. Wouldn't surprise me . . . if you put him up . . . to killing my daughter!"

Philippa's mouth worked like a bird's beak. "I would never—!" she sputtered. "I cannot believe this!"

"Speak up, boy," the duke said, wheezing. "Tell us . . . where you were this afternoon . . . when the shot was fired."

Drew glared, his eyes demon dark, his fingers curled around the silver handle of his knife. "In my room," he said, his words dropping like stones. "By myself."

"Hah! No alibi . . . should've known."

Gasping, the duke sat back in his chair.

The duchess rose to tug on the bell rope. "Don't be an ass, Hugh. You're making yourself ill."

"He's not ill, he's mad." All pretense of civility slid from Philippa's face, leaving it sharp as a hawk's. "Imagine, accusing Drew and me of such an atrocity! And all because that . . . that American bastard waltzed in here to curry the duke's favor."

"That's quite enough," Nicholas snapped.

The ball of tension in Elizabeth's stomach tightened. Pushing back her chair, she stood. "Stop this, everyone. I've not come here to lay claim to any inheritance. I wanted to meet my father, that's all. It's time each of you accepted that."

Philippa made a spiteful mutter. Drew ran his fingers along the knife blade. The duchess arched a regal eyebrow.

Nicholas wore a fierce frown; Elizabeth suspected he didn't approve of her drawing attention to herself. Deliberately she turned her gaze from him as she sat back down.

"That's my girl," the duke said, his breathing less raspy, his eyes more focused. "Knew you weren't greedy like the rest of the riffraff in this family."

Into the shadowed doorway came Mrs. Drabble, huffing and puffing, her pudgy hands laden with a silver tray. "Ain't no need t' ring, Yer Grace. I was bringin' yer curd tarts in a minute."

Adelaide motioned the housekeeper to the table, to set down the dish. "Fetch Dr. Marsh, please. And be quick about it."

Beady eyes widening, Mrs. Drabble obeyed.

The duke rubbed his knobby hands. "You come back here with him, Drabble, but tell him I'm fine. I've another reason for wanting his presence tonight."

Adelaide passed around the tray. What did Hugh Sterling have planned? Elizabeth wondered, toying with her tart and sickened by the delight he took in needling everyone. In a way she couldn't blame Philippa for her venom, Drew for his sulkiness, or Adelaide for her aloofness. How could Lucy Templeton have loved such a man as the duke? Perhaps he hadn't always been so malicious; perhaps the loss of his true love had soured him—

"You needed me, Your Grace?"

Startled, Elizabeth looked up from her plate to see Gilbert Marsh standing beside the duke. Dressed in the same plain brown suit he'd worn earlier, the doctor carried a small leather bag. His eyes flicked over hers just long enough for her to catch the glitter of emotion. No doubt he was displeased that she hadn't taken his medication and remained abed.

"His Grace had a spot of the asthma," Adelaide said. Marsh made a move to open his satchel, but the duke waved impatiently. "No, no. Damned tonic'll put me to sleep. Got to keep a clear head, tonight of all nights." Grinning, he gazed around the table.

"Get on with it, Hugh," the duchess said flatly. "There's no need for melodrama."

The duke snickered. "Practical as always, that's my Addie. Make yourself useful, Marsh; help me up. Bones get rusty from sitting so long."

The doctor extended a bracing arm and the duke levered to his feet. He looked so frail that Elizabeth felt a surge of sympathy. Mrs. Drabble rushed to take his plate. He flattened both palms on the tablecloth; the candlelight etched every line on his face, so that he looked like the sculpture of an aging warrior.

"Decided on a bridal gift for my daughter," he said. "Added a codicil to my will just this morning. Marsh and Drabble signed as witnesses." He paused, his violet eyes gleaming. "Except for what's entailed, I'm leaving the whole lot to Elizabeth."

Chapter 21

Philippa uttered a strangled squawk. Drew sat bolt upright. The duchess calmly continued to eat her tart.

Elizabeth's head throbbed; then her body went numb, even to the feel of the fork in her hand. She heard Nicholas stir in his chair.

"You can't do this," Philippa squeaked.

"It's outrageous," Drew snapped.

He flashed Elizabeth a look of such rancor that she felt chilled to the bone.

She managed to stand on shaky legs. "I'm sorry," she told the duke. "But I can't accept your money."

His wrinkled chin lifted in autocratic resolution. "You must. You're my only living child, flesh of my flesh, blood of my blood."

"I won't take so much as a cent from you," Elizabeth repeated. "If you insist upon leaving me an inheritance, I'll give it all to charity, every farthing."

His lips arched in a fossilized grin. "Charity, by Jove? A noble ambition for a nobleman's daughter. The Sterling School for Orphans, the Sterling Scholarship for Starving Artists..."

Philippa flung down her napkin. "This can't be legal. I'll call my solicitor. I'll . . . I'll have you declared incompetent—"

"And waste your pittance on legal fees?" the duke said, sneering. "Marsh and Drabble will testify I was of sound mind." He stared at the housekeeper, who hovered near the doctor. "Won't you?"

Chins jiggling, Mrs. Drabble nodded, though she looked none too thrilled to be the subject of Philippa's distress and Drew's scowl. Lips pursed, Dr. Marsh also inclined his head.

"There, now, you see," Hugh Sterling said, his ancient face bright with satisfaction. "My solicitors will be checking the document, though, just in case."

Philippa and Drew glared, their faces bearing a marked resemblance in the pinched rigidity of the mouth, the sharp line of the cheeks, the narrowed darkness of the eyes. Elizabeth couldn't blame mother and son for their fury; they had every right to feel betrayed. She herself felt hollow with shock, as much a pawn of the duke as they.

The duchess set down her fork. "Are you quite done, Hugh? I should like to retire."

"Never were much for fun, Addie. Too wrapped up in those horses of yours. Run along now—you must get your beauty rest." He cackled as the duchess made a dignified departure; then he closed his bony fingers around the silver-topped cane. Hobbling toward the door, he glanced around the table. "Pleasant dreams, everyone."

The instant the duke had gone, with Dr. Marsh and Mrs. Drabble following, Philippa shot to her feet and glowered at Elizabeth.

"You'll not get away with this," she hissed. "If I must approach the queen herself, you'll not touch a farthing of Drew's money. You're nothing but the duke's bas—" As she glanced at Nicholas, her angry voice choked to a stop.

"I would advise you," he said in a steely-soft voice, "to take care how you describe my wife."

His chair scraping back, he moved behind Elizabeth, his hands settling onto her shoulders. She welcomed the proprietary gesture; his warm fingers chased the chill from her veins and imbued her with the courage to gaze straight at Philippa and Drew.

"Oh, pooh," said a plaintive voice from the doorway, "have I come too late for dinner?"

Elizabeth whipped her eyes toward the girl walking into the dining room. "Cicely!"

"What the devil—!" Nicholas exploded, his fingers digging into Elizabeth's shoulders.

Clad in a dusty blue traveling gown, an ostrich-plumed hat perched jauntily on her head, Cicely strolled to the opposite side of the table and stopped beside Drew, whose sour expression sweetened to open admiration. With the careless elegance of a courtier, he tossed aside his napkin and stood.

"My dearest Lady Cicely, what a marvelous surprise."

As he kissed the back of her hand, her impish expression dissolved into adoration. "Oh, Drew, it's so very wonderful to see you again. I do hope you'll forgive me for barging in without an invitation."

"You're always welcome." Casting a sly glance at Nicholas's stony face, Drew added silkily, "After all, we're related now."

"In a loose manner of speaking," Philippa muttered.

The sudden sound of raised voices intruded from the hall. Though Elizabeth couldn't discern the words, the familiar tones of both speakers froze her blood.

Lifting her eyes to Nicholas, she blurted, "Papa's here! He's arguing with the duke."

Fingers gripping her skirts, she hastened into the shadowy hall, Nicholas close behind her. The angry voices grew louder; then she spied the two men standing outside the saloon. Miss Eversham hovered nearby, wringing her thin hands. Doctor Marsh stood watching, his lips compressed, as if he were annoyed at his patient being upset.

"Where is she?" Owen demanded. "I've a right to see my own daughter."

Hugh Sterling brandished his cane. "She's mine, by Jove! You'll not steal her away again... and you'll address me as Your Grace."

"Hah," spat Owen. "'You're fallen from grace.'"

"Don't you dare . . . spout the Scriptures at me," the duke said, wheezing. "Begone with you . . . you're not welcome here."

"I'm surprised you know the Bible when you hear it. I'll not move an inch until I see my daughter."

Elizabeth hurried forward. "I'm here, Papa."

Owen curled an arm around her waist. "See?" he told the duke. "She calls *me* Papa."

"And *me* Father, by Jove." He banged the cane on the oak planked floor. "You forget . . . if I hadn't been the man I was . . . Lucy would never have given birth to Elizabeth."

Owen tensed, his fingers balling into fists. "Watch what you say of my wife and my daughter—"

Appalled, Elizabeth stepped between them. "Please, stop this," she said, her eyes going from one man to the other. "I'm not a prize to be fought over. You might show some trust in my ability to love the both of you."

The duke's asthmatic hiss filled the silence. His abashed eyes slid away from hers and stared at his knobby fingers on the cane.

Owen combed his fingers through his thinning gray hair. "I'm sorry, Libby."

"I am, too," Hugh admitted stiffly, though he shot Owen a glare. "Time was when a man controlled who entered his house."

Dr. Marsh took the duke's arm. "Come along, Your Grace. You need to rest."

For once Hugh Sterling didn't argue. He hobbled forward to pat Elizabeth's hand. "Good night, little swan. I'll see you in the morning." With the doctor's help, the duke started upstairs.

Watching his halting progress, Elizabeth felt Nicholas's comforting hand stroke her back. She started to turn to him; then Owen's regard caught her attention. Regret shone in his hazel eyes, a regret that pierced her heart. Words of reconciliation pressed against her throat, yet she must wait for a more private time to speak.

Nicholas coolly eyed the governess. "I trust, Miss

Eversham, that you have an explanation for your sudden appearance here."

"Yes, my lord." Distress darkened her plain features. "But first, where is Lady Cicely?"

"Follow me."

Pivoting on his heel, Nicholas led the group back to the dining room. Philippa had vanished, leaving Drew and Cicely alone. The couple stood whispering in a shadowed corner, heads close, Drew holding her hands.

Nicholas glared at his sister. "What are you doing, young lady?" he said, his voice ominously quiet.

She whipped guiltily around, but held her chin pertly high. "Now, don't be angry, Nick. I've not acted against your command—you never forbade me to come here."

"I never anticipated your showing such exceedingly poor judgment, either."

"I accept full blame, your lordship," said Miss Eversham, hands clenching her sober gray skirts.

"No, you don't, Kate," Owen said. "The girl tricked you and ran off. She should accept the consequences of her own actions."

"Neither of you could have stopped her?" Nicholas asked.

"We barely managed to board the same train," Own said. "She threatened to make a scene when we tried to get her off."

The governess wrung her bony fingers. "I'm ever so sorry, your lordship. I did try to dissuade her."

"We'll discuss this further in private," Nicholas told his sister. "You'll have to stay the night, I suppose, but don't bother unpacking. You'll be leaving at first light."

"But I've come so far, Nick." Cicely's mouth settled into a charming pout. "Can't I stay for just a few days, please? London was so very tiresome."

"So was Yorkshire," Drew murmured, his eyes drifting to her lace-trimmed bodice, "at least until a few moments ago."

As Cicely coyly fluttered her lashes, Elizabeth saw

Nicholas's jaw tense. Laying a restraining hand on his sleeve, she said, "We're all tired. Why don't we talk this over in the morning? I'll ring for Mrs. Drabble."

As Elizabeth went to tug the bell rope, Cicely cast a look of longing at the remains of dinner.

"Mightn't I sit down for a moment? We were in such a crashing hurry to get here before dark that we didn't even stop to eat."

"Perhaps hunger will serve as a reminder of your rash behavior," Nicholas stated.

Her lower lip jutted out. "I'm not a child to be sent to bed without supper."

"I'll treat you according to the age you act."

She opened her mouth as if to retort. A blush suddenly colored her cheeks and her eyes grew watery.

"Come now, Hawkesford," Drew said. "No need to be so hard on the girl. She's sorry for acting impulsively."

Cicely looked up from beneath her lashes. "That's right, Nick," she said, her tone subdued. "I *am* sorry ...truly I am. Can't you find room in your heart to forgive me?"

Elizabeth bit back a smile. With her soulful eyes and her drooping shoulders, Cicely could have posed for a romantic rendition of repentance.

Mrs. Drabble spoiled the artistic effect by scurrying into the room. "Oh, fiddle," she panted, wiping her hands on the broad girth of her apron. "I'll be gettin' nowt done in th' kitchen, wi' all this answerin' doors an' bells an' such."

"We'll need two rooms prepared," Nicholas said. "One for my sister and Miss Eversham, and another for Mr. Hastings."

Taking Elizabeth by the hand, he rounded the table to offer his other arm to Cicely; his sister grudgingly accepted the escort. Drew slouched back into his chair and scowled at his wineglass. Reluctant sympathy tugged at Elizabeth. For all his profligate ways, what a blow it must be to have lost the assurance of a fortune.

They followed the grumbling housekeeper upstairs,

Miss Eversham and Owen bringing up the rear. Nicholas hung back as Mrs. Drabble led Cicely and the governess down the shadowed hall.

"Owen, I'd like to have a word with my sister. Could you wait inside with Elizabeth? There's been another attempt on her life and I don't want her left alone."

Owen started visibly. "Of course, my lord." Swinging to Elizabeth, he said hoarsely, "Are you all right, Libby?"

"I'm fine, Papa," she murmured.

She entered the bedroom, which was lit by tapers in the tall candlesticks on the writing desk and nightstand. Janet stood at the wardrobe, drawing out a nightgown. The maid bobbed a shy curtsy and retreated into the dressing room.

His face gray and his fists clenched, Owen turned toward Elizabeth. "What happened this time, Libby?"

Briefly she related the story, glossing over the danger in an effort to ease his worry. "Nicholas knocked me out of the way in time. He'll keep me safe."

"Bless my soul." Owen lifted a hand as if to touch her cheek, then dropped his fingers. "Are you sure you weren't hurt?"

"Just a slight headache from the fall."

Hands clasped behind his back, he paced the threadbare rug. "You mustn't stay here. Lord Nicholas should have realized that."

Elizabeth trailed Owen to the tester bed with its once-grand hangings of crimson Spitalfields velvet. "He did want me to leave, but I convinced him otherwise. Don't you see, Papa? I'll never be able to live free of fear until we find the person responsible for making these attempts."

Turning to her, he ran his fingers through his sparse gray hair. "I don't like this, Libby. Never did feel at ease in this old house, either." His expression grew distant and sad. "Lucy loved it, though. It was brighter here then . . . she had a way of lighting up the place with her laughter. Coming back makes me remember so much."

"You didn't live here at the manor house, though."

He shook his head. "At St. Mary's vicarage, a few miles away, toward Wrefton. But I became friends with your mother and as time went on, she confided in me more and more." His face settled into rigid lines. "Lucy badly needed a friend. She was torn asunder over the fact that she loved a married man, her cousin's husband."

"Why didn't you tell me before that Mama was related to the duchess?"

He looked puzzled. "Didn't I? I was so agitated that night we talked. . . ."

The sorrow on his face touched her heart. "When did you fall in love with Mama?" Elizabeth asked softly.

Owen sank heavily onto the bed, his elbows coming to rest on his knees. "From the start. She was the kindest, prettiest woman I'd ever known. When I learned the duke had gotten her with child I offered to marry her, of course. But Lucy refused, didn't want to burden me with another man's baby." He smiled wistfully at Elizabeth. "As if a sweet girl like you could be anything but God's blessing."

A lump formed in her throat, and Elizabeth had to swallow hard. "The duke claims he always loved me. But you said he renounced me when his heir was born."

Owen straightened, his features hardening again. "His visits dwindled once he had a son. That's how I was finally able to convince Lucy to marry me. She realized Hugh Sterling would never be the sort of father she wanted for you." Frowning, he tilted his head at her. "I trust you won't cast stones at your mother's memory, Libby. She might have acted rashly in having an affair, but she was a good woman, a woman with a heart full of love."

Hugging her arms, Elizabeth leaned against the velvet-draped bedpost. "Perhaps," she said slowly, "at one time I might not have understood. But now I know how it is to love a man."

"Aye," Owen said with a stiff nod. "And one day you'll know how it is to love a child, as well. I'm stay-

ing here with you, Libby. Not that I haven't faith in
Lord Nicholas, mind you, but two can watch out better
than one."

Though touched by the offer, she hesitated. "I'm not
sure the duke will allow that."

Hazel eyes darkening, Owen spat, "Hugh Sterling
always was a law unto himself. But don't you worry, I'll
have a word with him if he refuses me."

Alarmed, she sank to her knees beside him. "Please,
don't start another argument with the duke. He has a
bad heart; he mustn't be overexcited."

Owen sat as still as a statue. "You . . . care for him, do
you?" he said, his voice breaking with emotion. "Was
he . . . everything you'd hoped to find?"

Deeply moved, Elizabeth saw his agonizing fear that
she would renounce him. She threw her arms around
him, pressing her cheek to the familiar rough tweed of
his coat. "Oh, Papa, I care for him, but no more than I
would for an acquaintance. The duke may be the father
of my blood, but you're the father of my heart."

His arms tightened; she felt his chest expand with a
deep intake of breath. When at last he drew back, tears
sparkled in his eyes. "I'm sorry for failing you, Libby.
But at first I didn't realize you *needed* protection. I never
imagined even Hugh Sterling would stoop so low as to
harm his own daughter."

"But *is* the duke the culprit? Somehow I can't see
him in the role of murderer."

Grim lines creased Owen's whiskered face. "He's capable of anything, Libby. 'Be vigilant because your ad-
versary, the devil, walks about, seeking who he may
devour.'"

The gruesome words made Elizabeth shiver. Should
she fear the duke, or was her father's prejudice born of
jealousy? "Why didn't you tell me you'd gone to see
the duke in London, to warn him to stay away from
me?"

He lifted a graying eyebrow. "Would it have made a
difference to you?"

"Of course," she said, gently gripping his hands. "Because you did it for me, Papa."

The door opened and Nicholas strode inside. From his swift steps and disgruntled expression she guessed the interview with Cicely had not gone well.

Owen surged from the bed. "I trust you're not angry with Miss Eversham, your lordship. Short of using brute force, neither of us could convince Lady Cicely to return home."

Nicholas grimaced. "On the contrary, I'm grateful to you both for putting up with her pranks. This time she's gone too far."

"She told you of the other incident, then?"

Nicholas gave a curt nod. "Under duress."

"What other incident?" Elizabeth asked, glancing back and forth between the two men.

"I'd best let your husband tell you," Owen said, dropping a peck on her cheek.

"You've the last bedroom at the end of the hall," Nicholas said distractedly.

Nodding, Owen bid them good night. The instant the door closed quietly behind her father, Elizabeth repeated, "What incident, Nicholas?"

Removing his frock coat, he sent it sailing onto a gilt Queen Anne chair. "My sister behaved abominably toward Charles Garforth—and half of society, too, it seems."

"What did she do?"

"It happened yesterday at the Henley Regatta, a rowing competition. She was watching from the bank —alone apparently, because Miss Eversham had gone to fetch their tea and Aunt Beatrice was off greeting some friends."

"And?"

A dull flush seemed to tint his cheeks . . . or was it a trick of the candlelight? "Cicely was sitting in front of a screen of bushes. When she spied Charles's rowboat far in the lead, she . . . lifted her skirts and showed him her backside."

A giggle rose in Elizabeth's throat. "You're joking."

"No. Cicely claims to have acted on pure impulse, as if that should excuse her unseemly behavior."

Consumed by gales of laughter, she collapsed onto the bed. "Oh, Nicholas...can't you imagine...the look on Charles's face..."

"It's hardly amusing," Nicholas said, though the corners of his mouth twitched ever so slightly. "A boatload of people came around the bend and caught her in the act. The tale must be all over society by now."

"Oh, come now. She had her drawers on, didn't she? No one actually saw any bare skin."

"That isn't the point," he said, frowning. "Her reputation is surely in shreds."

Perching on an elbow, Elizabeth watched him unbutton his shirt. "Where's your sense of humor, Nicholas? I thought you'd gotten over being ashamed of the human body."

He flashed her a withering look. "I don't want my sister making an exhibit of herself. What man would want to marry a woman who'd behave so indiscreetly?"

Exasperation rippled through Elizabeth. "People will forget the incident the instant another scandal crops up. Society is likely gossiping more about the Earl of Hawkesford marrying an American artist. As for Cicely, it's only a matter of time before she accepts the fact that she loves Charles."

Nicholas's fingers froze on the last button. "She despises him."

Elizabeth shook her head. "I don't believe that."

Hands on his hips, he strode to the bed and stared at her. "What makes you so sure?"

She gazed boldly back, admiring the breadth of his bare chest. "What would you have done if I'd acted the way Cicely did?"

"Paddled your behind, by God."

"And then?"

Smiling, he came down on the embroidered coverlet and folded her in his arms. "Kissed you until you begged for mercy."

His lips brushed hers, his tongue seeking an entry

she willingly allowed. He tasted of wine and warmth, and she closed her eyes as desire melted her limbs and ignited her blood. She felt herself sliding into a vat of sweet, familiar pleasure, relishing the scent and feel of him, reveling in the knowledge that they belonged to each other.

After a time, he drew back. Running a forefinger over her moistened lips, he eyed her skeptically. "You truly think this is what Cicely wants from Charles?"

Nodding, Elizabeth let her hand drift over the dark, curling hairs on his chest. "Deep in her heart, yes. But she ran here, to her big brother, because she's afraid to face her feelings."

"Female logic," Nicholas scoffed.

"Ah, but remember how we resisted each other at first."

He grinned. "You do have a point there. I hope you're right."

She smiled softly. "Trust me. I trust you."

The light left his face, and he rolled onto his back to stare at the canopy with its gilded garlands and swans. "How can I allow Cicely to stay? I've my hands full keeping you safe."

A fist of fear squeezed her heart, but she kept her voice even. "Your sister isn't in any danger, Nicholas."

"I know," he said, his voice agonized. "But you are."

He pulled her onto the hard wall of his chest, his embrace desperately tight. Tucking her face into the crook of his neck, Elizabeth tried not to think of what lay beyond the safe circle of his arms. She longed to reassure him, but knew not the words. She could only wait and hope and pray. . . .

Regret twined around her heart. "Nothing has happened the way I'd thought," she murmured. "I came here wanting to find love from the man who fathered me. Instead, he's using me to thwart Philippa and Drew."

Eyes silver in the candlelight, Nicholas shaped his hands around her cheeks. "In his own way, Hugh Sterling does love you, Elizabeth."

"I tell myself that. But I can't help feeling hurt by what he's done."

He smoothed a strand of hair from her temple. "We'll talk to him tomorrow, love. Perhaps we can persuade him to change back the will."

"Yes, I'd like that." Cheered by the prospect, she lay her head on her husband's shoulder and began to plan the words she would use to convince Hugh Sterling.

The Duke of Rockborough stood before the suit of Persian armor in a corner of his bedchamber. Candlelight glinted off the perfectly polished metal, yet something didn't seem quite right. With the care of a connoisseur, he adjusted the long pike held in the gauntleted hand, aiming the wickedly sharp tip at the angle a knight would have used. There, the duke thought, satisfied with his handiwork.

Leaning heavily on his cane, he hobbled back to the tester bed and gingerly crept between the fine linens, his bones creaking as loudly as the bed ropes. Tonight he felt every one of his sixty-nine years. Perhaps he should have taken his sleeping draught instead of dumping it into the chamber pot when Marsh's back had been turned.

Yet once he'd settled against the plump feather pillow, Hugh Sterling smiled with glee. He'd wanted to stay awake tonight, to savor his triumph. Those leeches, Philippa and Drew, were like weapons; easy to manipulate if one possessed enough money and guile. Rubbing his knobby hands, Hugh reflected upon the events of the evening. By Jove, everything was shaping up so neatly—

Suddenly the door opened. "I see you're still awake," came the familiar voice, sounding not at all surprised.

The duke started. "What do *you* want?"

"I came to talk about Lucy."

"Lucy!" he snorted. "You must have been nipping at my store of brandy. What makes you think I'll speak of her to you?"

The visitor took a step closer. "I have to know if you truly loved her."

"None of your damned business. Now begone with you!"

"She loved you. I saw it in her eyes, so many times."

Hugh Sterling smiled. He stared into the distance, his aged face wistful with memories. "She did love me, by Jove, she did."

"Yet she was too virtuous to engage in a sordid affair. It's time you told the truth."

The duke's pensive mood altered to anger. "Who are you to lecture me? I'll not listen to your prattling!"

"You'll listen," the visitor whispered, advancing to the bed. "You owe me that much after all these years."

Fear invaded the duke. Impatiently he shook off the unfamiliar sensation. He feared no one... least of all the person standing before him. And he'd done nothing to be ashamed of, by Jove!

"I don't suppose it matters anymore," he said, shrugging. "All right, Lucy did have ridiculous scruples. Because of that, I could convince her to sleep with me only a few times."

"You forced her?" Horror weighted the voice.

"Nonsense." The duke shifted irritably beneath the quilted coverlet. "If she struggled a little, it was only inexperience. She wanted me. Even reached her pleasure, by Jove. I made a woman of her."

Looking stunned, the figure halted at the edge of the bed. "You raped Lucy. All these years, I believed you loved her, that she went to you willingly...."

Madness shone in those staring eyes. The duke glanced around for a weapon; a medieval dagger lay on the night stand. "I never raped her... and I did love her," he snapped in his most imperious manner. "Not that it's any concern of yours. Now get out of here!"

"No," the visitor said softly. "Your punishment is long overdue. You must pay for your sin."

The duke lunged for the dagger. With bone-crushing swiftness, the caller thrust Hugh Sterling against the mattress. Wheezing, he cursed his wasted body, cursed his weakness.

His heart hammered in terror as he gazed at those familiar eyes. Insane . . . how had he not seen the truth before?

This must be the person who'd shot at Elizabeth, who wanted her dead! In helpless fury, he fought, determined to protect his daughter.

The visitor seized the feather pillow, pressed it to the duke's face. Panicked, Sterling struggled harder, his lungs burning, clawing for air. The image of Elizabeth's lovely face blazed in his frantic mind. He couldn't die, not yet. . . .

Chapter 22

Elizabeth sat with Nicholas and Owen at one end of the massive dining table. Sunlight wandered through the long windows, setting dust motes to dancing and banishing the habitual gloom. Her body sated and her mind contented, she basked in the companionship of the two men she loved. Even the meal tasted better than usual, with steaming porridge, rashers of bacon, grilled tomatoes, and buttered toast with quince preserves.

Somewhere upstairs a door slammed. A few moments later, the sound of running feet approached. Mrs. Drabble rushed inside, her chins quivering with distress and her fingers twisting her apron. "It's th' duke," she gasped. "He's stone-cold dead!"

Elizabeth stared. Her mind reeled in shock. The teacup slipped from her fingers and clattered into the silver edged saucer.

As if from a distance she saw Nicholas's face whiten. Tossing down his napkin, he shot to his feet. "Are you sure?" he snapped.

Nodding, the housekeeper sniffed, dabbing at her squat nose. "I went t' bring His Grace th' mornin' coffee, like I always do. When there weren't no answer t' my knockin', I went on inside. He was layin' in the bed wi' his face white as snow an' his eyes starin'—" She blew her nose with the sound of a trumpet.

"Did you summon Dr. Marsh?" Nicholas demanded.

Mrs. Drabble nodded vigorously, her chins jiggling

in rhythm. "Aye, right off I rung." She made the sign of the cross. "I weren't goin' t' touch no corpse."

"Does the duchess know?"

"Nay, m'lord. She's gone. Out for her morning ride."

"I'll have to fetch Her Grace, then."

Bending to kiss Elizabeth's forehead, Nicholas said to Owen, "Watch out for her, will you? I shan't be gone long."

"Of course," Owen said, his face sober.

Elizabeth watched numbly as Nicholas strode out the door, the housekeeper at his heels. She felt hollow, drained of emotion, sapped of energy. Only a few short hours ago, the duke had been eating dinner at this table, his aging face alight with glee. . . .

Her blood chilled and she looked at Owen. "Do you suppose he could have been murdered?"

His hazel eyes widened; then he shook his head. "Why would you think that?"

"Maybe he stumbled onto the truth . . . the truth about who's trying to kill me. Maybe he forfeited his life for me—"

"Nonsense, Libby. You're grasping at straws."

"There's something else. . . ." She tried to make sense out of her jumbled thoughts. "I didn't tell you, did I? He'd rewritten his will, leaving his fortune to me. Perhaps someone hated him for doing so, enough to kill him. . . ." Her voice broke with horror and she buried her face in her hands.

Owen hastened around the table to drape a comforting arm across her shoulders. "I confess I'm surprised Hugh Sterling would make you his heiress," he said flatly. "Yet you mustn't blame yourself for his death. You said he had a bad heart. That's the likely cause."

"But what if—"

"Stop torturing yourself, Libby. For pity's sake, you haven't even heard what the doctor has to report."

"Yes. Yes, you're right." Taking a deep breath, she lifted troubled eyes. "Who would have thought this would happen? He was old and ill, yet so full of life."

"The sad truth is that we all dwell under the shadow

of death. Libby, I'd be a hypocrite if I professed any great grief. But I am sorry, for your sake."

A tremulous smile touched her lips; she reached up to clasp his hand, which lay on her shoulder. "I'm glad you're here, Papa. I don't know what I'd do without you."

Petticoats rustled as Philippa rushed through the doorway. She must have dressed hastily, for her gray hair stuck out like ruffled feathers from her black lace cap and the sash to her crape gown trailed like a pheasant's tail.

She wrung her hands. "How can you smile at a time like this?" she snapped at Elizabeth. "Haven't you heard about the tragedy the family has just suffered?"

"Yes, and I'm so very sorry," Elizabeth murmured. "If I may do something to ease your sorrow ... notify friends or relations, help make arrangements—"

"I've no need of *your* help," Philippa said stiffly. "You cared nothing for the duke. Why, you haven't even the decency to don proper mourning attire."

Elizabeth straightened her spine. "I've only just heard the news."

"Have you?" Philippa said, eyes narrowing to calculating brown beads. "Or were you the first among us to know of the duke's death?"

Elizabeth stared, bewildered. Abruptly her mouth went dry with shock and outrage. "Are you accusing *me* of murder?" she whispered.

Owen's hands tightened on Elizabeth's shoulders. "You've insulted my daughter," he said grimly. "I demand an apology."

"*Your* daughter?" Philippa looked perplexed; then her eyes rounded with disdainful recognition. "I remember your face, " she said slowly. "You're Owen Hastings, that vicar who ran off with Lucy Templeton."

"I am."

"Peculiar that the duke would die when you set foot in this house again." Philippa pointed a bony finger at him. "You must have been Elizabeth's accomplice."

Owen bristled. "You're as ill-tempered as you've

always been. You'll beg my pardon and Elizabeth's as well."

"What have you done now, Mother?" Drew said from the doorway.

Philippa lifted her chin defensively. "Nothing but ask a simple question."

"You slandered Elizabeth and me," Owen stated, "all but accused us of murdering Hugh Sterling."

Sober-faced and clad in a dark suit with a black arm-band, Drew strolled into the dining room. "Is this true, Mother?"

"He's twisting my words around. But perhaps the facts speak for themselves. Lady Elizabeth is the only one among us who benefits from His Grace's death."

Drew stared at Elizabeth; she couldn't fathom the intense emotion smoldering in those dark eyes. Hatred for her? Grief for his uncle? Or sorrow for the wealth he'd lost?

Looking back at Philippa, he said frostily, "I'm surprised at you, Mother. You've overstepped the bounds of propriety."

"Why, Drew! You've no right to address your mother in that tone."

"I've every right. I'm the Duke of Rockborough."

She uttered a chirp of disapproval. "Nevertheless, I am still your mother—"

"I'm in no mood for your prattle this morning. Apologize, will you?"

The command made her haggard face go rigid. She gawked at him; then her eyes slid away and she said in a grudging voice, "Do forgive me, Lady Elizabeth, Mr. Hastings."

"Of course," Elizabeth murmured.

Watching as Drew went to pour himself a cup of tea, she could not help but wonder at his disposition. Never before had she heard him speak so authoritatively to his mother. Had shouldering the responsibilities of the dukedom swept away his indolence?

The sound of footsteps drew her eyes to the door. Nicholas walked inside, followed by Gilbert Marsh. The doctor looked solemn, and his fair hair was mussed, as though he'd run his fingers through the thinning strands.

Rising, Elizabeth slipped her hand into Nicholas's. "Did you find the duchess?" she said quietly.

He nodded. "As she was riding into the stable yard. She's gone upstairs."

"May I offer my condolences . . . Your Grace?" Marsh said.

Acknowledging the sentiment with a nod, Drew set down his teacup. "I trust you've completed your examination?"

"Yes, do tell us," Philippa added, pressing a handkerchief to her beaklike nose. "If you've found anything . . . irregular, you are duty bound to inform the family."

His features swept clean of emotion, the doctor stood at the far end of the table. "I've little to report, your ladyship. His Grace apparently suffered an asthmatic seizure last night. The effect is rather like suffocation and his heart must have given out under the strain."

Leaning against Nicholas's solid warmth, Elizabeth felt a sweep of distress at the terror her father must have endured, the terror of trying to draw a breath.

"Are you quite certain?" Philippa asked sharply. "Is there any chance of foul play?"

Blinking in surprise, Marsh shook his head. "I saw no evidence of anything other than death from natural causes."

Philippa's shoulders sagged. She looked at her son, but he was staring out the window.

Marsh cleared his throat. "I've spoken to Her Grace and promised my help in making the appropriate arrangements. If you'll excuse me." Executing a brief bow, he departed.

The gathering drifted apart, Owen soberly going for a walk, Elizabeth and Nicholas returning to their bedroom. Nicholas dispatched Quinn and Janet to York to purchase mourning clothing. Alone with her husband,

Elizabeth felt her numbness lift, unlocking her emotions. Pressing her cheek to his chest, she wept, shedding not the stormy tears of grief for a lost loved one, but the quiet tears of sadness at losing the chance to know the man who had given life to her.

Nicholas drew her to an armchair of faded crimson velvet and cuddled her on his lap. Sunlight spilled through the opened window and the fragrance of wild herbs drifted from the gardens below. The air hummed with bees, the bright summer day a contrast to the bleakness in her soul. Elizabeth sought comfort in the steady beat of his heart, the supportive circle of his arms. As her weeping slowly ebbed, she drew in a deep, sighing breath.

"It's hard to believe he's really gone," she whispered.

His eyes soft, he scooped a tear from her cheek. "I know, love, I know."

Clasping his arms, she shifted in Nicholas's lap to study his handsome face. "This *is* just a dreadful coincidence, isn't it? For the duke to have died now..."

"You heard what Marsh said. Hugh Sterling was a sick man. This could have happened at any time."

Guilt reared inside her, and she swallowed the knot choking her. "I can't help wondering if I hadn't come here, if he hadn't been so agitated at dinner—"

Nicholas silenced her lips with a finger. "Hush, love. You couldn't have foreseen the future. I'll not hear another word on the matter."

She took solace in the conviction lacing his voice. Yearning swept her, a yearning so intense she could taste it, a yearning to escape the intrigue and danger of this house. "Oh, Nicholas, I can scarcely wait until we can go home, to live a normal life, to begin working again...."

An understanding smile gentled his mouth. "To finish that statue of me?"

And learn if she'd been awarded Lord Buckstone's commission, Elizabeth thought. Prudence kept her silent on the topic.

She lay her cheek against his shoulder. "To begin our marriage the way it ought to have begun, with joy and love and freedom from fear."

"I know, Countess." He tilted her chin up; his eyes were dark with desire, a desire that sent shivers of longing through her. His hand slid down her arm to her breast, offering a comfort that delved deeper than words. Softly he repeated, "I know."

The eighth Duke of Rockborough had a funeral befitting his status. Countless black-bordered notes had been sent out to the peers of the realm, and Elizabeth spent the better part of two days assisting the duchess in penning the letters. At Drew's command, an army of women from nearby villages spent several days cleaning the neglected manor house. Elizabeth was glad for the activity of directing the women, for it gave her a release for her pent-up energy. Despite all the scrubbing and polishing and sweeping, the house retained a gloomy aura, from the crape-hung door to the scores of floral tributes scenting the air.

Black-plumed horses drew the hearse to the tiny church of St. Mary's, where the eulogy lasted for over an hour beside the family's stone crypt. Afterward, the cream of English society crowded the house for the customary reception. Dignified in her widow's cap and crape-trimmed gown, the duchess accepted the condolences with an aplomb that won Elizabeth's admiration. Yet she couldn't help but wonder how much Adelaide truly lamented the loss of her husband.

Once the last guests had departed the next day, the family and beneficiaries assembled in the library for the reading of the will. The dismal gray afternoon required the candlelight of an immense chandelier. Above bookshelves crammed with musty tomes hung the age-dulled portraits of ducal ancestors. *Her* ancestors, Elizabeth thought, studying their reptilian eyes and antique costumes. She felt no kinship with those posed figures, no bond of shared blood. Was it the ever-present prickle of danger that made her so ill at ease?

Would she ever feel happy in this house, ever bring her children here to learn their heritage?

Thunder grumbled in the distance. Glancing around, Elizabeth saw only somber faces; Nicholas sat beside her on a sofa of well-worn gold brocade, the duchess in her widow's weeds occupied an armchair apart from the group, and Philippa perched like a sharp-eyed crow beside Drew. At the rear of the room a few of the old duke's employees gathered, including Mrs. Drabble and Gilbert Marsh, who had been given modest bequests.

Before a mullioned window stood the bespectacled Aubrey Dimsdale, partner in the legal firm of Cleggs, Dimsdale, and Faberley, Moorgate Street, London. Dimsdale's dry dissertation named a substantial amount for building an armory in which to house Hugh Sterling's collection of weapons. A dower house on the grounds and the stables were to remain under the lifetime control of the duchess, with the entailed Yorkshire estate going to Drew. The remainder, in the guise of vast properties scattered throughout England, went to Elizabeth.

As Dimsdale droned to a halt, Nicholas gave her hand a squeeze. "Wait here a moment, love," he murmured. "I'll make arrangements for transferring the deeds."

The instant he walked up to the solicitor, Philippa glared at Elizabeth. "I shall challenge this," the older woman hissed. "You may be certain of that." She glided out of the library, her black shawl flapping like the wings of a vulture.

Disturbed, Elizabeth wandered restlessly to a bookcase near the door. An icy suspicion nipped at her. Could Philippa have aimed her enmity at the duke? Though he had died of natural causes, might not Philippa have paid him a late-night visit and unwittingly provoked the fatal attack?

Gilbert Marsh walked past, his fair head bowed in contemplation, his boyish face cleansed of expression.

"Excuse me, doctor."

He swung to her; his blue eyes widened slightly, as if in surprise that she would address him. "Your ladyship?"

When he made no move to come nearer, Elizabeth closed the gap between them. "I've been wondering," she murmured, her fingers tense around the folds of her ebony skirt, "if the duke took his sleeping draught the night he died?"

"Yes. Why do you ask?"

"I was curious to know if the potion was so strong he wouldn't have awakened when he suffered the seizure."

Marsh eyed her warily. "I administered his usual dose of laudanum. It never before stopped him from summoning me during the night."

Her gaze lowered to the doctor's sober frock coat. So Philippa *could* have roused the duke. "I see. . . ."

"What is it you see, your ladyship? I trust you're not thinking I gave His Grace an overdose of medication."

Marsh held himself stiffly; the coldness in his eyes dismayed Elizabeth. "Of course I don't blame you, doctor. If anything, I must thank you for how well you cared for my father all these years." A thought occurred to her. "Where will you go now?"

He blinked, his eyes blank. "Go? Oh . . . you mean because the new duke won't be requiring my services. I suppose I shall look for new lodgings, perhaps in Wrefton." Marsh subjected her to an intent stare. "I shall be leaving as soon as I wrap up my affairs here. Good day."

Frowning, Elizabeth watched him walk out of the library. She had the distinct impression Gilbert Marsh hadn't voiced everything on his mind. Did the doctor, too, suspect someone in this house might have caused the duke's death? Could he be guarding a family member from scandal?

Hands in his coat pockets, Drew strolled to her. "My compliments, cousin," he drawled. "You've had quite the run of luck these past few weeks. First your marriage to Hawkesford, now your Sterling inheritance."

With steady eyes, she met his sardonic gaze. "I've no intention of accepting the bequest."

"Oh, yes, all those ragged orphans and starving artists." Drew uttered a self-deprecating laugh. "I'm sure they're far more worthy recipients than I could ever hope to be."

"Don't belittle yourself," she said gently. "It wasn't fair of my father to leave you without even the funds to repair this place."

"What's done is done." He stared at her from beneath lowered lashes. "I've been thinking... I can't afford to commission your services, but perhaps you'd erect a monument on the grounds in his memory." As if embarrassed at showing sentiment, he shifted his feet and mumbled, "Tradition, you know."

The suggestion warmed her heart. Had she been wrong about Drew's character? "I'd be happy to," she said. "I'm waiting to hear on another commission, but I can certainly start on the design."

"Hullo, there!" Waving, Cicely scurried through the doorway. "I've been waiting in the saloon *forever*," she said, fluttering her lashes at Drew. "What took you so long?"

"Congratulate me," he said, kissing her hand. "I am now officially the Duke of Destitute."

Cicely tilted her head in confusion. "The Duke of—? You mean your uncle didn't leave you any—?" Her cheeks flushed a pretty pink. "I don't mean to pry, Drew."

Her hand remained clasped in his. "You could never pry, my dear lady," he said, smiling into her adoring eyes. "Had I the funds, I'd sweep you away to the ends of the earth."

Troubled, Elizabeth watched the couple. This past week she had been so caught up in the funeral arrangements that she'd paid little heed to Cicely. Clearly the girl still fancied herself in love with Drew.

"Would you care to take a walk in the gardens?" Drew asked.

Cicely's eyes shone a deep blue. "Oh, yes—"

"Oh, no," Nicholas said, stepping between the two. "There's a storm brewing. I wouldn't want you to get soaked."

With a squeak of dismay, Cicely yanked her hand back. Drew arched an eyebrow at Nicholas. The men glared at each other, Drew lazily challenging, Nicholas blatantly disapproving.

The storm, Elizabeth decided, threatened to explode inside the house, rather than out. "Perhaps I could chaperon Cicely and Drew. We'll come back in if it starts to rain."

Eyes as gray as granite, Nicholas glanced at her. "No," he said bluntly. "I need to have a word with my sister."

Cicely's lips formed a pout. "Can't it wait, Nick?"

He shook his head. "We'll talk now. If you'll excuse us . . . Your Grace."

"Far be it from me to cause a family quarrel." Drew's churlish expression mellowed as he turned to Cicely. "Until later, my lady."

"Yes, Drew."

The worshipful glow in her eyes made Nicholas clench his jaw. Clamping his fingers around his sister's mauve silk sleeve, he addressed Elizabeth. "Come with us, please."

She nodded, though by the stiff set of her dainty shoulders, he knew she was annoyed at his high-handedness. At the prospect of soothing her irritation later, his loins tightened and his heart lightened.

Yanking his mind back to Cicely, he drew her out of the library and down a corridor. Elizabeth fell into step beside them, and a thunderclap mingled with the echo of their footfalls.

Cicely tried to break free. "You needn't manhandle me, Nick. I shan't run away."

"Indeed," he drawled, escorting her into a morning room decorated with the ubiquitous armor and weaponry. "You've proven yourself an expert at rash behavior."

"Oh, pooh." She sauntered away, hips swaying, as if

she were determined to prove herself a woman. "I've done nothing to be ashamed of . . . here."

Affection and frustration constricted his chest. "You've spent the past week flirting with a man who's known to be a libertine, a gambler, and a fortune hunter."

"I don't know why you say such things of Drew." Sighing dreamily, Cicely leaned against a glass case crowded with knifes. "He's so very handsome and exciting. And you can't complain about his social station. He *is* a duke, after all."

"With the morals of an alley cat."

"He acts the perfect gentleman with me."

Anger boiled inside Nicholas. "Of course. He's desperate to get his hands on your marriage portion."

Elizabeth stirred from her stance by a window. "We don't know that for sure. Perhaps if you were to supervise their meetings—"

His glare cut her short. She stared back coolly.

"Elizabeth is right," Cicely said, elevating her chin. "Drew cares for me, I know he does. *I* might not have gotten the looks in the family, but I can still attract a man."

"Of course you can," Nicholas said quietly. "That's not the point."

"It's only a matter of time until Drew offers for me."

The thought of his naive sister being taken in by a rogue like Drew Sterling made Nicholas's blood run cold. "He has nothing to offer you. And he won't have the chance to court you anymore. You're returning to London tomorrow."

Her eyes rounded in alarm. "No, Nick . . . I can't! Charles will. . . ." Cheeks reddening, she clamped her lips shut.

"I trust Charles to give you precisely what you deserve."

"You don't understand." She swept toward Elizabeth, seizing her hands. "You can convince Nick, can't you, please?"

Elizabeth smiled in sympathy. "If London isn't to

your liking, perhaps he'll let you go to Sussex, instead?"

Her voice rose into a question as she focused her lavender eyes on him. The entreaty on her fine-boned face dulled the edge of his anger, and he suppressed an unexpected grin. Perhaps she was right; Cicely truly feared Charles's displeasure.

"All right, then," he told his sister, "you may go to Sussex."

Hastening to him, she grasped his sleeve. "Oh, but Nick, what I *really* want is to stay here—"

"This is not a matter for discussion, Cicely. Go on and pack your things. You'll catch the first train in the morning."

She snatched her hand back and glared accusingly. "You never listen to me. I'm going to marry a man who lets me do as I please!" Wheeling, she stomped out of the morning room.

Thunder rumbled into the silence. Staring at the empty doorway, Nicholas wondered bleakly where he had gone wrong with his sister. Why couldn't she see he meant only what was best for her?

Elizabeth's arms looped around him from behind; he felt the gentle pressure of her cheek against his back. "Don't torment yourself, Nicholas. She'll soon get over her anger."

He turned, gathering her close, taking comfort in her familiar scent. "Why is she so blind to Drew's faults?"

"Because she's fascinated with what's denied to her. She spurns whatever comes too easily." Elizabeth lifted a wry smile to him. "Just as you'd predicted, even her interest in art has dwindled since you approved my teaching her."

He found no satisfaction in being right. "She's so damned headstrong. I can never make her listen."

Elizabeth reached up to touch his jaw. "Perhaps, my lord, you could try softening your manner. You do have a way of commanding rather than asking."

Nicholas stared down at her gypsy beauty. Guilt squeezed his chest as he remembered how he'd gov-

erned the direction of her life by refusing Buckstone.
He should admit the truth, should give her back the
honesty she always gave him.

And risk losing her?

He walked to a window. Lightning zigzagged against
the charcoal sky, chased by the snarl of thunder. "I
can't allow Cicely to stay here," he said, vanquishing
his uneasy thoughts. "She's heading for trouble with
Drew."

Elizabeth's sigh floated to him. "I know. It's a dilemma—you must do what's right for her, yet your disapproval only makes her want him all the more."

"Thank God she'll be away from his influence by tomorrow. I've enough to worry about with protecting
you."

A gust of raindrops spattered the glass panes. "No
attempts have been made on my life this past week,"
she said. "Do you suppose it's because of the duke's
death? I mean, if the culprit were Philippa or Drew,
they'd no longer benefit from killing me since it's too
late to change the will."

"I've considered that, yes." He turned to face her.
Against the stark black mourning gown, her skin was
milky smooth, her eyes a vibrant violet. "There is another possibility," he murmured, hating the need to
bring up the matter. "The culprit may have been Hugh
Sterling himself."

The color seeped from her cheeks. Her head moved
from side to side in denial. "I can't let myself believe
that, Nicholas. I just can't."

He took her hands in his. Her fingers were slender
and soft, yet he admired their strength as well, a
strength born equally of inner conviction and honest
labor.

"Circumstantial evidence is all we have to go on,
love. And we must consider the old duke."

"But why would he want to murder me?" she whispered. "He said he loved me. You believed him, didn't
you?"

Nicholas hesitated. "Perhaps there was a side to him we didn't know."

Her eyes clouded; a flash of lightning lit her distressed features. "I spoke to Doctor Marsh after the reading of the will," she said, her voice bleached of emotion. "I had the impression he was hiding something. Could he have known of a streak of madness in the duke?" She swallowed visibly. "Could my own father have wanted me dead because I was the reason Lucy left him?"

Remembering Hugh Sterling's devotion to Lucy, his treasuring of her letter over so many years, the way he'd mistaken Elizabeth for her mother when she'd first walked into his bedroom, Nicholas knew the chance could not be ignored. Not wishing to alarm her any further, he kept those thoughts to himself.

"I'll see what I can find out," he said, tenderly brushing back a stray wisp of hair from her temple. "I'll question Marsh myself."

Her face bleak, she nodded. "The headache powder," she said suddenly. "If Marsh gave me a poison, that would prove the duke's innocence."

He disliked dousing the hopeful light in her eyes. "I'm sorry, love. The medicine was a bromide, exactly as it was supposed to be."

"You received the test result from Thistlewood? When? Why didn't you tell me?"

"The report came by mail two days ago. You were busy preparing for the funeral."

Rain lashed the window as she took a step backward, her face taut with annoyance. "It wasn't fair of you to withhold the information."

"I meant only to spare you—"

"Spare me! Nicholas, we're speaking of my life. I've a right to know every detail, however small."

Her words cut into his heart. "I apologize, then. If I've been less than frank, it's because I love you and want to protect you."

The resentment fled her eyes. Coming to him, she rubbed her cheek against his chest. "Oh, Nicholas, you should know by now that keeping things from me is no way to protect me. It's because there are so many secrets in this house that I want none between us. The honesty of our love has given me the strength to get through this ordeal."

Honesty. The word festered inside Nicholas as his mind veered back to Buckstone. Trust shone in Elizabeth's eyes. Clasping her tight, unable to bear his haunting guilt, he pressed his mouth to her fragrant hair. She considered Hugh Sterling a manipulator, but she had no notion of the deceit her own husband had practiced.

His duplicity must end. Now.

Resolutely he leaned back to look at her. "I've not been entirely honest with you, Elizabeth."

Her brow puckered. "You've learned something else?"

"This has nothing to do with anyone here." Praying she'd understand, he took a deep breath. "It's about the commission."

"To design the memorial for Lord Buckstone?"

Nicholas nodded slowly. "Buckstone came to see you the day we were married." Seeing her eyes widen, he paused, then forced the words past dry lips. "He meant to award you the project, but I . . . turned him down."

Shock paralyzed Elizabeth. Only her heart continued to move, slamming in great, painful strokes against her ribs. She searched Nicholas's features for a grin, a telltale signal that he spoke a monstrous jest. Only sincerity and regret gleamed in his eyes.

Rain whipped the windows as mercilessly as the pain that scourged her soul. Strength poured into her limbs, and she pressed backward to escape his embrace. She retreated until the hard edge of a weaponry case met her spine.

"All this time I've been waiting, *hoping* to hear from Peter and it's been for nothing. You've known for nearly two weeks now. *Two weeks.* You knew even as we were speaking our wedding vows—" Her voice broke, her throat closing around his deceit until she could scarcely draw a breath. "You vowed to honor me, yet your words were a sham."

Hands outstretched, he took a step toward her. "Please, love, try to understand. I was afraid of losing you, afraid you'd go off to Ireland without marrying me."

His beseeching words burned in the kiln of her anger. "You might have trusted me. But you never ask, do you, Nicholas? If something doesn't suit you, you simply take matters into your own hands."

"I apologize. It was wrong of me, but I acted only out of love for you, I swear it."

"I know you had good intentions—that's your problem." She shook her head despairingly. "How many more times will you manipulate me for your own purposes?"

Remorse darkened his handsome face. "I'm sorry, love. I never meant to hurt you. It won't happen again."

"I wish I could believe that." Tears stung her eyes; she fiercely blinked them back. "I thought we were equals, Nicholas. But I've been a fool, a fool to think you would ever stop dictating my life."

Elizabeth ran from the room. Tears scalded her cheeks, half blinding her as she stumbled up the stairs. Thankfully she met no one; even her bedroom was empty. Sprawling across the embroidered coverlet, she buried her face in the pillow and sobbed out her rage and grief. The tempest of pain bruised her with all the fierceness of the storm battering the house.

Someone tapped on the door. She ignored the knock, yet the knob rattled and heavy footsteps approached. The mattress sagged. She tensed, bracing herself for Nicholas's touch, a touch she craved as much as she scorned.

But it was Owen's broad hand that caressed her back. "The earl asked me to check on you, Libby."

Distress and relief warred inside her. "I see he didn't care enough to come himself."

"He seemed distraught. Do you want to tell me what happened?"

Swallowing futilely against the lump in her throat, she shook her head.

Her father gave her shoulders a comforting squeeze. "Whatever disagreement you two have had, don't hold your feelings inside, Libby. Talk to him. 'Let not the sun go down on your wrath.'"

What was there to discuss? she wanted to cry out. Talk couldn't change Nicholas's autocratic nature. Talk couldn't restore her faith in him. Talk couldn't alter the fact that he'd caused her to lose the commission that would have been the armature on which to build her reputation as an artist.

Resting her wet cheek against the pillow, she stared out at the rain-washed windows. For a time Owen remained beside her; then he left the room, returning a few moments later with his Bible. Donning his spectacles, he settled into a chair. His familiar presence took the edge off her grief. Yet still she felt stranded, lost in a vast, dark wasteland of sorrow.

She half expected Nicholas to seek her out, to make another attempt to mend the rift between them. But he didn't appear, not even when a wide-eyed Janet delivered a dinner tray. Nor did he come as the early nightfall spread shadows throughout the bedroom. Owen lit a candle and continued to read. Elizabeth gazed up at the gilded swans on the canopy as the scene with Nicholas played over and over in her mind. The pain dulled to a gnawing ache. Squeezing her eyes shut, she found she could not close out the memory of his haunted voice.

I was afraid of losing you . . . I acted only out of love for you . . . for you . . . for you. . . .

Exhausted sleep enveloped her. Sometime during the night she had the vague impression of hearing low male voices, then later, feeling the warm pressure of Nicholas's back against hers and smelling the faint but potent scent of brandy.

Elizabeth knew nothing more until a loud banging

roused her. Groggily she pushed up on an elbow to peer into the charcoal shadows. She spied Nicholas donning his robe, heard a small thump and a hissing curse as he bumped into something.

The racket came again. Knocking, she realized hazily.

A key clattered in the lock; he swung open the door. Miss Eversham stood in the hall, the candlestick she held illuminating her sleep-disheveled hair and starkly agitated face.

"Forgive me, your lordship," the governess said, her words tumbling out in uncharacteristic haste. "It's Cicely! She's gone!"

Chapter 23

Elizabeth sat up straight in bed. The fog shrouding her mind lifted. "Cicely? What's happened to her?"

With a lean hand, the governess clutched together the edges of her prim night robe. "One of her suitcases is missing, along with some clothing. I'm afraid she's run off!"

"You're sure she's nowhere in the house," Nicholas snapped.

"Yes, my lord." Miss Eversham's homespun features were gray with distress. "She isn't in our room and I've looked everywhere downstairs."

"I can think of one place to check," he said, his voice tight with suppressed fury. "And, by God above, if she's there—"

His fingers clamped into fists. He stalked to the nightstand to light a candle; the flare of the match chiseled his face into a harshly molded mask. The murderous glitter in his eyes alarmed Elizabeth.

She scrambled from the bed, her crumpled skirts rustling against the linens. Already he was striding out the door and down the murky hall, Miss Eversham trailing him. Against the walls the suits of armor shone eerily, and the dark visor slits made Elizabeth's skin prickle. Her conjecture about Nicholas's destination tied her stomach into a sickening knot of dread.

Candle in hand, he marched straight to a room midway down the hall. He flung open the door and walked inside. She hastened after him, brushing past Miss

Eversham, who hesitated at the entryway.

The room had a distinctly masculine aura. A black frock coat lay carelessly over a velvet armchair. The dresser top held a handful of coins, along with a china bowl and pitcher set. A pair of riding boots leaned against a tall wardrobe, and the faint scent of shaving soap hung in the silent air.

Her chest constricted. Drew's bedroom. The four-poster bed was empty, the green coverlet neatly drawn to the pillows. Seeing the rigid lines of Nicholas's face, she couldn't decide whether to rejoice or panic in the fact that Cicely wasn't here.

"Have they gone off together?" she whispered, voicing her deepest fear.

"Undoubtedly." The word haunted the shadows; then his hand slammed hard onto a side table, sweeping away a half-played game of solitaire. "I should have seen this coming. God, I should have!"

His wrathful pain wrenched her heart. "What will you do?"

"Go after them, of course. And pray to God I can find Cicely before she ruins her life."

He strode out the door and past a white-faced Miss Eversham. Followed by the governess, Elizabeth ran after him into their bedroom, where he was already yanking off his silk robe. In the light of the candle, his broad bare back gleamed like bronze; his buttocks and thighs rippled with muscles.

Miss Eversham uttered a tiny gasp and retreated into the hall. Elizabeth walked slowly forward on legs weak with untimely desire. "I'll go with you," she said.

He thrust his arms into a shirt. "No, you'll stay here with Owen."

The sudden bitter memory of their argument swamped her. "Your wish is my command, m'lord."

Hastily buttoning the shirt, he sliced her a sharp look. "I suspect Drew's taken her to York, as it's the nearest city. They may plan to catch a train to London, and I'll have to ride hard to intercept them. You couldn't keep up, Elizabeth."

His explanation made sense, yet hurt still clawed her insides. Arms crossed, she watched as he sat on the bed to yank on his boots.

"Should I miss them," he went on, "I'll telegraph Charles to help in the search. I'll do my utmost to return before nightfall. In the meantime you'll be safe so long as you don't budge from this room." Nicholas surged to his feet, then added more gently, "Is that agreeable to you?"

Still smarting from his peremptory manner, she said, "Does it matter if it's not?"

He stood motionless, watching her, his expression as intense as a physical touch. Somewhere, a clock chimed four times. She could not draw her eyes from his tall, supple form. In the feeble glow of the candle, he looked lordly yet alone, overbearing yet beloved. A treacherous softening threatened the firm ground of her fury. Far more than symmetry of features made him handsome; his appeal arose from the kindness and courage and integrity beneath the outer shell of perfection.

"Elizabeth, I . . ." Unhappiness shaded his voice. He lifted a hand as if to caress her, then let his arm fall. Abruptly he pivoted on his boot heel and strode out, closing the door.

Caught in a welter of emotions, she sank beside the puddle of his robe and lifted the silk to her breasts. His quiet words felt engraved on her soul. What had he meant to say? That he needed her, wanted her, loved her? Without him, the future seemed empty and uninviting. Yet could love ease the pain of his betrayal? Could love compensate for the damage he had done to her career?

A knock broke the stillness. Alarm compressed her lungs and dried her mouth. She was all alone. . . .

She stood slowly, the robe slithering to the floor. Cautiously she asked, "Is that you, Papa?"

"Yes," came the muffled reply, "it's me, Libby."

With profound relief she opened the door. "Has Nicholas gone?"

His face drawn, Owen nodded. "And in a crashing

hurry. I pray to God he finds Cicely as swiftly as possible."

Trudging to a window, Elizabeth threw up the sash and leaned on the sill. The storm had passed and stars speckled the night sky. She drew in a gulp of damp, chilly air. Through the darkness she could distinguish the black square of the stable yard, the faint yellow pinprick of a lamp marking her husband's presence. Within moments the light was doused and the quick clop of horse's hooves drifted across the gardens. The sound grew fainter and fainter until it was lost in the chirp of crickets.

Kneeling by the window, she rested her chin in the cradle of her arms. Though Owen snoozed companionably in a chair, loneliness ached inside her. Nicholas was as vital to her life as breathing. She had known that, yet she had let her single-minded devotion to art subjugate her need for him. She'd clung stubbornly to her right to the freedom to choose her commissions, without considering that compromise was essential to marriage. Nicholas hadn't demanded the moon; he wanted only to keep her close. Because he needed her as much as she needed him.

The knowledge painted joy in the bleakness of her soul, like rainbows of color splashed onto a barren canvas. Other jobs would come her way, but never again would she find a man like Nicholas or a love as rich and remarkable as the one they shared.

Peace flooded Elizabeth, washing away the vestiges of pain and anger. She would find commissions closer to home, commissions that would let her devote time to both sculpting and her husband. The moment Nicholas returned, she would tell him of her decision.

She drifted into sleep until the bright morning sun poured over her. Cramped and stiff from her position by the window, she went into the dressing room and with Janet's aid exchanged the wrinkled black gown for a fresh one. The maid's incessant chatter brought a resurgence of anxiety to Elizabeth. Apparently the household staff hadn't yet learned of Cicely's disappearance with Drew. Would Nicholas succeed in finding his sister before she wasted her life on a rogue?

Miss Eversham stopped by to share a few worried words. Seeing Owen solicitously pat the governess's hand, Elizabeth wondered if an affinity were developing between the two. The possibility pleased her. Since her mother's death, Owen had been lonely, in need of companionship.

Once Miss Eversham had gone, Elizabeth found herself pacing restlessly. Nicholas's absence left her vaguely uneasy. She passed the time by questioning her father about the suspects, though he could shed no new light on the matter.

"Hugh Sterling's your culprit," he said. "You'll be safe now that he's gone."

She couldn't shake Owen's dogged insistence on implicating the old duke. Yet still her heart rejected the idea of her own sire cold-bloodedly wanting her dead. Where was his motive? Unless he truly *had* been insane...

In late afternoon Kipp came to the bedroom. "I was helpin' the men patrol outside, an' the doctor waved to me. Asked me to bring you this, yer ladyship."

He handed her a folded piece of paper. She scanned the note, and her heart leapt in excitement as she raised her eyes to Owen. "Doctor Marsh has been packing. He says he came across something that may have belonged to Mother."

Owen's graying brows lowered. "What could he possibly have of Lucy's? He was only a youth when she was here."

Curious, Elizabeth asked, "Did you ever see the two of them together?"

He shrugged. "On occasion; your mother took an interest in everyone. I recall Gilbert Marsh was an intense boy... devoted his time to doctoring everything from a bump on your head to colic in one of the duchess's horses."

"He treated me? He's never mentioned that."

"It was a long time ago. Likely he's forgotten, as you have."

Anxious to see what Marsh had found, she said, "Shall we go, then?"

Owen hesitated. "Lord Nicholas asked me to make certain you didn't leave this room, Libby."

Kipp hitched his thumbs in his lapels. "I'll 'elp you keep a look out. 'Is lordship says I'm a good watchman."

Elizabeth ruffled the boy's hair. "You're right about that. You see, Papa, I'll be quite safe."

"All right, then," Owen said, setting aside his Bible and spectacles. "Marsh is harmless enough. We'll go directly there and come straight back."

As they went downstairs, Kipp darted outside. Owen led Elizabeth through the maze of corridors toward the rear of the house. Uneasiness prickled her skin as they walked past glass cases of knives and guns. She had never grown used to seeing those instruments of murder; without Nicholas, the weapons appeared more ominous than ever. Even the suits of armor seemed to be watching her.

Near the kitchen, they met the duchess striding in through a back door. Adelaide wore her usual mannish riding clothes, and the only concession to her new status was the requisite widow's cap with its black streamers dangling from the back.

Nodding a regal greeting, she gazed at Elizabeth. "One of my grooms told me Hawkesford borrowed a horse early this morning. Now I've learned that my nephew is missing, along with Lady Cicely. So, they've run off together?"

"I'm afraid so," Elizabeth said reluctantly.

Brown eyes slitted, the duchess slapped a riding crop against her pant leg. "Hawkesford should have come to me. I could have organized a search party."

"He didn't want to create a commotion," Elizabeth explained. "The fewer people who realize Cicely's gone, the better his chances of bringing her back without ruining her reputation."

Adelaide arched a graying brow. "Quite so. You have my deepest apology for Drew's behavior. This is certainly one of his less than clever stunts."

Owen took a step forward. "It's not your fault, Duchess. None of us could have foreseen what's happened."

Tucking the riding crop under her arm, she graced him with a cool stare. "Mr. Hastings. How history repeats itself. You eloped with my cousin—and left St. Mary's in quite a lurch, I might add."

His hazel eyes twinkled. "That was some twenty years ago. I trust they've found a new vicar by now."

"A long-winded ass," she said, giving a snort of disgust. "Hugh's eulogy was no exception. You, Mr. Hastings, might have delivered the usual tedious sermons, but at least you saw the sense in brevity."

He chuckled. "It's good to know I've been missed." Taking Elizabeth's arm, he said, "Might we ask directions, Your Grace? My memory of this house fails me .. we're looking for the doctor's rooms."

"Turn left at the end of the hall." Adelaide pointed with her riding crop, then sent Elizabeth a piercing stare. "Do be careful in your wanderings, Countess. Remember, the person who took a shot at you has never been identified."

A chill slid down Elizabeth's spine. Did the duchess have a clue to the killer's name? Or was she herself the culprit, a madwoman warning her own victim?

"I'll stay close to Libby every moment," Owen said. "Good afternoon, Your Grace."

Adelaide nodded curtly and strode off, her thickset figure disappearing around the corner.

Subduing her uneasiness, Elizabeth walked with Owen down the hall. The doctor's door stood ajar and he rapped. "May I come in?"

"Yes, my lady."

Late afternoon sunshine lit the office. Except for packing crates stacked neatly against one wall, the room looked as tidy as ever. The drug cabinet held an array of bottles and jars. A pair of chintz-covered chairs sat before the tiny hearth, and the faint medicinal scent of carbolic tinged the air.

On the examining table, his long booted legs dangling, sat Pickering. Marsh swabbed disinfectant on the footman's outstretched palm. Seeing Elizabeth, Pickering jumped to the floor and came to attention. "Your ladyship! Don't mean to sit down on the job. I, er, got tangled in a hedgerow...."

Hiding a twinge of amusement, Elizabeth said, "I trust you haven't suffered a serious injury."

Marsh slid a glance at her. "One of the thorn pricks festered, that's all," he said, winding gauze around the footman's hand. "Keep this clean now, Mr. Pickering."

"Aye, sir. I'll be gettin' back to me duties." Cheeks beet red, Pickering bowed to Elizabeth, then scuttled outside.

"I received your note, doctor," she said. "You have something of my mother's?"

"Ah, yes. As I was cleaning out a dresser drawer, I found this tucked in the back." From a pocket of his frock coat, he drew forth a lace-bordered handkerchief. "It has your mother's initials on it."

Elizabeth took the folded square; though yellowed with age, the fine linen was as unwrinkled as if it had been freshly ironed. "LRT." Wistfully she smoothed a forefinger over the initials embroidered in cornflower blue. "Lucy Rose Templeton. Look, Papa."

Eyes misting, Owen scrutinized the handkerchief. "It's Lucy's work, all right. She always did have the prettiest hand at sewing."

Elizabeth sent the doctor a puzzled frown. "I wonder how something of my mother's came to be in your drawer."

Eyes on the handkerchief, he shrugged his slim shoulders. "You've seen the disorder in the rest of the mansion—the handkerchief must have been left there when I moved in. I thought perhaps you'd like to keep it as a memento."

"Thank you," Elizabeth said, warmed by the offer. "I've so few keepsakes from her life here."

"Think nothing of it." Walking to the desk, Marsh picked up the blue and white Spode teapot from beside a spirit lamp. "Would you care for a cup of tea? I've some brewed and I'd be honored if both of you would join me."

Owen frowned. "We should go back, Libby."

She hesitated, knowing her father was right yet unwilling to pass up the opportunity to do a little detecting. She must solve this mystery so she and Nicholas could live free of fear.

"Let's stay for a few moments, Papa? I've some questions for the doctor."

Marsh turned his back to pour the tea. "I should be delighted to help you, your ladyship. Please, do sit down."

His voice was pleasant, yet in the past he'd seemed to resent being questioned. Why was he willing today? His boyish features were amiable as he handed a china cup to each of them. Sinking into one of the chintz chairs, she wondered again if Marsh knew something vital. Maybe she could jar him into talking at last.

Owen stirred sugar into his cup. "I must apologize, doctor, for not greeting you the night I arrived. I didn't realize you were the same fair-haired boy I'd met so many years ago."

"We all change," Marsh said with a shrug.

"I should have guessed, though," Owen went on. "If you didn't have your nose in a medical encyclopedia, you were setting a bird's broken wing or soothing Libby when she'd skinned her knee."

"Those days seem long ago." Marsh watched thoughtfully as Owen tasted his tea. "I've always been interested in healing, in restoring the wounded to health."

The doctor offered Elizabeth a plate of brandy snaps. She took one of the rolled biscuits, though her stomach was clenched too tight for food. "Doctor, pardon me for changing the subject, but did my husband come here yesterday?"

Perching on the edge of the desk, Marsh looked surprised. "I haven't seen Lord Hawkesford since the reading of the will."

"Do you have any notion of why the old duke changed his will?"

"Notion? The reason is plain...." His blue eyes intently studied her over the rim of his teacup. "Because you'd returned home...where you belong."

His softened tone left her with a vague sense of disquiet. He was hiding something; she was sure of that much. "But why not leave the money to the duchess? Or to Drew...he was loyal to his uncle for so many years. He deserves an inheritance more than I."

"Deserves?" The doctor uttered a sedate laugh. "He's proven today that he doesn't deserve a farthing."

Blinking sleepily, Owen yawned. "You heard the news, then?"

Marsh inclined his fair head. "Lady Philippa was quite distraught over her son's disappearance. She called me this morning for something to quiet her nerves."

At least that explained why they hadn't seen the woman all day. "Doctor, may I ask your professional opinion on a matter of some delicacy?"

"Of course, your ladyship."

"It's about the old duke." She paused, hating to bring the subject out into the open, fearing the answer she might receive. Yet she must know. "I wondered if there were any chance he might have been... unbalanced."

Marsh's cup clattered into the saucer. A few drops splashed onto the polished wood desk; he leapt up to fetch a scrap of gauze from the cart beside the examining table. "Pardon my clumsiness, your ladyship," he said, carefully wiping the spilled liquid. "You startled me. Why would you accuse His Grace of lunacy?"

"I'm not accusing, only seeking your professional opinion." She sipped some tea to erase the dryness in her throat. "A week ago, someone fired a gun at me. Someone also hired a man in London to kill me." Her voice lowered. "I'm trying to identify the culprit, that's all. Certainly as a doctor you're qualified to diagnose madness."

Marsh's eyes looked curiously empty. "I've read some studies on the topic. I've a few volumes over here...." Rising, he went to a bookshelf and stared at the leather-bound spines, as if searching for a particular tome.

"'S what I been tellin' you, Libby," Owen said, his voice slurred. "Th' duke was unhinged. Any man who'd mistreat a wonnerful woman like Lucy's got to be mad...."

Bewildered, she gaped at him. Her father was slouched in his chair, his eyes half closed. Of course, he'd risen before dawn, but that didn't explain why he'd nod off when he took so seriously his task of protecting her. He couldn't have been nipping at the bottle again; she had been with him all day....

"I quite agree with you about Lucy, Mr. Hastings." Marsh's face remained unperturbed as he turned to stare at the older man. "In fact, I owe you my thanks for getting her away from the duke."

Owen blinked as if struggling to focus; then his eyes drifted shut. The china cup slipped from his fingers and smashed onto the stone floor, the shards skittering in all directions. The noise failed to rouse him.

Alarmed, Elizabeth set down her cup and hastened to his side. "Papa!" She shook his shoulder and his eyelids fluttered; then his head lolled against the back of the chair. "Papa, wake up! Dr. Marsh, do something! He must have suffered some sort of attack!"

A quiet snore slipped from Owen's lips.

"Don't worry, your ladyship," Marsh murmured smoothly. "He's merely sleeping."

Understanding swamped her in a sickening wave. She whipped her head around to gaze at the doctor. "You put something in his tea!" she accused. "What? What?"

"A dose of laudanum, that's all." His lips formed an earnest smile. "Trust me, Elizabeth. I could never harm a man who loved Lucy almost as much as I did."

Astonishment and dread roiled inside her. "What do you mean, you loved her?"

"Lucy meant more to me than life itself. The duke, however," Marsh went on, his tone turning brutal, "never felt as I did. All those years he had me fooled. He claimed he loved Lucy, but he finally admitted the truth the night he announced the new will."

"What truth? What are you talking about?"

"The truth about what he'd done to Lucy. She didn't want to have an affair with His Grace. But he preyed upon her foolish feelings for him and talked his way into her bed." Marsh's face crumpled, his eyes tortured. "He stole her innocence, forced her to lie with him. He raped her."

"No!" she gasped. "That can't be true. Papa would have told me . . . because Mama would have told *him*."

"Perhaps she was ashamed, ashamed that she'd found pleasure in his sin." Agitated, the doctor paced before the bookshelf. "I had to smother him, to make him pay. She was too good to be used, too gentle and kind."

Horror paralyzed Elizabeth. "You killed him?"

"I avenged Lucy's honor." Plucking a royal blue book from the crowded shelf, Marsh reverently flipped the pages. Elizabeth stood on shaky legs. Marsh held her sketchbook . . . the sketchbook containing the drawings of her mother.

"*You* were the thief who ransacked my lodgings," she whispered.

Sadness darkened his eyes. "I had to find the proof that Lucy still lived. And I have it, right here."

As he caressed the sketchbook like a lover, Elizabeth stared, trying to fathom his anguish. "I thought you were only a boy when my mother lived here."

"I was sixteen. Old enough to love with a man's heart." Gently laying the book on the desk, he stepped closer. The blankness in his eyes chilled Elizabeth.

"I ached to show my affection for you, Lucy. I ached to touch you, to kiss you. Do you remember the day before you left here? I worked up the courage to tell you of my love, but you..."

His voice choked; he lifted a pale, clean hand as if to caress Elizabeth's cheek. She backed away, her damp palms meeting the smoothly carved mantelpiece, her mind awash with fear. He thought she was her mother. He truly was mad.

Through the opened window drifted the clop of horse's hooves in the stable yard, the drone of bees in the herb garden. Quiet sounds, safe sounds. If he tried to overpower her, help was near....

"Please," she said in a low voice, "stay back or I'll scream."

He stopped short, hurt contorting his boyish features into a face she no longer recognized. "Don't shun me, Lucy. You did so that other time, but everything is different now. I'm a grown man. You can't say I'm too young for you. I'll cherish you, take care of you. The duke won't hurt you anymore."

Pity for his suffering overrode her fear. "I'm not Lucy," she said gently. "I'm Elizabeth, the Countess of Hawkesford. You need help, doctor. Let me take you to someone who can help you."

He shook his fair head, his smile beatific. "No, it's you who need help, Lucy. That letter Owen wrote to the duke said you were dead. But I know better. Let me heal you, Lucy, cleanse you of sin. We can share our lives... everything will be just as I've planned."

She glanced at Owen; he slept peacefully. She dared not leave him with this madman. Desperately, she said, "Your plan was for my mother. Look at me, doctor. I'm Elizabeth. Lucy had green eyes."

A faint frown creased Marsh's brow. "Don't try to confuse me, Lucy. You're as beautiful as ever." He took a step closer. "In a moment you'll be free ... free to live again with me. I've waited so long for you."

Reaching into his coat pocket, Marsh drew forth a dagger. Elizabeth's eyes fixed on the blade gleaming no more than a yard away. He intended to kill her!

Raising the knife, he started toward her. She

screamed and dodged. He lunged and slashed. The scalpel-sharp steel sliced her skirt, barely missing her calf.

Elizabeth dove for the door. He caught her sleeve and jerked her back around. His wiry fingers bit into her arm; his gentle lips smiled at her.

"Let me purify you, Lucy," he murmured. "Your blood will bring you back. It won't hurt but a moment."

His tranquil voice squeezed the breath from her lungs. The knife lifted, glinting in the sunlight. She yanked violently out of his grip. Her sleeve ripped; she stumbled against the tea table. Crockery crashed to the floor.

She felt herself falling, saw the blade plunging. Her elbow struck the hard floor. Sobbing with desperation, she rolled away and scrambled to her feet. He followed, his dagger raised, his smile profane.

Elizabeth bumped the hard edge of the desk. Heart slamming against her ribs, she snatched up the sketchbook. Utilizing all her strength, she swung at him. . . .

Chapter 24

"**I**'ll kill him," Charles vowed, taking the stairs two at a time. "If he's touched so much as a hair on her head, he'll die."

Nicholas followed the Marquess of Sedgemoor up the narrow steps of the hotel in York. "Don't do anything rash. For Cicely's sake, we mustn't attract everyone's attention."

Dark humor invaded Nicholas. Here he was, speaking like the voice of reason when murder blazed in his own heart. He burned to tear Drew Sterling apart limb by limb, to pluck out his fortune-hunting heart and cast it to the hounds of hell. Praise God the hours of frantic searching were nearing an end. Pray God they weren't too late. . . .

They emerged into a long hall lit by mid-afternoon sunlight. The floral carpet absorbed their swift footfalls as they searched the brass numbers on the doors.

Charles's boyish face looked grim with rage, his copper hair mussed, his ivory cravat twisted. "There," he snapped, marching toward the end of the corridor. "There's the room that bastard had the audacity to register in my name." Not bothering to knock, he wrenched open the door and surged inside.

Pulses pounding in fury and fear, Nicholas strode after his friend. He entered a small sitting room, genteel yet shabby. A twin globed lamp adorned a tiny side table. A drab green armchair dwelled beside the unlit hearth. Sitting a yard apart, at either end of a brown twill sofa, were Drew and Cicely.

He looked alarmed. She looked delighted. To Nicholas's immense relief, both were fully clothed.

She jumped up as Charles raced to her side. His hands gripped her shoulders, touched her cheeks. "Are you all right, darling?"

Her face glowed. "Oh, Charles, you came—"

"What did he do to you?" Pivoting, he charged Drew. "You bloody bounder!"

He yanked Drew from the sofa. His fist cracked against the young duke's jaw. The force of the blow sent Drew stumbling backward against the table. The lamp teetered and crashed, spreading the scent of spilled oil. Drew stood his ground as Charles lunged again. The smack of another blow rent the air. Drew went sprawling against the sofa, blood trickling from a corner of his mouth.

"Stop it!" Cicely screamed.

Fists swinging, Charles dove at Drew, who made no move to defend himself. A right-handed punch caught him in the belly. He doubled over, the air whooshing from his lungs.

Nicholas grabbed Charles and jerked him back. "For God's sake, leave off."

"He dishonored Cicely!" Charles paused to catch a breath. "I won't let the scoundrel get away with hurting her."

Tension knotted his arm, a tension echoed in Nicholas's own body. Yet he kept his emotions under iron control. "My sister isn't hurt. But she bloody well will be if there's a scandal over your killing Rockborough."

Charles glared first at Drew, who sat nursing his reddened jaw, then at Cicely, whose blue eyes were wide with shock. His gaze gentled and his muscles relaxed enough that Nicholas felt justified in releasing Charles.

"My thanks, Hawkesford," Drew said sardonically, dabbing a white handkerchief at his bloodied lip.

"Don't get overconfident," Charles snapped. "I'm

not done with you. I'll find another way to make you pay."

"But nothing happened," Cicely squeaked. "Drew kissed me, that's all."

Charles gathered her hands in his. "Thank God! We got here in time, then."

"Oh, pooh." She pulled away. "You don't understand. You see, I'd changed my mind. Drew was going to take me back to Swanmere."

"No doubt he was trying to lull your suspicions. England's most notorious rake doesn't give up after a single kiss."

She set her chin stubbornly. "It's the truth. Ask Drew."

Charles glowered. "Rockborough wouldn't know the truth if it kicked him in the face."

Nicholas glanced sharply from the duke to his sister. He looked disgruntled. She looked disillusioned. The door to the adjoining room stood ajar, the bed within neatly made. Perhaps . . .

"Well?" Nicholas prompted coldly.

Drew arched an elegant eyebrow. "Oh, do I get a chance at self-defense? I thought you'd already tried and sentenced me."

"Speak now or forever hold your peace," Nicholas said.

Straightening, Drew narrowed his dark eyes. "For what it's worth, then, I was intending to return Cicely home."

"You would say that." Charles slipped a possessive arm around Cicely's waist. "You'd say anything to weasel out of paying the piper."

Nicholas held up a restraining hand. "Let him speak. Go on, Rockborough."

Drew's eyes slid away, then returned, steady and bitter. "I knew Cicely saw running away as a lark, just another means of defying you, Hawkesford. I thought to use that to my advantage, to get her alone and . . ."

"Make certain you secured a claim to her marriage portion," Nicholas stated.

Drew shrugged defensively. "It's as easy to marry rich as poor. And she's a pretty girl. I wouldn't have minded. . . ." Glancing at Charles's thunderous expression, Drew cleared his throat. "However, matters didn't progress the way I'd intended. When I brought Cicely here, she . . . ah . . . changed her mind. Despite what people say about me, I've never forced a woman."

"You see?" Cicely said, tilting her pert face to Charles. "Drew was honorable enough to respect my wishes. You ought to thank him instead of thrash him."

"The queen will dance naked in Trafalgar Square before I thank that bastard," Charles growled.

She stepped away from him. "You're as pigheaded as my brother. As a matter of fact, you're worse. Nick at least listened to Drew."

"I've done enough listening. It's your turn to pay attention now. Come to think of it, you're the one who deserves a thrashing. For the worry you put Nicholas and me through today, as well as for that stunt you pulled at the regatta."

Alarm entered her eyes, yet she held her chin high. "You've no right to speak to me that way, Charles Garforth."

"I've every right," he said, advancing on her. "It's long past time I spoke my mind to you, Cicely Ware."

She retreated. "Don't you dare touch me." Her backside met the armchair. "Oh, pooh! Nick! Oh, Nick, help!"

Hiding his amusement, Nicholas crossed his arms and shrugged. "This isn't my argument. Besides, I don't want to cross Sedgemoor—he has quite the powerful right hook."

Charles stopped scant inches from her. "Don't think that once we're married you'll go running off to your brother for help. I intend to teach you to behave."

"You'll not teach me—" Cicely began scornfully. Her mouth dropped open. "Married? Whatever are you raving about? I wouldn't marry you if you were the last man—"

"I love you."

She stared.

Nicholas grinned. For once in her life his sister was speechless. And Charles had snapped out of his shyness at last. He pulled her into his arms and whispered something in her ear . . . something that made her blush and smile.

Nicholas turned to Drew, who sat morosely cradling his jaw. "Well, Rockborough, all's well that ends well."

"Pardon me if I fail to share your good humor."

Feeling charitable, Nicholas advised, "When you return, you should have Marsh take a look at that jaw."

"That quack? No, thank you."

A sliver of suspicion pierced Nicholas's satisfaction. "Why are you always scornful of the doctor?"

"He's just an odd sort, that's all. Keeps to himself."

"How so?"

Drew shrugged. "Oh, lots of ways . . . while we were in London he was forever trotting off on little private errands."

Nicholas's stomach clenched. "What sort of errands?"

"He claimed to be observing new techniques at a hospital, but he never once learned anything to aid my uncle. Just handed out sleeping potions, same as always."

"Do you have any idea where he really went?"

"Probably to an assignation with a woman . . ." Drew paused, his puffy lips curving into a cynical smile. "Or come to think of it, maybe he gets his jollies with other men."

"I see."

With feigned nonchalance, Nicholas turned away. He tried to thaw the ice invading his veins, but the chill of doubt remained. Was Marsh the murderer? Had he been stealing away in London to watch Elizabeth? To meet with the man in the porkpie hat?

Remembering the doctor's secretive manner, Nicholas suddenly pictured Marsh skulking about, hiding in a tangle of yews and shooting at Elizabeth. Fear strangled him. Elizabeth was at the house with only

Owen to protect her. Owen would never suspect the doctor; Owen was convinced the duke was the culprit. Marsh might visit her on a pretext, draw a gun and fire. . . .

Stepping swiftly to the door, Nicholas addressed Charles, "I'm returning to Swanmere. I trust you'll see to Cicely's safety."

"Of course, but—"

Nicholas didn't wait to hear the reply. Half running, he leapt down the stairs and out to the stables to fetch his horse. He rode through the congested back streets of York, heading toward the city gates and the rolling countryside beyond.

Dear God, if he were to lose Elizabeth. . . .

Pain wrenched his gut; guilt badgered his heart. During the long ride back, regrets pounded his mind in rhythm with the swift pace of the horse's hooves. He'd been dead wrong to refuse Buckstone and then delude her about the commission for so many weeks.

You never ask, she'd said. *If something doesn't suit you, you simply take matters into your own hands.*

He had acted too bloody arrogant from the start. He'd expected her to change her life to suit his expectations. She wanted their marriage to be a partnership, yet he'd bulled ahead and made a decision that rightfully belonged to her alone.

How many more times will you manipulate me for your own purposes?

Nicholas shifted uncomfortably in the saddle. He'd swallow his pride and make amends. He's ask Buckstone to give her back the commission. He'd rearrange his business and political schedule. He'd find the time to accompany her to Ireland.

I've been a fool to think you would ever stop dictating my life.

In his mind he saw her tear-misted eyes glittering with accusation and pain. Elizabeth had every right to resent him. God, what if she decided their marriage had no future? What if she made up her mind to leave him?

What if she died? What if he never again held her in his arms, whispered love words in her ear?

Cold sweat bathed his palms. He kicked the gray, urging the horse to a swifter pace. Moorland stretched in all directions, a vast treeless expanse as desolate as his heart. Yet like his heart the land pulsed with life. The wind carried the sweetness of warm grass. A few shaggy sheep trundled over the rocky hillsides. Puddles from yesterday's storm dotted the landscape. His horse startled a red grouse that flew out of the bracken alongside the rutted road.

If only he could so easily flush out Elizabeth's assailant. His mind veered back to Marsh. What connection might have existed between the youthful Marsh and Lucy Templeton? Was the doctor the madman?

Taking a deep breath to calm his violent heartbeat, Nicholas forced himself to consider the other suspects. What of the duchess? Gruff and aloof, she had ample reason to resent the lovechild of an affair between her husband and her cousin. Yet Adelaide seemed too straightforward to indulge in stealth. And Philippa? She might be vindictive, but would she fire a gun from the bushes? As for Drew... After today, Nicholas felt sure the new duke was honorable in his own indolent way, too honorable to commit murder.

He passed the gate house and started down the avenue of elms marking the winding drive to the manor house. Spurring the gray onward, he prayed Elizabeth had passed a quiet day in their bedroom. If anything happened to her...

His fingers tautened on the leather reins. Anxious and aching, he rode hard, paying little heed to the cool beauty of the woodland bordering the moors. At last he caught sight of the broad expanse of sheep-cropped lawn leading to the stark stone mansion.

Cantering past the forecourt, he headed his lathered mount toward the stables. At the rear of the house, grooms and stable lads crowded the outer door to Marsh's rooms.

Nicholas's blood ran cold. Fear tumbled wildly

through his mind. He swung from the saddle and ran across the yard. *Please, God ...*

"Let me through," he commanded.

The men parted. Several snatched off their caps. Nicholas surged into the doctor's office. Before the hearth a table lay overturned. Broken crockery strewed the flagstones. Pastries and spilled tea littered the floor.

Owen slouched, snoring, in a chintz-covered chair. Sleeping?

Pivoting from the incongruous sight, Nicholas saw the mannish figure of the duchess bent over a woman seated in the other chair. A woman whose ebony hair cascaded over a gown of mourning silk. Her sleeve was ripped, exposing her milk-white flesh.

His heart ceased beating. Sick with dread, he shoved aside the last few men.

"Elizabeth!"

Adelaide straightened.

Elizabeth tilted up her face, wan yet infinitely beautiful. "Nicholas, you're here...."

The light in her eyes chased the chill from his veins. Falling to his knees, he caught her close, crushing his mouth to the silk of her hair, breathing in her familiar scent. Her body felt fragile and sweet, warm and alive.

"She's fine, Hawkesford," the duchess said. "Only dreadfully shaken."

"What happened?" he demanded.

Elizabeth drew back. "It was Marsh," she murmured, her voice desolate. "He's responsible for everything. He put a sleeping draught in Papa's tea. Oh, Nicholas, the doctor loved my mother... he thinks I *am* my mother. He came at me with a knife...." She glanced down and shuddered.

Following her gaze, he saw an antique Scottish dirk lying on the hearth. Her skirt bore a jagged slit, testimony to the blade's razor edge. His mind reeled with horror and guilt. He'd come so close to losing her. So bloody close ...

"Marsh killed Hugh," Adelaide said furiously. "I had doubts about that chap, but never any evidence. The more I thought about Elizabeth coming here to visit the doctor, the more I realized I had to come check on her." She shook her head in self-disgust. "I was almost too late. . . ."

Nicholas looked sharply at the duchess. "When did this happen?"

"Only a few minutes ago. As I rushed toward Elizabeth, Marsh got past me and into the house. Your men and some of mine went after him."

Elizabeth grasped his wrists. "Kipp went, too," she said in alarm. "I tried to stop him."

Rage propelled Nicholas to his feet. "I'll find Marsh."

"I'm coming with you."

When she started to rise, he pressed her firmly into the chair. "Absolutely not. You'll stay with the duchess."

She set her chin obstinately. "And what if Marsh comes back?"

Adelaide scooped up the dirk. "Let him. I'll cut the scoundrel's heart out."

Her protectiveness warmed Nicholas's soul; her conviction inspired his confidence. "My thanks, Adelaide."

She shrugged, though her eyes settled with wistful fondness on Elizabeth. "She always was Lucy's pride and joy."

Nicholas caressed his wife's cheek, soft as swansdown. "And mine now, as well." Pivoting, he drew his derringer and sprinted from the room.

Dread throbbed inside Elizabeth as she watched his broad back vanish. She surged up, swinging toward the duchess.

"I'm going after him."

"Don't be an ass. You shouldn't get within a furlong of Marsh."

"Would you sit by while someone you loved was in danger?"

The duchess stared, her brown eyes slitted, her sturdy hand grasping the dirk. Her nostrils flared like a horse's as she sucked in a deep breath. "Hawkesford

will flay me alive. Ah, well, at least promise you'll stick
to me like a burr."

Elizabeth nodded, though mentally she vowed to do
whatever was necessary.

Adelaide glanced at the group of sturdy stable men.
"One of you, stay with Mr. Hastings. Come along, Elizabeth."

Boots crunching the broken bits of porcelain, Adelaide headed through the doorway. Petticoats swishing,
Elizabeth hastened to keep pace with the duchess.

Adelaide glanced back, her equine face alight with
dry humor. "You should wear trousers, Countess.
They're far more practical."

"Believe me, I shall return to trousers . . . as soon as
my life returns to normal." Elizabeth's smile died.
"Where do you suppose Marsh went? There must be a
thousand places he could hide."

The knife gleamed dully at the duchess's side. "I've a
notion," she said grimly. "Perhaps he fled to the room
where Hugh seduced your mother."

A distant thudding grew louder as they hastened up
the main staircase. At the far end of the corridor, Elizabeth spied a group gathered around Hugh Sterling's
chambers. Nicholas battered the closed door with his
shoulder. The panel broke open with a splintering
crash.

"Take care, your lordship," Pickering warned. "The
bugger's got Kipp—"

Nicholas strode into the bedroom. Heart pounding,
Elizabeth rushed down the hall and past the men.
Peering around Pickering's lanky form, she took in the
macabre setting at a glance, the guns and swords and
spears scattering the room, untouched since the duke's
death.

Before the suit of armor brandishing a pike in its
gauntleted hand, Marsh held a white-faced Kipp im-
prisoned. Horror choked her. One of the doctor's arms
was clamped around the boy's chest; the other pressed
a wickedly curved knife to Kipp's slender throat.

Madness glittered in Marsh's blue eyes. "Drop your weapon," he snapped wildly.

"As you wish." Nicholas opened his fingers; the pistol thumped to the carpet. "Just don't hurt the boy."

"Stay away," Marsh warned. "I don't want to kill him . . . I only want Lucy back."

"Then release him," Nicholas said soothingly. "Come with me and I'll help you find her."

The knife quivered against Kipp's throat. "Help me?" the doctor said, his voice dwindling to a whimper. "You think I'm a lunatic. I won't be put away. I won't be trapped in a place where I can't find my Lucy."

Kipp's brown eyes shone round and scared. She alone held the key, Elizabeth realized. The key to secure his safety.

Squelching a surge of fright, she stepped boldly forward, making a wide arc around Nicholas. "I'm here, Doctor. Your Lucy."

She heard Nicholas's sharp intake of breath, felt the alarm radiating from him. Yet she knew he dared not forestall her . . . not yet.

Marsh gave a start as his eyes focused on her. "Lucy?" he asked in a quavering voice.

"Yes," she murmured. "You can let him go now."

Seraphic peace softened the doctor's face as he let loose of Kipp. Panting, the boy crumpled to the floor and stared up at the doctor.

"My dearest love," Marsh whispered, his eyes never leaving her face. "You're finally here. Come to me."

He held his arms open, the curved knife glittering in the last rays of the setting sun. Elizabeth wet her dry lips. Why was Kipp still cowering at the doctor's feet? A tiny frown began to form on Marsh's angelic face. She had to humor him as long as Kipp remained in danger. She took a step forward.

Seizing her arm, Nicholas yanked her back. "No!"

Marsh waved the blade. "Don't touch her! She's mine!"

He started to charge, but Kipp rocketed his small

body upward. Arms flailing, Marsh fell back, onto the armor. The suit teetered, then collapsed with a metallic crash. His slim body tumbled atop the pile. An unearthly scream rent the air. Blood blossomed around the pile point protruding from his chest.

A moment of silence stretched into an eternity of horror. Then Adelaide raced to Marsh, ahead of the footmen and servants.

Sickened, Elizabeth buried her face against Nicholas's chest. Though Marsh lay dead, she could still hear his shriek reverberating in her head. The murmur of voices finally penetrated her shock and she lifted her face.

"Kipp?" she asked. "Is he all right?"

"I'm 'ere," the boy said, and she realized Nicholas held an arm around the boy's shaking shoulders. His eyes were wide, his face pallid. "Blimey, I didn't mean fer the doctor to grab me like that. I was only tryin' to capture 'im."

"You took a senseless risk," Nicholas snapped, yet his severe expression mellowed. "But you did save Elizabeth's life."

Kipp brightened, thrusting out his liveried chest. "Aye, I did at that."

"Let's get out of here," Nicholas growled, guiding Elizabeth out the door and down the hall.

Once alone in their room, she said, "Did you find Cicely?"

"Yes. She'll be arriving with Charles soon." Nicholas took hold of Elizabeth's shoulders, his grip none too gentle. "You stubborn American. You shouldn't have come upstairs. For that matter, you should never have left this bedroom in the first place. Aren't you ever going to learn to listen to me?"

Her heart overflowed; despite his gruff manner, love radiated from him. "When you learn to stop commanding me, my lord."

Remorse softened his handsome face. "Forgive me, Elizabeth," he said, his palms cupping her cheeks. "I swore I'd stop telling you what to do, but I suppose it'll take time for me to change." His voice dropped to a husky whisper. "Will you allow me that chance?"

She smiled. "You were only trying to protect me . . . and I love you for that."

"I love you, too." Yet his brow remained furrowed. "I want you to know, Countess, that the instant we return to London, I'll speak to Buckstone and convince him to—"

Laying a finger over her husband's lips, Elizabeth silenced him. "I don't need that commission," she murmured, her words heartfelt. "I'd rather spend my life sculpting you and loving you."

Epilogue

"**H**old that pose."

"Indeed. You try sitting still with twenty pounds of squirming baby in your lap."

"The two of you look charming. Justin, give Mama another big smile."

Pencil flying over the sketch pad, Elizabeth captured her son's beaming face, the two front teeth, the adorable violet eyes. He perched restlessly in his father's lap, his chubby body clad in a sailor suit. Winter sunshine poured through the windows of the conservatory, and gleamed on tousled chestnut locks the exact hue of Nicholas's neatly groomed hair. Justin babbled and waved at her.

"My sentiments precisely," Nicholas said, grinning at his son. "Your mother's quite the beauty. You should have seen the admiring looks turned her way when we walked into the Meltons' ballroom last night."

"They were staring at *you*," Elizabeth retorted, sketching the breathtaking angles of his face, angles that still fascinated her even after a year and a half of marriage, even after a thousand renderings on paper. "All those prim and proper ladies were secretly longing for a night in your bed."

"Jealous?"

"Always."

"I want only you, Countess."

The tenderness shining in those silver gray eyes washed Elizabeth in delicious serenity. The pencil stilled in her hand; the fountain murmured in harmony with her quickened heartbeat. Her blood warmed under the impact of his sensual smile, his loving expression. Wanting him, she leaned forward in her chair. . . .

Justin reached up and yanked at his father's perfectly knotted cravat.

Aiming a severe scowl at his son, Nicholas peeled off the offending fingers. "Enough of that, young man."

Unperturbed, Justin cooed and patted his father's smooth-shaven cheek. An indulgent grin softened the chiseled corners of Nicholas's mouth; Elizabeth hastened to catch the expression on paper.

"Scamp," he growled. "Only six months old and already you can circumvent me as easily as your Aunt Cicely."

"Did I hear my niece's name mentioned?"

Majestic as Britannia on the prow of a ship, Lady Beatrice sailed down the winding flagstone path, her navy silk gown rustling, the plume on her velvet hat wagging.

"We were comparing Justin's behavior to Cicely's," Elizabeth said, quickly drawing her swan trademark in the bottom corner of the paper.

"He's a perfect angel. Aren't you, darling?" Beatrice smiled at the boy; Justin burbled in delight. "But oh, that Cicely." She shook her head in fond disapproval. "Imagine, attending the ball in her condition. And Charles even allowed her to dance!"

Setting her pad on the worktable, Elizabeth hid a smile. "Pregnancy is natural and wonderful. It's no cause for a woman to hide herself in shame."

"How utterly American," Beatrice sniffed, though no rancor colored her words. "Well, at least Cicely's confinement is drawing near. Perhaps having a little one will calm her madcap ways."

"Or perhaps," Elizabeth murmured, "she'll always be Cicely."

"I hope so," Nicholas drawled. "If my sister hadn't

stolen away to study with a certain sculptress, I wouldn't be happily married today."

His eyes sought Elizabeth's; the softness on his face brought a familiar wave of fulfillment.

"Humph." Despite her hauteur, Beatrice had a suspicious sheen in her gray eyes as she looked from her nephew to Elizabeth. "Come along, Justin, say your good-byes. We're going to visit your Aunt Cicely and Uncle Charles."

Nicholas hugged the boy close. "I love you, son. Be a good lad now, and don't pull your great-aunt's hair."

Elizabeth went to gather Justin into her arms. The feel of his small body made contentment curl around her heart. His faintly milky scent enveloped her as she planted a kiss on his silken cheek.

Over his tousled mop of hair, she gazed at Beatrice. "Where are Papa and Miss Eversham?"

"Waiting in the carriage. I am quite capable of fetching my own grandnephew."

Beatrice efficiently took hold of Justin; his chubby fingers reached for her pearl earrings. "Here now, my little lord, you must learn to behave the way you're supposed to," she scolded, carrying the baby out of the conservatory.

"Whether she realizes it or not," Nicholas said, "my aunt has become a bit unconventional herself lately. You've changed us all, Countess."

Wistfulness touched Elizabeth. Clasping her hands, she took a step closer. "Does that bother you, Nicholas? To have society label you an eccentric for marrying me?"

A lazy smile lit his handsome features. "Come here."

"Yes, my lord." Willingly she took his outstretched hand, let him draw her onto his lap and fit her against his hard shoulder.

"Society can go to hell," he murmured. "My life would be empty without you. You've taught me to be open, given me my precious son, shared so much of yourself."

His words lifted her heart. She raised a hand to

grasp the ring hanging from its silver chain inside her blouse. "Oh, Nicholas, I feel so blessed to have you and Justin. This ring has truly been a talisman."

"Hugh Sterling would have been proud to see his grandson."

A bittersweet sigh escaped Elizabeth. She tilted her head to study her husband's face. "Drew was proud, too. When I was finishing the memorial in Yorkshire last week, did you notice the way he took to Justin? He seems to have mellowed lately, and I had the impression he's lonely beneath all that ducal cynicism."

"He'll have sons of his own someday. Especially if he wants to gain control of the generous trust fund you set up for his children."

"I want him to marry for love, not money. I want him to be as happy as we are."

Nicholas nuzzled her ear; a delicious shiver slipped over her skin. "Happy," he murmured, "is too mild a word for the way you make me feel. Do you remember the first time you sat in my lap?"

"Mmm . . . yes. You touched me. . . ."

"Like this." His hand drifted downward over her breasts, seeking the womanly shape of her waist, the roundness of her thigh. Dewy warmth bathed her as his fingers stopped just shy of their goal.

"I touched you, too." Desire trickling through her veins, she discreetly shaped her hand to the virile proof of his love. "This is how I've always wanted to sculpt you . . . magnificent . . . extraordinary . . . the perfect man."

He sucked in a sharp breath. "Praise God you used a fig leaf. It's rather disconcerting to know all of London has been gawking at the statue of me on display at the Royal Academy."

She laughed. "The head is Apollo's. No one need know that flawless body is yours, my darling."

"No one but you. One of my fondest memories is the night you finished that statue, the night we made love here in this room, with the moonlight silvering your skin and camellia petals showering your body."

"I remember, too," she grumbled teasingly. "I was sore for days from that stone floor."

He tweaked her nose. "Next time you can get on top."

"How gallant. Who says there'll be a next time?"

"I do." His fingers traced the valley formed by her Turkish trousers. "I adore you, Countess. I'd love to show you how much."

"Now?" She gasped as his fingers worked a familiar magic. "Anyone could peer in the windows."

"Come now, you were the one who taught me to be adventurous."

"To a point. Enough's enough."

"I'll never have enough of you."

His fingers continued to stroke her intimately; she struggled to gain the breath and the willpower to speak. Brushing a kiss against his jaw, she said, "Nicholas Ware, can't you ever behave the way you're supposed to?"